Meant for You

Meant for You

A Novel

Pandora Frank Hamilton

MEANT FOR YOU
A NOVEL

This is a work of fiction. All of the characters, names, incidents, organizations, and dialogue in this novel are either the products of the author's imagination or are used fictitiously.

iUniverse books may be ordered through booksellers or by contacting:

iUniverse
1663 Liberty Drive
Bloomington, IN 47403
www.iuniverse.com
1-800-Authors (1-800-288-4677)

Because of the dynamic nature of the Internet, any web addresses or links contained in this book may have changed since publication and may no longer be valid. The views expressed in this work are solely those of the author and do not necessarily reflect the views of the publisher, and the publisher hereby disclaims any responsibility for them.

Any people depicted in stock imagery provided by Getty Images are models, and such images are being used for illustrative purposes only. Certain stock imagery © Getty Images.

ISBN: 978-1-5320-7048-8 (sc)
ISBN: 978-1-5320-7047-1 (e)

Library of Congress Control Number: 2019902837

Print information available on the last page.

iUniverse rev. date: 03/29/2019

To my husband, Ronnie

I was meant for you.

ACKNOWLEDGMENTS

I would like to take this opportunity to thank friends and family who have contributed their time, talents, and expertise to the writing of this novel. I hope my readers enjoy this story of love, hope, and forgiveness in the face of loss, grief, and deception. Life is not perfect, and the most innocent actions often result in the most disastrous consequences.

Thank you to my test readers, Marty Wooldridge Younts, Janie Hackney, and my mother, Wonda Frank, for their ideas, corrections, and encouragement.

Thank you to Mandy Lawrence for giving me a new perspective and approach. It took a lot of extra hours, but it worked.

I want to express my appreciation to Raeann Shaak Allred of Dawn's Bridals for her ideas and descriptions of bridal gowns and bridesmaids' attire. It truly is a beautiful world.

Thank you to Roger Tripp for his advice regarding the working environment and education of attorneys. There is no doubt Roger sports the most creative socks in the world of law.

Lastly, I want to thank my husband, Ronnie, and our son, Michael, for listening to me rehash simple sentences and for giving me their honest opinions. I love them both more than they will ever know.

PART ONE

1969
Beginnings

CHAPTER 1

Susan Anderson

Susan Anderson's eyes opened to an alien world, an alien life, a new life. The opaque sunlight filtered through half-open windows covered by ancient venetian blinds. The faded metal slats had seen better days. The brightness mocked the darkness within her soul. The heat of summer had set in, spreading its veil of humidity over her skin, rendering a sheen of salty perspiration. The overhead ceiling fan swirled the warm, moist air throughout the room, providing no comfort for the body or spirit.

For one brief moment, Susan had no idea where she was or how she'd arrived in this foreign place. She sat upright and peered from left to right, then left again, her actions mimicking someone attempting to cross a street. But there was no street, no traffic, no vehicles to avoid, only the quiet whispers of the others. Her heart and stomach bowed to the pressure of abandonment and the loss of everyone and everything she'd ever loved.

She fought to comprehend her surroundings, which resembled a hospital ward. Sterile, stark, green. She wrinkled her nose as she surveyed the oversized room. She generally liked the color green, but not this one. This shade should have been discarded as a failure, its formula permanently erased by the designer. The worn black-and-white tile floor evidenced the scuff marks of a thousand soles. The ceiling, a mass of water-stained squares, begged for the relief of a coat of out-of-the-can white paint. The sun's reflective rays did nothing to improve the appearance of the unappealing room. Emotional clouds descended on her heart, blocking any semblance of life-sustaining sunshine. Perhaps she should have died too.

Her heart plummeted, and a sadness overtook her being as she recognized her surroundings. She was in an orphanage. It was 1969, and she was twelve years old. She'd lost her mother, her home, her world. She was no better than a stray animal left on the doorstep of a stranger's house. She was certain she would survive physically, but would she survive emotionally?

Life without a father had not been so bad. She'd heard people say you don't miss what you've never known. She found that to be true. But she'd a mother, a wonderful mother, and now she was gone. Susan's heart ached; she missed her mother terribly. Tears formed, quickly spilling over and coursing down her cheeks in wet, salty trails. A box of tissues had been strategically placed on the small metal nightstand next to her bed in anticipation of her flood of tears. She yanked out two tissues and let the tears fall. She welcomed the pity party that followed, with wracking sobs that echoed down the hallway. She was confident she was not the first or the last to shed a tear at the Cabot Home for Children.

Susan calmed herself after more than a few moments of tearful, heartbreaking sobs. She threw away a mountain of damp, sticky tissues and sat on the edge of her bed. There were three other beds in the room, two of them occupied by girls who appeared to be close to her age. She noted their attempts to offer her some degree of privacy. She assumed they had suffered the same fate, only earlier in their youth. It was now her turn in this unfortunate game of childhood solitude and self-pity.

Susan had been introduced to the girls who shared her room the previous evening. Their names were Jackie and Roberta. Both seemed hesitant toward her. Susan couldn't blame them; she felt hesitant toward them as well. Trust would not come easily. Misplaced trust exacted a heavy toll.

She missed her bedroom in the old apartment that she'd shared with her mother. She'd loved the oversized purple-and-white flowered wallpaper and her white wooden bedroom furniture. Her mother had allowed her to pick her own bedspread, and she'd chosen bright shades of purple-and-pink striped fabric with matching fluffy pillows. She often sat propped on the pillows, reading books from her small personal stash or the public library. She'd read by the light of her purple-and-white mushroom-shaped lamp. It was the coolest lamp Susan had ever seen. Her mother had bought it for her at a gift shop in Chapel Hill.

In the days that followed, Susan learned from Jackie and Roberta that the three of them would be entering the seventh grade at Cabot Junior High School in August. They were quick to inform her that in addition to the children's home students, it was also the school attended by children of the wealthiest citizens of Cabot. The children of Cabot's upper crust were generally unkind to those living at the children's home. Susan's new roommates told stories of how they and others had been mistreated and bullied. Susan agreed with her newfound friends that staying out of the limelight was best. Susan would strive to become a nobody, to blend in with the crowd. She was convinced the further she stayed on the outskirts of the complicated societal class structure of junior high school, the easier life would be. She would do as she was told by her teachers—keep her head down and bring no attention to herself. It sounded good in theory. She would discover, however, that theories often have the opposite outcome when they play out in real life.

CHAPTER 2

Barbara Leigh Anderson

Barbara Leigh Anderson was Susan's mother. She was considered by many to be a beautiful woman. Her long brunette hair and deep brown eyes bespoke her complex personality and deep-seated soul. Susan was constantly reminded of her mother as she gazed at her own reflection in the mirror. She'd inherited her mother's hair and eye coloring but didn't consider herself comparable to her mother's beauty. Her mother often laughed, saying her complexion was a combination of fair to partly cloudy. Her warmly tinted skin took on a golden glow in the warm summer sun, hinting at an ancestry of Native American and European influence. Her slim waist and perfect feminine proportions were the product of an active lifestyle. She enjoyed being outdoors and was an avid runner long before it was fashionable. She was considered tall but carried her height as regally as a queen. She personified a deep and intelligent being, able to debate any topic of the day or solve any problem with a combination of intelligence and common sense.

Barbara Anderson was a native of Ferndale, Kansas, the daughter of strictly religious parents. Her parents were in their forties and had given up hope of ever having a child. Susan assumed her mother loved her parents, though she disagreed with their extreme views. Her mother never said in so many words, but Susan suspected her mother was an abused child. Barbara did not believe in physical punishment for children, holding the opinion that other options could be used for discipline. Punishment consisted of sending Susan to her room or taking away privileges. Susan's conscience punished her more than her mother ever could. Guilt came easy for Susan.

Religion was a hotly debated topic between Barbara and her parents as she transitioned from adolescence to adulthood. Barbara described a number of discussions and arguments that led to her leaving home. Barbara's interpretation of the Bible differed greatly from her parents'. Barbara described God as loving, leading his followers in faith and hope with forgiveness and love going hand in hand. Her parents' version was more along the lines of fire and brimstone with no leeway; once guilty, always guilty. Forgiveness had strict stipulations. Susan's mother once told her if people felt worse when they left a church than when they entered, they were at the wrong church. She described God as forgiving and loving because humans were imperfect. She thought God made them that way so they would need him, similar to a child needing a parent.

Barbara considered herself a free and inventive spirit, loving books, school, and learning. She valued education, especially for women, and graduated at the top of her high school class. She read aloud to Susan every day, bringing the characters of books, poetry, and short stories to life.

Many evenings, especially during warmer months, Barbara and Susan sat in silence on their little porch, no need for conversation, each sensing the other's thoughts and emotions. They were extensions of each other. Their family was complete. Barbara devoted her entire being to Susan. She never dated; said she'd already found love. Susan often wondered if her mother was referring to her father. Barbara had friends from the hospital where she worked and their small apartment complex but spent very little time socializing with them.

She spent her free time taking care of Susan. They were a team; Barbara loved her daughter, and Susan adored her mother. Barbara instilled in Susan the qualities of love, kindness, joy, prayer, and the value of education.

As a child in the late thirties prior to the United States' immersion into World War II, Barbara and her parents visited the North Carolina coast. It was an extended vacation, visiting churches that shared the same belief system as their church in Kansas. Her father spent the entirety preaching at a host of churches. During their trip, Barbara fell in love with the Atlantic Coast and its ever-evolving beauty. She'd never seen the ocean before and was intrigued by the rolling, frothy swells. She was mesmerized as each wave made its noisy arrival, a unique and unstoppable marvel of Mother Nature. As she cupped her hand over her eyes, she noted the reflection of millions of sparkling gems on the ocean's surface, twinkling like faraway stars in the night sky. The white effervescent waves soothed her soul as her nose tingled in the scented breeze, its brine-laden aroma lending a tropical perfume to her senses.

Barbara's parents disliked the moisture-drenched environment and the powdery sand, but she loved it. She relished the feel of the sand's massaging warmth beneath her feet, and her skin took on the golden hues of a summer tan. The offshore sea breezes lifted her hair in a cacophony of waving tendrils. The resonating melody of the ocean mesmerized her with a flurry of crashing waves against the gently sloping shore. The whitewashed shells pinged against one another, tousled by the stirring, pungent surf. The songs of the gulls signaled their feathered, web-footed companions and human visitors alike. She laughed as the pipers raced to and from the water's edge, stealing tidbits of sea creatures, the curious wee birds forcing the smooth shells open with their sharply pointed beaks, consuming their meal greedily.

Barbara could not swim, yet her childish innocence gave her courage to venture into the unknown depths. She trusted her senses while jumping the buoying waves, defying her parents' rule of staying in knee-deep water.

In the end, standing at the ocean's edge, peering out over the waters of creation, Barbara felt a closeness to God. The magnitude of God's presence and his peace overwhelmed her with the serenity of creation's beginning, Genesis. She observed the fine line between sea and sky with childish wonder, drawing her into its mysterious aura. Barbara was saddened when the time came to leave and vowed to return someday.

As Barbara's high school graduation approached, she made the decision to apply to colleges in North Carolina. She was confident this was where she was meant to live. She had no intention of returning to Kansas when she finished college. She was accepted by the University of North Carolina at Chapel Hill for study in nursing. She excelled in her classes and was frequently asked by faculty members if she would be interested in medical school. She declined, stating her desire to be in direct contact with patients. She felt she could play a more significant role in healing with a close proximity to patients on an hour-by-hour basis, meeting their needs with patience and kindness.

She graduated second in her class from UNC–Chapel Hill and accepted a nursing position at Cabot Memorial Hospital in Cabot, North Carolina, a small town nestled in the southeastern third of the state. She was happy to remain in North Carolina, a state with a pleasing climate and numerous beaches for vacationing. Her decision would lead to a life unsanctioned by her parents and society, ultimately bringing both her and her child to their knees.

CHAPTER 3

Paternity

The 1950s was not a popular time to be an unwed mother. In most cases, a pregnancy out of wedlock resulted in the father's offering to marry the mother as soon as possible. The infant was claimed premature but fooled no one. The girl's situation was discussed in hushed whispers among the town's gossip circles. Unplanned pregnancies occurred more often than one might imagine, many families discovering in later years that Grandma or a Great-aunt was pregnant when she married. The boy offering to marry the girl might or might not be the father but felt the need to take on the responsibility of raising the child, freely giving the infant his name. Through the years, wedding dates were altered or conveniently forgotten, covering for unplanned pregnancies. Many modern-day descendants would be surprised to see their heritage laid out in DNA analysis, realizing their ancestors were not who they thought they were.

Susan's grandparents disowned her mother the day she told them she was pregnant. She informed them she had no intention of getting married and planned to raise the baby on her own. They said it went against their religion to have a grandchild out of wedlock. Susan was curious as to where it said in the Bible that you should disown your child when he or she did something you didn't like or disagreed with. She guessed the part of their Bible that spoke of love was missing. The part about forgiveness was missing too. She wondered how parents could disown a child so quickly because of one mistake. Her mother was perfect in Susan's eyes.

Barbara Anderson never revealed the identity of Susan's father to anyone. Susan's birth certificate said *Unknown* in the space provided for the father's name. Susan was puzzled as to why her mother chose not to name a father. Who was he, and what were the circumstances that prevented her mother from identifying him? Susan knew babies had fathers, and she had one out there somewhere. Maybe her father didn't know of her existence. Possibilities swirled in Susan's mind.

Susan began questioning her mother about the identity of her father when she started school and repeated her inquiries most birthdays. Her mother promised, with each query, she would tell Susan when the time was right. Susan asked her mother when that time might be, and her mother smiled, closed her eyes, and said to wait; Susan wasn't old enough to understand. Her mother reassured her and promised she had enough love for two parents. Susan never felt unloved, but her curiosity was not assuaged.

By her eleventh birthday, Susan had gathered enough courage to once again ask her mother about her father's identity and her mother's relationship with him. Susan began her conversation by asking her mother if she loved him. Her mother explained that she loved him, but circumstances prevented them from being together. Before Susan could ask her mother another question, her mother turned and walked away silently. Susan thought she saw her mother wipe her eyes. That would be the last time Susan would have the opportunity to ask about her father.

Susan suspected her mother had worked with her father at some point. She suspected he was a doctor at the hospital. On the few occasions she'd visited the hospital, she'd met some of the doctors on staff there. They were courteous, but no one stood out. None of them showed any interest in Susan, leaving her to question her suspicions. Perhaps she'd been wrong, or her father had moved away to another town or hospital. His identity would remain a mystery.

CHAPTER 4

Beach Memories

Susan smiled as she recalled memories of her mother and their vacations to Myrtle Beach. They planned their beach trip for the last week in July each summer. He mother drove their 1963 Chevrolet Corvair packed with everything they would need for a week's stay. They rode the entire trip sunglass-clad, top down, with radio blaring. They sang at the top of their lungs and didn't care who saw them. They passed more than one car in which the inhabitants were shaking their heads, laughing. They waved excitedly, giggling at their own antics. It was a happy time.

Susan's mother rented the same cottage each year. It was owned by the family of one of her colleagues at the hospital. The owners lived in Conway, South Carolina, and vacationed at the beach cottage for part of the summer, renting the cottage to people they knew for the rest of the warm-weather season. Each spring, Susan's mother reserved the beach cottage for their annual midsummer getaway.

The small white clapboard cottage was located across the street from the Atlantic Ocean. It had two bedrooms and a bathroom with an antiquated claw-footed tub. The front porch was enclosed with shabby screens pocked with small holes stuffed with tiny wads of cotton to keep out mosquitoes and a multitude of other insects. Rocking chairs lined the porch for the best views of each morning's sunrise and allowed the cooling sea breezes to flow into the shady oasis each afternoon. The porch made for a perfect observation point for a curious preadolescent girl. Susan observed the fascinating populace treading the broken, sand-covered sidewalk. Over the years, she observed more than one person tripping on the uneven pavement, spilling ice cream scoops or snow cones they'd purchased from the ice cream shop just a block away.

The tiny kitchen, with its ancient gas stove, scratched pine cabinets, and deep iron-clad sink, welcomed Susan and her mother with the ghostly fragrance of meals past. The oak floors and knotted pine walls and ceilings had seen better days, but they didn't mind; they loved this little cottage. It welcomed their annual pilgrimage with a comforting air of familiarity. The ceiling fans in the bedrooms and living room kept the humid air on the move, cooling with as much of a breeze as could be expected in the tropical heat. Susan and her mother seemed to luck out, experiencing not a single rainy day. An occasional thunderstorm rattled the windows in the evenings after they'd retired from their day of sunny adventures, but the next morning brought with it a bright golden sunrise, promising a full day of splashing in the waves and building sand castles.

As soon as they arrived each year on a sun-drenched Saturday afternoon, Susan and her mother shopped for their week's worth of groceries at the little mom-and-pop grocery store out on Highway 17. It was called Jacobs' Grocery. Everyone at home said the prices were twice as high at the beach grocery stores, but her mother liked the sweet elderly couple, Bill and Wonda Jacobs, who ran the little store. They remembered Susan and her mother each year, calling them by name.

Susan's mother cooked eggs and bacon for breakfast with orange juice or milk. Her mother's coffee, with its early morning aroma, added a most intoxicating scent to the sea breezes wafting from the open windows. She'd allow Susan a small portion with a liberal amount of milk and sugar. Susan nicknamed it chocolate coffee. It was delicious and made her feel very grown-up.

Lunch consisted of fried bologna sandwiches with mayonnaise and mustard or fresh tomato sandwiches, slathered with mayonnaise and a good shake of salt and pepper on fresh white bread, oozing a sweet pink broth. They'd eat their way through two or three bags of potato chips, with her mother's homemade oatmeal-raisin cookies for dessert. There was something about the sea air that made everything taste better.

They cooked dinner a few evenings with a fare of meatloaf or fried chicken with fresh green beans, corn on the cob, and locally grown cantaloupe. Leftovers meant the pair could stay out on the beach a little longer the next day, skipping the evening's meal preparation. Cold fried chicken or meatloaf sandwiches tasted delicious after a hot day on the beach. If they were lucky, the grocery store had a fresh shipment of shrimp, and her mother boiled them in spices and lemon slices. They'd eat them on the front porch, throwing the peels in a small bucket between the two of them.

Susan and her mother made the trek to the local seafood restaurant, Mack's Fish House, a couple of evenings during their trip. Mr. Mack had been the proprietor for years, with his sweet wife, Dearie, manning the cash register. He employed two young men in the kitchen and could be heard barking out the orders as the teenage girls working as waitresses clipped them to the ticket carousel. The three men worked their culinary magic and produced a delicious fare of fried fish, shrimp, oysters, french fries, and hush puppies. The chalkboard menu offered scallops when they were available. The restaurant's coleslaw and tartar sauce were homemade daily by Dearie. She mixed them by the gallon, and they were consumed eagerly by locals as well as tourists. Typically, Mr. Mack was a little on the gruff side, but Susan could coax a little smile from him by complimenting his fried treats. Mr. Mack truly had the best fried shrimp and flounder anywhere. His hush puppies melted in your mouth, especially when dipped in his wife's homemade cinnamon-sugar–butter concoction. The french fries were batter-dipped, and there were customers whose entire order consisted of plates of the crispy golden fries. Susan and her mother stuffed themselves and pretended to waddle their way to the car, eliciting laughter from anyone watching their antics.

Susan thrilled at their visits to the Pavilion, just up the street from their cottage, where they played pinball and rode carnival rides. She and her mother giggled delightfully with every bounce or drop, temporarily taking their breath away. They'd indulge in icy snow cones, with Susan choosing grape and her mother choosing cherry. They'd compare tongues, a silly contest to determine whose was the brightest color. Her mother always won.

Susan was fascinated by the mechanical contraption that pulled taffy in the beachside candy store. She stood at the window, watching the long, jointed arms go 'round and 'round, pulling the sticky wads of spun sugar. Just when it looked as though the revolving arms would lose their bundle of sweet, sticky delight to the unforgiving floor, another arm saved the day by appearing from below the huge wad of colorful candy, grabbing and pulling with more tenacity than before, mesmerizing Susan. Her mother bought a box filled with a flavorful rainbow of the gooey candy each year, with the intention of taking it home. None of the soft treats ever made it to the end of their vacation week.

Swimming and wading in the ocean kept Susan and her mother busy during their sun-filled days. Her mother rented oversized navy-blue rafts for both of them with large white painted numbers. Susan had learned how to swim at the city pool in their hometown at an early age, so she felt comfortable swimming on her own. Susan recalled flipping off her raft, convinced she'd gone under the water a good ten feet, though once she opened her eyes, she could see wavy, milky sunshine, distorted by the mesmerizing movement of the water above. She immediately sensed this was the direction to swim. It was then that she realized she was in waist deep water. All she needed to do was stand, leaving her safe in the roaring waves.

Susan and her mother sat on an old bedspread in their bathing suits, observing the sights and sounds of vacationers, here just like they were. The beach was a place of amusement and relaxation. It offered a respite from the day-to-day activities of work and school. It was the closest thing to paradise Susan could imagine.

By the end of their vacation, Susan and her mother sadly packed the car after what seemed like a mere few days and headed home, leaving behind their happy place. They'd take one last walk on the beach before heading home. The lone saving grace of the long drive was stopping by their favorite produce market and purchasing a small basket of fresh peaches. Susan recalled how juicy and sweet they tasted, each fuzzy treat perfectly ripened on the tree. Her mother made a peach pie and a freezer of peach ice cream when they returned home.

After a few pensive days, the mother and daughter returned to their routine and reminisced about their trip. Each year Susan's mother had the film from her camera developed and printed at the drugstore on Main Street, and she made a small photo album of their annual trip. Though they visited the same places and generally did the same activities each year, every photo book was unique. Most pictures were taken of Susan playing on the beach or enjoying rides at the Pavilion, but Susan took a few of her mother. On one occasion, the camera slipped from Susan's sweaty hands, and she took a picture of her mother's feet in the sand. They laughed at the picture, and it became one of their favorites. Her mother occasionally stopped other beachgoers and asked them to take a picture of the two of them. Generally, these pictures were posed, but Susan remembered one taken as her mother reached down and tickled her, just as the camera snapped. The resulting look on Susan's face was priceless. Her mother laughed so hard she admitted she'd almost wet herself. Her mother framed the humorous picture, placing it on the television in their living room. Life could not have been better for the mother-daughter pair.

CHAPTER 5

The Great Silencer

The tiny family of two had a good run—that is, until 1969. Susan's mother didn't tell her at first, but she'd found a lump—a lump in a place where there shouldn't have been one: her breast. She sat Susan down and explained the diagnosis, making sure Susan understood. She would undergo surgery and everything would be back to normal.

Much to their disappointment, the surgeon couldn't get all of the cancer; it had metastasized, spreading to her lungs, bones, and brain. It was growing aggressively with no way to slow it down. Barbara fought a valiant fight. Susan was convinced God would not let her mother die. She would be alone without her mother. God did not abandon children. He loved her. He wouldn't take her mother away.

Susan was old enough to help her mother at home with household chores. She was convinced her mother would get well, and they would live just as they had before the diagnosis. She helped clean the apartment and could make a few simple meals, mostly sandwiches. They ate a lot of sandwiches.

In time, her mother became too sick to live in their home and had to be hospitalized. She had been out of work for two months. They had no income and were living off her mother's savings and money in her retirement fund. Susan was sent to live with Diane, one of her mother's friends from the hospital. She finished sixth grade with Diane dropping her off and picking her up from school each day.

Susan's mother made the decision to call her parents in Kansas when she entered the hospital. She had not communicated with them in almost thirteen years. They hung up before she could explain that she needed help. Susan recalled walking into her mother's hospital room that cool, drizzly day and seeing her mother hang up the phone. Her mother dropped her face into her hands and wept. Susan didn't know the reason for her mother's despair but sat on the bed by her side and wept with her.

Susan's grandparents made no attempt to contact her or her mother after that day. Susan never met them and never knew what happened to them. From that point, Susan considered them dead.

Susan's mother died the day after she finished sixth grade. She sat at her mother's bedside holding her hand. At that point her mother was not conscious, but Susan wanted to think her mother knew she was there and sensed how much she loved her. Susan talked to her mother, touching her face gently. She looked like a porcelain angel, her complexion ghostly pale, lying in the worn hospital bed. Susan was lying beside her mother with her head on her mother's shoulder, her hand on her mother's cheek, when she breathed her last breath. The nurses, many of them friends of her mother, were kind to Susan and didn't make her move away until she was convinced her mother wouldn't start breathing again. They tearfully stood back as Susan kissed her mother goodbye.

Barbara Anderson was buried three days later in the city cemetery, her grave covered with beautifully arranged flowers in a rainbow of colors. Susan wanted to pick up every basket and wreath, throwing them as far as her small arms could fling them, screaming at the top of her lungs. She didn't care where they landed, as long as they were nowhere near her mother. Her anger was at an all-time fever pitch. God was not on her list of favorites. He'd let her down. She found no solace in the well-meaning words of comfort expressed by those mourning her mother's death or the minister who'd officiated the funeral. Their words rang hollow in Susan's ears. No mother, no father, no family—and shortly, she would be homeless. It was not fair. And to add salt to her emotional wounds, the secret of her father's identity died with her mother. Death was the great silencer. There was no peace in buried secrets.

Susan spent the next three weeks with Diane. A notice was placed in the legal notices of the local newspaper that Susan had become a ward of the state. If there was a father in the community, this was his opportunity to come forward. There was no response. No one claimed her.

Diane found a buyer for her mother's car. Susan could not bear to watch as the new owners drove it away that Friday afternoon. She remained inside, crying uncontrollably. All of the furniture was sold, and Diane took her mother's clothes since they fit her. She promised not to wear them while Susan stayed with her. They boxed up Susan's clothes, some personal items, and all the photos and photo albums her mother had assembled over the years. Susan would be allowed to keep them. Diane and her mother's attorney put all the money from the sale of her mother's belongings into a trust fund for Susan. She would have access to it on her eighteenth birthday. She would need the money for living expenses and college when she was deemed an adult by the state of North Carolina.

Susan's single treasure was an emerald ring that had belonged to her mother. It was a princess cut with three diamonds flowing away on each side, set in a thick gold band. Susan assumed she'd bought it for herself or that it was a gift from her parents; she never told Susan its origin, and Susan never thought to ask. Her mother wore it on special occasions, like church or a girls' night out. Susan had admired it for as long as she could remember, trying it on, with her mother's permission, and then returning it to the white satin-lined box when she was finished. It was beautiful and, Susan suspected, very expensive. She would guard it with her life.

Diane delivered Susan to the Cabot Home for Children on a hot afternoon, dripping with humidity. The sky threatened an evening marred by thunder, lightning, and torrential downpours. Diane hugged Susan and promised to visit when she was able. Susan never saw her again.

CHAPTER 6

Expectations

Day-to-day events and activities kept everyone busy at the children's home. Each child was responsible for cleaning their personal space. Tidiness and cleanliness were high on the list of chores. Children were expected to make their beds before breakfast. No article of clothing was left unfolded, and dresses were hung in the shared closets of the girls' dormitory rooms. Susan noticed some of the other residents traded off chores. She didn't mind folding clothes but hated dusting, so she folded Jackie's laundry in exchange for Jackie dusting their shared space.

The residents seemed cheerful and happy for the most part, and Susan was pleasantly surprised at how well she was treated by staff members and the other children residing in the home. There were many reasons children had been placed there. Like Susan, some children were there because they had no family. Others lived at the home temporarily because their parents couldn't take care of them, or they caused excessive trouble in their families. Some of the children had been taken away from their parents permanently by the court system. Susan made every effort to make her time pass quickly, staying busy with chores or reading in her spare time.

Susan was puzzled to discover, two weeks after her arrival, that she would receive a small allowance each month. She was instructed by the hall mother to refrain from discussing her monthly disbursement with any of the other children, as she was the only child who received extra money. She didn't ask the source of the money at first but grew curious as time passed. The amount of money wasn't much by any means, but it was more than anyone else received. Susan gathered the courage and approached the hall mother early one afternoon while most of the children were on the playground. Susan sensed she was uncomfortable with giving an answer, and Susan wasn't sure she would respond. The hall mother looked up and down the empty hallway, making sure they were alone, before motioning Susan into her office. She shut the door, pointed to a chair for Susan, walked across the room, and turned toward Susan while leaning back on her desk. Her forehead was drawn together into a scowl. Uncertainty filled Susan's mind. Maybe she was in trouble for asking about the money. Maybe the hall mother would be in trouble if she gave an answer.

"Susan, I really shouldn't tell you this, but I'm going to make an exception. Do not discuss this with any of the other children. Do you understand?"

Susan slowly nodded her head as she comprehended the hall mother's statement.

"You will be inviting trouble, which will be bad for you and the administration."

Susan feared the consequences of her question and started to say she didn't need an explanation. She would be happy to go back to her room none the wiser. The hall mother took a deep breath and began. "You have a benefactor, an outside person. The Children's Home does not know who this person is, and he or she gives money so you can have everything you need. This person also makes a sizable donation to the home for the benefit of all the children. The home initially turned down the money but rethought the donation, considering it would help everyone, not just you."

"And you have no idea who this person is?" Susan questioned, puzzled. Could it be a friend of her mother's from the hospital? Maybe a group of friends had pooled their money? Maybe Diane? Maybe her grandparents? Any way she looked at it, everyone benefited, not just her.

"No, we have no idea. It is delivered in cash." She offered no additional comments.

"Thank you, Miss Freedle. I'll keep this to myself," Susan promised, her voice a whisper.

"You're welcome. You may go back to your room now."

Susan walked slowly down the hallway, questions swirling in her mind. Who was this benefactor, and why was he or she interested in her?

CHAPTER 7

Settling In

Susan's first summer ended with a cookout for all the children at the orphanage. It was sponsored by a local church and featured hamburgers and hot dogs. A group of men from the church hauled in various charcoal grills and coolers filled with soft drinks and chilled side items. Susan savored every bite, especially the French onion dip manufactured at the local dairy. Her mother occasionally bought the creamy onion-and-herb–laced dip to eat with their potato chips. As she thought of her mother, her chest tightened, and she found it difficult to breathe. Her mother had died nine weeks earlier, but it seemed as though a lifetime had passed. She looked around, hoping no one noticed her panicked state. Realizing no one had, she relaxed, silently talking herself down from the perilous ledge of emotions. She made a concerted attempt to focus her attention on a bowl of homemade vanilla ice cream when it was placed in her hands by one of the ladies of the church. The lady smiled at her, and Susan made every effort to return the smile.

"Is everything okay, dear?" she whispered.

"Yes," Susan answered in a weak, trembling voice, her head down, eyes drawn to the chilly bowl. "I just miss my mother." She sniffed as she wiped a tear away with the back of her hand.

The lady's smile brightened as she reached down and hugged Susan. She spoke in a kind voice. "My name is Margaret Penninger. What is your name?"

"Susan," she choked out with a sniff.

"It's nice to meet you, Susan. If you need anything, just let me know. I'll be glad to get it for you."

Susan's response came out much stronger. "Thank you, Mrs. Penninger."

"You're welcome." She patted Susan on the shoulder and turned to walk away. Susan watched as Mrs. Penninger walked to the dessert table, wiping her own eyes with a handkerchief she pulled from her dress pocket. Their paths would cross again, and Susan would sense she had an ally. For some unknown reason, Margaret Penninger appeared to understand Susan and her grief.

Susan suddenly realized that Margret Penninger was the first person outside the children's home she'd spoken with or who'd spoken to her since she'd arrived in June. There was another world out there, one that Susan assumed had ceased to exist. She hoped to find herself back in a world of normalcy someday.

CHAPTER 8

Passing Time

School started in August, and Susan was relieved to see the faded yellow bus creep up the driveway's broken pavement. There were forty-nine children on the bus, twenty-one junior high students and twenty-eight who attended high school. The children at the home had the bus all to themselves. It was a short ride to and from school, lasting ten minutes on a good day. No one bothered anyone on the bus. The students talked softly and kept their hands to themselves. Susan would have read a book if the ride had taken longer, but with such a short jaunt, there wasn't enough time to warrant retrieving a book, reading a few pages, and then closing it and putting it back in her book satchel when the bus arrived at school. Everyone was on their best behavior, knowing if they caused problems, they would be in serious trouble at the orphanage. No one wanted any part of that kind of trouble. Susan had witnessed two boys fighting earlier in the summer, and she'd heard their punishment was quick and severe.

Susan worked and studied diligently; school was easy for her. She excelled at academics and became the go-to person when kids needed help with their homework. She took on the role of hall tutor.

Susan was pleased to find that the children's home housed an extensive library with row upon row of books in all genres and topics, fiction and nonfiction. She suspected many of the books had been castoffs from other libraries. Children were allowed to check out one book at a time, but it seemed, more often than not, Susan finished her chosen book on a weekend when the library was closed. The home's librarian, Mrs. Frank, who'd retired from the public schools, volunteered in the library three days a week. She allowed Susan to check out two books at a time when she saw what a voracious reader she was.

"I promise to take good care of them," Susan assured Mrs. Frank.

Mrs. Frank playfully swore Susan to secrecy—she must tell no one—and gave Susan a wink.

Reading became Susan's escape, along with her love of the outdoors. Sadly, the outdoor play equipment was quite old and rusty. Susan wasn't sure it would hold up much longer without repair or replacement. After swinging on the oversized swings, children would walk away with brown hands from the rusted chains secured to the weathered wooden seats. It took ten minutes of scrubbing to remove the powdered rust stains. There was a baseball field on the expansive orphanage property. The boys usually monopolized it, but the girls joined when they were offered the chance.

The older kids held jobs around the orphanage: the boys helped with janitorial duties, and the girls worked in the cafeteria. Everyone stayed busy; the staff kept an eye open for loiterers, assigning them jobs, no matter how menial.

Christmas was bittersweet for the residents of the children's home, particularly those with no outside family. The home's residents became a close-knit family, wishing each other a merry Christmas and sharing decorating duties with a mismatched assortment of ornaments and decorations. A Sears Wish Book came in the mail, and it became just that—a book of wishes and dreams. It was passed from child to child, each impatient for a turn. Many of the children made lists of gifts they would choose if given the opportunity. They were realistic, knowing they wouldn't receive the items, but it gave them hope, something to wish for, satiating their dreams. The catalog eventually fell apart from usage, and many of the pages were saved and treasured by some of the younger children.

The church that had sponsored the back-to-school cookout held a Christmas party for all the children's home residents. A grandfatherly gentleman played the role of Santa in convincing fashion. Each child received a bag of gifts, according to age and gender. Susan's bag included a new twelve-pack of pencils, a journal, an ink pen, a box of colored pencils, and a gift certificate for a new piece of clothing at a local department store. That meant a shopping field trip. It had been months since she'd shopped for her own clothes. She and most of the others were excited at the opportunity to pick out something for themselves.

Susan and her mother had enjoyed an occasional day of shopping. They didn't buy a lot but loved to look at and try on new clothes. At the thought of her mother, sadness encompassed her being. This was her first Christmas without her mother. She dropped her head slightly and felt tears threatening to fall. Would she ever be able to think of her mother without grief overwhelming her? Not that she could ever imagine.

CHAPTER 9

Top Honors

Junior high school progressed quickly for some and slowly for others. Susan was one of the fortunate ones who breezed through. She loved school. Watching others fail was disheartening. She observed friends who performed poorly in school and felt pity for them. Living in the children's home was temporary, academic struggles were permanent and affected a person for a lifetime without intervention. Susan made a sincere effort to help the children who struggled in any way she could.

Susan made a concerted effort to keep a low profile at school by following class rules and completing assignments in the time allotted. She was one of the first students to raise her hand in response to teachers' questions. She had a small circle of friends that generally kept to themselves during breaks and lunch. She didn't think she stood out in the school environment. Little did Susan know, she was being watched by her teachers.

The school's guidance counselor, Miss Olsen, summoned her to the guidance office two months before the end of school. Susan was unsure of the reason and couldn't remember any infraction she might have committed. Miss Olsen started the conversation by saying that Susan's teachers had noticed her willingness to work and study. They wanted Susan to be successful in life after high school. She questioned Susan's plans after graduation.

"I've asked you here today to talk to you about what you think you might want to do when you grow up. Have you thought about college?" Miss Olsen said with a smile.

"Well, my mother was a nurse, and I've thought about the medical field, maybe nursing or medical research," Susan replied hesitantly.

"Have you thought about becoming a doctor?"

"No, not really. I don't know if my grades would be high enough."

"We think your grades are excellent; as a matter of fact, your grades are the highest in the eighth grade."

"My grades are the highest in the eighth grade?"

"Yes, and I would like to help you sign up for college prep classes next year in high school.

"That sounds great; thank you."

Miss Olsen smiled at Susan and patted her on the shoulder as Susan left her office. "I will always be here for you. If you need anything, please let me know. I think you should get back to class. Here is a note to explain your tardiness."

She handed the note to Susan and sent her on her way. As Susan arrived to class, her math teacher smiled. Susan didn't know at the time, but he'd been one of the teachers who'd referred her to Miss Olsen.

Junior high graduation was a week away, and the entire eighth grade exuded excitement, both in anticipation of summer vacation and entrance into high school the following fall. Students had signed up for next year's classes the previous week. They would be freshmen in high school. Susan was happy with all of her choices: Algebra I, US History, Shakespeare, basic grammar and composition, typing, biology, home economics, and mandatory study hall. Her year would be full, but she wasn't nervous; she was excited and thrilled to be challenged academically. Most of these classes were college prep, and she viewed home economics as being a life prep class, so it felt like a winning plan.

Susan and the other eighth-graders participated in the graduation ceremony on the last day of school. The school's music teacher played "Pomp and Circumstance" on the piano while each student marched in step, wearing their nicest outfits—girls in white dresses and boys wearing white shirts and ties. Susan spotted two of the Cabot Home for Children administrators seated in the parent section of the gym. She guessed they were representing the fourteen eighth-graders since their parents would not be there. She hadn't given much thought to the fact that a small group of students would be recognized with trophies and a small financial award for academic excellence. The names were announced down to number two. Applause was moderate, with a few catcalls from two proud fathers. When number one was called, it was Susan; she stood up and walked toward the stage to thunderous applause. The school staff and audience stood, clapping. Everyone seemed to know her and was happy to see her acknowledged as the top student in her class. It was indeed an honor. Susan was presented a small trophy, with her name and "Top Student 1971 Cabot Junior High School" engraved on it, and an envelope. She was overwhelmed; she'd never received this much positive attention from so many people. It was then she thought of her mother. Tears blurred her vision, and she quickly wiped them away, appearing to be overcome by the recognition. Her English teacher, Miss Smith, snapped three pictures of her shaking the principal's hand and promised to mail one to her at the orphanage. She was true to her word, and the picture arrived two weeks later. Susan sat down long enough for final remarks to be made, and then the graduating class marched out to classical music, again presented by the music teacher. As the students reached the hallway outside the gym, Susan's small group of friends surrounded her to congratulate her and ask, "What's in the envelope?"

"I don't know. Should I open it?" Susan said timidly.

A chorus of *yes* came tumbling from the group, so she opened it. There was a fifty-dollar bill in the envelope with a letter of congratulations. Susan was shocked; she'd never seen a fifty-dollar bill before, much less received one. She quickly sought the orphanage administrators and asked them to take her financial treasure for safekeeping so she would not have to be responsible for that much money at school. They assured her they would take care of her prize until she arrived home later in the afternoon. That would be a substantial deposit on her future college education. Her trophy sat on her nightstand all summer. She thought how proud her mother would have been. She then thought how proud her father might have been, had he known.

CHAPTER 10

High School

The summer of 1971 passed quickly for the children and teenagers at the orphanage. The first day of high school arrived, and excitement combined with a bit of apprehension filled the air of the dormitory rooms. The teens raced to open the windows as they boarded the bus that hot August morning for the short ride to school. They anxiously entered the front doors of Cabot Senior High School, picked up their class schedules, and headed to an expanded homeroom, where their teachers explained school rules, and they completed forms for their school records. Their first-period class would be shortened accordingly, keeping the rest of the day on schedule.

Susan walked quickly up the ramp to the second-floor science lab for her first-period biology class. As she walked into the classroom, she recognized many of the faces from junior high school. Susan quickly spotted her friend Debbie. They'd shared classes in eighth grade, and Susan asked if she could sit with Debbie. Debbie obliged with a smile and said, "Sure." The tables seated two, so Susan hurriedly grabbed the chair, just in case someone else had the same idea. The two girls talked for a few minutes about their summer vacation until the teacher entered the noisy classroom. The students quieted quickly since he appeared eager to begin. He introduced himself as Mr. Kriesowsky, but everyone should call him Mr. K. He began calling each name from his class list, followed by a comical mix of responses from the anxious group.

"Here."

"Yep."

"Here."

"Yes."

"Here under protest"—this from the soon-to-be-discovered class clown, which was followed by muffled laughter.

Luckily, their teacher had a sense of humor. He laughed and said, "I'll be expecting this same enthusiasm when the class dissects frogs."

"Yuck!" everyone chimed in, faces contorted with disgust. He shook his head with a grin and moved on to the next name. He'd almost finished calling roll when the door opened and a young man walked in, hesitantly at first, then appearing to gain confidence as he walked from the doorway to the front table that served as the teacher's desk. He handed Mr. K. a sheet of paper. The teacher took it, added a name to his class list, and then pointed to a seat that happened to be at the table next to Susan's.

Susan hadn't seen him before. He hadn't been a student at Cabot Junior High; she was sure she would have noticed. Susan was not alone in her infatuation, by the looks he received from the other girls in the class. His blue eyes, curly dark-blond hair, and tanned physique made him appear as the quintessential lifeguard at the country club pool. Susan couldn't help but stare. Female hormones rose to precarious levels. It was obvious all the girls were smitten with their new classmate.

In the meantime, Mr. K. called the last name: "Richard van Allen Pierce II."

The late arrival answered, "Here. You can call me Rick."

"Okay, Rick Pierce." He slowly wrote a note beside the new addition's name in his class roll book. "Okay, class, here are my class rules and requirements."

Susan listened intently, writing notes as a reminder to herself and to take to the children's home so the hall mother would know what was required for her classes. Class ended with assignments and an extremely heavy biology book, which had seen three previous caretakers, according to the names written in the owner section inside the slightly frayed front cover.

Debbie was registered for a different second-period class, but the two friends would meet afterward, sharing classes for the remainder of the day. It was nice knowing there would be a familiar face in her classes. They each promised to save a seat for the other in their third-period class and simultaneously said, "See you in a little while." They both laughed and waved as they walked in opposite directions down the locker-lined hallway,

Susan headed for her US history class. She'd heard the teacher was a stickler for discipline without a hint of humor. She walked into a stark environment, with plain cork bulletin boards devoid of decoration except for a smattering of loose staples and bent thumbtacks. She quickly concluded the rumors about her history teacher were true. She'd been warned in advance that this would be the most challenging—and most boring class—on her schedule.

As roll was called, she noticed the new student was sitting in this class as well. There were no comical responses from the first-period class clown. He answered with a polite "Here."

Susan couldn't help but steal a peek at the new member of the class of 1975, sitting slightly behind her at an angle, a couple of rows toward the window. She could not have picked a worse moment because just as she did, he peered across two rows of desks at her. She quickly diverted her gaze back to the teacher. She was embarrassed having been caught and turned a deep crimson. She focused her attention on the chalkboard, where the teacher was writing an outline for the first week of class. She continued to steal glances at the new guy, thinking how lucky it would be to be his girlfriend. US History was going to be a long, boring class that would last for the next 180 school days. Susan had no doubt she was capable of making an A, but she was worried her attention would be drawn to this new male student. Where had he come from? Where had he attended school up until now?

During lunch on the first day of school, Susan noticed Richard van Allen Pierce II, aka Rick, sitting with the upper clique of students in the cafeteria. He behaved as though he knew them; he probably lived in the same high-end neighborhood. That meant he was already out of reach, and Susan gave up before she made her first attempt to flirt with him. Why would he show any interest in her? He belonged to the group of kids whose parents were the Who's Who of Cabot. These were the children of doctors, lawyers, and business leaders. Whether their money was old or new, she knew they had lots of it. They also had attitude, most of them not good. They looked down at the rest of the world from their high, self-appointed perch. Susan purposely stayed away from them. Situations never turned out well when people like her found their paths crossing that of the high-ups. Ordinary kids steered clear because that was the sort of trouble no one wanted.

And there he was, right in the middle of them. So much for the thought, yet she couldn't help but glance at him from time to time. Susan hadn't been attracted to many of the boys at school, and there were no boys at the children's home that held any interest for her. But this boy was different. She couldn't put her finger on it, but she knew there was something about him that would hold her interest for a long time to come.

By the end of school on the first day, Susan had a stack of books and an equally tall stack of homework. College prep classes assigned homework from day one. *I might as well get used to it*, she thought. *I have many more years of school ahead of me.*

As Susan walked to the bus, she noticed Rick standing out front, waiting in the car-rider group. A sleek silver Mercedes rolled up; he opened the back door and climbed in, throwing his books on the seat ahead of him. She could see someone she assumed was his mother, a pearl-encrusted, perfectly coiffed blonde, who looked as though she had stomped bugs bigger than herself. Susan quickly determined this was not a nice woman by the scowl on her face. Susan sensed an air about the woman, as though she could take a sizable man down with her stare. The woman rolled up her window and drove into the main driveway, blowing her horn at a car that obviously had the right-of-way. It didn't seem to matter to her. Susan hoped her own path never crossed that one.

The older kids at the orphanage were expected to have a job when they entered high school. They received a small allowance for working. Susan's job was serving in the cafeteria. Cooks did the actual food preparation, but the older kids were assigned to serve, wash dishes, and clean tables. Susan, Roberta, and Jackie lined up every evening during the school year to serve whatever items were on the daily menu. On weekends and holidays, they served all three meals, eating their meals after the other children had been served. The girls thought they looked atrocious in their hairnets and were thankful no one outside the home would see them. Each of the three girls had long hair and begged the cafeteria manager to let them wear their hair in ponytails. She told them they could, but they still had to wear the dreaded hairnets.

Susan smiled at the kids shuffling through the line, especially the new ones or the little ones. She remembered being appreciative of every smile she'd received in her first few months. She'd just marked her third year and was accustomed to the routines, rules, and regulations. Children were given opportunities to spend their money, but Susan chose to save hers. She already had a small allowance and new clothes, so she didn't need to spend her extra money. She was saving for a car. It was a long shot—the worst thing the administrators could say was no—but she would bide her time and be on her best behavior. Maybe—just maybe—they would say yes, and she would have enough money to buy some sort of vehicle when she turned eighteen. It didn't have to be new or fashionable; she only needed wheels, minimal transportation. A girl could at least dream.

CHAPTER 11

Rick Pierce

Rick was anxious about entering Cabot Senior High. He'd never attended public school, only private. A few friends from Stone Brook School were transitioning to the city's public high school. Most of the kids from his neighborhood went to Cabot Senior High as well. Stone Brook had been a haven for the wealthiest families of Cabot and the surrounding area, marking a tradition for some, with parents and grandparents as alumni of the highly touted private school. Only the wealthiest and most intelligent children were accepted and educated within its walls. Stone Brook was limited to serving students through the eighth grade. On two previous occasions, parents and board members had seriously discussed the option of extending the student population through the twelfth grade, but their ideas never moved past the discussion stage. Offering competitive high school classes was more of a challenge than elementary and junior high curriculums. It never came together, so here he was.

On the other hand, he was relieved to be in public school. His mother did not have the influence here that she had at Stone Brook. His mother imposed her control over every aspect of his life. He hoped she would back off and allow him to gain some independence during high school and date who he wanted, when the time came. The first afternoon's antics in the parking lot did not bode well. He'd wanted to crawl under the seat when she'd cut off the other car. His mother had made an ass of herself on the first day of school. He'd pleaded with her to let him ride the bus to school. She laughed and told him riding the bus was out of the question. She made it perfectly clear that she had standing in the community and would not allow her only child to engage in any activity that could be remotely compared to others below her standard of living. Rick found it was easier to give in than argue with her. He knew he would not win. That was the conclusion he and his father had come to a long time ago. Life was much easier when his mother came out on top, winning whatever battle they fought.

From the time Rick learned to ride a bicycle, he could, more often than not, be found at his friends' houses. Most of his friends did not like his mother. The overwhelming complaint was that his mother was just plain nosy, making every effort to spy on them. The boys had no plans to cause any trouble, but they were boys and were at an age where privacy was of upmost importance.

His mother didn't allow a pool in their yard and hated teen music. Rick begged for a pool table for the basement, but she nixed that idea as well. He didn't know what he was supposed to do, with nothing at his house to entertain his friends, so he took to his bike and either hung out at a friend's house or the country club pool during the hot summer months.

Rick looked forward to tryouts for the high school basketball and baseball teams. His private-school teams were competitive, and he'd been an integral part of their success. Stone Brook had given special attention to children with talents in sports. Football was not offered—not enough boys to make a team—but basketball and baseball were huge, with significant wins over teams from much larger schools. Rick felt confident he would have a chance to play both of these sports at Cabot. For now, football season would be starting, and he looked forward to Friday night home games. He accepted that his mother would drop him off unless she and his dad stayed for the football games, which he highly doubted. He hoped they didn't. That would give him a chance for social time with his friends.

Rick spotted a group of teens from his neighborhood on the first day of school as he entered the cafeteria. They invited him to sit at their table, and the gossip began. Rick had no interest in teen drama, and this group was the epitome of drama, especially the girls. They talked trash about everyone, finding something insulting to say about everyone in the cafeteria. He surveyed the room and observed ordinary kids enjoying conversations with their friends. He didn't see anything to judge. He noticed that most of the other kids looked much happier than his group. He could see genuine laughter and smiles, kids happy to see each other after the summer break. He saw friends. Rick also spied the girl he'd caught staring at him that morning in his biology and US history classes. He recognized her look of embarrassment when he caught her. Her softly curled dark hair and brown eyes were pretty against flawless skin, not pockmarked with acne like many kids their age. It was too bad she wasn't friends with this group. It would be nice to get to know her. But then again, if she was a part of this group, her outer beauty would be negated by the ugliness on the inside. Rick sensed she was as beautiful on the inside as she was on the outside. He'd keep an eye on her, just in case he got the opportunity to talk to her. Something about her had caught his interest.

CHAPTER 12

Partners in Slime

The second day of biology class brought with it change. Susan walked into class, and before Mr. K. began taking the class roll, he commented that students shouldn't get too comfortable in their present seating arrangement. This was not good news since she and Debbie had already decided how they would divide dissecting duties and other, what Debbie considered *icky* science experiments. Susan didn't mind the icky stuff.

"Okay, everybody, I see some empty seats and we are going to fill them. Everyone will need a partner. I'm going to start here in the front and we will fill in as we go. Be prepared to move." Mr. K. instructed.

Susan looked around the classroom, taking note of the empty seats and wished the teacher would let those with a partner keep them without rearranging the entire class. Mr. K. barked out instructions impatiently. The students moved slowly, most unhappy with the new arrangement.

Susan's breath froze when she realized her new lab partner was the new student Rick Pierce. She looked at Debbie with wide eyes and Debbie winked sensing what she considered Susan's good fortune.

"Well, I guess we're partners." Rick stated softly.

"Um, I guess so." Susan replied without making eye contact.

During the switch, Susan bumped Rick's arm, sending an electric shock through her body. She jerked and looked at him. He stared back at her, and she sensed he'd felt the same jolt. They smiled nervously at each other and turned back to the teacher, who'd already started class.

High school was a busy time, and the days flew by. Susan continued helping kids on her hall with their homework after she finished hers. None of the other teens was enrolled in college prep classes, so their homework questions seemed easy enough to her. The children's home had a study room where residents could do their homework, and Susan spent much of her evenings there, finishing her studies, helping others, and reading. Anyone causing too much noise or any sort of trouble was booted from the room without fanfare.

A month into the semester, Susan considered she'd never had a friend who was a boy. Rick Pierce was nice enough, and they seemed to be growing as friends. She learned from their conversations that he'd attended private school through the eighth grade—that was why she hadn't seen him before. He seemed happy to be in public school. He said he liked the freedom. She told him she lived at the Cabot Home for Children since her parents were dead. He expressed his condolences but asked why she didn't live with her grandparents. Susan told him they were dead too. It didn't seem so far-fetched; they probably were dead by now. She felt no remorse for her untruth, though she told herself she should have. Still, it was hard to feel remorse for people who denied her existence.

Rick and Susan were friends in class, but they didn't socialize outside of class—no hall conversations, no cafeteria conversations, though they ate in the same lunch group. Rick continued to sit with friends from his neighborhood, while Susan sat with her own group of friends. Susan didn't push it; being nice in class was one thing, but being nice to someone in public was different, especially in the complicated societal hierarchy of high school.

Each Monday morning, Rick excitedly described the Friday night football games or the weekend Duke football games. He informed Susan that his dad and grandfather had gone to college at Duke, and he thought he would go there too. His family members were attorneys in a law firm in Cabot, and he planned to go to law school, like his father and grandfather. Susan told him her mother had gone to Carolina and had been a nurse. She hoped to go there for undergraduate and medical school.

"Wow, medical school. That's cool. Do you like blood?" Rick said, wrinkling his nose.

"Doesn't bother me in the least. I don't mind blood, but what I really want to do is help people." Susan replied with a strong voice and a conviction she hadn't heard in herself before that day.

"Well, I think that's great. You sound like you'll be a great doctor."

"Thanks."

"Miss Anderson, Mr. Pierce," their biology teacher announced for all the class to hear, "May we start class now, or would you like to share your conversation with the rest of us?"

Susan's face bloomed bright red and, interestingly enough, Rick's face equally flushed. They both dropped their heads and mumbled something resembling *sorry*, and class started.

As the school year progressed, Rick and Susan's friendship deepened. They laughed and started a little rivalry between Duke and Carolina, joking with each other about wins and losses. It was fun, and Susan found herself looking for Rick outside of class more and more. She stole glances at lunch or in the hallway. She noticed he reciprocated those glances with a nod of his head and a smile.

By their junior year, Susan and Rick's relationship had grown to socializing in the hallways and sitting together at lunch. They had a few friends in common and sat with them during their lunch breaks. Susan noticed the questioning stares from Rick's group of friends, and she didn't think they approved of his choice, but he didn't seem to care. They'd occasionally call out to him after he'd worked his way through the cafeteria line, but he smiled, waved his hand in a greeting, and moved on to the small table he shared with Susan and their mutual group of friends.

Sandra Penninger proved to be a favorite friend for Susan. She was one of the most genuine, down-to-earth people Susan had ever met. She was one of the high-society girls, but one would never suspect it by her friendly, inviting personality. Sandra was a senior. She had a steady boyfriend who'd graduated a few years earlier and would finish college when she graduated from high school in the spring. She swore Susan and Rick to secrecy when she told them that she and Don planned to get married after he'd worked for a year. They wanted to buy a house. She planned to be a secretary and would have a year of business school under her belt when they married.

"My mother is going to have a cow, but frankly, I don't give a shit. I am not going to nursing school," Sandra whispered to Rick and Susan during lunch one day, leaning over her lunch tray, glancing back and forth between them. Sandra's mother was trying to convince her to go to nursing school, but Sandra didn't like the idea of dealing with sick people. The thought of blood and "bodily gunk" nauseated her. Sandra admitted she'd not inherited any of her mother or father's medical genes; she did not have the stomach for anything in the field of medicine. Her mother had worked as a nurse before marrying her father and was content to be a stay-at-home mom, raising their children. Sandra added, with a wrinkle of her nose, that she dreaded the first skinned knee when she had children. She'd probably throw up. Her mother would have to get over her decision. She was bound and determined to fight her mother's choice for her career to the bitter end.

Susan liked Sandra very much—she didn't play immature games like most teenage girls. Susan called her a Renaissance woman and admired Sandra's tenacity, forward thinking, and willingness to stand up for herself and her beliefs.

"I'm not sure what you mean by that, but it sounds like a compliment, so I'll take it," Sandra told Susan. They grinned at each other, shrugged their shoulders, and laughed out loud. Susan sensed she had an ally and a friend outside of the orphanage. It felt good.

CHAPTER 13

Janet Pierce

Janet Pierce was a very proud mother. Rick, her only child, was a junior marshal for the upcoming graduation ceremonies. His grades qualified him, along with ten other students, who she assumed were deserving of the honor. She was confident she'd raised him well. He was a good son who planned to follow in his father's footsteps in the law office. He'd inherited his parents' intelligence and good looks. Someday, he would inherit her money.

Janet and her husband, Richard, planned to attend graduation to proudly witness their son lead the class of seniors. She made sure all of her friends knew about her son's honor, including her bridge club, women's church circle, and her ladies' civic group. She made sure Rick had a new white dress shirt, black suit, tie, and shoes to round out his graduation apparel. He would look very handsome with his marshal sash. Her best friend, Margaret Penninger and a few of her other friends had children who were members of the graduating class. She would be sure to speak with each of them at the ceremony, offering her congratulations.

Graduation evening arrived, and Janet was bursting with excitement. She made sure to mention that her son was a junior marshal as she greeted friends and acquaintances on the way into the auditorium. She noticed Richard eyeing her strangely. She didn't know what his problem was, but he was not going to ruin her night. To those attending the ceremony, it was a night to celebrate the graduating class, but to Janet, it was about her son. Richard reluctantly agreed to attend after much badgering in the week prior to graduation.

"I don't see why we have to go. Rick's not graduating. Can't he go by himself? He can drive himself," Richard complained.

Janet was beside herself. "Don't you want to see your only son on his special night?"

"Not really. He'll be escorting the seniors. Janet, this is not his special night. You do realize this is not his graduation, don't you?"

"But we have to be there; we must be there. We're his parents. All the other junior marshal parents will be there. It would look terrible if he had no family there."

"I highly doubt all the other junior marshal parents will be there. I just don't see the need."

"Well, you and I will be there; this discussion is over," Janet stated with the sharp finality of a judge's gavel as she marched out of the room.

The graduation ceremony proceeded as planned, and Janet was satisfied with her son's role in the evening's ceremony. The only disappointing part of the evening was the comical mix of class clown/valedictorian, who presented a memorable graduation speech. Janet thought it was silly and juvenile. She observed Richard laughing and was embarrassed that he would fall for such an undignified oration. She hoped whoever gave the speech next year would present a speech with sophistication and decorum.

As soon as the ceremony concluded, Rick approached his parents. He was not alone; he was accompanied by a girl. She was wearing a white dress with a marshal sash matching the one worn by Rick. Janet wasn't sure where this was going, but she didn't like it. She didn't immediately recognize the girl, but something looked familiar about her.

"Mother, Father, I want you to meet someone. This is my friend, Susan Anderson. She's in all of my classes. She's the reason I made an A in calculus. She's the chief marshal," Rick said excitedly.

Susan held out her hand, shaking Janet's and Richard's hands cheerfully.

Who is this girl? I've never seen her before, Janet thought. "Hello," she said suspiciously and then added, "You're the chief marshal?"

"Yes, I am. It's nice to meet you," Susan said to both Janet and Richard.

Before Janet could say more, she heard someone calling Susan's name repeatedly from across the auditorium. It was Margaret Penninger's daughter, Sandra, who also was waving her diploma wildly for Susan to see her.

"I need to go, but it's nice to meet you. Your son, Rick, is a very good friend." With that, Susan walked through the crowd to the other side of the auditorium, embracing Sandra with a joyful hug.

Janet still couldn't put her finger on what was familiar about Susan Anderson, but something was the same as ... as what? Or who? She'd have to think about it. Something about that girl piqued her memory; she'd have to figure it out. She knew one fact for sure: she did not like the look in her son's or that girl's eyes. Guilty attraction was written all over their faces.

"Isn't she great? She's really smart too. She could go anywhere she wants for college. I think she's going to be a doctor and will probably go to Carolina after we graduate," Rick eagerly professed and then turned away to talk with some friends who'd just received their diplomas.

"Did you recognize her, Richard?" Janet asked.

"No, should I? She's just one of Rick's classmates."

"Something tells me she's after him," Janet replied suspiciously.

"I don't know. It looked more like he was after her," Richard said with a slight smile.

Janet noted his response. She was not amused.

CHAPTER 14

Strike Three

Rick had started driving to school as soon as he'd received his driver's license. He breathed a sigh of relief as he was liberated from the confines of the back seat of his mother's Mercedes. He was certain he had the most embarrassing mother in town. Everyone talked about how embarrassing their parents were, but his mother had to be the worst. She was rude and looked down on every human being she met.

Rick's first real defiance of his mother's wishes came in the form of a cheap eight-track tape player, sloppily installed in his car by his friend Mitch Penninger. Rick's new car was black, sleek, and very expensive. He would never forget her reaction to the purchase—she'd been mortified. He'd driven into the driveway with the music blaring from every speaker. His mother, dressed for gardening, walked from behind the house with a stern frown, carrying a trowel in her gloved hand. She'd more than likely been tending her prized roses. He swore she loved those stupid flowers more than him or his father.

"What have you done to your car? I could hear that awful noise from a mile away!" she yelled as he parked his car in the driveway, music continuing at a high decibel level. She stomped to his car. "What in heavens name do you think you're doing? What will the neighbors say? Turn that thing off!"

"How do you like it, Mom? It's an eight-track tape player. Mitch and I installed it this afternoon." He knew he'd baited her; she hated to be called Mom.

"I don't like it, and your father will make you take it out. You look like a drug addict, and you're acting like one too!"

"Mom, I don't think having an eight-track tape player in my car makes me a drug addict. I think it makes me a normal teenager. I like good music, and I can pick out whatever I want to listen to, you know? Plus, it's my car; you told me so, remember?"

Her face turned crimson, and Rick was in his glory. *I've stolen her proverbial goat and tied it out of reach. Ha-ha!*

The coup de grace was his father's approval of the menacing music maker when he arrived home after work. He liked it and gave Rick his blessing. He handed Rick a twenty-dollar bill and told him to buy more tapes. Rick suspected it was an act of defiance on his father's part by the suspiciously gleeful look on his face. *Ha-ha number two*, Rick thought.

Rick's mother didn't speak to him for two days—two of the most peaceful days of his life. He whistled as he walked through the house, yelling goodbye to her each morning as he left for school, letting the door slam a little louder than was necessary. It was glorious! *Ha-ha number three! Strike three, Mom; you're out!*

Rick drove into the student parking lot on the first day of his senior year and made his way into the building at the back entrance. With schedule in hand, he headed toward homeroom, talking to friends and classmates along the way. He peered down the hallways, searching for one face in particular—Susan Anderson. He hadn't been in contact with Susan over the summer. They hadn't communicated during any of the summers between their years in high school.

The kids at the home didn't have phones, and the girls were not allowed to date until they were seniors. But now, the class of 1975's senior year had arrived. Excitement filled the air. Plans for college were in the works for a number of his friends and classmates. This would be a year of *last times*.

CHAPTER 15

Seniors at Last

Susan was thrilled to see a familiar face first thing in the hallway—Rick Pierce. He must have spent the summer at the pool. His tan was perfect, and his blue eyes were the color of ice—hot ice. Susan smiled and waved shyly when she spied him. He walked across the hall around a group of giggling girls to speak to her when he spotted her. She freely admitted to herself that she felt more than friendship with Rick. She was attracted to him; call it a crush, call it whatever you wanted, but she liked him, more than a lot. The sight of him made her heart flutter, sending a warm flush over her cheeks. He'd hinted last spring that he would've asked her to the prom if the children's home had allowed her to go. She wasn't sure if he was serious, but he had inquired as to whether the high schoolers at the home could go to prom. She sadly told him the boys and girls were only allowed to go their senior year.

Susan recalled prom night last spring, sitting on her bed, imagining what it would be like to dance the night away. She identified with Cinderella. The following Monday, the juniors and seniors eagerly shared their experiences. Everyone agreed the band was fantastic, playing lots of great music with just the right mix for slow dancing. Susan was envious and would have loved to have gone. Now that her senior year was here, she would have her chance to experience all the events she'd heard about the last three years.

The children's home loosened its reins when residents were high school seniors, providing counseling to assist in the transition to adulthood and independence. The graduating seniors would be transitioned out two weeks after graduation unless they were under eighteen. Underage teens who graduated remained until their eighteenth birthdays, when they were considered adults by law.

Susan would be heading to college next fall but would live on her own during the following summer. The thought of independence brought with it mixed feelings of excitement and a small degree of apprehension. Susan felt relatively confident she would be ready. She would have to be ready, whether she was prepared or not.

Susan laughed when she spied Rick as she walked into Advanced Science, her first-period class. She walked directly to his lab table and sat down.

"Want to be my lab partner?" she asked with a smile.

"Yep," Rick said with a nod of his head.

They'd been lab partners in their ninth-grade biology, tenth-grade chemistry, and eleventh-grade physics classes, with both making A's each year.

"Are you ready for more icky stuff?" Susan said with a grin.

"Yes, as long as the future doctor handles the worst of it," Rick said softly, gazing into Susan's warm eyes.

"I think I can handle that request." Susan laughed softy, prepared to do battle with whatever deceased, formaldehyde-soaked creature their teacher placed in front of them.

Susan was excited that she and the other seniors from the orphanage were allowed to attend home athletic events, including football games, on Friday nights. A small bus from the children's home transported the seniors to the games, but Susan didn't mind the bus ride. It was worth it if it meant she could socialize with friends, especially Rick Pierce. The two of them made plans to meet and sit together. He spread out a blanket, protecting them from direct contact with the metal bleachers. They sat close, sharing body heat and stolen glances. The sensation of Rick's body sitting next to hers sent shivers from her heart to the tips of her fingers and toes; their shoulders and hips touched. She'd been attracted to Rick from the start and their closeness here only enhanced her feelings. This was like a date. Susan had never been on a date. She didn't know what to expect but guessed a date was whatever a couple wanted it to be. She was aware that dates usually ended with a kiss—normal dates, that is, where a boy drops off a girl at her house. This would be different, though. Would Rick kiss her? Could they steal a kiss? Would he try? She didn't know but was eager to find out.

The end of the game approached, and Rick asked if she wanted him to walk her to the bus. She replied yes, and they sat, outwardly appearing to be engrossed in the game, but neither would be able to describe any play or score for the remainder of the competition; their attention solely was on each other in anticipation of what was to come. The final horn sounded, and the game was over. Rick took Susan's hand and led her down the bleachers. They walked hand in hand through a darkened area of the parking lot toward the orphanage bus. No one was close; students and fans had dispersed quickly. The bus was about twenty-five yards away when Rick slowed to a stop. He faced Susan, took her chin in his hand, and kissed her. It was electric. She wanted more and sensed he did too. He leaned down and kissed her again, this time with more … more of everything. They parted, opened their eyes, and smiled, not an innocent smile but a knowing smile, a provocative smile. At that moment, their relationship changed. It was no longer a simple school friendship or a trivial crush. It became a necessity; Susan needed him. She longed for him—someone she could love, someone she could trust, someone who would love her back. Susan knew, in that instant, Rick was the one for her. They were meant for each other. She couldn't imagine being with anyone else.

They walked hand in hand to the bus, with Susan dreading the moment they would draw away from each other. The moment was almost painful as he let go of her hand; her heart mourned the separation, mourned the moment they were no longer touching.

"I'll see you Monday. Meet you at the front entranceway." Rick whispered as he leaned over, brushing his lips against her ear.

"Yes, you will," Susan replied softly, eyes closed, her voice barely audible, every nerve in her body standing at attention.

They smiled at each other, and Susan climbed the steep steps of the bus. There were eleven students on the bus, and a collective "woohoo!" could be heard. Susan sat in her seat with a blush that rivaled any sunset. She didn't want anyone to see the grin on her face; she let her long wavy hair fall to drape her face while pretending to search for an item in her purse.

Monday morning dawned, and with it, an atmosphere of anticipation that was hard to deny. It didn't matter that it was a school day; it was a joyous day. Susan knew she would see Rick again. She couldn't wait for the bus to arrive at school.

Some of the kids asked what had happened at the ball game, but she didn't say anything, didn't let on; she was not the type to kiss and tell. She explained that she and Rick were very good friends but silently admitted to herself it was so much more. She was in love with him.

The bus drove into the school parking lot, and Susan spotted Rick standing at the front entrance, waiting, smiling. She stepped off the bus, walked across the parking lot, and met his twinkling eyes with hers. He took her hand, lifting it to place a gentle kiss. They both laughed, and after spying no adults in sight, Rick leaned over and kissed Susan's perfect lips. She beamed an endless smile, and the two of them walked hand in hand into the school building. Rick escorted Susan to her homeroom and reluctantly let go of her hand with the promise of seeing her in first period. It would be an excruciatingly long twenty minutes.

CHAPTER 16

Blooms of Fall

September led into fall, which found Rick and Susan inseparable. The couple was a staple at their school's home football games. Homecoming, the most popular week of the school year, was fast approaching. Every day was assigned a different theme, from '50s Day to Tacky Day to School Colors Day. The children's home staff helped the high schoolers with their outfits. The children's home had a room in back of the seldom-used auditorium with costumes and pieces of odd clothing that could be easily improvised for themed events.

Susan excitedly assembled outfits for each themed day. For her '50s outfit, Susan found a poodle skirt and an old pair of saddle oxfords that were a size too large. She rolled down a pair of white oversized socks and pulled her hair into a long ponytail. *Perfect*, she thought as she peered into the mirror of the hall bathroom. She stood for an extra moment, studying her reflection, and realized how much she looked like her mother. Her long brunette hair and brown eyes were a constant reminder of the person she'd loved most. She was happy the memory of her mother did not bring tears for a change.

Susan smiled as she walked outside to the school bus, knowing Rick would be waiting for her in his '50s outfit. He was a pretty good sport about dressing up for the homecoming themes. Some of the students refused to participate. *Adulthood is so close*, Susan thought. *Why not enjoy being a kid a little longer and have a little fun?*

The week's grand finale would be the homecoming dance on Friday night after the football game. The seniors from the home were allowed to go to the dance, and Susan was excited for her first dance. Rick promised to escort her.

The homecoming dance was everything Susan imagined. The band, a group of guys who'd graduated a few years earlier, played all the latest music. She wished the night could last forever. She'd found happiness—true happiness—with Rick. The pair danced to every song. The slow dances were her favorite, with Rick holding her close. She could hear the gentle thumping of his heart as she laid her head on his shoulder. She was convinced she could never love another heart as much as she loved this one. She pulled back to peer into his eyes, and he leaned over slightly to gently kiss her. It was easy to tune out their surroundings; their attention was centered on each other, blocking out everyone and everything, save for the music. The lights were low, and they were unaware they were being watched, but many did observe them, including eyes and ears that would report to Rick's mother the following morning.

CHAPTER 17

Hitting the Fan

Saturday morning found Rick with a smile on his face. He was in a good mood and had straightened his room and made his bed before he skipped down the stairs for breakfast. He was in love with Susan Anderson, plain and simple. She was everything he could ever want. She was sweet, kind, smart, and beautiful. He couldn't imagine life without her.

As he sat down for breakfast, his mother asked if he'd enjoyed the homecoming dance. He excitedly responded that it was the best dance he'd been to as a high schooler. He realized a moment too late that his reply had been a little too enthusiastic. He could sense her immediate suspicion by her facial expression. He was unaware that the mother of a classmate had made a call to his house early that morning, reporting his choice of dancing partner—his only dancing partner—the previous night.

"Did you dance last night?" his mother asked.

"Yes, I did," he replied happily, again a little overly enthusiastic.

"Who did you dance with?" his mother asked, eyeing her sugar-topped grapefruit.

"Um, a girl." He was a little more reserved, sensing the tone in his mother's voice.

Janet stopped eating and eyed Rick. "What girl? What's her name?"

"Just a girl from school." Rick became wary of his mother's questioning and knew trouble was brewing.

"Just a girl? I asked you her name. Who is she?"

"Her name is Susan Anderson. You know her; you met her at graduation last spring. She was a junior marshal like me. She's really smart; we're in college prep classes together." Rick thought this explanation was good enough, but it only added fuel to the fire.

"Who are her parents?"

"Well, she lives at the Cabot Home for Children. She doesn't have any family. I think her mother was a nurse at the hospital years ago, but she died. I don't know when her father died—I think when she was little or maybe before she was born." Rick paused before adding in a louder voice, "I don't know what that has to do with anything. She's really nice, and I like her, okay?" He knew this conversation was inevitable, but he didn't feel any better now that it was out in the open.

"An orphan? She's an orphan? No, this will not do. You cannot date a girl from that orphanage. I don't care how smart she is; she is not for you."

"I beg to differ with you."

"Excuse me? You"—Janet made the hand motions of quotation marks—"beg to differ with me? I think not. Neither your father nor I will allow this. This relationship is over."

"No, it is not over. Frankly, I love her and will see her all I want. We have classes together; there's nothing you can do about that!" Rick replied with satisfaction.

"You love her? You do not love her; you don't know what love is!" his mother shouted.

"Well, I guess you're right. I see very little love here at home between you and Father!" Rick yelled at his mother.

"That is enough! This is over; we will not discuss it again." His mother threw her napkin on the table and stormed out of the room, leaving Rick to stare at her retreating figure as she hurried down the hall and slammed the dark-paneled mahogany bedroom door.

He angrily stood and turned to walk upstairs to his room, taking note his mother did not correct his retort on the status of her marriage to his father.

Later that afternoon, Rick lay on his bed, contemplating how he could change his mother's mind about Susan. He knew his mother would like Susan if she spent some time with her. Maybe he should invite Susan for dinner. He would convince the staff at the orphanage to allow Susan to have dinner with his parents, giving them a chance to get to know her. He knew it was a stretch, but he would bring Susan to his house on a Saturday afternoon, have dinner, and then return her to the children's home later in the evening. It was worth a try.

Rick decided to visit the children's home the next weekend. He would talk to Susan about it the following week at school. High school residents were allowed visitors. Susan had explained a few weeks earlier during lunch that dates were allowed for seniors. The only stipulation was that they had to take place on the grounds of the orphanage, whether in one of the small parlors or outside in one of the common areas. Children were not allowed to leave the orphanage property.

Susan had jokingly invited him to practice their golf skills on the driving range. She'd explained that the children's home was surrounded by fields that had once been used to grow vegetables and grain for flour, keeping the orphanage supplied with fresh food during the growing season. The fields stood empty now, with the advent of large quantities of food delivered with the ease of a phone call. The largest field was mowed weekly and had been converted to a makeshift driving range. The kids loved it, and some of them became quite skilled at driving and putting. A small putting green was added later as a project by one of the men's groups in town, and it kept many of the boys and more than a few of the girls busy practicing their skills. The driving range also served as a perfect place to socialize and spend dates. Members of the local country club donated three sets of used golf clubs and a large supply of worn golf balls. Competitions were held between the younger children, gathering the tattered golf balls scattered throughout the field. They hunted the balls like Easter eggs. Susan jokingly teased Rick that she'd gotten pretty good and challenged him to a driving and putting contest with a wicked, sideways grin. He returned the grin; challenge accepted.

Rick approached Susan with the idea of visiting her at the orphanage. He hoped she would say yes. He suggested the following Saturday afternoon and said they could practice their golf swings on the driving range. She accepted his request eagerly, and the date was set.

Saturday afternoon arrived, and Rick purposely didn't tell his parents where he was going. His mother eyed him with curiosity when he told her he was going to a friend's house to watch a ball game. She asked for a name and phone number of his friend. He gave her the name of a friend who lived in another neighborhood but told her he didn't know the number and thought the number was unlisted. This was the beginning of a string of lies he would tell his mother, not because he enjoyed lying but in an attempt to satisfy her overzealous curiosity. She'd brought this on herself by forcing his hand. She was the reason for his lies. He hoped she'd give him a break and back off a little. In a matter of months, he would leave for college, and she would have to loosen the strings, whether she was ready to or not.

He drove to the orphanage with a sense of excitement. He wasn't sure of the protocol, but was sure Susan would fill him in on the rules and regulations. He didn't want to cause any trouble for Susan and wanted to be welcomed back in the future.

He arrived, parked in a faintly marked visitor spot, and walked into the main office. He signed in and told the receptionist his name and who he wished to visit. Susan was called on the intercom, and she quickly rounded the corner with a radiant smile. She hugged him and led him, holding his hand, to one of the small parlors.

Rick was nervous, an emotion he experienced rarely. It would be an atypical date, but he would make the best of the opportunity to spend time with Susan outside of school. It felt good to sit with her and talk without dozens of kids milling around them. They'd talked for half an hour when Susan suggested they go to the driving range and hit some balls.

"I thought you'd never ask," Rick said with a grin, pulling Susan close to his side with his arm around her shoulders.

"I've gotten pretty good at this," she said, raising her eyebrows with a sly grin that looked a little like a dare.

"You do understand I've been playing golf since I was old enough to hold a club, so game on, Miss Anderson," he said with a laugh.

They walked out to the newly mowed field hand in hand, not letting go until they picked up their clubs.

Rick arrived home by five o'clock. He entered the house through the French doors in the den from the patio. He was afraid his face would betray him so he took a deep breath and relaxed, knowing he would have to face his mother sooner than later.

"Did you have fun?" she called when she heard him walk into the kitchen.

"Yes, I guess you can say that. I'm getting a soda and going to my room. Call me when dinner is ready." That was all Rick could say without sounding guilty. Yes, he felt guilty but quickly pushed his guilt-ridden thoughts to the back of his mind, burying them deep in his subconscious. He kept telling himself he hadn't started this trouble. It was his mother's fault.

Rick visited Susan two more times before he broached the subject of taking her to meet his parents. Susan was a little hesitant. Rick made every effort to assure Susan his parents would welcome her.

Susan agreed to the visit, and, surprisingly, the administrators gave her permission to leave campus for the evening. The next Saturday, she would be allowed to leave at four and return by seven thirty. The couple would have time for dinner and a brief visit. Rick promised he would have her back on time.

The Saturday afternoon of Susan's visit arrived. She would be meeting his parents for a second time, the first being their brief encounter last spring at graduation. The conversation between Rick and his parents in planning Susan's visit had been interesting. His father agreed it would be nice opportunity for them to get to know Susan. He would be happy to grill out on the covered patio; the fall weather was cool but would make for a comfortable evening.

Rick's mother, on the other hand, was quiet. Rick didn't know whether he should interpret this as a good sign or a bad one. She agreed they would like to see Susan again, a change from her reaction when he and Susan had gone to the homecoming dance together. He added that he'd dropped by the children's home to see her briefly. He held his breath, waiting for his mother's reaction. She remained quiet, but he could sense her psychological wheels turning. He hoped for a pleasant evening, allowing Susan a chance to escape the confines of the children's home.

Rick and Susan had described their families to each other during lunch early in their relationship. He sensed how much Susan loved her mother by the tears that welled in her eyes. Susan hadn't known her father since he'd died before she was born. He wished his relationship with his parents was better, much like Susan's had been before her mother died.

Rick described his parents to Susan, explaining his mother had graduated from Meredith College. Her claim to fame was that she was the first runner-up in the Miss Raleigh beauty pageant. She blamed the talent competition for her loss, saying it was impossible to beat a professional ballerina. Rick laughed, saying she would have won Miss America if nagging was considered a talent. He'd also said this to his mother and knew she did not consider it a source of amusement. His mother had inherited a sizable fortune, as well as multiple properties and a priceless jewelry collection, when his grandparents died.

His parents had met in Cary, North Carolina at a cocktail party for up-and-coming political figures in the early fifties. They married after his father finished law school at Duke and settled in Cabot, his father's hometown. They'd moved into his great-grandparents' house, which had stood empty for a number of years and needed updating. His mother remodeled the entire house, bringing it back to its former glory. His father worked at the law firm Rick's grandfather founded with two of his friends after law school. Rick hinted that his parents' marriage wasn't a happy one. He described his father as choosing to play golf or working long, tedious hours at the law office of Pierce, Morehead & Grant, where he'd made partner years earlier. He guessed his parents were either too financially invested in their marriage, or each was too stubborn to leave the other. He didn't see any reason for them to stay together otherwise,

Saturday afternoon arrived, and Rick excitedly picked up Susan at four. They rode directly to his house. He lived fifteen minutes away, so the drive was shorter than the young couple would have liked. They held hands while Rick drove, with the volume of the eight-track tape player turned high enough to satisfy teenage ears. Susan's smile was infectious, and he found himself glancing at her with a broad grin on his face. They arrived at his house and were greeted at the door by his mother, who was overdressed for the occasion. *Why is she wearing a designer dress for a cook-out?* he thought. He was wearing a pair of old jeans and a plaid shirt, and Susan was dressed in jeans and a top he'd seen her wear at school. He noticed Susan looked anxiously at his mother's outfit and then to her own clothes. Susan was wearing her mother's emerald ring,

Meant for You

which matched the green trim of her top. He'd noticed it sparkling in the sun on their drive.

Rick encouraged Susan to call his parents by their first names. He thought *Mr. and Mrs. Pierce* sounded stuffy and pretentious; plus, all of his friends called them Janet and Richard. Susan was hesitant, saying she preferred to address his parents formally. Rick assured her he'd never heard anyone call his mother Mrs. Pierce, other that the housekeeper and caterers who worked for his parents.

"Mother, this is Susan Anderson." Rick cheerfully introduced the two women. "And this is my mother, Janet."

"Hello, Janet, it's nice to see you again," Susan said timidly, extending her right hand to shake Janet's, the emerald ring glittering in the light.

"It's Mrs. Pierce, if you don't mind," Janet corrected Susan with pinched lips.

"Oh, I'm sorry, Mrs. Pierce; please excuse me." Susan's face blushed with embarrassment.

"Oh, Mother, everyone calls you Janet; lighten up," Rick said with a roll of his eyes.

Rick escorted Susan into the exquisite home, giving her an abbreviated tour of the first floor. His mother followed, keeping her distance. She didn't utter a word.

Dinner was a stiff affair, with steaks grilled by his father, stuffed baked potatoes, a salad, and yeast rolls purchased from the local bakery on Main Street. The pecan pie came from the same bakery. His mother made it known, swiftly and without a doubt, that she did not bake.

The evening's conversation was guarded, with Rick doing most of the talking. He noticed Susan talked very little, only answering direct questions from his mother or father. He found it interesting that his mother complimented the emerald ring Susan wore and said it looked familiar. *She must have seen one similar to it when she*

.

65

was shopping, he surmised. He noticed his mother eyed the ring throughout dinner, brows furrowed, deep in thought.

After returning Susan to the children's home promptly at seven thirty, Rick lied when he commented that he thought the evening had gone well. He didn't want to hurt Susan. He'd taken note of his mother's reaction to her but held out hope she would change her mind. It was obvious his mother did not approve of Susan, but there would be plenty of time for her to come around. All his mother needed was the opportunity to get to know Susan. Plus, she had to change her mind; he planned to be with Susan for a long time to come. He planned to marry her someday.

CHAPTER 18

Unhappiness on Every Front

Janet Pierce was furious. Her son had brought home a girl from an orphanage, of all places, a poor girl, a nobody. This was not at all what she had planned for her only child, sole heir to her money. She'd had a bad feeling about that girl when Rick introduced them at the graduation ceremony last spring. She'd sensed trouble brewing then. She'd told Richard something was going on between Rick and that girl, but he wouldn't listen. Men were useless.

Why on earth didn't that private school have a high school? This would've never happened if Rick had gone to high school at Stone Brook. Contact with undesirables would have been nearly impossible there. He would have been in school with his kind, their kind, her kind. Now it was ruined. All her plans were ruined. Janet's blood boiled at the nerve of that girl calling her *Janet*. She was proud of the look she'd given Susan. That should teach her. She hoped she'd scared the little money-grabber.

To make matters worse, Richard had the gall to say he liked the girl after Rick left to take her back to that place. He thought she was pretty, smart, and nice, a very sweet girl. He said he hoped this was the kind of girl Rick would marry someday. He'd smiled and walked out of the room, humming to himself. She'd been left to stand, motionless, in shocked disbelief, eyes wide, her mouth hanging open.

Janet fumed and sputtered as she straightened the kitchen, taking her anger out on an innocent dish towel, slinging it across the room against the credenza, nearly toppling a vase of fresh flowers. She walked to the bar, poured a healthy shot of bourbon, and downed it with one swallow. This was Janet's hidden talent, and she found plenty of time at home alone to practice. It wasn't ladylike, but she wasn't feeling much like a lady right now. She closed her eyes and calmed her breathing. She'd have to get rid of that girl, one way or another—but how?

The following Monday, Janet called her best friend, Margaret Penninger, to set up a lunch date later in the week. Margaret would know what to do about that girl. Yes, Margaret would know exactly what to do. Hadn't she steered Sandra to her fiancé, Don? Don had graduated from business school and had taken over management of a multimillion-dollar factory that employed hundreds of local workers. The fact that his family owned half of the company was of no consequence. He would have been successful whether his family had money or not. But this Susan girl, she was nothing, had nothing to build on. Rick said she would be a doctor someday—big deal. She could say anything she wanted. Saying something and doing it were two different things and becoming a doctor required years of college and study and lots of money, and this girl had none.

Lunch with Margaret was always an amusing experience. She had the ability to make Janet laugh and cry in the same breath. She claimed to have such a boring life, but the stories she told … Janet wasn't sure how many of Margaret's tales were true; she suspected Margaret stretched the truth, adding drama and a healthy dose of exaggeration. But Margaret was known for her advice. She always seemed to see the situation for what it was and give counsel in a most advantageous manner with a positive outcome.

Margaret was caught up in wedding plans for her daughter, Sandra, on the day of their luncheon. The wedding would take place the following summer at their church, with an elaborate reception at the Cabot Country Club ballroom. Margaret was eager to share all the plans and preparations for the wedding. She appeared quite miffed with her daughter's lack of enthusiasm for the upcoming ceremony.

"Do you know Sandra had the gall to say she wished she and Don could elope?" Margaret complained. "And Jack pipes up and offers to give them ten thousand dollars to do it now—elope! I was appalled! Can you imagine telling a child that? No one appreciates me. Why, if it weren't for me, there would be a tacky little wedding reception in the church fellowship hall with peanuts and lime-green punch. I have worked—no, slaved—to give this family some degree of class and decorum, and you see what thanks I get!" Margaret sat huffing and puffing, shaking her head. "And to top it off, every time I ask Sandra what she wants me to do about this or that, she replies, 'Do whatever you want to, Mom,' like I have all the answers. I just don't understand. She won't finalize the list of bridesmaids, and we need to go shopping to find a wedding gown. I cannot get her to understand it will take time to get dresses and have alterations completed. You know, you should be thankful you don't have a daughter. The boys aren't nearly so troublesome."

"My dear Margaret, I'm sure everything will turn out beautifully, and they will thank you for your time and effort. They will appreciate you like you deserve when it's all said and done."

Margaret sat for a moment, took a drink of her sweet tea, and agreed with a nod of her head, somewhat reluctantly. "I wish they'd appreciate it now. Don's mother has worked with me a little, but she has all boys and has no idea what it's like to prepare for a daughter's wedding. All she has to do is buy a dress, rent a couple of tuxedos, and hire a planner for the rehearsal dinner." Margaret stopped talking to take in a deep breath and eat a bite of her shrimp salad.

Janet interpreted this as a break in the conversation and ventured the topic she'd called Margaret to discuss.

"Margaret, I have a problem. Rick brought home a girl, and I need to get rid of her before their relationship goes any further. She's a nobody, not the daughter of someone like us. She's an orphan; lives at that children's home over on Danbury Church Road. I cannot have this. I don't understand how this has happened." Janet hesitated, wrinkling her brow, peering down at her half-eaten congealed salad. "Damn that private school. They should've had a high school for our children. Rick has been brought up better than this. What does he see in her? And to make matters worse, Richard likes her. Said she was the type of girl Rick should marry someday. I think he said that just to piss me off!" She sighed in exasperation. "Well, I'll tell you this—he succeeded!"

"Janet! Don't talk like that. It's not like you to use that sort of language."

"Sorry, it slipped out. You know I don't use that kind of vile language. I am so angry. I can't get anything accomplished because I'm thinking and worrying about Rick."

"Well, Janet, maybe he feels sorry for her, or maybe it's a little bit of rebellion. And it was just a date. It's not like they're getting married." Margaret sighed and confessed to Janet, "I wasn't going to tell you, but Mitch came home and told Jack and me that the school kids call Rick and Susan 'the Jock and the Orphan Nerd.'"

"Oh my God!" Janet's horrified reaction was revealed in her expression as she dropped her face into her hands.

"Frankly, I don't like it one bit. Mitch said she is very nice and extremely smart." Margaret made an effort to console Janet. "You know, now that I think about it, I remember her from the cookouts and Christmas parties our church sponsored for the children's home. Her name is Susan, right? Well, I just don't think it's appropriate to call the two of them names. It's just not right. Janet, I think this relationship will run its course. You know how teenage boys go through girls. I guarantee you that in a few months, this will be over, and he'll be dating someone like my Sandra."

"I don't know. I think he's had eyes on this girl for a while. He introduced her to us last spring at graduation. She was the chief junior marshal." And then, in a barely audible whisper, Janet mumbled to herself, "Cheater."

"Oh, I remember her at Sandra's graduation. She is quite pretty and smart too, hmm." Margaret shook her head, sighing. "Janet, it will be all right. I promise. Really, this girl is not so bad; it could be much worse."

Janet didn't look convinced. "You'd think differently if it were one of your boys, and you know it," she replied sharply, leaving Margaret temporarily speechless.

CHAPTER 19

Class Rings and Things

Susan was wearing Rick's class ring. She could hardly believe her eyes as she admired the ring on her hand. Rick had given the ring to her the week after what she considered the mostly disastrous dinner with his parents. He'd gotten down on one knee, like a proposal, asking her to be his steady girlfriend. She was ecstatic. It was far too large for any of her long, slim fingers, so her roommates helped her melt wax from an old candle they found in the supply room and filled in the gold circle to fit perfectly. She found herself sitting with her chin balanced on her left hand, the heavy class ring pointed outward in plain view for all the world to see. It was a constant reminder of how much she loved Rick.

Susan didn't know if Rick's parents knew of the gift, but she surmised they might not approve, particularly his mother. She could imagine his mother's look of displeasure. The gift was temporary; the ring was not hers to keep, and she wouldn't wear it forever. Maybe something with a diamond would replace it someday. Rick had hinted of a more permanent replacement as he admired it on her hand. She could only hope. She would gladly return it as an even trade for an engagement ring.

She guarded the ring, making sure it was safely hidden in her secret place with her mother's emerald ring when she wasn't wearing it. This was especially true when she was serving in the cafeteria line. There would be dire consequences if it ended up in a pot of soup or stew. She imagined a thin layer of oily wax coating the surface, with the heavy metal ring swimming at the bottom of the pot.

Susan noticed that Rick's hair was longer than usual, and he had not shaved in a week. He'd mentioned in passing he wanted to let his hair grow a little longer and maybe grow a mustache and a beard— not outlandish, just enough to bug his mother. He said he'd cut it by the time graduation pictures were taken. He had limits on his appearance, keeping the beard and mustache neatly trimmed. He'd pointed out most of his favorite rock band members had long hair and beards, so why not? Susan had to admit he looked handsome and a little rakish, plus his beard and mustache tickled with every kiss, adding an exotic sensation. It was becoming more and more difficult to squelch her desire for him, and from what she could tell, he felt the same way toward her. She feared their bodies would eventually overtake common sense and good judgment. Maybe it was good she lived within the confines of the children's home; temptation was kept in check.

CHAPTER 20

College Plans

Rick and Susan were busy making college plans that fall. Rick hoped to drive his car to college, giving him the opportunity to see Susan anytime he wanted. He would be at Duke, and she would be at Carolina. It was a short drive between the two campuses. He hoped they could make their relationship more intimate, as both of them would be living in dormitories with visiting hours, doors that locked, and roommates who went home on weekends. He and Susan would finally have the privacy they wanted without prying eyes and ears. He sent in his application for the early admission program and was notified within three weeks that he had been accepted. He and Susan were left in shock when Susan received a rejection letter. How could this have happened? Susan was on target to be the valedictorian of their class, which they both assumed would make her a prime candidate for premed and medical school. Both he and Susan were crushed. They found it impossible to hide their disappointment from their friends and each other.

Susan was left to quickly research premed schools and pick another to apply to. She settled on the University of Virginia in

Charlottesville. It appeared she would be in line for a full scholarship. The acceptance letter came quickly, and it was settled—but they were heartbroken. Their plans for the following fall were ruined. They would see each other maybe once or twice during the school year, if at all. They sadly brainstormed ideas for ways they could see each other while living nearly 200 miles apart.

Rick informed his parents of Susan's rejection from Carolina in passing during dinner the following week.

"I guess you will find out anyway, but Susan didn't get into Carolina. She has been so excited about going there. She doesn't have any idea why. None of the counsellors at school can figure out why she wasn't accepted. Her grades are excellent—all A's—and her SAT scores are near perfect. It doesn't make sense. In my opinion, any university would be lucky to have Susan as a student." He sat perplexed at the dining room table, shaking his head.

"So they didn't give her any reason?" His dad asked.

"No, just a letter saying she wasn't accepted and wished her luck in the future."

"That's too bad, she's such a smart girl. I'm sure she will find another university that would be glad to have her as a student." His mother replied.

Rick eyed his mother suspiciously and mentally questioned her seemingly complimentary comment.

When they'd finished dinner, his mother stood and walked to the kitchen. He could have sworn he saw her smile as she turned the corner.

CHAPTER 21

The Invitation

After a long yet mild winter, spring was just around the corner. The winter had been filled with basketball games, and Rick had been one of the top scorers for the varsity team. He was thrilled to see Susan sitting in the bleachers, cheering for him. Her bright smile and soulful brown eyes gave him a mental pat on the back. The look of joy on her face was contagious. She was on his side. No games, no drama, just love, happiness, and trust—something he'd witnessed very little of at home. He didn't know where his parents' marriage went off the rails, but he'd quickly realized that the kind of marriage he wanted was very different from theirs. The sort of marriage he desired would be with Susan Anderson. They were a team; they supported each other; they communicated on the same level and shared a love he couldn't imagine having with anyone else.

Spring arrived with warm breezes, flowers, and the gentle unfurling of tiny green leaves. Rick's next step in his and Susan's relationship would be asking Susan to the prom. His immediate thought was that she would take it for granted, but he would make it official with a verbal invitation. Their relationship had continued to deepen, much to his mother's disapproval. *She'll just have to deal with it*, he thought. *If she wants to make herself miserable with worry over my love life, so be it. It's her problem.* His dad appeared to like and approve of Susan, which seemed to irk his mother all the more. Rick silently laughed over that development. It didn't take much to aggravate his mother, and he found it quite comical. She had no idea how much she annoyed many of the people she came into contact with, and turnabout was considered fair play.

He wasn't sure how the prom worked for girls at the children's home. He knew girls shopped for dresses and guessed they had their hair done. He would ask her after school. He didn't tell his mother who he was inviting; he knew she would not approve, but she had to know it would be Susan. His mother continued to make it clear she was not happy with his choice of Susan Anderson as his girlfriend. She made suggestions of girls in the neighborhood who she thought would be suitable dates. He ignored her. Susan wasn't wealthy or high on the social ladder, but that didn't matter to him. She was a good person, kind, smart, and pretty—very pretty. Just his type. They had fun together and would have a future together. He was in love with her.

"Yes!" Susan shouted when Rick asked her to the prom and then whispered, "I love you."

"I love you too," he whispered softly. Then he became serious. "Can you get a dress? Do you need money?"

"No, I don't need any money." Susan laughed. "I can get a dress. I have enough extra money to buy one. You sound so nervous."

"Yeah, I don't know what came over me, you live in a different situation, and sometimes I'm not sure what to do or say."

Rick was relieved by Susan's reply. She wore kindness on her shoulders like a mantle; she understood that her living situation wasn't always easy to maneuver for outsiders such as he.

CHAPTER 22

First Steps

Susan intended to buy a car—an old, faded-green Volkswagen Bug—for her eighteenth birthday. She would need transportation in June when she graduated, and now seemed to be the perfect time. She'd spotted it a few weeks ago, sitting in a yard with a FOR SALE sign on the main road between the children's home and the high school. The car's year was close to the time she was born, but she didn't care. Her excitement built with the possibility of owning her own transportation.

She'd been a model student, never causing trouble, always helpful and kind to all the kids and grown-ups at the children's home. She guessed her request would be something new for the staff, and it would set a precedent. She simply wanted to drive to and from school. The staff could check the mileage; she didn't care. It was just a few miles, and she would drive it joyfully. She promised to follow every rule to the letter. The staff would not regret a positive decision. The old Bug had an engine, a steering wheel, and four tires. That's all she needed. She approached the administration with her intention to buy the old car and could hardly believe her luck when they approved her request a week later. She knew from the beginning that if she messed up, they would never consider this option for anyone again. The administrators made it clear they would keep close tabs on her; it would only take one screw-up, and her driving days would be over until she moved out the following summer.

Susan proudly drove to school the next Monday morning in her new-to-her set of wheels. She was aware that she had the worst-looking vehicle in the high school parking lot, but she didn't care. She had wheels. She had freedom. She had independence—sort of. No more bus rides. Freedom never felt so good.

As she parked her car, she observed the student parking lot behind the high school with amazement. She found it hard to fathom how people could afford such expensive cars for teenagers. She guessed that very few of these kids truly appreciated what they had. The outlandishly expensive vehicles were possessions, weapons of boastfulness and pride—and expected. Anything less would have been an insult to a teenager's level of standing in the high school hierarchy. No punishment or remorse was apparent when transgressions were committed by these elite beings. They cleared every criminal hurdle unscathed.

But Susan knew differently. She would witness their brown bags containing beer bottles and marijuana joints passed from car to car when they thought no one was watching. She was an insignificant nobody. What interest would she have in these illegal forays? She wouldn't tell; therefore, they paid her no attention. Susan guessed no one would listen if she reported the activities anyway. Money talked, and the courts listened. Her descriptions of illegal drug and alcohol use would fall on deaf ears. She pretended not to notice and minded her own business. She was nothing and would stay nothing in their eyes.

CHAPTER 23

The Luck of the Draw

Rick drove into the high school parking lot Monday morning. It was partially filled with vehicles—a mix of old and new, shiny and dull, clean and mud-caked cars and old trucks. He pulled into a spot on the front row typically reserved for seniors. He noticed an old faded-green Volkswagen three spaces down. Standing beside it was Susan. Rick usually met Susan at the front door of the school as the children's home bus parked down the driveway. Why was she in the student parking lot? Had she driven that rundown car to school? How could she do that while living at the home? She waved to him, and he walked over.

He looked from her to the car. "Is this yours?"

"Why, yes, it is!" she replied excitedly. "I bought it last week for my birthday. I wanted to surprise you. I can drive to and from school—that's it—but I'm okay with that. I'm free!"

She grinned from ear to ear and laughed—and Rick thought it was the most beautiful laugh he'd ever heard, gently lilting and genuinely happy.

He blinked and looked at Susan as if seeing her in a new light, a mature light. She was beautiful. Her long brunette hair was pulled back in a ponytail, which suited her. Her hauntingly deep brown eyes drew him into a world he knew had not always been happy but one that she'd made the best of, despite losing her mother and home. She was taller than most girls, standing a few inches shorter than him, which allowed him just the right angle to view her face with perfect dimples that creased with each smile. Her joy was contagious, and he returned her smile, making inquiries about the specifics of her car—the year, model, how many miles, how she'd managed to find it. She excitedly explained every detail as they headed to homeroom, hand in hand.

"I think it may have been green in a former life, but now I'm not so sure." She laughed, her eyes twinkling. "The gears drag a little, but they're okay. I've practiced all weekend driving around the parking lot at the children's home. I'd take you for a ride, but the staff is really strict and would see more miles than necessary, and I'd be in trouble."

It dawned on Rick, unexpectedly, how much Susan appreciated what she had. The old dilapidated car was hardly worth more than a couple of hundred dollars, and in that instant, he realized how much he and his friends took for granted. None of them truly deserved what they had; it was just a matter of who their parents were and the money that flowed—the luck of the draw.

CHAPTER 24

A Night of Stars

The day of prom arrived on a sunny Saturday, the first weekend of May. It was unusually warm and humid for that early in the summer season. Susan had settled on a cobalt-blue gown with rhinestone-encrusted spaghetti straps from a local bridal shop. She'd spotted it on the clearance rack and tried it on, with encouragement from her friends. Everyone in the shop assured her the dress was perfect. With a pair of moderately high-heeled silver sandals, it hung perfectly on her tall, slim frame without requiring alterations. A local retired hairdresser volunteered her services, styling each girl's hair for the yearly event. Susan's hair was curled, with select locks held in place by rhinestone clips, showing off her pearl teardrop earrings that had belonged to her mother. She truly had no idea how beautiful she was, though her friends repeatedly assured her.

Rick could hardly take his eyes off her when he picked her up from the lobby of the children's home. They rode hand-in-hand to Rick's house for photos before heading to the restaurant for dinner. Susan was taken by surprise when Rick's mother complimented her on her dress and hair. His mother snapped a number of photos of the young couple. Rick's father was quick to express how well the young couple complemented each other, which was out of character for his usually quiet self. Susan noticed his mother's wide-eyed looks at his father's remarks.

Rick bought Susan a simple nosegay of white roses with baby's breath and a boutonniere for himself to match. They made a stunningly handsome couple. They were off to dinner at Evelyn's, a charming restaurant in Cabot that featured a resplendent menu. The candlelight dinner was exquisite and unlike anything Susan had experienced.

I could become accustomed to this lifestyle, if given the opportunity, she thought.

The couple rode the short drive to the Cabot Country Club Ballroom and danced every dance that evening. Much to their surprise, they were crowned prom king and queen later that night. Susan bubbled with excitement as she adjusted her rhinestone tiara. Rick grinned at her during their solo dance and kissed her lightly on what he considered the softest, most perfect set of lips he would ever be privileged to kiss. The night could not have been more perfect.

CHAPTER 25

Graduation

Graduation rapidly approached following the prom. The ceremony bringing an end to high school would take place the first Friday in June. Final days were filled with completion of classwork, yearbook presentations, the senior picnic, and graduation practice.

The evening of the graduation ceremony arrived, the air electric with excitement. The auditorium was packed with family and friends of the graduating class. Family members were beaming with pride, and a low murmur could be heard throughout the auditorium. Decorations of feathery white mums and roses in the school's colors filled the oversized vases on the stage, and banners were hung celebrating the graduates of the class of 1975.

Susan stood near the front of the line of girls. The boys and girls would march in on opposite sides of the gym, filling in the long rows. They'd practiced earlier in the week, with the boys joking around, but no one joked this evening. Everyone took the evening's ceremony seriously. Some of the graduates would be the first in their families to receive a high school diploma, and this would be a historic evening for them.

The ceremony proceeded to the address by the valedictorian, and Susan walked confidently to the podium.

The audience applauded, and there were whispered comments:

"You know, she's an orphan."

"She's so smart."

"It's hard to believe she lives at the orphanage."

"She is such a pretty girl.

The applause died down, and Susan welcomed everyone to the ceremony. She began by expressing her wish that her parents could be here. She described the graduates' road, which had led to this night, as fulfilling, and she thanked her classmates for their support and encouragement of each other.

"We are all in this together," she said. "I've heard old age referred to as your golden years, but I disagree. Youth should be considered our golden years. Being young brings with it opportunity—opportunity to do and be whatever we can imagine, whatever we are willing to work toward. I want to give each of you a challenge. Don't ever stop educating yourself. Take a class, read a book, train for a new job, or work to advance in the job you have. Be a lifetime learner. And don't forget to love those around you. Tonight will be the last time we are together. There are classmates here tonight we will never see again. Take a moment to look around and bid each other farewell. This place is a part of you; it is a part of your history. It is a part of each of us—we share this one distinction. Treasure the memories, remember the good times, and learn from the bad. Treasure them all. Congratulations, class of 1975!"

The graduating seniors were the first to rise with a standing ovation in response to Susan's speech; then the audience stood, the applause growing louder before gradually dying away. Susan wiped the tear traveling down her cheek and smiled at her classmates for the last time as a student at Cabot Senior High School.

PART TWO

1975
All Good Things Must
Come to an End

CHAPTER 26

Bliss

Susan and Rick were inseparable during the summer following their high school graduation. They spent long, lazy afternoons at the lake, swimming or soaking up the bright sunshine. They were young and in love. Their days were perfect. Susan learned to water ski under Rick's skilled tutelage, only losing her balance on the first takeoff; she rose on the next try, quickly mastering the skill.

Rick's parents did not own a lake house, but many of his friends' parents did, and the couple took advantage of their invitations, spending sunny afternoons boating and sunbathing. Their evenings were spent at the movies, socializing at Bertie's Drive-In, indulging in their famous caramel milkshakes, or walking the aisles of the nearby mall, perusing the shops. It didn't matter where they went or what they did as long as they were together.

Susan felt fortunate to have found a summer job at a local diner as a waitress during the morning shift, serving up plates of eggs, bacon, grits, and stacks of the restaurant's famous buttermilk pancakes. The Country Home Diner was the only local restaurant that served genuine maple syrup with their all-you-can-eat pancake platters, making the diner a favorite food destination. Susan received a free meal with each shift, and she took advantage of the perk, consuming her share of the golden pancakes along with crispy smoked bacon and fluffy scrambled eggs. The food offerings were as good as advertised.

Susan temporarily moved into a tiny studio apartment on the outskirts of town, where she spent the summer before leaving for college. She lived on money from her inheritance, savings, and a newly discovered trust fund, the source unknown to Susan. The apartment was fully furnished and included pots and pans, dishes, and bed linens. It could be considered a halfway house for those fresh out of high school desiring a step toward independence. The tenants were on their own but were monitored by the manager and his wife, who lived in one of the larger apartments downstairs, with a view of the common front door. Since most of the residents were under twenty-one, with some being former residents of the children's home, they were expected to be in by midnight and were not allowed overnight guests. The rules were strictly enforced, and anyone caught breaking them became homeless within twenty-four hours.

Rick's mother had not warmed to Susan and seemed more on edge now than ever. The relationship between Susan and Janet Pierce appeared to deteriorate at an accelerated rate as the summer progressed. It was as if Janet knew something—something unpleasant. Susan frequently caught Rick's mother watching her and felt a sense of unease. Susan was aware that Rick's mother didn't care for her; she was convinced it stemmed from her lack of parents, money, or social status, but it appeared as if there was something more. Susan couldn't put her finger on it, but there was something Mrs. Pierce knew—or at least thought she knew. Rick appeared oblivious to her actions and spying. He never mentioned it; therefore, neither did Susan.

Summer's end and the move to college rapidly approached. Susan would be moving into her dorm the third Saturday in August, and Rick would move to his dormitory at Duke the following week.

Their last evening was filled with promises—promises to write, promises to call when they were able, and the promise to meet back in Cabot during Thanksgiving vacation. Susan had made arrangements to spend the long Thanksgiving weekend with her friend Debbie, who insisted that Susan travel to North Carolina for the holiday. Susan happily accepted the invitation, as it would give her the opportunity to spend time with Rick.

All of Susan's belongings were packed into her car the night before her move, ready for the long trip the next day. She tossed and turned the entirety of that last Friday night, partly excited to begin college but also concerned and saddened by thoughts of separation from Rick. It was easy to make promises, but a long-distance relationship would make or break the couple. The *break* part was what worried her. What if Rick found another girl? What if the two of them didn't have time to write? Their relationship was more than a crush; it was real. They were in love. She truly hoped they'd marry when they finished college.

Susan and Rick had received their college addresses earlier in the summer and their letters began filtering in approximately two weeks after their arrival at their respective universities. They didn't write long letters; they were short, to-the-point notes of love and *I miss you*. Susan quickly realized she had nothing to worry about with their relationship; she and Rick were as strong as ever. They each made new friends and spoke of them in their letters. They described their exploits as college freshmen and counted down the days until Thanksgiving. In the process of counting the days, they hatched a plan, one that would ultimately define their relationship. They would spend the night together in an out-of-the-way hotel before returning to school, following their Thanksgiving break. They were both ready to take this step in their relationship. This would seal their love for one another.

Their plan went off without a hitch. They each left Cabot on Sunday afternoon after saying their goodbyes to their respective families and friends and proceeded to drive fifty miles to a hotel they'd planned as their destination. And everything was perfect, with the exception of one tiny detail. Neither of the teens had brought birth control. Susan admitted she was too embarrassed to purchase any, thinking that Rick would bring something. Rick had considered buying condoms in Durham, but he'd chickened out at the last minute. It was the first time for both of them, but they would be careful. There were more types of birth control than condoms or pills. The both laughed nervously as Rick asked Susan again if she was ready for this important step forward. She assured him she was; they were both ready to take their relationship to the ultimate level.

The couple drove separately to the hotel, with Rick taking the lead and Susan following a short distance behind. They arrived within a few minutes of each other and checked in as Mr. and Mrs. Pierce. The hotel manager glanced at their ring fingers questioningly. Rick laughed nervously, explaining that they had eloped to South Carolina this past weekend and were on their way home; they would be picking out rings later. The manager relaxed somewhat, though he continued to eye them with a small degree of suspicion.

"Room twelve. That will be $43.29. We prefer cash if you've got it. I will need a credit card in case you leave any damages."

"We promise we won't damage anything." Rick tried his best to reassure the manager.

"Sorry, hotel policy." The manager waited patiently, tapping his fingers on the counter, taking the card Rick handed to him after Rick had some difficulty prying it from his leather wallet.

"Be back in a minute with the key and your card," the manager stated dryly.

"I didn't know you had a credit card," Susan whispered.

"Yeah, my parents gave me one for traveling and to buy gas and stuff. We have to be careful. We don't want to leave any damages because my mother gets the bill," Rick said with some concern in his voice.

"We'll be okay, Rick. We're both respectful, and we won't break anything. What are the chances anything will happen, you know?" Susan reassured him.

"I guess you're right; let's go." He took the card and keys from the manager, grinning at Susan, knowing this night would alter their lives forever. Neither realized how true this would be.

Susan awoke as the last stars faded in the dawning light and stretched her arms and legs, yawning. She momentarily forgot her surroundings and disorientation clouded her vision and mind. It was seven fifteen. Upon realizing she was in bed with Rick, her heart nearly jumped out of her chest. She sat upright, realizing she was naked, and quickly pulled the sheet over her, turning her gaze away from Rick. She feared he would spy her crimson blush, the perfect shade of guilt.

Last night had begun on the shy side for both of them. Desire soon dissolved all traces of modesty. The proof lay in their lack of attire as the sun rose in the pink-tinged light, their clothing scattered in small puddles across the carpeted floor of the hotel room.

Rick opened his eyes and appeared slightly disoriented as well. He reached for Susan's arm and pulled her to him in a firm embrace. His reluctance to release her spoke of both fear and protection—fear of never experiencing this feeling again and his need to protect her from a world that hadn't always treated her well. He curled his arm around her bare shoulders in a provocative embrace, laying his hand across her breast. Her breath froze at his touch, her body tense with erotic anticipation.

"You know we have to leave soon, don't you? You have a class at ten, right?" Susan reminded him. Looking up at his strong jawline, she realized their connection to each other would never be the same; innocence was a thing of the past. Passion was their future.

"Yeah, I know." He took a deep breath.

By the time Rick rose from the bed, Susan had jumped from the opposite side, gathered her clothes, and dashed into the small bathroom. She had nearly a four-hour drive ahead of her; Rick's drive was much shorter.

"Are you okay today?" Rick asked with concern in his voice.

"Yes, I'm fine. I'll be glad when this drive is over. I have a class today at one. Thankfully, my biology professor let us know he would be out of town today, so my morning class was canceled." Susan walked to the dresser, slinging her purse over her shoulder.

"You know I don't want you to leave," Rick, standing just a few feet away, said in a low, husky voice.

"I don't want to leave either." She started to tear up, remembering their separation when leaving for college back in August. She wiped her eyes, daring to look away from Rick for only a brief moment.

"It won't be long. You're coming to stay with Debbie for Christmas, aren't you?"

"No, she didn't invite me, but I'm trying to figure something out. It's strange when you have no family to visit during holidays."

"Well, one of these days, I'll be your family. How does that sound?"

"I wish it was now."

"We both have career goals and years of school until we reach them. We won't be in school forever. Remember, school is temporary. Just hang in there, okay?" Rick reassured, pulling her close to him.

"I guess when you put it that way, I understand. It's just not easy. My brain knows you're right, but my heart hurts. I feel like I'm drowning."

Rick tilted her chin, their eyes meeting, both deep, lipid pools of desire. "It will be worth it in the end." And he kissed her deeply.

He reluctantly released her, picked up her bag along with his, and headed for the door.

"Geez, this door is stuck again," Rick said as he pried the door open.

The couple walked out into the cool November morning, slamming the pesky door with authority. Unknown to either of them, the vibration of the door closing ended the life of a small, glass lamp that sat precariously on the edge of a flimsy side table. The sound of breaking glass was muffled by the thick avocado-green shag carpeting.

"Did you hear something?" Susan asked Rick.

"Hear what?" he replied, heading for their cars.

"Nothing, I guess. Let's go turn in the key. Don't forget to tell the manager about that door. It seems to stick every time we try to open and close it."

"I'll do that. It was really stuck this morning. I didn't know if we'd get out." And he walked quickly to the office.

She waited for him beside her car, her heart breaking. She wiped away tears with a tissue in the chilly morning air. It took every bit of self-control for Susan to remain calm as Rick kissed her one last time before both of them departed on their separate journeys. As soon as Susan could no longer see Rick's car, her emotional dam burst. She found a parking lot on the side of the road, stopped, and sobbed uncontrollably, having no idea when she would see him again.

CHAPTER 27

Green but Not with Envy

The weeks following Thanksgiving crawled at an unnervingly slow pace. Susan missed Rick terribly and was plagued by the flu during final exams. She assumed she'd caught it from her roommate and some friends who'd been deathly ill during the last week of classes. The symptoms were excruciating. She couldn't remember having thrown up so much. She'd eaten a small hamburger for dinner and could have sworn she threw up two pounds of hamburger meat during the night that followed. She couldn't imagine ever eating a hamburger again. Studying for exams posed a challenge. Her grades were all A's going into exams, and she worried they would fall due to her illness. She eked out A's on her exams and sensed the Christmas holiday would give her the rest she needed to recuperate.

Susan's heart dropped when Rick's letter arrived, explaining she wouldn't see him for the entirety of their winter break. He seemed just as disappointed as she. His mother was the culprit. She'd made plans for Rick to visit family in Florida, where he would spend Christmas and New Year's. She'd already bought the plane tickets, he explained. He wouldn't return to North Carolina until two days before the spring semester started.

So Janet Pierce was up to her old tricks again. Susan was convinced Mrs. Pierce would continue to interfere as long as she and Rick were together. Would Mrs. Pierce accept Susan as a daughter-in-law, and if not, how would the couple manage? If only Janet could truly see how happy she and Rick were, she would relent. Maybe she would soften with a grandchild or two someday; Susan could only hope.

The university made temporary living arrangements for the few students with no place to go for the month-long winter break. Students were able to rent rooms at a discounted rate from a small, locally owned hotel in Charlottesville. Susan drew money out of her trust fund, hoping she'd have better luck next year. She would have taken some pleasure from the opportunity for privacy, but she was sick. The flu symptoms did not relent as the week of Christmas passed, leaving Susan in a miserable state. Had she gotten so stressed from constant studying that she couldn't shake the illness? Stress could do strange things to the human body. Food didn't stay down, and when it did, she was so nauseated she didn't know how she would eat the next meal. She bought a box of saltine crackers and a carton of cola, both of which seemed to momentarily calm her agitated stomach.

By the first of January, Susan was still waiting for her period. She'd skipped one in high school after the disastrous dinner with Rick's parents. The next month it arrived right on time. Her feminine stash had not been touched since two weeks before Thanksgiving. After a second miss, she knew something was wrong. She considered a worst-case scenario but then pushed the idea out of her mind as soon as it entered. *No, it can't be. That doesn't happen the first time.* She and Rick had been careful. She gained a small degree of confidence and breathed a sigh of relief, convinced the case of the flu had changed her body rhythms. *Yes, that has to be it.* She'd give it another few days, and her body would straighten itself out. But it didn't.

CHAPTER 28

Hatching a Plan

The credit card bill arrived in the mailbox two weeks after Thanksgiving. Janet generally handled the household bills, including all the credit cards and utilities. On more than one occasion, she'd hidden the amounts from Richard. She couldn't understand how money could go out so quickly.

She opened Rick's credit card bill and glanced at the list of charges. *The Monterey Inn? What's the Monterey Inn?* She checked her calendar and the date matched the Monday after he'd returned to college following Thanksgiving. Had someone stolen his card? The amount was fifty dollars. She reached for the phone on her small kitchen desk and dialed the operator.

"Yes, we have a number," the operator stated blandly and gave Janet the number.

Her fingers shook as she dialed the number.

"Hello, Monterey Inn. Can I help you?"

"Yes, I have a question. I think my son spent the night at your hotel a couple of weeks ago. He thinks he left his watch there, plus he had a charge for fifty dollars on his credit card. His name is Richard van Allen Pierce." Janet saw fit to tell this tiny fib; she had to get to the bottom of this matter without delay.

"Oh yes, he and his wife stayed here. A lamp was broken; that's the reason for the charge. We cleaned the room completely and didn't find any belongings. As a matter of fact, I cleaned that room myself. I remember because I found the broken lamp. They were a sweet couple. Said they had eloped to South Carolina. They were a nice-looking couple, him blond and her a brunette. I did think it sort of strange since they arrived in separate cars. Hated the charge for the lamp, but they knew any damages would result in a charge on his credit card, you know?" The manager droned on with Janet becoming angrier and more impatient with every word.

"Thank you," she blurted and hung up.

So he and that girl met up and spent the night in a hotel room, pretending to be married. Common slut, taking advantage of her son and her money. She walked by the nearest mirror, glancing in it, and was shocked at her appearance. Her face and neck were a splotchy, mottled red. She stopped in her tracks, making an effort to breathe deeply. She needed to calm down and think about this rationally. She had no doubt they had sex. Did they think they would get by without being caught?

Her first reaction was to call Rick. She dialed the number to his dormitory and immediately hung up. She thought for a few minutes, calming her senses, and realized she could approach this from more than one angle. Should she tell Richard? Should she call Rick first and get his explanation?

She had to break up this little relationship—and soon. And then an idea hit her: why tell anyone? Rick and that girl stayed in touch with letters. Letters written frequently. Rick had told her so a couple of months ago. So stop the letters. Stop all deliveries to Rick. His roommate was a nice young man who had promised Janet to look after Rick in a private conversation at their first meeting, as Richard and Rick were unloading Rick's belongings on freshman move-in day. He promised to keep his eyes open as she slipped a one-hundred-dollar bill into his hand. Rick was none the wiser.

The time had come to call in the favor with the promise of more money. She recalled Rick was in class now—she made sure to memorize his class schedule—but his roommate might be available. She called and luckily, Rick's roommate, Dan, was in their shared dorm room. She knew her request sounded odd, but with the promise of more money, Dan agreed to remove any letters from their mailbox. Rick usually left his mailbox key on his desk; it would be easy to swipe the key and wouldn't be difficult to censor the mail. Dan knew Susan's handwriting well and would take care of the letters.

"Oh, and by the way, there will be another letter from Susan, except it will be typed; the envelope will be typed as well. He should get that one. Can you handle this for me? I'm depending on you. This is not the girl for Rick; he just hasn't figured it out yet."

Janet's next step was to write the letter from Susan, breaking up with Rick. It had to be short and sweet—well, not too sweet. Rick would be upset, but he'd get over it. The right girl would come along, and he'd be happy to be rid of Susan. *He'll thank me someday,* she thought. *Well, not thank me, since he'll never know, but he'll have no regrets. Susan Anderson doesn't deserve him.*

Janet set out to write the letter. She went through ten drafts before she was satisfied with the results. She was surprised when she checked the time and realized she had spent all morning and part of the afternoon composing the letter that would put an end to all of her problems.

"Okay, let's see—one more read-through," she said aloud to herself.

Dear Rick,

    I don't know how to begin this letter, but I'm going to try. I have been thinking about our relationship. You and I have spent lots of time together, and it has meant the world to me. But I have to admit that the feelings I have for you are not as serious as I thought, and I think we should take a break from each other. I've started dating someone here and found that my feelings for you have changed. I wish you well, and maybe our paths will cross again someday. Please do not contact me again. It will be hard for both of us, but we will be okay. I wish you all the best.

Take care,
Susan

And that was it. Janet knew she had one step left in her plan. Drive to Charlottesville, Virginia, mail the letter, and drive back home. The letter had to be sent from Virginia to make it plausible; it was just that simple. A Cabot postmark would give it away. Janet called her friend Margaret and canceled their lunch at the tearoom the next day. As soon as Richard left for the office, she left the house. She was on a mission, and it could not be delayed, not for one more minute.

Richard kept a constant eye on Janet's car. She would run a car to death, given the opportunity. He quizzed her on a weekly basis— Did she have a full tank of gas? Were there any engine lights on that would signal trouble? How many miles did she have before her next oil change? When he thought about it, he'd grab her keys and check for himself. Her knowledge of car care was limited to inserting the key, starting the engine, steering, and operating the trunk lid. She generally got three to four months on each oil change, and he'd never known her to use more than a tankful of gas in a week. This was the reason he sat scratching his head on this overcast Saturday morning. She'd logged close to five hundred miles on her car in one week. He'd just checked her car last Saturday. He knew she had to stop for gas somewhere. Where had she gone? She was two hundred miles over her oil mileage, and the car was on empty. He didn't think he could get the car to the gas station without running the engine dry, as well as taking it in for an oil change. He knew he had a conversation-starter for dinner that evening.

"So what have you been doing this week? Been traveling?" Richard asked Janet.

She choked on her iced tea, and her face drained of color when she looked up at him, her eyes wide. For the first time in their marriage, he saw fear in her eyes. What had she done?

"Oh, I did a lot of shopping this week. You know, we've got that thing next weekend, and I wanted a new dress, and you know I need shoes, a purse, and jewelry to match too. It's a formal event." Janet lowered her eyes to her plate. "But I couldn't find anything. I drove everywhere. I'll try again next week. I heard about a little shop on the other side of Raleigh, but it was not what I thought it would be, very disappointing."

Richard noticed she seemed to slowly gain confidence as she described her week. He was satisfied with her explanation, considering he wasn't aware of any reason she should lie to him.

CHAPTER 29

Waiting

Days passed and still no sign of a period. This was not a good sign. Susan's nausea continued, and she decided to visit the campus infirmary. She'd heard they did pregnancy tests. Her mind continued in its state of denial while her body gave in to the symptoms.

Nothing could have prepared her for the shock of the positive result. Susan walked out of the infirmary in a daze. A dozen questions formed in her mind on her walk back to her dormitory.

Contacting Rick would be her first priority. What would he say? What were they going to do? And her pregnancy was not her only worry. What would happen with their college plans? How soon could they get married? Would he marry her? What would his parents say? A multitude of questions raced through her mind at a dizzying pace, only to be repeated five minutes later with no answers.

Susan gave in to the dread and dialed the number to Rick's house. She was desperate to contact him. She'd left multiple messages at his dorm desk before and after Christmas break to no avail. None of her calls was returned. She had not received a letter from him in some time, which was strange; his letters usually arrived like clockwork. She'd failed to receive any communication from him since a few weeks after Thanksgiving. He'd spent Christmas and New Year's in Florida, so the opportunity to see him or talk with him was zero. The silence was deafening. What was going on? Her panic was getting the best of her nerves, not to mention the nausea and vomiting. She'd weighed herself a couple of days earlier and had lost two more pounds. Didn't pregnant women gain weight? She didn't think this was a good sign.

The phone rang three times; the voice of Janet Pierce answered. "Hello."

"Um, hello, Mrs. Pierce?"

"Yes, may I ask who is calling?"

"This is Susan Anderson. I was trying to get in touch with Rick, and he hasn't returned my calls. Can you give him a message for me?"

"I'd be glad to, dear. Do you want him to call you?"

"Uh, yes, that would be great. Thanks. He has my number."

"Thank you, dear." And Janet hung up.

Susan sighed and waited. She waited for Rick to call; she waited for him to write. Nothing, no calls, no letters, no communication. *If I didn't feel so horrible, I'd drive to Durham and find him.* The spring semester had started, and she was covered in classes, labs, and homework—three research papers due in two weeks and tests next week. She prayed for a break, but no break came. She checked the calendar and calculated she must be about two months pregnant and decided she should see a doctor. Her health and her baby's health depended on it.

In the meantime, Susan confided in no one of her pregnancy, not her roommate or any of her friends or classmates. *Put on a happy face and smile*, she told herself. *Bury yourself in class work, and never let on anything is wrong. No one must know, at least not yet.*

Her call to the doctor's office came with a quick response when she explained her predicament. Immediately following her examination, the gynecologist sat down with her in his office to confirm her pregnancy and question her plans. She explained she didn't have any plans yet, could not reach the father, and was in panic mode. She had no idea where to go from here.

"Have you thought about adoption?" Dr. Adams questioned.

"What? Give it away?"

"Yes, are you able to care for your baby? Do you have help?"

"No, I don't know how I would care for a baby and go to school. I guess I could get a job. I'd have to quit school, though. I don't have any family. You see, I'm an orphan. My parents are dead." Susan hung her head, making little eye contact with the doctor.

"There is an alternative for you to think about, okay? There are couples who cannot have children of their own. They are wealthy and would help you financially. You would be compensated well for your contribution to their family."

"Compensated?"

"Yes, compensated financially. They would give you money. They pay all of your hospital and doctor bills. They provide housing during the pregnancy; most girls don't tell their families or friends, leaving fewer questions to be asked later. It's not as uncommon as you'd think. Attorneys draw up a contract, everyone signs it, agrees to the terms, and everyone comes out a winner. It's really quite simple."

"What do you suggest?" Susan asked softly.

"Well, Susan, I can't suggest anything, but I want you to think long and hard about this decision. Be honest with yourself. Consider all your options."

"Okay, I will. I promise. I'll call you as soon as I decide."

"That sounds good. You strike me as a smart young woman. I'm sure you will make the right decision for you and your baby," Dr. Adams said with a note of compassion in his voice.

Susan walked out of his office, her heart heavy with the decision she'd already made in her mind.

CHAPTER 30

Regret

Rick knew his mother would love Donna; she was one of them, a fellow member of the upper echelon of society. After receiving the break-up letter from Susan following their night together, he was left in shock. Susan spelled it out, leaving no doubt that she wanted to move on, though maybe their paths would meet again later in life. Rick didn't understand, couldn't comprehend how their relationship faltered so quickly. There were no signs in her previous letters or their night together that could have led him to believe she was unhappy. Everything had gone perfectly. So where had the relationship gone wrong? He didn't know; he'd probably never know. She made it clear in her letter she was finished.

Well, he guessed he could be finished too. But it wasn't that simple. He should have cut class and driven to Virginia the minute he read the letter. He should have called her dorm. He should have passed on the trip to Florida. Regrets. Regrets for what he should have done. Regrets for what he did. Or maybe it was guilt? Guilt for what he did and didn't do; no good outcome from any of his decisions. He was the loser anyway he looked at it, and it was bad.

Where should he go from here? His heart was broken. He loved and hated Susan Anderson in the same breath. She'd hurt him to his very core. How would he get past this? His friends encouraged him to get out, meet new girls. There were lots more fish in the sea waiting for someone like him. His friends took turns making the case that girls loved a guy on the rebound. He'd get all the pity he could stand.

The mixer with the sorority from Meredith proved to be a gold mine of feminine prospects, a grand opportunity to lick his wounds. Some say the third time's the charm, and the third girl he met introduced herself as Donna Creighton. Within the first ten minutes of their introduction, Rick knew her parents lived in Raleigh, her father was a North Carolina Supreme Court judge, she was a political science major with a prelaw concentration, she was wealthy, and she thought he was just the cutest guy she'd ever met.

And that was the beginning of their courtship. Their relationship grew from there, with Donna being the predominant driving force. On their second date, she asked Rick if he was the marrying kind. He was speechless; he had no reply. He thought she was joking. *The marrying kind? Isn't this a little early to be talking about marriage?* He probably should have run, but she was easy in the way guys like girls to be easy. She was easy on the eye and, as it was rumored, easy in bed.

Though he fought it, Rick couldn't help but think of Susan. He missed her. Susan and Donna were both beautiful women in their own rights, but their personalities were polar opposites. Donna was the storm; Susan was the calm after the storm. When he thought of Susan, his heart and stomach dropped into his shoes. He felt the burning, scorching sensation of losing something that could not be replaced. A regret he likened to the sinking feeling of losing an irreplaceable treasure. It was a destructive pain that repeated over and over until he was sick of the memory, a tape loop he could not control. Why couldn't he shake her memory?

His mother consoled him during their trip to Florida, though he knew it was not heartfelt—no love lost. Rick knew his mother's feelings for Susan had not changed, despite his best efforts. One fact about his mother: she never changed her mind, no matter the evidence presented before her. If she thought someone was guilty, they were guilty to eternity. An accused person would not fare well with his mother as a member of the jury.

He observed Donna and saw a confident, smart, attractive young woman who always appeared at the top of her game. She dressed impeccably, and her blonde hair was fashionably long with the perfect amount of curl. She was a beauty. She had money, and she knew how to use it. Her family treated the service staff in their home as second-class citizens, and Donna never made small talk with them. They were beneath her. She handed out orders like a seasoned general and demanded the respect she knew was due. Her family's checkbook was ancient, old money. Her nose remained tilted toward the sky; humility played no part in her vocabulary. She knew what she wanted, and she went after it. And, as Rick shortly realized, she wanted him.

Susan, on the other hand, was intelligent, gentle, and sweet and a natural beauty. She was kind to everyone, whether one was a member of the upper crust or a housekeeper. On more than one occasion, he'd noticed his mother's scowl as Susan exchanged kind words with the wait staff at social functions. She was appreciative of anything anyone did for her.

Rick had yet to hear Donna say thank you or offer a positive word of encouragement to anyone. She more often complained that service was slow or food wasn't cooked to her specifications; seldom was anything prepared to her liking.

He was still convinced he would have been happier with Susan, but he didn't think Susan would have survived in his world. She was too good, had too much compassion and good-heartedness, and had too much of a conscience. Even as a part of him still loved Susan, he was aware that his life would be much easier with Donna. She would be accepted into his family and society with open arms. Everything would be easier—holidays, birthdays, family events; the list was endless. Susan's presence would have remained an uncomfortable reminder of her initially awkward entrance into his family's society. His mother could be polite to a fault, but they would walk on eggshells, constantly keeping up their guard, knowing that as soon as he and his mother were alone, he would face tirade after tirade regarding his choices in life, particularly anything that could be attributed to Susan.

Ultimately, Donna would be his choice. He'd learned from the best—his father—that men should let women do as they please, or men's lives would be a living hell. So why not go with the flow? He could adapt. His life would be much easier and happier in the long run with Donna by his side.

CHAPTER 31

Ah, the Question

Rick and Donna began dating as soon as they returned from winter break. He made the thirty-minute trek to Meredith once or twice a week for dinner dates and occasional visits to Donna's parents' home in Raleigh on weekends.

Donna was head over heels in love with him, and he was certain he loved her. She clung to him when they were together, constantly looping her arm through his or resting her hand on his thigh, making it obvious she was ready for the next step in their relationship. They were perfect for each other. She was suited to him and the life he led. She understood power, prestige, and money, especially money. So why did he question his choice?

Donna's parents welcomed him with open arms from the start, inviting him for weekends of golf and dinner parties. He anticipated their reaction as he opened the satin-lined burgundy-velvet box. They treated him as if he were their son. Donna's mother, Liz, beamed when he thanked her for the slightest act or favor.

Two-carat perfection was how the jeweler described it. He stared at the diamond engagement ring that had set him back a large sum of money. Thank goodness for trust funds. Donna was worth it; she deserved it; she expected it. But why did it feel the tiniest bit not right? His thoughts wandered to a dark-haired girl, all alone in the world. If someone had asked him a year ago, he'd have said Susan would be the one he was proposing to this week. But she was okay; she'd told him so in her letter. That damn letter. He'd kept the letter in a shoebox under the bed in his dorm room, hidden from his roommate and the rest of the world. The letter was sterile, lifeless, and possessed none of the heart or beauty of her expressions. When he touched it, he couldn't feel her presence in the fabric of the paper. No scent, no touch, just an alcohol sterility that communicated *Go away, goodbye*. This was not the Susan he knew and loved. Oh crap, he'd said it again. He had to stop doing that. Susan Anderson was not a part of his present or his future, and he did not love her. He kept telling himself that he needed to get over her. Susan had no feelings for him; she'd moved on, and he should, too.

He looked at his reflection in the mirror and said aloud, "You love Donna, and you are going to propose to her over spring break at your parents'. What's done is done. Susan Anderson is not for you. Period. End of statement." His brain comprehended, but his heart stubbornly refused to listen.

Rick and Donna arrived at his parents' home Friday evening, just in time for cocktails and steaks on the grill. His mother instantly loved Donna, just as he'd predicted. What was there not to love? Donna was beautiful, blonde, smart, and rich. Her golden hair was curled perfectly, her neck adorned with a 14-carat-gold add-a-bead necklace, and she was outfitted in a pink Lacoste shirt with a crisp khaki skirt and Bass loafers. If he didn't know better, he would swear she was the inspiration for preppie Barbie.

Rick introduced Donna to his mother as the couple walked through the open French doors from the brick-paver patio.

"Mother, this is Donna Creighton. Donna, this is my mother, Mrs. Pierce."

Rick recalled the embarrassing moment when he'd introduced Susan to his mother. That introduction had gone bad from the start. But this introduction was different. His mother immediately chastised him and gently took Donna by the arm, ushering her into the room.

"Call me Janet. All of Rick's friends call me Janet. Mrs. Pierce sounds so formal and stuffy. Sounds like my mother-in-law, God rest her soul."

Rick wrinkled his forehead, thinking his mother was formal, stuffy, and a snob.

"Now, Donna, what is your major? What country club do your parents belong to? You know I went to Meredith too," Janet gushed.

"Whoa, Mother, take a breath," Rick interjected, fearing she would scare Donna into silence.

"Well, I'm just so interested in this beautiful young lady." And his mother scowled at him.

"Mother, why don't we discuss it over dinner. Donna and I would like to at least get our bags out of the car and get settled before you start the third degree." Rick frowned, thinking his mother was overacting.

"Okay, but hurry. I want to get to know this lovely young lady," Janet said sweetly, tilting her head slightly, her voice a soft purr.

The suitcases were unloaded, with his bag dumped on his bed, dirty laundry pouring from every zippered opening. Donna's bags were deposited in the guest room down the hall. He had a sneaky suspicion she would end up in his bedroom before the week was over. She'd hinted earlier that if they had the house to themselves, they would get to know each other even better. She pretended to be a virgin, but Rick knew better. Some time ago, he'd had a moment alone with her roommate, who was eager to talk. She'd discovered Donna with a boy in their dorm room the second week of classes, which was absolutely forbidden by residence hall rules. They were almost caught. Donna's roommate also knew Donna was taking birth control pills. Donna's mother knew, but her father did not.

After unpacking his bag and depositing a mountain of dirty clothes in his bathroom hamper, he walked downstairs to find his dad preparing to grill huge T-bone steaks. In general, his father spoke very little, just the basic "How's school? Getting all A's? When do you leave?" How his father won nearly all of the cases he'd tried, Rick did not understand. It wasn't that his father's law skills were subpar; his father's knowledge was exceptional. It was the fact that Richard Pierce was a man of few words at home, yet one of the most eloquent speakers Rick had the opportunity to witness in a courtroom. Go figure. He surmised his mother talked enough for the both of them. She made up for his silence with her constant chatter.

Dinner proceeded with nonstop questions and answers between the women. His mother was beside herself when she discovered Donna's father was John Creighton, a North Carolina Supreme Court judge. His mother was in her element. Donna's parents, John and Liz Creighton, lived in Raleigh, and Donna was a political science major. Donna planned to go to law school and practice until she had children. At that statement, she gave Rick a sideways look with a smile and hesitated slightly.

Rick wondered if Donna had seen the tiny velvet-covered box he'd hidden in his duffel bag. He didn't think so, but maybe girls could sense when a proposal was in the works.

The week progressed just as Rick imagined it would. His mother planned every day down to the minute. He and Donna had very little time alone. The opportunity presented itself for them to spend some romantic time alone later in the week, with his parents attending a business dinner with the partners in his father's law firm.

An early dinner of take-out pizza, and their Thursday evening was set. He had to admit that Donna was quite the pro. His experience with Susan the previous fall prepared him for what to expect when a girl was inexperienced. Donna was not inexperienced in any way, shape, or form. Her participation in their lovemaking was pleasant, and she coyly admitted she was taking birth control pills in anticipation of their advancing relationship. Rick had to admit it was a pleasant experience, and he looked forward to a lifetime of love and companionship that the ring in his bag would foretell. Donna returned to her room before his parents arrived home later that night, and surprisingly enough, his mother didn't check on either of them. He had the sneaky suspicion his mother wouldn't object to their spending the night together or would actually encourage it.

Rick planned to take Donna to the lake on a romantic picnic and pop the question. His plan might have worked, had the weather cooperated. The day was breezy and cool, with large, puffy clouds occasionally covering the sun. Napkins and plates blew away in the wind, and the two of them constantly played chase with some errant object, leaving them no option but to eat out of containers of fruit salad and potato salad while clutching their ham-and-swiss sandwiches. Donna found no humor in the situation, and her continual complaining made the day a bust. Rick's disappointment was coupled with stray thoughts of the past summer spent with Susan. She wouldn't have complained; she would have laughed and joked about his botched proposal. Rick knew the day and proposal must be perfect for Donna; she would never forgive him if there was one tiny imperfection.

He resigned himself to defeat and went to plan B. Saturday would be their last evening, celebrated with dinner at his parents' supper club. That would have to do; his last opportunity before they were due back at school, ready for the last weeks of their freshman year of college. He would have preferred a quiet setting, but on second thought, Donna and his mother would find the attention of a restaurant full of club members exhilarating.

Saturday evening arrived with the excitement of the supper club Spring Fling dinner. This was Rick's chance for the perfect proposal. And as planned, as soon they finished dessert, he got down on one knee and took the plunge. Donna was ecstatic.

"Yes, yes, yes! I will marry you!" She grabbed him, nearly toppling him over, both laughing and admiring the ring. His mother jumped to her feet, having no idea of his plan, and grabbed the newly engaged couple.

"Oh, my goodness, Rick! You didn't tell us. This is so exciting; we have a wedding to plan. Champagne for everyone!" his mother gushed with excitement.

Bottles of champagne were brought from the bar, popped, and poured as everyone excitedly toasted his and Donna's upcoming wedding. His father's reaction was one of silence. Rick noticed that his father did not drink the champagne but held the glass briefly before placing it back on the white linen–draped table. His father studied him with raised eyebrows and a questioning gaze. It was obvious from his father's expression that he was not on board with Rick's decision. Maybe he should have consulted his father before moving forward with his plans, but it was too late now.

CHAPTER 32

Happiness in the Eye of the Beholder

"I'm engaged!" Donna screamed into the phone, her mother on the receiving end of the late-night call.

"You're what?" her mother's shocked voice shouted.

"I'm engaged, Mom. Rick proposed tonight at dinner. I am so happy. Rick is wonderful. I'm getting married!"

"That was a short dating period, don't you think?" her mother replied.

Donna ignored her mother's comment. "Let me talk to Daddy; he'll be thrilled."

Donna's mother motioned her father to the phone, her eyes wide, lips pursed lips, slowly shaking her head.

"Hi, sweetie, your mom says you have something to tell me. It's awfully late, don't you think?"

"Daddy, I'm engaged … to Rick. I'm getting married! I am so excited! I'm coming home next weekend so Mom and I can start shopping for a wedding gown. We've set the date for August. Let me talk to Mom again!"

Donna's father handed the phone back to her mother without Donna missing a beat.

"Mom, I think we should go to both of those bridal shops downtown first. I've got to pick out something soon so it can be ordered and arrive in time to be altered for my portrait."

"Are you sure you and Rick should be getting married so soon? Your father and I think he's a wonderful boy, but shouldn't you at least wait until both of you finish college?" Liz Creighton's concern was evident in her voice.

"No, Mom, we don't have to wait. We will both stay in college. We've already discussed how we can study together. Aren't you happy for me? Don't you want me to be happy?"

"Well, yes, we do. We just want to make sure you've thought about this and realize you need to finish your education," her mother replied cautiously.

"We've already discussed it, and it's a done deal, Mom; no reason to fret. You always do this. Anytime I have an idea, you disapprove. Don't you want me to be happy?"

The recurring theme—her happiness—reared its ugly little head for a second time.

"You know your father and I want only the best for you, and your happiness is important to us." Mrs. Creighton hesitated slightly. "Well, I guess we need to go shopping, then, don't we?" Liz followed the usual family protocol of giving in to Donna's demands. After she hung up the phone, she walked into the den, facing her husband. "I guess we have a wedding to plan."

"How much is this going to cost?"

"Well, it's not every day your only daughter gets married, so I would say a lot."

CHAPTER 33

In Hiding

Susan's life flipped upside down in a matter of days. Giving up her child for adoption was the right decision. She'd thought long and hard about adoption, considering her mother's pregnancy. Her mother had kept her. Probably never thought of giving her away. But Susan knew hers was a different case. Her mother had an established career and income. Her mother was older and mature. Her mother was able to take care of herself and a baby. Susan sadly possessed none of those qualities.

A few of her friends became suspicious of her perpetual green color and loose clothing. She was thankful when her second trimester took a turn for the better, with food staying down and a general feeling of well-being. She joked with her friends that since her bout with the flu and what she described as a misdiagnosed food allergy, she felt much better and had gained some weight. Luckily, she was able to hide the extra pounds with her clothing and assorted jackets while the weather was cool.

As soon as Susan finished her last exam, she moved into a small apartment less than a mile from campus. It was furnished with basic furniture. The adoptive parents provided linens and kitchenware. Susan would wait out her last trimester in private with no summer classes. She shopped for groceries across town, leaving her apartment rarely. She would remain in the small one-bedroom apartment for the duration of her undergraduate class work. She admitted it was better than sharing a room in a dormitory. The lack of privacy made it difficult to study the amount she needed for premed classes, not to mention hiding her growing pregnancy. Having her own bathroom was a perk; she'd never had a bathroom all to herself. Though her plans were set, and she would be taken care of financially, she knew she had some trying moments ahead of her. She was alone and would have to care for herself after the baby was born. She was due in August. Shortly afterward, she would be back in college for the fall semester, giving her little time to heal and rest. She purposely refused to let herself dwell on her decision to give up her child. She'd made the right choice, yet thinking about it was painful. She made up her mind she would live as if nothing had changed and concentrate on the future. It all sounded good in theory, but would she be able to pull it off and make it a reality? She thought she could.

CHAPTER 34

Lucky Number Eleven

June's Bridal Creations was the upscale bridal shop in downtown Raleigh. The dark timber and beveled-glass door led to an interior designed for royalty, or at least the illusion of it, making one long to trace one's ancestry to blue bloods. The hardwood floors were polished to a mirrored shine. The creamy antique-satin sofa and matching wing chairs were positioned perfectly. Creamy flocked wallpaper adorned the elongated walls. The pale-blue floral area rugs were spotless. Mahogany tables were placed strategically throughout the waiting area, with mixed vases of pearl-white floral arrangements. This was not a bridal shop for the faint of wallet. It was known throughout the city that June Satterfeld, the owner of the shop, prided herself on her ability to find a gown for every taste. Very few customers left without finding the gown of their dreams.

It was apparent June loved her shop and her career. Wedding planning was usually a once-in-a-lifetime event, and she strove to make it a pleasurable experience for the bride, her mother, and the entire wedding party. Her ability to accessorize and match veils to each bride's tastes and gown was uncanny. She was good at what she did, and the community recognized it. Her shop was sought after by brides from the Raleigh–Durham area. She placed great value in the power of word-of-mouth advertising. A large wedding could bring in enough business for a half a dozen or more future gown sales, not counting the bridesmaids' and mothers' dresses. June Satterfeld could never be accused of turning away a bride, no matter the bride's budget, but appointments were almost always necessary, with few exceptions. Donna Creighton was the exception. Appointments were made days in advance, with the waiting list ranging into weeks during the peak bridal season. June understood Donna was the exception to every rule. Creighton money was old but spoke volumes. She'd take this appointment herself, leaving her two assistants to handle their other clients for the morning. Donna's call to June on Friday morning was a surprise, and it took some juggling to rearrange everyone's schedules, but it could be done. Donna described her idea for the perfect gown, making sure June understood her preferences and dislikes. Lace, but not too much; hundreds of pearls; slim waist; and the neckline a little on the low-cut side to show off her figure.

"It's my wedding, not my funeral. I don't want to cover everything up," Donna said bluntly.

June worked late into the evening, personally choosing gowns that might fit the taste and wallet of the Creighton's only child. Clients such as Donna did not have the patience or time to waste on gowns that were unsatisfactory. She must love every choice. If not, her attention would fade and she'd walk out empty-handed.

Saturday morning arrived, and Donna's excitement could not be contained. She ate very little at breakfast and—what shocked her mother most—was dressed and ready to leave thirty minutes early. She and her mother arrived at the bridal shop promptly at ten o'clock, ready for their first day of wedding preparations.

Fifteen gowns were waiting for her, ready for the decision of a lifetime. By number five, the day was looking like a failure. Too tacky, sleeves too puffy, too much lace, not enough lace, no pearls—the list went on and on. By gown number ten, the appointment was looking grim, but lucky number eleven was withdrawn from the plastic cover, and Donna's eyes lit up.

"Oh, I like that. I really like that one," Donna whispered as June hung the gown on the polished brass hook. This one appeared to fit every stipulation. Donna turned her back to the mirrors, stepped into the gown, and pulled it over her arms, making sure to keep her eyes averted from the image reflected in the triple set of mirrors. June fastened the back of the gown and told Donna to turn around to face the mirrors. June fluffed the hem, letting it float to the floor like a blanket of snow. Donna opened her eyes, and someone in the room whispered quietly, "That's the one." The statement would be recalled by all in the room, but no one could remember saying it. The dress was perfect.

Liz Creighton could not have asked for a more positive or productive day in the preparations for her daughter's wedding. Donna's wedding gown, shoes, and veil were now on order. Hopefully, other plans and preparations would fall in line as easily as today's. The problem? She couldn't shake the bad feeling, an omen of sorts. As happy as Donna appeared, Liz didn't think it would last. The problem wasn't Rick Pierce; he was a wonderful young man. He was kind, mature, sensible, and smart. He brought out the best in Donna. She'd been in a perpetually good mood since she and Rick began dating. He could not be nicer or more suited to being a perfect husband. The problem was Donna. She was not suited to being a wife—or at least not a cooperative one. Every decision would be hers to make; the happiness of the household would depend on her mood of the day.

Liz wanted the best for her daughter, but she was also realistic. She made up her mind to have one last talk with Donna, making sure she understood how marriage worked and the sacrifices couples made for one another. She hoped to talk Donna into waiting. She'd quietly spoken with June at the bridal salon, asking her point-blank if the order could be delayed or canceled. June promised to hold the order for a few days until she got the final word from Liz. Liz was thankful for June's consideration since she'd put down a sizable deposit.

"Donna, can we talk?" Liz hesitantly asked as she walked into Donna's pink-themed bedroom.

"Sure, what is it?" Donna replied, not taking her eyes off the bridal magazine filled with pictures of bridesmaids' attire.

"Are you sure this is what you want?" Liz asked cautiously.

"What I want? Do you mean my wedding gown? Yes, I love it, I knew the moment I put it on." Donna looked at her mother, shrugging her shoulders.

"No, the gown is perfect; I agree. Maybe I shouldn't phrase it quite that way. Um …" Liz hesitated; then she headed into a topic akin to shark-infested waters. "Not what you want, but what you should do, making a mature decision about getting married."

"What are you saying? I shouldn't be with Rick? I shouldn't be happy? I thought we'd gotten past this. Mom, don't you trust me?"

Liz continued, passing on answering Donna's question. "Your father and I are concerned. We don't want you to make a mistake. Marriage is serious; it's permanent. I know trying on wedding gowns and being the center of attention is fun, but marriage is serious. It takes commitment, compromise, and patience. My concern is that you are more in love with getting married than being married. Your wedding should not be the highlight of your marriage. Do you understand what I'm saying?"

"So you hate me and Rick too," Donna fired back.

"No, we love you, and we like Rick too. He's a wonderful young man. We just don't understand why you need to get married so quickly. You just met a few months ago. All we ask is for the two of you to date a while, get to know each other a little better, give it a little time. It's okay if you want to be engaged. If the two of you are meant to be together, it won't be a problem. Do you understand what I'm saying?"

"Mom, we know we love each other and see no reason to waste time. We are meant for each other." Donna looked her mother square in the eye. "And you—or daddy, for that fact—will not question me again. Do you understand?" Donna did not blink or look away.

Liz stood frozen in her spot; she'd been chastised by her teenaged daughter in her own home. She would not question Donna again.

CHAPTER 35

The Happy Couple

The bride's parents hosted an engagement party on Easter weekend. It was a grand affair, with invitations extended to a number of state political celebrities. The governor of North Carolina and other high-ranking officials were in attendance. The event would be the first social event of the spring for the Who's Who of Raleigh society. The caterer did not disappoint, and champagne flowed freely in crystal flutes, with toasts for the happy couple.

Donna flitted among the guests with ease, introducing them to Rick and his parents. Janet Pierce was in social heaven. She made no attempt to hide her delight with the party and the attendees. It was like a dream—she repeated those words throughout the weekend. Her son was marrying into *this*. She couldn't be happier. Rick should thank her someday, but he wouldn't, would he? He would never know the lengths she'd taken to rid him of Susan Anderson and make it possible for him to meet someone suited to his social standing. She would have to be satisfied knowing that she alone was responsible for these wonderful events, for without her intervention, none of this would have been possible.

Three bridal showers were planned, each taking place within a four-week span in June, including one in Cabot with all of Janet's friends in the country club banquet hall. Stacks of gorgeously wrapped gifts were piled high on the long table, specifically designated for the silvery-white and creamy-eggshell–colored packages arrayed with fluffy bows of white, cream, and varying pastels. Donna relished opening the vast array of gifts and carefully unwrapped each package with gentle tugs on the paper and delicate bows. She tore one bow, and everyone teased her that she a Rick would have at least one child. She blushed, a smile lighting her features. Janet and Liz clapped with the promise of grandchildren. The assortment of gifts was worth the effort with a multitude of china place settings, silver, crystal, linens, and small appliances.

Janet's accompanying luncheon was fabulous, with tomato aspic, curried chicken salad, lemon-dill shrimp salad, croissants, assorted vegetable salads, and cream puffs with whipped cream and strawberries. The beautifully decorated mini-tiered cake served for dessert would have been appropriate for a small wedding in itself. Janet spared no expense for her future daughter-in-law. Over two hundred invitations were sent, with all but six affirmative responses. Those invited but unable to attend made sure to send a gift, keeping in mind that a no-show to an event hosted by Janet Pierce meant a lifelong grudge. Janet adhered to strict rules of etiquette. She'd made an example of a former friend some years ago when the woman was a no-show to a luncheon Janet hosted for a local charity. Janet made the poor woman's social life miserable by convincing their mutual friends to disinvite her to all their luncheons and activities. Janet could not hide her smugness when the woman and her husband sold their house and moved to a community in a rural part of a nearby county.

CHAPTER 36

Two Weeks' Notice

Smiling. Rick could sense himself smiling. He was happy. He stood in the stark white hallway and could hear gentle laughter floating from the open doorway to his left. He gingerly peered into the brightly lit room. Who was laughing? He slowly turned, looking around the room. It was empty, but the laughter continued. It was a sweet, endearing, feminine laugh. He unconsciously repeated his turn around the room, and it took shape, giving off a peaceful persona. Blue. The walls were pale blue. Gauzy, white curtains fluttered gently in the breeze from the open window. He could see trees and mountains in the distance; it appeared to be summer.

He turned back to the room in slow motion and noticed a dark-haired woman sitting in a chair, wearing a white gown that covered her arms and legs. She was cradling an infant. She seemed familiar, like someone he should know, but who was she? Her name stood poised on the tip of his tongue. What was her name? He moved a step closer; her laughter was infectious. He smiled at her.

Something about the woman made him happy. He walked— more like glided—across the room and peered at the infant wrapped in the light-blue blanket. It must be a boy. The woman cooed and talked sweetly to the tiny baby, continuing her gentle, angelic laughter. Rick stood transfixed to his spot, just steps away. She didn't seem to notice his presence in the room. He kept repeating to himself, "I know her. I know her. My God, what is her name?" His smile slowly transformed into a frown. His forehead wrinkled with confusion. "Why can't I say her name? Why can't I remember?"

His inability to identify the woman was agonizing, seemingly driving him to madness. He rubbed his temples with both of his hands, his joy transforming to torture.

"Please, God, help me!" he yelled to the ceiling.

Rick awoke, drenched in sweat, his heart racing at an alarming rate, and he could have sworn he was having a panic attack. He was to the point of hyperventilating. He verbally willed himself to regain composure. "Calm down; just calm down; it's okay; it was just a dream." Eventually, his breathing and heart rate returned to normal as he dried the sweat from his forehead with the cool cotton bed sheet. And then it hit him. He rapidly drew in his breath and knew the woman's identity. It was Susan Anderson. He sat upright in the bed with his head in his hands, his elbows propped on his knees, his mind far outpacing his breathing and heart rate. Why? Why dream of Susan? Why now, of all times? And a baby? Why would Susan be holding a baby?

Her presence in the dream was happy, and he was happy to see her, though her identity was just out of reach, tormenting him into a prison of confusion.

Was this a sign? An omen? Was he making the right choice? Shouldn't he be dreaming of Donna? Would Susan haunt his dreams? Why was there a baby in his dream? So many questions and no hope for an answer.

With two weeks to go until the wedding, Rick began doubting himself and his decision. Was this a wake-up call or just a case of cold feet? There were signs that he and Donna were meant to be together, but there were also caution signs, hard to ignore, that maybe they should wait—or maybe they shouldn't be together at all.

Rick didn't want to be a statistic, didn't want to be divorced in five or ten years. His was a desire to be married once. *Until death do us part*, he thought. He should talk about this to someone but who? He couldn't tell his parents; that would upset their whole existence. He couldn't talk to Donna; she would freak out. None of his friends seemed to possess the maturity level to give him sound advice. An exorbitant amount of money had been spent in deposits, with more promised to caterers, florists, the banquet hall, and the church, not counting formal wear and dresses—so many dresses.

Just suck it up, he thought. *Everything will be okay. It will work out.* He and Donna were meant for each other, weren't they?

CHAPTER 37

And Baby Makes One

The contractions started lightly at first. The tightening reminded Susan of the cramps she'd experienced during her period. Beyond the contractions, Susan didn't know what to expect. The doctor had talked very little about labor, and Susan regretted not asking more questions. She'd been too embarrassed to ask, realizing too late she should have been more inquisitive. Suddenly, fear clouded her thoughts, and she started second-guessing herself, doubting her decisions and actions thus far. During her last appointment, Dr. Adams instructed her to call the hospital when the contractions were seven minutes apart. She forgot to ask if she should start timing when a contraction started or when it ended. That would make a difference, depending on the length of the contraction. He'd instructed her to leave for the hospital when she'd progressed to that point. *What possessed me to think I could do this on my own?* she thought with worry.

The upside of keeping a pregnancy secret? She would be able to resume her life with no one the wiser. The downside? She had no one to help her; no one to drive her to the hospital; no one to comfort her. She was alone. Was she destined to face the rest of her life alone? She lowered her head and prayed, "Dear Lord, please help me—" Another contraction gripped her, this time the tightening stronger and more painful. Her abdomen not only felt the pain, but it radiated into her extremities, leaving her weak at the knees and nauseated. Fear set in, and she worried she would not be able to drive herself to the hospital.

She considered the situation for a brief moment and made the decision to leave for the hospital. They couldn't turn her away, could they? Waiting too late to leave for the hospital would be devastating, for both her and the baby.

She quickly called the doctor's office, informing the nurse she would be leaving for the hospital as soon as she hung up. Dr. Adams would be contacted to prepare for the delivery. His office was in charge of contacting the adoptive parents so they would know she was in labor.

Susan placed her hand on her swollen belly and whispered, fighting tears, "Baby, this will be our last day together. I hope you have a wonderful life. I love you, and I hope you understand why I'm doing this. I promise I will never forget you, and I will love you until the day I die." She added weakly, "Please forgive me. I just don't know what else to do."

Susan could only credit the grace of God for helping her drive to the hospital. At the first stop light, a contraction gripped her fiercely. The car behind her beeped its horn when the light turned green. She didn't know how many times; she hadn't heard it at first. The contraction took every bit of consciousness she possessed, making her choice to drive herself a poor one. She panicked, realizing her water could break at any time.

She made the fifteen-minute drive to the hospital and parked in the emergency room parking lot. She locked the door of her car after pulling out her purse and a small suitcase. She walked a few yards, her confidence building. She could do this.

As soon as the positive thoughts crossed her mind, a contraction locked in on her quickly, causing her to drop her suitcase and lean against the nearest car in the parking lot. She didn't know if she could make it any further. She called to a man walking through the parking lot and asked him to get someone to help her. He immediately read the situation and ran to get a nurse from the emergency room with a wheelchair.

It was a hot day in the South—sweltering, some would say—and Susan was pouring perspiration, fearing she would collapse.

"Oh, dear Lord, please help me," Susan whispered repeatedly.

She thought she might faint if help did not come. She fought the urge to vomit, breathing deeply, her right hand supporting her belly, and her left, burning against the trunk of a blue sedan parked slightly across the line.

Susan gave birth to a healthy 7 pound, 4 ounce baby boy that evening at 8:47. The date was Wednesday, August 11, 1976. Her baby's birthday. This date would be forever engraved in her memory.

Susan spent the next two days in the hospital, her stay paid for by the adoptive parents. Her school tuition, books, and expenses, including her apartment would be paid as well, until the day she finished medical school. She thought they must be very wealthy to be able to afford all these bills.

She'd made up her mind beforehand and declined to see the baby in the delivery room. She did not want to form a bond with the infant. For the time being, it was out of sight, out of mind. *It's better that way*, she thought. Form no bonds now; therefore, no bonds to grieve later.

She was surprised the next day when a nurse walked into her room with an infant in her arms. And a camera.

"What is that?" Susan asked with a worried look. "I don't have a baby."

"Miss Anderson, the adoptive parents have asked for a picture of you holding the baby. It was their only request." The nurse offered the explanation, which made no sense to Susan.

"But I'm … I'm not—" Susan stammered.

"It won't take but a second. Here." And the nurse handed the infant to Susan. "Smile," the nurse said and snapped the picture.

Susan didn't smile; her look was forlorn with a deep-seeded sadness. She was barely able to make eye contact with the impersonal camera. And then it was over. The baby was whisked away, with Susan barely glancing at his face. The baby had wispy blond hair with sapphire blue eyes. *Rick.* That was all she could think—he looked like Rick.

Was this a mistake? Should she change her mind? She was painfully aware she had thirty days, according to the contract she signed. She sat, eyes closed, tears gently falling down her cheeks, not bothering to wipe them away. She would not change her mind. She would spend today grieving, but tomorrow would be different. She vowed there would be no more tears, no regrets, no second thoughts. This was a new beginning for everyone—for her, her baby, and Rick. Yes, Rick too.

She hoped Rick was happy. She guessed he must be since he was getting married this Saturday. She remembered the clipping announcing his engagement that Debbie had sent last spring. Her mother's death had been devastating, but the loss of Rick was almost worse—worse because he was still in the world yet belonged to another. Any chance she and Rick had to be together was over. They were finished. Frankly, it would kill her to see him again, especially with a new wife and a future family. She sniffed and wiped her nose, weakly wishing him well. He and his new wife would have children and live happily ever after. Without her. The end.

Saturday arrived, and Susan was discharged as soon as the doctor made rounds.

"Well, Miss Anderson, you can go home today. A nurse will be in to help you dress. All of your vitals look good. You will need to rest, so don't overdo it. Call my office on Monday to set up your six-week appointment." Dr. Adams signed the chart and walked out the door.

The nurse entered the room with Susan's discharge papers and reviewed the instructions with her. "Remember, most women take it easy for six weeks. You should too."

"Well, I'll try. School starts in a couple of weeks, and I'll be back in class. I guess studying could qualify as time to rest, right?" Susan replied with as much commitment to the nurse's suggestion as she could. "Can I ask you a question?" Susan asked hesitantly.

"Sure."

"Have the adoptive parents picked up the … uh … the …" Susan couldn't bring herself to say the word.

"Baby?" the nurse replied easily.

Susan stammered again. "Yes … um …"

"Yes, they left yesterday. The infant was in good condition and was discharged from the hospital." The nurse continued to write notes on the discharge papers.

"Oh, okay."

"Are you all right? You seem a little distracted."

"I'm fine. I was just thinking about …"

"About what?" The nurse stopped looking at the paperwork and turned to Susan, patting her hand gently.

"Oh, nothing. It's not important." Susan smiled weakly.

"Okay, then, do you have someone coming to drive you home?"

"No, I can drive myself. My car is in the emergency lot out back. I drove myself here Wednesday."

"You drove yourself here while in labor?" The nurse stared at Susan, wide-eyed.

"Yes, I don't have any family, and none of my friends could drive me."

"What about the baby's father? Where is he?"

Susan knew she had to lie at this point; there was no other way. She'd lied for the temporary birth certificate, stating that the father was deceased. She had to keep it up. She teared up, which wasn't difficult at this point and said, "He's dead. He died in an automobile accident before I knew I was pregnant."

"I am so sorry." The nurse leaned over and gave Susan a gentle, motherly hug.

"It's okay. I'm fine now. Time to go back to school. I'm prelaw at Duke University." There; she'd lied again. One lie quickly led to another. It couldn't be helped; she didn't want to leave a memory trail. If the nurse knew someone at UVA, it would be all over. Susan wanted no trace to haunt her.

"You really shouldn't be driving; actually, you should not drive for two weeks," the nurse said, expressing her concern.

"Well, I'm sort of all I've got right now. I'm staying here locally for a couple of weeks, and I'll be fine. I promise to go straight home and stay put." Susan thought she would definitely go straight home; she was exhausted. She couldn't remember the last time she'd had a decent night's sleep.

An employee of the hospital walked in, pushing a wheelchair. Susan gingerly sat, holding her purse and small suitcase on her lap. She was wheeled downstairs to the emergency room exit. She walked to her car, unlocked the door, and climbed in. She drove straight home, staying true to her promise.

CHAPTER 38

Something Old, Something New, Something Borrowed …

The Saturday of Rick and Donna's wedding was typical of summer in the South—hot, dry, and sweltering. Most of Raleigh's lawns were brown and crisp with a lack of rainfall and temperatures in excess of ninety degrees for the months of July and August. The only exceptions were the irrigated lawns of citizens who appeared to be immune from the city's water restriction guidelines. They were lush and green, with no evidence of the hot, dry weather that had plagued the eastern half of North Carolina.

Donna initially hinted at a reception under a gargantuan tent on the back lawn of her parents' home, since their red-brick colonial sat on three lots, with plenty of room to spread out. A resounding *no* could be heard for blocks from her father. Frankly, he did not want hordes of people trampling his property. His groundskeeper kept his lawn and landscaping immaculate. It would take weeks to recondition the grounds to their former state if Donna got her wish. He argued there would not be room for cars to park on the street in their gated community; therefore, a more public site for the reception would have to be chosen.

The wedding was taking place at St. Paul United Methodist Church in Raleigh, the largest church in Wake County. The reception would be held at Maxton Hall and Gardens. This was the most architecturally pleasing location for wedding receptions and formal events in the city. Guests could choose from the cool ivory interior, gracefully decorated with crystal chandeliers, three walls of French doors, and vases of fresh flowers, or the gardens, shaded by towering oaks and a multitude of flowering trees that seemed perpetually in bloom throughout the warm-weather season. Flowers and plants were always at their peak, manicured to perfection.

The church's bridal room was built for the comfort of a wedding party ranging from small and intimate to a host of bridesmaids too numerous to keep track of, as they prepared for their march to the music of Handel, Pachelbel, or other great composers.

Donna's bridesmaids arrived with dresses, hats, shoes, accessories, and attitudes in tow. What a day this would be.

Rick's father was his best man, and he'd chosen a group of fraternity brothers and a few high school friends, including Margaret's sons, Mitch and Roger, to serve as groomsmen.

Rick sat in the small room reserved for the groom and best man, awaiting the ceremony. His mother entered the room in a fluff of pale-blue silk. He had to admit she'd never looked prettier or happier. Her pearls were perfectly matched, and a flawless white orchid corsage graced her shoulder, matching her white-satin elbow-length gloves. She was a beauty in her mother-of-the-groom couture.

She pinned his boutonniere in place on his smooth, tailored lapel and kissed his cheek for the photographer. She smiled for half a dozen more pictures, including two with his father.

This was going to be a good day, with all the females happy. His mother told him Donna looked absolutely lovely, the most beautiful bride she'd ever seen, and that Donna was eager to join him at the end of the aisle. She exited the room in a flurry of icy silk, leaving him to stare at the door. His father left the room to keep an eye out for the minister, who would let them know when they were to enter the sanctuary.

Rick pulled his wallet from his tuxedo pants, checking for some cash to give the limousine driver as a tip, and remembered the secret compartment—the compartment that held a piece of his past, one he'd almost forgotten. He pulled out the picture he'd placed there less than two years ago and stared at it.

He could hardly believe his relationship with Susan was over. He could not accept it for weeks, but today, his life would change. Susan was his past; Donna was his present and future. There was a beautiful woman waiting to spend the rest of her life with him. He needed to give her all of him—100 percent. No holding back. Rick mentally vowed he would not disappoint her.

He considered the picture, touched Susan's face, smiled one last time at her image, and then tore the picture into myriad jagged pieces. She'd never belonged to him, only borrowed for a brief moment in time. She'd made it perfectly clear in that damn letter. He dropped the torn pieces into the trash, along with the cello bag from his boutonniere. He walked away, clearing his mind of the past, looking forward to his future—his and Donna's future. His father called from the door, announcing it was time to take their places at the front of the church. Rick took a long, deep breath and readied himself for his new life, leaving the past behind.

CHAPTER 39

Rice Promises

Rick and Donna's wedding couldn't have been more perfect. The music, the flowers, the bridesmaids' dresses, the wedding gown, not to mention the reception, the food, the champagne, the string quartet, the dancing—everything had been absolutely perfect.

The bride and groom raced joyfully through a shower of rice and were off to honeymoon in Charleston, South Carolina, for a week before settling back into their sophomore year at college.

Janet Pierce returned to the church with her husband to collect Rick's clothing. Richard chose to wait in the car, and she promised she wouldn't take long. She'd just gather Rick's belongings and would be back quickly. The housekeeping staff was already busy cleaning the church, removing the floral arrangements to ready the sanctuary for the next day's Sunday services.

Janet made her way to the groom's dressing room through the arched walkway. She opened the door and immediately spied Rick's clothes neatly draped over a chair. She had not raised a sloppy child. She'd brought a bag to gather everything, wishing to leave nothing behind. She and Richard would be staying at a hotel that night, but would return home tomorrow morning after breakfast with Donna's parents. While gathering the last of Rick's personal items, Janet spied the crumpled cello bag that had held Rick's boutonniere in the trash. She picked it up, touching it gently, smiling at one last remembrance of the day—and noticed what appeared to be torn pieces of a photo in the bottom of the trash can. She fished the pieces out and crudely matched the edges together, recognizing the photo of Susan Anderson. She drew in her breath in shocked recognition, raising her hand to cover her mouth.

What? Why did he have that girl's picture? Where had he hidden it? What happened here this afternoon?

Richard had said nothing about a picture; probably, he didn't know. Janet was under the impression this relationship was over months ago, when Rick brought Donna home to meet Richard and her.

With a worried wrinkle in her finely shaped, manicured brows, she voiced her concern aloud to herself. "Is this really over?"

CHAPTER 40

Something Blue

Susan drove her car into the parking lot of her apartment complex, breathing a sigh of relief. She'd made it, though she'd scraped the gears more than once during the drive home. Changing gears would be tricky for a few days, seeing as she would need time to regain her strength. She sighed and parked in a space not far from her front door, thankful the space was open; she didn't think she could walk much farther than the ten or fifteen feet between her car and her apartment door.

She was tired. She'd hardly slept in the hospital, as she kept questioning her decision to give her baby away. Deep in her heart and conscience, she knew she'd made the right choice, but it gave her no solace, no respite from the guilt and emotional turmoil that would follow her the rest of her life.

The happiness she'd experienced with Rick had been an illusion. If he truly loved her, he would have called or written. At least he could have driven to Charlottesville to break up with her in person. She was at a loss as to what had happened in the days following their weekend last November. The engagement announcement

141

she'd received from her friend Debbie last spring said it all with the stabbing pain of reality. He'd met someone else.

Today was Saturday. Susan thought for a moment, and her heart fell into the pit of her stomach. Rick was getting married today. Was he already married? She didn't know what time it was right now, and she didn't know what time the wedding ceremony would take place.

Susan closed her eyes for a moment. Tears formed that distorted her vision when she opened her eyes, making the world appear foggy and dreary, though the hot sun was shining high in the hazy blue sky. She picked up her purse and small suitcase from the back seat and made her way into her small apartment. She dropped her belongings on the carpeted floor as she walked through the living room and gently lowered herself to the worn sofa. She leaned her exhausted body sideways, slowly lying down. She had no desire to put even the slightest bit of pressure on her stitches, the resulting proof of her effort to push Rick's son from her body. Whether from sheer exhaustion or a miracle, she slept.

Susan awoke later in the afternoon, recalling no dreams, for which she was thankful. She opened her small suitcase and removed her maternity clothes. She stuffed them into a garbage bag, along with the mismatched assortment of pregnancy pieces she pulled from her small, cramped closet. She opened the bottom drawer of her worn secondhand dresser and reached inside, removing the rubber band–bound stack of letters. She held them in her hand for a moment, visualizing the sender with closed, tear-filled eyes. She stood, took a deep breath, and walked to the garbage bag. She stuffed the stack of letters into it without hesitation. She carried the bag to the dumpster, sliding the heavy door open with all the strength she could muster. She heaved the bag into the dumpster, and it landed with a dull thud, stirring a sickening odor and disrupting insects from their resting places. She turned away, wrinkling her nose with disgust, experiencing a bout of nausea. She walked away, leaving the door open, her strength depleted. Frankly, she didn't care.

She'd bought the maternity clothes at a secondhand store months earlier, and it was apparent their usefulness was over. She'd mended small tears and loose seams resulting from repeated laundering and worn, threadbare fabric. The letters she'd received from Rick represented shattered dreams and broken promises. She wanted no part of them now. It was time to move on.

Susan walked back to her door and stepped inside, feeling the cool air of the window air conditioning unit. She made herself a bologna sandwich and crawled into bed, though it was seven thirty in the evening, and the sun still sat above the horizon. She would sleep until nine the next morning. Her new life would begin that day. She vowed never to speak of her child or Rick Pierce again—to anyone.

A few days following her solitary homecoming, a plain white business envelope arrived in Susan's mailbox, postmarked Cabot, North Carolina. There was no return address, and her address was typed in black ink. She slid her finger under the sealed flap of the nondescript envelope and pulled out a newspaper clipping. There was no note attached to the clipping, the sender remaining anonymous. Susan read the heading, devastated. Tears ran down her cheeks as she silently read the wedding announcement:

Creighton–Pierce

Miss Donna Elaine Creighton of Raleigh, North Carolina, and Mr. Richard van Allen Pierce II of Cabot, North Carolina, were united in marriage Saturday, August 14. The nuptials took place at St. Paul United Methodist Church in Raleigh, North Carolina, in a 3:00 p.m. ceremony before the Rev. Raymond George O'Roark. A program of music was presented by Dr. Marie Franklin Pinckney, organist, and Mr. Samuel Kinard Bost, soloist.

The bride is the daughter of Justice and Mrs. John Aaron Creighton of Raleigh, North Carolina. She is a 1975 honor graduate of Jefferson High School in Raleigh and is currently attending Meredith College, studying political science with a prelaw concentration. She plans to pursue a career in law.

The bridegroom is the son of Mr. and Mrs. Richard van Allen Pierce I of Cabot, North Carolina. He is a 1975 honor graduate of Cabot Senior High School and is currently attending Duke University, majoring in prelaw and history. He plans to pursue a career in law.

Given in marriage by her father, the bride wore a white gown designed with a regal Queen Anne neckline and long, bell-shaped sleeves with lace appliqués. The empire-waist bodice was accented with Alencon lace appliqués embellished with seed pearls, which flowed into the front skirt. The full A-line chiffon skirt extended into a chapel length train. Finishing both the skirt and train was an Alencon lace border at the hemline. Complementing the gown was a beaded Alencon lace Juliet cap, accented with a full length chapel veil encircled with an Alencon lace trim. The bride carried a bouquet of white roses, leather-leaf fern, and baby's breath, accented with white satin ribbon.

The bride was attended by her college roommate, Miss Suzanne Patricia Burke of Raleigh, who stood as maid of honor. Bridesmaids included Miss Teresa Louise Smith of Greensboro, Miss Rebecca Justine Hill of Fair Bluff, Miss Karen Alaina Andrews of Cary, Miss Lee Ann Parker of Albany, Georgia, Miss Tippy Gwendolyn Pope of Durham, Miss

Madelyn Kay Reed of Hickory, Miss Stephanie Ann Hendricks of Raleigh, Miss Kimberly Annette James of Raleigh, and Miss Elizabeth Cox Brand of Charleston, South Carolina.

The bridesmaids wore petal-pink chiffon full-length dresses designed with a bateau neckline and a short flutter sleeve. A simple pink satin ribbon accented the waist. Completing the bridesmaids' ensembles were white wrist-length gloves, dyed to match peau de soie shoes, and a pink tulle-brimmed hat adorned with a pink satin band. Bridesmaids carried nosegays of pink roses, white carnations, and baby's breath accented with petal-pink satin ribbon.

The groom's father stood as best man. Groomsmen were Mr. Mitchell Jackson Penninger of Cabot, Mr. Roger Carl Penninger of Cabot, Mr. James Carson Baker of Cabot, Mr. Steven Paul Graham of Chapel Hill, Mr. Michael Scott Hamilton of Boone, Mr. Edward Duvall Spencer of Durham, Mr. Gregory Charles Atwood of San Antonio, Texas, Mr. Thomas Hoyle Williams of Greensboro, and Mr. Douglas Keith Moore of Richmond, Virginia.

After a weeklong honeymoon in Charleston, South Carolina, the couple will make their home in Raleigh.

The remainder of the wedding announcement had been clipped off, but Susan didn't need to read anymore. She'd just given birth to Rick's son one week ago, and now she sat reading his wedding announcement. He was married to someone named Donna Creighton—well, Donna Pierce. Mrs. Rick Pierce. Mrs. Richard van Allen Pierce II. Devastation did not come close to describing Susan's emotional state.

CHAPTER 41

Newlyweds

The majority of Rick and Donna's early marriage was spent studying, giving Rick cause to question his decision to marry before completing his college education. Life was not always easy with Donna. She was spoiled, and it was obvious her parents had rarely denied a request or desire. She was a handful, to put it lightly.

He had a trust fund, which he started drawing from when he turned eighteen, and an allowance from his parents. Donna's parents were generous with her allowance, keeping the newlyweds in an upscale Raleigh apartment situated between Duke and Meredith. The newlyweds' parents paid their college tuitions. Both were preparing for law school, and many of their classes coincided. Rick encouraged Donna to transfer to Duke, but she wanted to stay at the smaller women's college.

Rick's primary concern during the early days of their marriage was that Donna would become pregnant. This would derail their plans. As their classes became more intense, their sex life declined. Their dating, engagement, and honeymoon days were filled with the promise of a physical relationship, but all that changed the moment they walked through the door of their apartment upon returning from their honeymoon. He didn't know what changed, but the physical parts of their marriage were few and far between. He had to admit when Donna was in one of her moods and wanted something, she hung onto him like a second skin. Once her goal was achieved, she lengthened the distance between them again. The promise of a loving, physical relationship dissolved into a pendulum of moods that swung from love, to anger, to indifference.

Donna continued to heavily socialize with her friends on weekends when she wasn't studying, leaving little time for Rick. Her maturity level—or lack of—became apparent immediately. Her alcohol consumption increased from not only wine but mixed drinks when she could get someone twenty-one to purchase the assortment of rum and vodka she craved.

Rick knew he'd made a mistake. Not one of his friends discouraged him from marrying Donna. As a matter of fact, all of his friends told him it would be the best decision of his life. They only saw the fun side of her; they couldn't see her dark inner side.

Why had she changed? She continued to be the apple of his mother's eye. They loved each other. Visits to his parents were filled with luncheons, cocktail parties, and dinners at the country club, with dancing into the late hours. Rick was exhausted when they returned to their apartment on Sundays after a weekend with his parents in Cabot. Visits with Donna's parents weren't much better; they continued to dote on her and felt the need to entertain her as if she were a toddler. It was sickening to watch.

He knew how he'd gotten into this predicament; he'd fallen victim to a rebound relationship. His failed romance with Susan pushed him toward an emotional quick-fix when he should have stood back, taken a deep breath, and refrained from making ill-advised decisions about dating and marriage. He'd refused to allow himself to grieve for Susan and the consequences of his actions would haunt him for a lifetime if his and Donna's marriage didn't improve.

He wouldn't leave Donna, but how could he stay? He was headed for the mirror image of his parents' marriage, and it concerned him. The only solution was to persevere through college and hope that Donna would mature with law school, a career, and motherhood. He hoped his and Donna's marriage would improve with time because it couldn't get much worse.

CHAPTER 42

Moving On

Susan's residency was both exhilarating and tiring. She worked long days in preparation for her future as a physician. She found it difficult to witness patients suffer and worked diligently to heal them. She came to grips with the fact that everyone didn't get well. She'd experienced the failure of modern medicine, recalling her mother's illness and suffering in the last days of her life. There would always be illnesses and diseases with no cure. But as she would come to realize, many patients did get better or at least improved, and she found that part of medicine to be fulfilling. She celebrated with her patients when they rounded the corner to healing and improved health. She vowed her bedside manner would be commensurate with her ability to diagnose and heal.

She occasionally recalled the memory of a tiny blond baby with sapphire-blue eyes and the opportunity she'd been granted in exchange for him. There was no way she would have been able to afford years of college, fulfilling her medical degree requirements. Now she would complete her medical degree with zero debt. Was the trade worth it? Yes, she thought it was. One life sacrificed for many; that was how she justified her decision. His life would be better financially and emotionally, and so would hers. She had to live with this mind-set; there was no other. The regret would be too painful to bear. She'd been given the opportunity to save lives, lives that could be lost otherwise. She promised herself she would make a difference in the world. She delegated the image of a tiny baby to the dark recesses of her mind and planned for the future, a successful future, fulfilling her hopes and dreams, dedicating her medical mission to her mother's memory. She was confident her sacrifice would be worth it in the end.

CHAPTER 43

A Matter of Trust

Years of undergraduate school and law school did not bring about the change in Donna's demeanor that Rick had anticipated. Her maturity level declined, if that was possible, and her ability to compromise reduced to level zero.

Donna and Rick graduated with their undergraduate degrees and finished law school in the allotted seven years, both completing their law degrees at Duke University. Time may have flown for some but dragged its heels for Rick. He was happy to be finished with college but dreaded the move to a full-time life with Donna, granting her every wish and whim for the next forty or fifty years. He would have to work diligently to keep her emotionally and financially secure.

Donna made it known very quickly she would not work after the pregnancy and birth of their first child. Rick was puzzled as to why she'd continued law school when she clearly did not wish to practice law for any period of time. She'd wasted thousands of her parents' dollars for an education she had no intention of using.

The young couple shared classes in law school and interned at the same law firm in Raleigh. Rick suspected his wife was keeping an eye on him, protecting her investment. Donna kept close tabs on him, though she accused him of being nosy when he asked where she was going or where she'd been. Most of the time, she didn't seem interested in him romantically, though she made it clear she didn't want anyone else to have him. She mentioned early in their marriage that she did not tolerate extramarital affairs. The topic was brought up during a dinner party with friends after everyone had generously imbibed in the evening's alcoholic offerings. The evening's participants laughed off the subject until Donna expressed her opinion. She left no doubt that she did not believe in extramarital activity and would not tolerate it; she'd take her spouse for everything he had. She eyed him after completing her speech with a resoluteness that left him feeling duly warned. He squirmed slightly in his chair and felt a pang of quilt, though he was just an innocent bystander at this point. The evening had a somber tone for a few moments before the conversation switched to sports, with good-natured ribbing between college rivals Carolina and Duke. Rick filed Donna's conversation into his subconscious. He had no plans to cheat, but knew she kept a close eye on him and would drain his finances if he strayed.

Rick's return to his hometown of Cabot was, for the most part, a positive experience. In general, he was glad to be home, glad to be part of the city where he'd grown up. He looked forward to working in the law office with his father and the law partners; his relationship with them was positive. He'd maintained a presence in the office since his elementary school days.

Donna's move, on the other hand, was quite the opposite. She wanted no part of Cabot, North Carolina, and reminded him daily. She complained, describing her new home as piddly, boring, and low class, with no decent ladies' stores or entertainment. She couldn't understand why Rick wanted to live in Cabot and not a large city such as Raleigh or Charlotte.

Rick was happy with boring at this point. He'd tired quickly of the fast-paced city life in Raleigh and found the slow-paced lifestyle of Cabot a welcome relief.

Donna studied for the bar at her parents' beach house at Ocean Isle. She spent the summer after law school there, leaving Rick on his own in their rented condo. Rick opted to work for his father's law firm while studying, committing himself to gaining valuable experience. It would elevate his skills and give him the opportunity to engage in conversations that would enhance his skills in the real-world workplace. His plan paid off when he passed the bar on his first attempt. He was ecstatic, as were his mother and father. Donna, on the other hand, was not impressed. She did not pass and couldn't understand why she'd failed. She claimed to have studied meticulously for months. She insisted her days sunbathing on the beach were few and far between, though Rick doubted her claim when he looked at the darkened bronze tone of her skin and her sun-bleached blonde hair. He surmised she'd spent most of her time on the beach and minimal hours studying.

Rick understood why his wife expected to pass the bar. It was simply because she was who she was, the daughter of a state supreme court judge. Rick knew it didn't work that way; there were no favors granted by the North Carolina Bar Association. Donna came home to stay at the end of the warm-weather season and half-heartedly studied for a second attempt. He offered to help her, but she resisted, saying she could do it herself. He noticed her frustration level growing with occasional terse replies to simple questions. In the meantime, she mentioned that a friend from college was pregnant, catching Rick's attention. He noticed she seemed happy when talking about the prospect of motherhood. His fear of an unplanned pregnancy had made him extra careful while he and Donna were in college, but college was finished now. Maybe a baby would give her something to do and give her a positive look at the future. His mother would be thrilled to be a grandmother. Rick considered the present state and future of his marriage and decided to suggest to Donna that they try for a baby. This could be the solution to the score of problems that had marred their marriage so far.

Donna needed a cause, a job, and as time progressed, it became obvious she would not pass the bar. Money and years of college wasted. His father's law firm offered her a paralegal position, which she refused vehemently. Both Donna and his mother argued the job was far beneath their social status. With a public career out of the question, Rick chose to approach the subject of parenthood.

Donna was ecstatic. The excitement in her voice and eyes was contagious, and she became a different person overnight. She was happy, excited, and significantly slowed her alcohol consumption. She wasn't what one would consider a heavy drinker, but as the afternoon approached each day, she could be found in the living room or patio, consuming her chosen cocktail. He suspected she drank during the day while he was working, though he couldn't prove it, since he arrived home after six most days, and she was well into her happy, inebriated mood by then. He and Donna needed to have a serious talk about her use of alcohol. Research pointed to the fact that expectant mothers and those who were planning to become pregnant should abstain from all alcohol consumption.

Donna stopped taking birth control pills, and she and Rick waited a couple of months before having unprotected sex, giving her body a chance to rid itself of the effects of the contraceptives. She was ecstatic when she missed her period a short three months into their efforts to become pregnant. She immediately drove to the pharmacy for a pregnancy test. Disappointment was written all over her face when it was negative. Her period started two days later. She would have two more false alarms in the next year, leaving her in a depressed state.

Donna's personal efforts to thwart her drinking were admirable in the first year but began to fade as time progressed when she didn't become pregnant. She began sneaking a glass of wine at dinners with his parents at the club when she thought no one was paying attention. Rick wasn't sure what she drank when he was at work. The bottle levels of their small bar at home stayed consistent, though he wouldn't be surprised to find a secret stash hidden away. Slowly, the evening cocktails returned in earnest. Her interest in sex waned to a level slightly above zero. She was a pro at putting on a happy face in social settings, but her disappointment was clearly evident in the privacy of their home. With her disappointment came an ever-increasing consumption of alcohol.

As her periods continued each month, a new degree of depression set in for Donna. They'd bought a house, and in her early excitement, she'd furnished the nursery, confident she would become pregnant. After months of negative results, she closed the nursery door, refusing to open it for the housecleaners.

Rick looked around the room while Donna was out of the house and found a thick coating of dust on the mahogany crib, dresser, and changing table. The walls had been painted a soft gray, ready to add colorful accessories denoting the gender of the new addition. Instead, the room was depressing, the stark gray color signifying the cloud hanging over his and Donna's marriage and their inability to have a baby.

Months led to years, with the two of them nearly abandoning their dream of having a family; their marriage was precarious at best. Donna spent more and more time at her parents' in Raleigh, and Rick devoted most of his time to the law office. Their intimate moments were few and far between, but there was no thought of using birth control. It became evident they didn't need any.

PART THREE
1986

Few things in life are guaranteed
The sun will rise, the sun will set
We will be born, we will die
Some will find love, love will find some

CHAPTER 44

Hit Restart

For some, time flies; for others, time is dragged, kicking and screaming, clinging to the tattered remnants of the past. Depending on the day, Susan's life could fall into either category. Time flew when she was stressed, overworked, or too busy to notice. Time came to an abrupt halt when memories reared their ugly heads. Grief, loneliness, and regret seeped into her thoughts when she least expected them. No matter how hard she pushed them back to the recesses of her subconscious, she could not staunch the flow.

Susan couldn't decide which past event was worse—the grief of losing her mother, Rick, or her child. Loneliness and regret made their way to the forefront, rendering her powerless to stop them—regret for the decisions she'd made, for what she did and didn't do. She second-guessed herself on every front, though she was well aware she'd done the best she could, given the circumstances. She made every effort to recall happy memories, especially of her mother before she became sick and of Rick while they were in high school, but her brain had a way of remembering what it wanted, leaving Susan with a sick feeling in the pit of her stomach.

In time, Susan's past evolved into more of a dream. When she least expected it, the past came flooding back, sometimes in waves, other times like creepy things that go bump in the night, setting her nerves on edge. She found herself reliving her mother's death, the loneliness of adolescence, and her lost child. Her thoughts were intermingled with haunting memories of Rick and how much she'd loved him. She knew a part of her would always love him.

Susan completed her medical degree and was offered a position at Cabot Memorial Hospital in the emergency department. Debbie, her friend from school, worked in the administrative office of the hospital and called her about the opening, begging her to apply, offering to put in a good word. Susan's classwork and clinical expertise spoke for itself. She was happy yet a little anxious to be returning to her hometown. She was no longer the orphaned teen who had left Cabot years ago. She was a grown woman with a medical career, ready for the life she was meant to live. She still had a few friends there, and she would be near her mother's grave. She'd not been able to visit her mother's gravesite in a couple of years, and it would be comforting to place flowers there in her mother's memory. She thought her mother would be proud of her.

Susan couldn't help but consider the possibility that Rick lived there, but she quickly concluded they had little to no possibility of coming into contact with each other. She could not think of one instance where she would possibly see Rick Pierce, with the exception of a grocery store, restaurant, or department store. The possibilities were minimal at best. She wouldn't waste her time worrying. If she saw him in public, she'd be cordial, say hello, and make herself scarce as quickly as possible.

Susan's hometown was located close to the coastal areas of North Carolina, and she looked forward to living near the beach again. It had been years since she'd had the opportunity to go on vacation, and a trip to the beach would do her good.

Emergency services had been Susan's favorite rotation in her medical training. Many of the medical students shied away from the emergency department, but she found it challenging. She found one could make a difference quickly, virtually at a moment's notice. She prided herself on her bedside manner, a necessity in the ER. Family members and friends were most likely functioning in a state of panic and needed a steady rock to lean on during their visit. Susan made every effort to be the calm during the storm. She made sure each patient and accompanying family member or friend was aware that she was there to help. Though a number of patients' illnesses or wounds were not severe, Susan made sure she and the staff were always ready for whatever situation faced them.

Susan saw a number of patients who had no insurance, no regular medical doctor. She treated them no differently than insured patients. Compassion was her number-one priority. Between her residency and tenure in Cabot, she'd delivered nine babies in the ER. Most of the new mothers waited until it was too late to call their obstetricians, so *tag*—she was it. These moments of new life never got old. She did her best to resist reliving her own child's birth, and it was in these moments she was reminded she'd made the right choice. Not that she wouldn't have loved her own child, but she loved him enough to allow him to live a life with opportunities she would never have been able to provide for him, had she kept him. She would have struggled for a lifetime, with her child paying the price. It was an outcome she could live with and be satisfied.

Parents frequently brought in babies and children with high fevers and cuts or broken bones from falls, sometimes in need of a single stitch, sometimes a line of multiple stitches. Susan made every effort to comfort parents and children. In many cases, parents seemed to panic more than their children. Susan recalled an occasion when a six-year-old boy with a deep gash in his leg watched the entire procedure, all seventeen stitches. He never cried or fretted; all the ER staff looked on in amazement. She and her staff were somewhat surprised since his mother threw up in the cubicle trash can before they started.

Susan smiled as she recalled the most humorous case she'd experienced in the emergency room. It involved a newlywed couple in their forties. She'd diagnosed the wife with shingles. The wife thought she'd experienced a severe allergic skin reaction and was in a fair amount of pain. As the wife returned to the waiting room, she worded her diagnosis in a most unfortunate way, saying to her new husband, "You'll never believe what's wrong with me."

Her husband, pale and eyes wide, promptly passed out before his wife could explain. When he regained consciousness, she explained her diagnosis. He swallowed hard and said he thought his wife was pregnant. His wife laughed first and the staff joined in, as she further explained her shingles diagnosis. Her husband wiped his forehead and seemed to say a silent prayer; then he joined in with the laughter. This was the first and only time in Susan's career a diagnosis of shingles was a good thing.

Some of Susan's more serious patients involved accidents, strokes, and heart attacks. These were serious and involved a group of medical professionals who worked together like a well-oiled machine, forming an effective team in their care of patients and their families.

Sadly, all of her patients did not survive. Some cases were far too advanced or the patient passed before she could help, but she did everything in her power to help and heal in every way possible.

Susan's childhood experience with the death of her mother helped her understand loss and enhanced her feelings of empathy for those who lost loved ones. She found she could place herself in their positions, assisting those who found it difficult or nearly impossible to deal with life or death situations.

The hospital gave her the opportunity to escape an empty life. She'd rented an apartment in Cabot, one built recently in a newly developed area just outside the city limits. It was a one-story end unit with no upstairs neighbor; no noisy footsteps emanating from the freshly painted, white popcorn ceiling. The kitchen was well appointed, and she put forth good effort to cook small meals with no more than two servings, saving one for a workday evening. Cooking at eight o'clock in the evening was not her idea of fun after a twelve-hour shift at the hospital. She kept sandwich ingredients and usually ate one if she was too tired to cook.

Susan's neighbors were nice but stayed to themselves. They were mostly young married couples with whom she had little in common. Her free time was boring yet predictable. She had a few friends at work, but they were mostly nurses with different schedules, so their outings were infrequent.

Susan found that her relationships with old friends from high school were different now. Most of them were married with children. She had little in common with them, and their interests were no longer compatible. The exception was Sandra Penninger Shaeffer. They'd initially bumped into each other at the local downtown bookstore. They excitedly hugged each other, each talking simultaneously. Sandra was happily married with two young children, and Susan explained that she was working in the local hospital emergency department. They exchanged phone numbers and promised to call and meet for lunch.

After their initial lunch date, Susan and Sandra made time to meet and have lunch every other week, renewing their friendship. Sandra had not changed, still the ever-witty and funny lady. She was a secretary at her husband's company and worked part-time now that she had children. Sandra joked that the company could not run without her, so she worked part-time to keep everyone in line. She congratulated Susan for achieving her medical degree and laughed about her mother's idea of nursing school for her, pretending to gag. The two old friends laughed until they had tears running down their faces. Susan was pleased to have Sandra back in her life. Their lunch dates gave her a chance to laugh, forgetting her empty social calendar.

"I've been meaning to ask you—whatever happened to Rick?" Susan asked during a lunch date with Sandra, her heart beating swiftly in her chest so hard she could feel it in her ears.

"Oh, he's been married for years. I think I heard he and his wife tried to have a baby sometime back. I don't know what happened because they don't have any children. Maybe they changed their minds. They live over in the Country Club, maybe half a dozen blocks from his parents. I guess they're okay. I don't run into them much. Most of my and Don's friends are parents of our children's friends or couples whose husbands work at Don's company." Sandra hesitated, then continued. "If you don't mind my asking, what happened to you and Rick? You two were a great couple, and everybody thought you would get married. After you moved to Virginia, it's like everything came apart. I went to his wedding the next summer; both my brothers were groomsmen. It was over the top, no expense spared. I'll tell you this—her parents must be loaded. So what happened?"

"He just stopped communicating with me. One day, the letters and phone calls just stopped. I guess he'd met his future wife and fell in love. I just sort of moved on," Susan explained, picking at her lunch. She found it difficult to make eye contact with Sandra.

"So he didn't officially break up with you? He just stopped calling? What a jerk. I thought he was better than that. I am surprised. I've seen guys do that when they thought girls were getting too close or maybe in trouble—you know what I mean—but I never thought Rick would do that, especially to you." Sandra paused and then said, "Well, good riddance! You deserve better."

Sandra didn't realize how close to home she'd come with her comments; how close she was to the secret Susan had kept hidden from the world. Sandra let her know quickly and decisively that she should date. Sandra would check into the single professional men at her husband's company. Susan assured Sandra she was not interested, but Sandra made it her goal to set Susan up on a date. Susan secretly hoped there was no one available.

Susan generally ate lunch in the cafeteria at the hospital when she was working. She didn't skimp at lunchtime since she worked day-long shifts. It would be late in the evening before she would have the chance to eat dinner. She made sure she had a hot meal each day at work. The hospital cafeteria had good food, cooked from scratch. It was fresh, not processed. The hospital was quite forward-thinking, with nutrition being an important part of the healing process. The hospital had been awarded a significant grant toward proper nutritional support of patients and the differing types of needs based on illnesses. Those who worked at the hospital benefited from the healthy philosophy. Daily specials changed, with an assortment of offerings each day. Today was no different, and Susan inched through the line, making her choices. She paid the required amount and sat down at an empty table. Most of her meals were eaten solo.

CHAPTER 45

Bob Carson

Bob Carson resigned himself to the fact that Sherry was gone. Her passing had not been unexpected, but no matter how much he'd prepared, he was not ready for the finality of her death. She'd died ten months ago from what doctors termed a rare brain tumor, glioblastoma. It was advanced and incurable. He'd felt powerless as he observed Sherry battle the cancer. Watching her drift into the depths of the illness had been torture. They'd been married nineteen years. After her death, he didn't know what he would do. He found no reason to put one foot in front of the other for days. He sat mired in grief, pity, and isolation. He was forty-five years old and couldn't imagine living the rest of his life alone, yet he had no desire to date anyone. No one could take the place of Sherry. Frankly, going on a date scared the hell out of him. Who would want a man his age anyway? According to television, dates had gotten a little racy these days. He had no desire for any of that. Call him old-fashioned, but modern-day relationship antics were not his idea of what an appropriate date should be.

Bob attended a support group once a month at the hospital for people who'd lost wives, husbands, or a significant other. As a result, his emotional state was much improved. The problem was, he felt uncomfortable with some of the women attendees and the suggestive hints they made. They appeared to be sizing him up for their next husband. He was not ready to begin looking for a companion in the near future.

Today, two of the ladies had asked if he wanted to meet at the local coffeeshop up the street from the hospital for a cup of coffee. He politely declined and walked toward the restroom. He hoped they wouldn't follow him or wait outside in the hallway. He checked his watch and, after five minutes, walked out the door, relieved to see the hallway empty.

The idea of a cup of coffee sounded good, considering Cabot was in the chilly throes of winter, and he walked to the hospital cafeteria. The hospital coffee was always fresh and it would be nice to sit a moment, enjoy a cup, and then head back to the office. The amount of new projects was generally slow during the winter in the landscaping and concrete business but would pick up in a month or two in anticipation of spring planting and decorating plans.

Bob walked into the cafeteria, took a cup, and held it to the dispenser, letting the hot coffee fill to the brim. He raised it slowly, taking a small sip so as not to spill it on himself or the floor. He paid the cashier and walked into the seating area. He glanced around the dining room and spied a few occupied tables with individuals and small groups engaging in early lunch conversations. He noted one table by the courtyard windows where a young doctor was sitting, and he studied her for a brief moment. She was attractive. Her dark hair was pulled back into a ponytail, which suited her. She appeared to be in her late twenties or early thirties, much younger than his forty-five years. He made an effort to exercise daily and eat mostly healthy food. He considered himself fit for his age. He had the beginnings of a little gray at his temples but hadn't experienced any hair loss, which he thought was a plus.

He silently considered asking the young woman if he could sit with her. Something about her drew his attention; he couldn't quite put his finger on it, but something was there. The worst thing she could say was that she wasn't interested in his company, and he would move on. Success depended on effort. In actuality, he had no desire to date anyone. It was just that she looked lonely, much like he'd been these past months. Maybe he would make a new friend.

"Do you mind if I sit here?" Bob peered at the young woman with a questioning look, resting his hand on the back of the chair to her right.

"Um, okay, sure." She appeared to rearrange herself in her chair.

"How's the food here? It looks pretty appetizing for hospital food." Bob continued to stand, eyeing her plate. He inwardly groaned, realizing his question sounded juvenile.

"Actually, it's quite good. A little extra ketchup makes it even better." The woman laughed nervously.

"I didn't see anywhere else to sit …" Bob glanced around the room and then looked back at her.

He watched as she scanned the room, eyeing plenty of empty tables and chairs. She looked up at him, questioningly, raising her eyebrows.

"I didn't want to sit alone," Bob said in an embarrassed tone, dropping his gaze to his coffee cup, and then sheepishly making eye contact with her again.

"Well, that explains it," she said with a dimpled grin.

Bob extended his hand to shake the woman's. "Hi, my name is Robert Carson. My friends call me Bob, so I guess I'm Bob Carson." He hesitated. "That sounded pretty stupid, didn't it? Let me start over. I'm Bob Carson, and you are?"

"Dr. Anderson, Susan Anderson." She smiled as she reached up to shake his outstretched hand. His calloused handshake was firm but gentle. Bob sat down in the chair to her right, resting his left hand in front of him on the smooth Formica table. The cafeteria's recessed lighting reflected off the gold wedding band he'd continued to wear. It caught his eye, and he noticed Susan seemed to glance at it more than once.

"I take it you work here?"

"Yes, I'm a doctor in the emergency department."

His eyebrows raised slightly. "That's quite a job. I bet working in the ER can be quite stressful at times."

"It is but quite rewarding. I'm blessed with the opportunity to help people every day," Susan replied easily. "Are you visiting someone?"

"No, I come here once a month for a grief-support meeting, but I think this one was my last. My wife died last year, and the last ten months have been pretty tough. I'm doing better now." He paused, glancing down at his wedding ring. "I know I have to move on with my life. She would be disappointed in me if I grieved my life away."

"You must have loved each other very much."

"We did," Bob said sadly, thinking of Sherry on their wedding day for some reason.

"What about your children? How have they coped with the loss of their mother?"

"We didn't have any. We just never got around to it." They both fell silent for a moment; then Bob continued. "Do you have any children?"

"No, I don't have any children. I'm not married. Guess I just haven't gotten around to it."

Bob nodded his head in acknowledgment and took another sip of his coffee. He noticed Susan checking her watch.

"I'd better finish and get back to work. It was nice talking to you," Susan said, smiling.

Bob hesitated. He couldn't believe what he was going to say, but he decided to act on it. "I know this is a strange thing to ask since we just met, but would you like to meet for dinner sometime?"

She smiled without hesitation. "That would be nice."

"How about this weekend?" Bob said, her smile boosting his courage.

"I work Saturday, but I have Sunday free. Do you have a restaurant in mind?"

"Have you eaten at Evelyn's?"

"Oh yes, that's one of my favorites."

"It's a date!" Bob was embarrassed by his sudden enthusiasm. "Meet you at six thirty?" He made an effort to reel in his emotions.

"I'll see you there," Susan replied.

Bob smiled to himself as Susan stood and exited the dining area. Something about Dr. Susan Anderson intrigued him.

CHAPTER 46

Decisions, Decisions

It was five o'clock Sunday afternoon, and Susan had yet to decide on what to wear for her dinner with Bob Carson. Obvious flaws were noted in every dress she pulled from her closet. Neckline too high, neckline too low, too short, too long, not her color—why did she buy that? After a fierce vetting process, she was left with two dresses, one black and one sapphire blue. Susan held the blue in front of her, then the black, peering into the long mirror. Realizing the mirror would be no help, she stuck out her tongue at her reflection, gently laughing at herself. She switched the dresses seven times, back and forth in front of her like a yo-yo. She considered Bob had most likely seen way too much black in the past ten months, so she returned the black one to her closet and hung the blue dress on the large brass hook at the top of her bathroom door. It was fashionable but of a classic style, with a square neckline, fitted silhouette, and long, slim sleeves. She chose a simple silver chain with matching earrings that sparkled when she tilted her head. She studied her hair and pulled out the curling iron. Simple curls would do. With a few twists of the curling iron, she thought she looked presentable. She finished with a little tinted moisturizer, mascara, blush, and lipstick. She eyed herself in the mirror, thinking, *This is as good as it gets.*

Evelyn's was an upscale restaurant for a small city like Cabot, tasteful, with soft candlelight, white linen napkins, and hunter-green tablecloths. Each table was accented with miniature floral arrangements in shades of white and cream with various greenery. The chef moved from the rat race of Chicago to the town of Cabot years earlier, bringing a superb menu enhanced by seasonal choices.

Susan recalled dinner at Evelyn's the evening of her senior prom. It returned her to a time of happiness. She and Rick had shared an intimate dinner there in the spring of 1975. It was her first visit to Evelyn's and her last, until recently returning to Cabot. On her first visit, Rick introduced her to escargot. She was hesitant at first—snails? She recalled swallowing hard, just thinking of eating the slimy little creatures. Rick assured her she would love them. "Just give the delicacy a try," he'd said. After her first courageous taste, she was hooked. The decadence of the buttery garlic appetizer was as delicious as the aroma hinted.

Susan generally ordered the same dinner of Maryland crab cakes, complemented by a unique Dijon sauce. She could hardly resist the grand finale of the decadent made-in-house mocha chocolate cake, sharing a bite or two with dinner companions. The layered dark chocolate cake was deliciously delectable and had a fluffy mocha icing resembling chocolate whipped cream accented with a hint of espresso. It made her abandon all logical thought with an unmatched desire to lick the plate. The taste was exquisite.

Susan arrived at Evelyn's at six twenty-five. It was dark and cold. She shivered, considering that dresses were not made for winter. Thankfully, winters in this part of North Carolina were usually milder than the ones she'd experienced in Virginia during college and were of shorter duration as well.

Susan was not fond of winter. She could feel dread seeping its way into her consciousness as fall settled into the rhythm of chilly nights and shortened days. While others reveled in the joy of cooler temperatures and brightly colored leaves, Susan could feel a sinking apprehension deep in her soul. For Susan, the darkness heightened by the time change and onset of cold weather was depressing. The flagship holidays of Thanksgiving, Christmas, New Year's Eve, and Valentine's Day were lonely for people like her, those with no family or significant other. Dark and cold, dead foliage, and lifeless, empty trees symbolized the season. She eagerly volunteered to work fall and winter holidays. She wouldn't be lonely if she was working, surrounded by her colleagues.

The new year had begun, and she considered the possibility of someone to spend Valentine's Day with this year if this date worked out. Bob Carson seemed nice enough, a little old for her, but she guessed this evening would tell the tale. *Tonight is just a date, isn't it? Oops, used the D-word*, she thought.

Susan parked her car a few yards from the entrance and walked quickly through the heavy, ornately carved front door into the restaurant, making every effort to stay warm. The door closed tightly behind her with a whoosh of frigid air. The night was cloud-covered, with a few snowflakes drifting from the overcast sky. The weather forecast called for flurries, but no accumulation was expected on roads or highways. This area of North Carolina, unlike the mountains, rarely saw measurable snowfall, but when it did, the roads were a nightmare. Not a loaf of bread or a gallon of milk remained in the grocery stores. Thankfully, there would be no problems tonight, just a blustery cold front accompanying a northwest wind, giving the sensation of blowing over ice.

Susan walked into the foyer of the restaurant, keeping her coat close, relaxing in the entranceway's warm interior. There was no sign of Bob Carson, so she decided to ask the maître d' if there was a reservation. The maître d' indicated no reservation for Bob Carson. She wondered if she'd been stood up.

The maître d' asked if she'd like to sit at the bar and wait. Susan considered his suggestion and followed him to the bar area. Opting to leave her coat on, she sat at the lone empty table. She ordered a half glass of Chardonnay. If Bob didn't show, she'd drink her wine, leave, hit a fast-food drive-through, and go home. Her flannel pajamas and blue fuzzy robe would be of great comfort on this cold night. *It's just that simple, isn't it?* But it wasn't that simple. Susan was lonely. The thought of being abandoned again sent her heart tumbling into her stomach. Her track record with men was not good. Her luck was not good. Earlier, she'd sensed tonight would change her luck, but doubt began creeping into her thoughts, aiming for her newly gained confidence.

Her drink arrived. She paid for it and took a sip. It wasn't bad; actually, it was quite pleasant, nice and dry with a hint of oak and pear. She settled back to relax, enjoying the warmth of her coat and the warm air drifting from the overhead vent.

She heard someone call her name, but it wasn't the voice she was expecting. It was a voice that had lain dormant in her subconscious for eleven years. She would have gladly gone a lifetime without hearing it again. It was the voice of Janet Pierce.

Susan went into panic mode and tried to think of an escape plan. She longed to crawl under the table, but hiding was not an option; she'd been spied.

Susan stood a good three inches taller than Janet, though she'd always felt belittled by the woman. As she sat in the cushioned chair, she was forced to look up at Janet, a blow to Susan's already precarious emotional state. Susan couldn't help the flood of emotions and memories the sight of Janet brought back. It was as if Janet had known her before their first meeting, as if she'd hated Susan long before their first meeting, like she'd known a dirty little secret. Susan sat wide-eyed in puzzled panic.

"My, my, how are you, Suzanne?" Janet drawled.

"It's Susan. I'm well, thank you, and you?" Susan replied. Janet Pierce knew her name and knew it well.

"Oh, simply marvelous, as always. Are you here with your family?" Janet briefly glanced around the restaurant, as if looking for someone. Susan found it hard to believe Janet would ask that, considering that Janet knew Susan had no family.

"No, I'm meeting a friend."

At that moment, a wonderful, slightly familiar male voice called from behind.

"Hello, Susan, sorry I'm late. I decided to take a shortcut and forgot the road was closed for repairs. My, you look beautiful."

Susan smiled up at Bob and saw he was dressed in a dark charcoal wool suit and tie.

"And who might this gentleman be?" Janet eyed Bob.

Susan prepared herself to say Bob Carson, but that was all she could say; that was all she knew.

"Bob Carson of Carson Concrete and Landscaping," Bob interjected, extending his hand to shake Janet's.

"Yes, that's why you look so familiar. Your company designed the landscaping for my side garden last year. So nice to see you again. I hope you two have a lovely dinner." And with that, Janet turned abruptly and maneuvered her way through the restaurant, spying her husband and their table.

"Do you know her?" Bob asked with a concerned tone in his voice.

"Yes, it's a long story for another time. She doesn't care for me, and we'll leave it at that."

Later, Susan would explain Janet Pierce's dislike for her. Bob guessed most of the story before she could explain that she'd dated the woman's son; he recognized the look. He'd been on the receiving end of the same look from the mother of a girl he'd dated in high school. He recalled the woman's ire at her daughter's dating a nobody who worked with his hands.

Bob replied with some concern, "I feel like I need to protect you right now for some reason."

Susan relaxed a little at his comment; she didn't have a problem with that idea at all, and her tremulous smile was all the encouragement he needed.

"I want to apologize again for not being here on time. I guess I was a little excited about our date and forgot the road closure on East Alton Street." Susan immediately picked up on his use of the D-word. "You know how the best of intentions can get you in trouble?" Bob explained.

Before Susan could answer, the maître d' came to escort them to a quaint table for two by the window. The night outside was dark and cold, but both the table and company were warm and inviting in the soft candlelight. Susan ordered the other half of her glass of wine, and Bob ordered one as well. She noticed his wedding ring was gone.

"So you own Carson's Concrete and Landscaping. I've heard of your company. I don't have a yard, but I've heard some of the other doctors talk about your work. They say you are the best in town."

"Well, we certainly try. We have a landscaping division that can work wonders. It's not inexpensive, but it is worthy of a magazine spread, if I say so myself. My father started the concrete company when I was young. I majored in horticulture and landscaping at NC State. My dad added the landscaping division into the concrete company after some convincing from me. My dad wasn't on board at first. You know how bad concrete looks fresh—plain and raw with square edges?"

"I do. Did your dad finally come around?"

"Oh yes, when he saw what I could do, he changed his mind quickly. He passed away a few years ago, and I took over the entire operation. I'm an only child. My mother died about twenty years ago from breast cancer, right before I married Sherry."

The color drained from Susan's face, and she struggled to keep her breathing even. She softly voiced, "My mother died from breast cancer when I was twelve."

Susan was relieved to see the waiter bringing their dinner. It had taken her a few moments to regain her composure. The mention of her mother's death always left her short of breath and off balance. After a few moments, she was able to breathe evenly again and enjoy her dinner. She'd ordered her favorite crab cakes, and Bob, prime rib.

Dinner broke the conversation, and Bob neglected to ask about Susan's father. Susan didn't know if the fact that she was the daughter of a single mother would be troubling to him. She would be honest. She would not hide the truth.

"I've eaten here on a number of occasions and have never been disappointed. I usually order the prime rib, seeing as I do not cook it at home." He hesitated slightly. "Now I do grill a mean steak. Maybe you would like to have dinner at my house sometime." His comment came out as more of a statement than the invitation she thought he meant it to be. "I know we haven't finished this dinner yet, but would you like to have dinner with me at my house? I don't want to be pushy or anything. I just thought it would be nice to see you again."

"I'd like that," she replied sincerely, a smile enhancing her dimples.

The waiter took their empty plates and asked if they would care for dessert. Bob looked at Susan and said, "Would you like to share a piece of chocolate cake?"

"Yes, I was hoping you'd ask; that's my favorite," she said enthusiastically.

"Mine too." And Bob grinned at her.

The cake was devoured, and the plate was scraped as clean as could be without the disintegration of all manners. Susan checked her watch—eight forty-five. Where had the time gone? She'd certainly enjoyed the dinner and looked forward to the possibility of seeing Bob Carson again.

"I guess I need to be heading home," she said reluctantly.

"When will you be off again? Maybe one day next weekend?" Bob asked.

"I won't be working next Saturday."

"Would you like to have dinner at my house? I know it's winter, but I grill year-round. Steak is my specialty."

"I would love to," Susan replied sincerely.

"Can I pick you up?"

"I don't want you to go to any trouble"

"It's no trouble. How about I pick you up at five o'clock. You can help me with the salad."

"It's a date." Susan immediately realized that she'd just said the D-word.

"Yes, it's a date," Bob said, smiling broadly. "I do want to ask you one question."

A moment of panic hit Susan. What was his question? Was it about her family, her father?

"What's your address?" Bob asked.

CHAPTER 47

The D-Word

Bob arrived at Susan's apartment at five o'clock Saturday evening. Susan was ready and waiting by the front window. She'd looked forward to their date all week. He knocked on her door, and she greeted him with a smile, donning her wool coat. He drove a high-end late-model SUV. The interior was warm and comfortable.

She'd forgotten to ask where he lived; the subject never came up during their dinner at Evelyn's the previous weekend. As they neared his house, the route seemed oddly familiar. It slowly dawned on her these were the same streets she'd ridden to the Pierce home. Two left turns instead of two right turns, and they entered a gated drive labeled Cambridge Estates. The homes and grounds were picturesque. Even the cold and drab grays and browns of winter could not diminish the beauty of their elegant brick and stone work. Bob turned into the curved drive of a magnificent Colonial Revival home. The evergreens appeared to keep the grounds in a perpetual state of life. The setting sun gave the brickwork a golden glow. Bob's house was beautiful—and huge.

"You have a lovely home," Susan said with awe.

"Thank you. It belonged to my parents, and I couldn't bear to sell it when my dad died. They bought it out of foreclosure and brought the beauty back to its classic stature. It had stood empty for a number of years and needed some work. Sherry and I sold our house and moved here. I've remodeled the inside, but the exterior is classic, and I wouldn't change a thing."

The interior of the house proved to be as classically beautiful as the exterior. The living room was highlighted by a finely detailed fireplace and an exquisitely ornate tray ceiling. The kitchen featured double stoves and ovens with intricate tile work. The house also boasted five bedrooms, five and a half baths, a formal dining room, a huge pantry, a roomy den with a theater-style television, and a small office. The sizable laundry room dwarfed Susan's one-bedroom apartment.

"Wow, this is a big house. I love the kitchen. Did you do the tile work?

"Yes, I did. Took me two weeks, but I think it turned out perfectly. I know the house is big, but I don't think I could part with it. Lots of good memories." Bob hesitated for a moment.

"I have plenty of ingredients for a salad in the fridge if you want to take a look. I'll get the steaks out and let them rest for a while before I grill them. Would you like a glass of wine?" Bob retrieved two wine glasses from the cabinet.

Susan laughed. "Yes, I thought you'd never ask."

"Red or white?"

"Whatever you're having."

"Chardonnay it is."

With glass of wine in hand, she set out to explore the designer refrigerator. She chopped and sliced the mix of lettuces, tomatoes, cucumbers, carrots, and radishes until she was satisfied with the results. Bob had baked potatoes prior to leaving and had wrapped them in foil, setting them back in the warm oven. The steaks were perfectly marbled.

"How do you like your steak?" Bob asked Susan.

"Medium rare—is that okay?" Susan replied.

"Great! Just the way I like mine."

The steaks were grilled, salads dressed, and steaming potatoes opened to add creamy butter and a dollop of sour cream with a sprinkle of chives.

"This looks and smells fantastic," Susan remarked, smiling at Bob. "You're a good cook."

Bob smiled back at Susan. "I put forth good effort, if nothing else."

They both ate, intermingled with occasional comments about cooking for one and how neither of them was a fan of that. They both agreed they would rather cook for a small group than for themselves.

"That's why I eat in the cafeteria at work. The food is fresh and tastes good. I try to cook on my days off and save some for evenings when I come home. Seven-thirty or eight o'clock is awfully late to start cooking dinner. Every so often, I go through a drive-through restaurant and bring dinner home. Those usually aren't the most nutritious meals. I don't like eating in restaurants alone," Susan said matter-of-factly.

"I agree. I would rather eat at home than alone in a restaurant. I grill better than I cook on the stove, so I usually have something in the freezer or fridge to grill. Vegetables are a little tricky, but I usually find something that will do in a pinch. My wife cooked, but she liked me to grill. She took care of the sides." Bob's voice dropped off at the end of the sentence, and he looked at his plate for a moment, his throat constricting a bit.

Susan reached over and covered his hand with hers. "I know you loved her very much, and I'm sorry she's gone."

Bob sniffed slightly and then looked at Susan. "I'm sorry. There are still moments I find myself missing Sherry, but I'm okay, really; I'm fine. I guess it would be sad if I didn't feel her loss at some point, wouldn't it?"

181

"That's exactly right. I wouldn't expect any less of you. It means you are human and a human who has found love in his life. I'm saying that as a compliment." And she smiled a sweet smile, gave his hand a gentle pat, picked up her glass, and offered a toast. "To the loves we have lost. May they rest in peace and know we will love them to the end of our days."

Bob picked up his glass and touched hers with a gentle *ping*. He took a sip, followed by a smile for Susan as he peered deeply into her warm, sensuous brown eyes.

After the dishes were loaded in the dishwasher, Susan and Bob sat in the living room talking about college days at their respective schools. At that point Susan decided to tell Bob about her mother— that she'd been a single parent.

"My mother was a single parent and I have no idea who my father is, my mother never told me. My mother died when I was 12 and I was placed in the Cabot Home for Children. I grew up there and graduated from Cabot High School. I was the Valedictorian."

"You haven't had it easy, have you?"

"No, but I made up my mind I would go to college and make an effort to be successful for my mother. I think she would have been proud of me."

"I think she would." Bob smiled.

Susan did not tell him about her relationship with Rick Pierce or her child. It would do no good to explain old love interests; at this point in her life, it didn't matter.

"Oh my, I didn't realize it was already eleven o'clock. I guess I need to take you home."

"Yes, I guess so. I've had a lovely evening. You have a beautiful home," Susan said again, looking around the living room, at the ceiling, and toward the foyer. "I hope I can visit again," she said before she caught herself. It sounded forward, too forward. She'd enjoyed the evening and was interested in seeing Bob again, despite their age difference, but she wasn't sure he was ready for a relationship. He was so emotional when he mentioned his late wife.

I'll accept whatever comes of our relationship, she told herself. *If it's meant to be, it will happen.*

As Bob drove Susan back to her apartment, the night sky was clear, with stars sparkling brightly. The moon sat above the horizon. She was an avid moon-watcher; she had been from the time she was a small child. She remembered gazing with wonder at its presence in the night sky; sometimes it appeared as a small sliver, scooping a bit of water or as a glowing white orb, full and bright. Many nights, clouds did their best to cover it, but with the tiniest, thinly veiled break, the moon reappeared, comforting her. She pointed it out to Bob, explaining her fascination,

"I must admit I'm a moon junkie. When I was a child, I always thought it was God looking over me when I saw the moon. It gave me a sense of peace, especially after my mother died. I spent many nights propped on the windowsill, praying."

"I'm sure it gave you hope and comfort, being alone and all," Bob said compassionately, briefly glancing at Susan.

"Thank you. I'm sorry to be so forward. I don't usually confide in others like this, but you seem like a nice person, and I trust you, though we've only known each other a couple of weeks."

"Well, I think we can remedy that. Would you like to go out for dinner one evening this week? No more meeting at the restaurant. I'll pick you up this time. Is it a date?"

Bob could see Susan's smile in the light of the instrument panel as they drove into a parking space outside of her apartment, the SUV coming to a halt.

"Yes, it's a date."

Bob walked her to her front door, gave her a gentle kiss on her lips, hugged her, and thanked her for a wonderful evening. He walked back to his SUV and backed out of the parking space. As he left, he waved to Susan, a smile on his handsomely lined face. Susan waved back with a smile and the best feeling she'd experienced in years. She looked toward the moon and murmured, "Thank you."

Over a span of months, Susan and Bob could be found together every evening and weekend she wasn't working at the hospital. Bob ate lunch with her in the hospital cafeteria at least once a week. During these lunches, they often recapped their first meeting and their personal thoughts about each other that cold January day, laughing at their interpretation of meeting at the restaurant, both of them fearful of the D-word. They agreed fate had been kind to them that day. The probability of years of living alone would have taken a toll on both of them. They both confessed they didn't want to be alone for the rest of their lives. They became a romantic couple, with the added bonus of being best friends. They joked that neither had to bring the other home to meet their parents. No awkward parent introductions, hoping for the best but fearing the worst. Susan had experienced the worst with Janet Pierce.

Susan couldn't quite put her finger on the reason, but her love for Bob felt different than the love she'd had for Rick. It was strange. She loved Bob and wanted to spend the rest of her life with him. She eventually chalked up her feelings to teenage crushes versus mature romantic relationships. There was room for only one man in her heart, and it was Bob Carson. Every thought of Rick Pierce was pushed to the far recesses of her subconscious. Rick Pierce was the past; Bob Carson was her present and, hopefully, her future.

CHAPTER 48

The M-Word

Susan and Bob became engaged at Thanksgiving in 1986. Bob popped the question following dinner at Evelyn's, a ten-month celebration of their first date. After dinner, a bottle of champagne was delivered to their table. With a questioning look on Susan's face, Bob dropped to one knee, pulled a blue velvet box from his jacket pocket, and proposed.

The ring was exquisite—a perfectly cut oval diamond surrounded by sparkling sapphires, set in a platinum band. Bob shyly told her he remembered the sapphire-blue dress she'd worn on their first date and how beautiful she looked. Susan was on the verge of tears by the time Bob finished his proposal. He described how he felt about her the first time he saw her in the hospital cafeteria; how he knew there was something special about her.

She wiped her eyes and reached out her arms to hug and kiss him. She realized he was still holding the open ring box and laughing. She pulled back and held out her left hand for Bob to slip the ring onto her finger. Everyone in the restaurant clapped and cheered as if they were a part of the planning of the evening's proposal. Susan waved shyly to the cheering crowd, settling down to admire her engagement ring. It was the most beautiful ring she'd ever seen, much less owned. Her mother's emerald ring was beautiful, but her engagement ring was spectacular.

"I have a matching wedding band," Bob said, gazing longingly into her eyes.

"I can't wait to see it, hopefully soon," Susan replied.

"Yes, soon, don't you think?" Bob said. "I think that would be perfect."

Susan took a week of vacation after Christmas. She and Bob simply went to the courthouse and were married in a private civil ceremony. They had agreed that since neither of them had any family to speak of, there would be no formal wedding ceremony. They kept their wedding plans a secret.

They spent the first two days of marriage moving Susan's belongings to Bob's house. When all of Susan's belongings were unpacked and put in place, Bob made a suggestion he'd thought about for a few days.

"Would you like to go to the beach for a real honeymoon?"

"That would be wonderful. Where do suggest we go?" Susan asked eagerly.

"We could go to Fran and Greg Mason's cottage on Oak Island." Bob explained that his friend Greg Mason and his wife owned a beach cottage there. They'd been offering him a week at the cottage for the past year. The newlyweds took them up on their offer, excited to spend their honeymoon on the island. It would be quiet now, but with a warmer-than-usual forecast, they packed a few shorts and T-shirts and hoped for the best.

The quaint, raised-foundation cottage had a simple white clapboard exterior with a broad front porch and a screened back porch just off the kitchen. The simple exterior belied the comfortable interior, decorated with beach-themed appointments. There were three bedrooms and two baths, with a large combination kitchen and dining room. The living room overlooked the street, which separated the house from the elevated two- and three-story oceanfront homes. Slivers of the Atlantic Ocean could be spied between the assortment of gray, white, and blue beach houses. The sun's reflection glistened off the gentle waves.

Susan sipped her coffee while seated on the comfortable cushioned loveseat on the front porch on their first morning, wrapped in Bob's arms. The feeling of security was now a part of her new normal. Susan had survived emotionally tumultuous moments but sensed those days were behind her. She'd found someone she could trust, love, and spend the rest of her life taking care of and being cared for each and every day. There was no drama. Dealing with drama, especially in-law drama, was the downfall of more than a few marriages. She could feel her heart pounding faster and her anxiety rising just thinking of Janet Pierce. She hoped Janet was happy now, because her unhappiness was like a poison to those surrounding her. Susan mentally shook her head and knew she would never have to think of Janet Pierce again.

Susan gently voiced her pleasure with their honeymoon choice. "Wouldn't it be nice to stay here forever?"

"You know we have to eventually go back to work, but I'm with you; this is heaven, don't you think?" Bob gently whispered in Susan's ear.

Susan laughed the sweet laugh Bob had fallen in love with the first moment he heard it. "Yes, this is heaven."

Most of the island restaurants closed during the winter months, so the newlyweds' dining choices were limited. They purchased groceries at the local grocery on the mainland and cooked most meals themselves. On their forays through the island streets in search of an open restaurant, they passed a few houses listed for sale. One in particular caught both Bob's and Susan's eyes, and they drove back and forth three times, contemplating it.

"Someone is going to think we're casing the joint." Susan laughed nervously.

"Okay, just one more time. Make sure you write down the phone number on the sign. Here's a piece of paper. I don't have a pen on me. Do you have one in your purse?" Bob said in a businesslike tone.

"I do. Let's see, um, okay, I got it." Susan wrote down the number, and they agreed to call the next day.

"You know, it would be nice to have a place here. We could spend vacations at the beach and maybe bring our family here." Susan eyed Bob as he glanced her way.

"And what family might you be talking about?" He grinned and reached over to take her slim hand with the platinum band and matching diamond-and-sapphire engagement ring, picking it up to place a gentle kiss.

"Oh, I think we could work on that. What do you think? I suppose that would be a good project for us, maybe the sooner the better. We're not getting any younger, old man." Susan giggled, using her pet name for her new husband, considering the wide gap in their ages.

"I suggest we get started on that project right after dinner. What do you think?"

"Count me in!" And Susan giggled like a happy teenager, thinking, *Oh, love feels so much better than loneliness.*

The next few months were a flurry of activity for the newlyweds. They put in a bid for the beach house and suddenly were the owners of a vacation home on the coast of North Carolina. The house was in need of some cosmetic work but was, for the most part, inhabitable from day one. Both the front and back of the house boasted porches that ran the width of the house. They'd bought it furnished with a beach-themed ensemble of sofas, easy chairs, and a white wooden dining table with matching chairs—bright and airy. The walls were painted shades of pastel blues, greens, and yellows. The old wooden floors were refinished and glowed with new life. A new refrigerator and stove were installed, and the kitchen was ready. Accessories were added, along with plump sofa pillows and seat cushions for the dining room chairs. The couple could be found at their newly acquired escape every free weekend and every week of vacation. They named their beach house Summer Solstice, agreeing that every day spent there, no matter the time of year, would be like the first day of summer. It was their happy place.

CHAPTER 49

At Last

The spring of 1987 arrived with daffodils, fragrant green grass, and rain. Soaking, pouring rain. Just when the sun peeped its tiny self from behind the swirl of angry clouds, the clouds planned their revolt and poured again. Rick noticed the yard needed to be mowed, but the groundskeeper couldn't get to it for another week.

Donna Pierce was miserable, suffering from a lingering stomach virus. The symptoms dragged on for days. She vomited after each meal, causing concern for her and Rick. He'd gone to the grocery store a couple of days ago because she hadn't shopped in two weeks. She said the smell of the deli counter had driven her out, and she wasn't going back until she felt better.

"Are you still sick?" Rick repeated his question before and after work.

"Yes, I feel awful. I'm going to the doctor tomorrow. I made the appointment this afternoon. You can fix yourself a sandwich. I'm going to lie down." And with that, Donna slowly stepped on the bottom step of the staircase. She didn't make it any farther before she dropped to the floor.

Rick ran to her, picked her up, and laid her on the sofa. He ran to get a cool, wet washcloth from the guest bath and laid it across her forehead.

"What happened?" she asked groggily.

"I don't know, but I'm going with you to the doctor tomorrow. I'm driving. No arguments."

"Well, Mrs. Pierce, you are pregnant," the doctor said as Donna and Rick sat staring, not moving or reacting.

Finally, Rick asked, "Are you sure?"

"Yes, 100 percent. Mrs. Pierce, you said you haven't had a period in a couple of months, said you lost count of the weeks, right? And the pregnancy test came back positive. Yes, you are going to have a baby."

Rick hugged Donna, each laughing and tearing up simultaneously. It had been years since they'd thought of trying for a baby, so the news was a shock. The couple had given up hope of ever having a child. Rick knew his and Donna's parents would be ecstatic with the promise of finally being grandparents.

As soon as Donna's first trimester ended, her nausea and lightheadedness subsided. She soon reverted back to her old, self-absorbed habits, spending lots of Rick's money on decorations for the nursery and baby clothes. Donna and her mother or mother-in-law spent days debating clothing choices, highchairs, car seats, diapers, and anything else that could be purchased for the soon-to-be new member of the Pierce family.

On the day of the sonogram, Donna's excitement could not be contained. Rick could sense she hoped for a girl. He didn't care whether it was a girl or boy; he would be happy with a healthy baby. He'd questioned her consumption of alcohol in the early days of her pregnancy, but Donna ignored him. He let it drop but hoped there would be no lasting effects from her questionable behavior.

"Do you want to know the gender?" the technician asked the expectant couple.

"Yes, we do," Donna quickly said.

"Well, do you see that?" The technician pointed to something on the screen.

"Yes, so?" Donna said hurriedly.

"It's a boy," the technician said with a big smile. "You are having a little boy."

"Are you sure?" Donna asked.

"Yes, very sure."

"Does everything look okay?" Rick asked.

"Everything looks just fine."

Rick was relieved. *So far, so good. Maybe Mother Nature will be forgiving of Donna's poor health habits.* He had to admit she'd been a model expectant mother since the doctor's initial diagnosis.

From the moment the technician announced the gender of Rick and Donna's baby, the color blue invaded their life. The nursery furniture was dusted and polished to a sheen. The walls received a fresh coat of pale-blue paint with snowy-white trim. Blue cushions for the rocking chair, blue rugs on the floor, blue sheets, bumper pad, and blankets for the crib. Tiny blue-and-white outfits lined the closet on miniature blue hangers, and blue sleepers were neatly folded and placed in the dresser. Life was looking up for the Pierce family; all the females were happy.

CHAPTER 50

Carson, Party of Three

The first year of marriage brought with it a new member to the Carson family, a baby girl. Susan became pregnant within the early weeks of their marriage. She wasn't surprised. Getting pregnant was way too easy for her. She could imagine that in the years before birth control, she would have been one of those mothers with fifteen children. Bob was thrilled with the promise of parenthood. Months before Susan was to deliver, Bob filled the nursery with clothes, furniture, stuffed animals, packages of diapers, and so much more. They decorated the room, painting the walls a gentle creamy white, which could be accented with blue or pink. Susan and Bob chose not to know the gender of the baby, wanting it to be a surprise when the baby was born.

Susan didn't tell Bob about her first child. She'd vowed to herself she would never speak of him again. She debated whether she should rethink her decision to keep her secret but remained convinced a confession would only bring hurt to an otherwise perfect marriage. She could not bear to hurt her husband in any way. His love and devotion was priceless, and she would keep this secret where it belonged—in the recesses of her memory, hidden from the rest of the world. Bob was her second chance for love and for being a mother. She grew more excited each day at the thought of motherhood.

When the time came, she and Bob religiously attended childbirth classes, and she pretended to know much less about giving birth. Her medical training was a convenient cover for her knowledge of childbirth, more knowledge than the average woman would have before pregnancy with a first child. She was well aware of the pain of giving birth and held a small bit of dread in the back of her mind. She would make it, though; she knew she would be okay, and Bob would be in for the experience of a lifetime.

Julie Elizabeth Carson was born on a cool, crisp afternoon in late October. She was beautiful and perfect. Her silky black hair was tousled, and her blue eyes shown between finely lashed eyelids, squinting in the bright lights of the delivery room.

Bob was beside himself. He stopped everyone he met in the hallway of the maternity ward and told them he was a father. Susan chuckled to herself at the thought, guessing some of his audience probably thought he was a little old to be a father, maybe more the age of a grandfather. He was a little miffed when three different people asked him which infant was his grandchild while observing through the wide expanse of windows in the nursery. Susan was much quieter and cradled her daughter.

The interesting part of the newest family member was that Julie Elizabeth Carson came out of the womb defiant. She never cried but actually scowled at Susan, pursing her lips and wrinkling her tiny nose. Susan could have sworn her baby daughter smiled at Bob when he held her while frowning at her. The newborn's scornful look was a signal, and Susan knew she was in for trouble. It was obvious Julie would be a daddy's girl. *Whatever happened to the wonderment of having a little me?* Both she and Bob were easygoing, calm, and mild-mannered, but it was apparent Julie would be a little spitfire. She would be opinionated, smart, and confident. In the meantime, Susan would have to deal with this innocent-looking little cutie with the obstinate, stubborn, day-old princess attitude. She sighed and decided this would be an interesting ride. She gazed at her newborn daughter and whispered, "My sweet, sassy girl, you know you are mine and Daddy's. We will love you forever, and we will live happily ever after. I promise."

CHAPTER 51

Arrival in Blue

The birth of Richard van Allen Pierce III was a historic event for both the Pierce and Creighton families. The cold, dark November night heralded a joyful moment for the two intertwined families. Donna's delivery was typical, with eight hours of labor and a strong cry from the newborn baby boy.

"We'll call him Richie. How does that sound?" Donna looked questioningly at Rick.

He nodded his head in agreement. "Richie it is. That sounds perfect." He smiled at the sight of his son.

Donna cradled the newborn, reluctantly releasing him, placing the infant in his grandmother's arms. His wispy blond hair and blue eyes were a mirror of Rick.

Unbeknownst to any of the group of joy-filled parents and grandparents, he was the second mirror of Rick Pierce. The first, an eleven-year-old, lived happily in a world far from Cabot, North Carolina.

In the Pierce and Creighton families, Richie was doted on and might have been spoiled as well, but in actuality, Richie Pierce was a most gentle, kindhearted, caring, and intelligent child. Richie's personality reflected none of the ostentatious superiority heaped on him by his mother and grandmothers. His gentle character made him a favorite friend of children in his nursery school. Richie's mild manner became the benchmark for defining the perfect child, as parents of his classmates compared their own children's poor conduct to his seemingly flawless composure.

"Why can't you be nice, like Richie?"

"Why don't you share like Richie?"

The comparisons went on and on. This proved to be a blessing and a curse for Donna. Richie was invited to every child's birthday party, pool party, and numerous playdates. The blessing side was his popularity. All parents want their children to be liked and accepted by those around them. The curse side was every child wanted a part of him, rich and poor. Every friend—and he had many—wanted him close. Donna allowed Richie to attend every event to which he was invited. She inwardly grimaced when the activity or party did not meet with her expectations.

CHAPTER 52

What Are the Odds?

Susan shook her head, ashamed of her parenting skills. She didn't know what to do with Julie, and to top it off, Bob was no help. He was useless when it came to parenting. Susan loved her husband dearly, but his parenting skills were horrible. He spoiled Julie beyond all reason, giving in to their daughter's every whim.

Susan herself had been the quintessential cooperative child. She did as she was told and never spoke out of turn. She did her chores and never sassed her mother. She came home and did her homework with the work ethic of a successful businessperson. Julie, on the other hand, was obstinate, sassy, and brave. Her confidence grew to levels unmatched by other children her age. Julie questioned every move her parents made; her personality was nothing like Susan's or Bob's. Susan and Julie looked like mother and daughter on the outside, but Julie's cute appearance belied the little demon inside. With kindergarten just around the corner, Susan worried how Julie's behavior would manifest itself at her new school and her reaction to her teacher's authority. She'd spent her preschool years in a local church daycare with both Bob and Susan working. Julie had been somewhat cooperative, but she was smart, and she knew it. She had no qualms about calling out an adult if she felt she was right. And the little stinker was right most of the time. She was entertaining to be around and was usually on her best behavior in public, but her obstinate side reared its ugly head at home, much to her parents' dismay.

As kindergarten neared, Susan wasn't sure who was more excited, Julie or Bob. School would start next week and kindergarten orientation was that night. Susan's latest battle with her daughter centered around purchasing a book bag for school.

"Daddy, why can't I get a book bag today? I need one today, Daddy. Please take me shopping. Mommy won't buy me one, but you will, won't you, Daddy?" Julie cajoled her father.

"No, let's wait and see what your teacher says tonight at school." Bob put forth good effort to persuade his daughter to wait.

"Nobody wants to do anything I want to do." Julie left the room, pouting, crossing her arms over her chest, trying her best to stomp her tiny feet on the tile floor.

Susan let out a soft sigh after her daughter's rude departure. "What are we going to do with her?"

"I don't know, truly I don't." Bob looked at the floor, shaking his head. "I thought she'd calm down with age, but her terrible twos and headstrong attitude don't seem to be fading."

"Thank you for standing up with me. You know her go-to strategy is to divide and conquer, and her targets are us." Susan peered at Bob with a look of gratitude.

"Well, I guess we old people have to stick together, don't we?" He laughed and then gave Susan a gentle kiss. "It's us against a five-year-old, and frankly, I don't like our odds."

The kindergarten classroom was an interesting place—everything appeared in miniature. Miniature desks, chairs, tables, kitchen sets, even rocking chairs. Bob and Susan, along with every other set of parents, eyed the pint-sized chairs and pondered the best approach to sitting in the wee torture devices. Standing against the back wall seemed more advantageous than sitting, and many of the fathers chose this alternative.

Bob contemplated his descent onto the minuscule chair. "I guess gravity works on the way down, but we may have to be helped up."

"I'll help you, old man." Susan snickered under her breath, eyeing Bob as he dropped to the chair. She had to admit the chairs were not the most comfortable, but they suited a group of five-year-olds to a T.

The children had been escorted to the multipurpose room to engage in introduction-to-school activities. This separation kept the active little ones busy without interfering with the parent/teacher meet-and-greet. The classroom teachers would review a plethora of information in the form of a mustard-colored packet filled with handouts and forms to be completed.

Susan peered around the classroom, but she didn't recognize any of the other parents in Julie's class—until a new set of parents entered the room. Her breath caught in her throat when she recognized the father. Her stomach instantly filled with hot acid, and she blushed hotly, the sensation resembling being set on fire. She swallowed hard, tearing her gaze away from the man in an attempt to focus on the kindergarten teacher's explanation of lunch payments. She touched Bob's hand and forced a tremulous smile.

CHAPTER 53

To the Surface

Rick could hardly believe Richie would be starting kindergarten next week. It seemed like yesterday he and Donna had brought him home from the hospital, a sweet bundle dressed in blue. Rick considered himself and Donna lucky to have Richie. He was their miracle baby. Donna was diagnosed with a severe case of uterine fibroids, and both of them knew she would not be able to carry another child. Richie would carry all of their hopes and dreams on his small shoulders. This would appear to be an immense burden for his son, but Richie handled it with kindness, grace, and dignity beyond his years. He was a bright child, perfect in every way.

Richie's excitement was contagious. He bounced around the house singing a song he'd learned in nursery school about kindergarten being the best place on earth. Rick couldn't help but smile at his son's enthusiasm.

"Hurry, hurry, hurry!" Richie called from the garage door. "We're going to be late, Mama. Come on, Daddy. Hurry!"

"We're coming dear." Donna called. "Just wait a minute; we're coming." She finished applying her lipstick, smoothed her dress, and walked down the carpeted staircase.

Their ride was noisy with Richie's questions about his new school. The funny thing was, he answered most of his own questions. Rick couldn't help but smile with a father's pride as he glanced in the rearview mirror and saw his son sitting in his car seat, talking away to no one in particular.

Rick and Donna had considered enrolling Richie in a private school, but there seemed to be a scarcity of them in the area. Stone Brook School had closed some years earlier due to enrollment deficits. Janet Pierce could not believe Rick and Donna would send her grandson to public school, but Rick had no problem with the idea. Donna put up very little argument, and the decision was made to send Richie to the local elementary school.

Parking was at a premium; all the spaces were taken within a short walk to the front doors. Rick dropped off Donna and Richie at the front walkway and proceeded to park on the side of the wide driveway that led away from the school building. The weather was hot and humid on that mid-August night, and Rick was thankful for air conditioning. He'd not thought to change his clothes and wore the suit and tie he'd worn to the law office that day. By the time he made the trek to the front door of the school, he was covered in a fine coating of perspiration. He walked into the lobby of the elementary school and immediately felt the cool rush of dehumidified air as it hit his exposed skin. He sighed with relief.

The staff member seated at a table in front of the office asked for their child's name. She gave them Richie's room assignment and packet of information and escorted the inquisitive young man to the multipurpose room to join in the activities with his classmates—the future graduating class of 2006, though no one was thinking in those terms with a group of hyperactive five-year-olds.

Rick and Donna walked down the hall, counting off the room numbers until their son's classroom appeared around the corner.

As they entered the classroom, they noticed the room was near full with tiny chairs, arranged for parents to sit. The teacher had already begun her presentation but paused to allow them to find a seat. A cursory look around the classroom allowed Rick to recognize a few sets of parents. He and Donna wound their way over to sit next to the parents of a boy in Richie's preschool class. They lived a few blocks away from the Pierces, and their son was an occasional playdate for Richie. A few of the parents shifted to different chairs to make room for Rick and Donna, standing slowly with the help of one mother who looked as though she frequently worked out at the gym. Faint laughter was heard as parents grunted to stand up. The kindergarten teacher continued by introducing herself to the newcomers and dove back into the information needed for the nervous parents. Rick made another cursory look around the room to check for familiar faces, and his gaze halted on a mother sitting across the room. He recognized Susan Anderson immediately.

It's been close to—what?—eighteen years since I last saw her? The weekend of Thanksgiving 1975. An avalanche of emotions stormed their way into his brain, with a mix of anxiety and excitement leading the way. She hadn't changed at all, still as beautiful as she was in high school. She was a thirty-something woman now, and age had only enhanced her beauty. She was sitting with a man who looked more like a grandparent but who Rick assumed was her husband. She looked happy.

As the orientation concluded, the kindergarten teacher dismissed the parents, who then proceeded to the multipurpose room to collect their excited kindergarteners. Rick's eyes followed Susan through the rush, only losing sight of her in the mass of parents and children in the multipurpose room. He found himself hot and cold at the same time, a basket of nerves and emotions. He'd denied his feelings for her a thousand times, but in that moment, he knew a part of him was still in love with Susan Anderson.

203

CHAPTER 54

The Enforcer

Susan was delighted to see Julie making lots of friends in her kindergarten class, though the relationship that concerned her was Richie Pierce. Julie talked about him every day after school. It was Richie this, or Richie that. Hardly a dinner conversation went by without mention of him and whatever had happened in their kindergarten class that particular day.

"Richie and I played in the kitchen during Centers, Mommy. The teacher told us we had to go to different centers, but we didn't listen. She looked at us and shook her head. We talked about our families today too. I told my class that my mommy is a people doctor, and my daddy is a tree doctor. Everybody laughed, and I told them it was true. Richie didn't laugh." Without provocation, Julie then announced that Richie was her best friend. She repeatedly asked to go to his house to play. Susan didn't know how much longer she could put Julie off; her young daughter could be quite persuasive—and persistent. But Susan could not imagine herself at Rick Pierce's house.

The invitation came in the mail two weeks into November, a birthday party for Richie Pierce. The party was being held at the most popular birthday spot in town, Roma's Pizza Parlor. The draw of a pizza buffet, huge game room, and the exclusive party room was a draw for fashionable birthday parties and celebrations for the elementary-school crowd. Susan put off the discussion as long as possible but finally faced the inevitable and sat Julie down to explain why she couldn't take her to Richie's party in the only way she felt she could—by lying. Susan didn't like lying to her child, but the circumstances necessitated it. Susan was fairly convinced Rick's wife would not know her history with him, but her presence at the party would be awkward, not only for her but, she suspected, for Rick, as well. And what about his family, particularly his mother? Susan could see the questions forming in Julie's mind as she explained she couldn't take her to the party because she might have to work, and even if she didn't have to work, she had housework taking up all afternoon.

"Daddy can take me," Julie argued, firmly convinced that her father would do anything she asked him.

"I don't think Daddy would enjoy a six-year-old's birthday party at a pizza parlor," Susan said, trying her best to convince her daughter.

"Yes, he would. We play games and have cake and take presents."

"I don't think Daddy wants to play pinball or anything like that, okay? Daddy will be busy and won't be able to take you."

"He would for me. Daddy would do anything for me."

"I would what?" Bob walked into the room just in time to hear Julie's statement, and she immediately ran to him, jumping into his arms, eyeing Susan with a sneaky gleam in her eye.

"Daddy, you would take me to Richie's birthday party, wouldn't you?"

Susan could have given her daughter a swift, not-so-gentle pat on her backside for using Bob to get her way. Bob still spoiled Julie rotten, making it nearly impossible for Susan to make her daughter follow the rules of the house. Susan, unfortunately, wore the title of *enforcer.*

"Sure, I would. Why do you think I wouldn't? Susan, are you working Saturday?" Bob asked, wrinkling his brow at the thought.

Susan tried to think fast and come up with a plausible excuse. "No, I'd planned to clean out some closets and thought it would be hard to stop and start again."

"Why don't Mommy and I both take you to the party? How does that sound, sweet girl?" Bob hugged Julie tighter and kissed her on her forehead.

"Yay, I'm going to Richie's party! I'm going to Richie's party!" she sang, bouncing around the room. She bounced a couple of extra times in front of Susan and gave her mother what Susan had come to recognize as the "hairy eyeball." Susan's chest dropped in defeat. *What am I going to do with these two?* Bob had taken on the role of not only father but grandfather. He was Daddy in every respect, except discipline, which made him the grandfatherly image who could see no wrong in his daughter's actions. He'd admitted he could not bear the thought of correcting his daughter, leaving the job of discipline to Susan. It was a formidable position at best, only to be undone every time Julie went over her head to Bob. Susan knew she'd been defeated again in her own home—those two against her one.

CHAPTER 55

Happy Birthday

"I'm happy; she's happy. What's the problem? She has her life, and I have mine," Rick said as he stood in the corner and discreetly argued with his mother over the noise of twenty excited five- and six-years-olds without making eye contact. He watched Susan and Bob Carson, while Donna flitted around the room, guiding the children in the direction of the games and activities.

"Have you ever told Donna about that girl?" Janet whispered. She continued to observe the children playing party games in the huge private party room, but her face held no joy or happiness. Her lips pursed between comments; her brow was deeply furrowed. Rick knew this was not the party his mother would have planned for her only grandson. It was noisy and what his mother considered cheap. She'd put on a happy face when Richie announced his party plans, but he saw her groan inwardly at having to show up at a pizza parlor. His mother had saved Richie's gifts for a private party at her home the following afternoon. She told him and Donna she'd bought a small birthday cake and would add six royal blue candles to the cake for Richie to blow out in the privacy of her own home.

The Creightons were driving to Cabot, and Janet made it clear her grandson would have a respectable party, without all this noise and brashness. She told Rick in private she would not have attended this party, but Richie made her promise she would, and she would keep her promise to her only grandchild.

"I never saw the need to tell Donna about Susan. I don't know why that would be important; it really doesn't matter at this point. We've never discussed our dating histories," Rick explained. "For some reason, Richie and Julie have become best friends at school. All Richie talks about is Julie. I didn't know she was Susan's daughter until recently. I remember seeing Susan and her husband at the kindergarten open house, but the children were separated from the parents, and I didn't see which child belonged to her when the event ended. Would I have chosen Susan's daughter as Richie's best friend? Probably not, but I won't discourage him from being her friend either."

"Why not? It would be easy to steer him in a different direction. Susan obviously knew where she was taking her daughter for a birthday party today. She shouldn't have come." Janet's eyes narrowed to slits.

"Mother, they're innocent children. What's the problem?" Rick could not understand why his mother was behaving this way, though he should've realized her feelings toward Susan would never change. Her disdain for Susan had not lessened in the years since he and Susan had dated. Many years had passed since the break-up letter, but it appeared his mother was still living in the past and couldn't move forward. He could see that Susan was happy with her husband and posed no threat to his and Donna's marriage. Why would his mother continue to hold a grudge? It made him wonder if she knew something he didn't.

"I just want the best for my grandson. My problem is that when the past comes back into our lives, it's not always good. We don't need someone ruining Richie's party." Janet tilted her head down slightly, shaking it from side to side, her eyes closed. She inhaled and let her breath out slowly.

"Well, I will not discourage my son from a kindergarten friendship. Besides, as soon as they're in different classes, they'll lose interest in each other."

Even as he tried to convince his mother, he was not convinced himself. He could see Richie and Julie laughing and talking as if they were alone. They were doing a fairly good job of ignoring all the other children at the party. His gut feeling was that they would be lifelong friends, regardless of any degree of parental interference. Rick didn't see any reason to discourage them; they were cute together, and they were both good kids. Friendships were important growing up, and if this was the worst thing that happened, they would be a lucky group of people.

PART FOUR

2006
The Truth about
Life and Death

CHAPTER 56

Firsts and Lasts

Susan found it hard to believe Richie and Julie would be graduating from high school in six short weeks. They'd both attended their last prom this past weekend. The weather held out, though thunderstorms had been in the forecast. It was April. The day was warm, so the girls didn't have to wear sweaters with their dresses. She'd taken tons of pictures. Julie, Richie, and their dates tired quickly of the fanfare, but they didn't complain. The four of them made the trek from house to house—they were all only children and seniors, and they understood how important it was for their parents.

They would soon be considered adults. It seemed like only yesterday Julie and Richie were going to each other's birthday parties, playing T-ball, and having playdates. Where had the time gone?

Weeks in advance, Susan and Bob planned dinner with their daughter the evening before graduation day. They made reservations at Evelyn's, well aware the restaurant would be packed with happy graduates and their families. Susan wanted it to be a special evening for her daughter.

Julie, Richie, and a group of their friends would be spending the week following graduation at the Carson's beach house. They would be eager to leave early in the morning after graduation for their first foray into adulthood—a week without parents. Susan prayed they would use good judgment. They were good kids, but a little freedom could lead to a lot of trouble in a hurry.

Susan and Bob invariably made a big deal out of special occasions because Julie was their only child. Every occasion was a first and a last. She would be attending UNC Chapel Hill in August, and they secretly hoped she would opt to stay at school on weekends with home football games to make the best of her time in college. Bob and Susan would miss their daughter but encouraged her to engage in all aspects of college life while she was there. "Study hard, but take time to have fun and be a typical college student." Susan recalled her days in college. She had so little social life and wanted her daughter's experience to be different. There was a time to study, and she would need to do that, but she also needed time to loosen up and make memories that would last a lifetime, discover new friendships, and participate in extracurricular activities just to have fun. Adult life would be here soon, and as Bob had told Julie, it was then she'd have to be a grown-up; no more acting like a child.

CHAPTER 57

Richie Pierce

Richie Pierce truly loved his mother, but didn't know what she expected from him. He'd done everything in his power to please her. From his first day of school, he'd made good grades, stayed out of trouble, played sports, and recently received his Eagle Scout award. What else did she want? She'd chosen every extracurricular activity for him. She wanted him to be a three-sport athlete, though he was only interested in baseball. She didn't understand but finally relented when she saw how good he was at baseball and how bad he was at football and basketball. He was sure she loved him and was proud of him, but enough was enough.

Her latest complaint was college. His mother was not happy with his choice of college or his major. She constantly needled him about changing his plans. She wanted him to go to Duke like his dad and be a law major. She couldn't understand why he wanted to major in business or go to Carolina. She'd brought up Julie Carson and hinted that he'd been coerced by Julie to go to UNC with her. He'd explained that his choices for college and his major were just that—his choices. His mother argued she would never see him if he went to Carolina, making accusations that he would stay on campus on weekends just to spend time with Julie and his friends, ignoring his family. He admitted to himself she was partially correct on that point. He needed to get away, and college was the perfect opportunity.

Control—his mother always wanted 100 percent control over him. In his opinion, times were changing. In private, his dad took his side over his mother's. His dad had supported Richie and his decision to attend Carolina, and he'd encouraged Richie to major in whatever subject he desired, not what everyone else thought he should pick—namely, law. Richie had no desire to attend law school and would not be a part of the law firm. He didn't want to argue with his mother, but his college major was his decision, not hers.

During their latest rift, he guessed he'd crossed the line when he reminded her she'd finished law school but never passed the bar. That brought on a whole new level of anger. His dad had told him last fall of his mother's inability to pass the bar, and he probably shouldn't have said anything, but he couldn't let it go. He had so little ammunition against her; it was more than he could resist.

This morning had been a battle of wills, the old argument rearing its ugly head again regarding his choice of college. He left as soon as he could, leaving half of his breakfast on the table, heading to school earlier than usual. He, Julie, and some close friends were going to make plans at lunch for their graduation beach trip. He was unsure how his mother would react to that news. Would she okay his idea or veto it with her brand of justice? He'd find out soon enough. The small group of friends were planning to stay at Julie's parents' beach house, so their trip was free except for food, gas, and entertainment. They'd have a great time; he was certain. Julie's parents had already given the teens permission to use their house, so very little planning would be necessary. The new graduates could chill for a week, celebrating their entrance into adulthood and independence. They'd have a blast riding the waves, sunbathing, eating out with no parents, and staying up all night if they wished.

Richie walked out the door with a slight smile and a suggestive whistle. It was a wet morning and still a little dark, but he felt a strong urge to get away. He didn't want anyone to get the wrong idea; he loved his mother, but right now, he didn't like her very much.

CHAPTER 58

A Day to Forget

Susan had worked the day shift since her first days at Cabot Memorial Hospital, seven to seven in the emergency department, and she liked it. She worked three days on, with three days off, giving her time to spend with her family and go to church when she had Sundays free. Bob was a good cook and picked up the slack on days when she worked late, so they didn't starve. She'd noticed Julie seemed to enjoy much of his cooking more than hers. He'd kept Julie in the kitchen with him for as long as Susan could remember, and some of his skills had rubbed off on her. Julie had learned early on how to peel potatoes, snap beans, fry fresh yellow squash, and make meatloaf with extra ketchup, a family favorite. They ate what one would consider simple meals at home, with a few forays into fine dining. Bob and Julie had always been close, and cooking was just one more activity they happily shared.

Susan recalled driving to work that Friday morning. It was raining heavily, with scattered thunderstorms left over from a passing cold front, the squall line stalled over the eastern third of North Carolina. She found it nearly impossible to see the road, especially since it was still dark outside. Daylight Saving Time was wonderful in the evenings, but mornings were dark and dreary when she drove to work for the seven-to-seven shift.

Some days were unforgettable, and this would be one of them— in a horrible way. It would change the world as everyone knew it. The ER received an urgent call from a paramedic with an ambulance inbound, carrying a male victim involved in an automobile accident on Deer Path Road. The road was aptly named due to year-round deer sightings, and occasional accidents resulted from the large population in the area. The victim was an eighteen-year-old male with multiple broken bones, probable internal injuries, and traumatic head injury. They were performing CPR; the patient's heartbeat had stopped twice, and they were attempting to get the patient's heart beating now. The paramedic's voice was grim, offering little hope without immediate intervention.

When the ambulance arrived, the patient was rushed into an examination room in cardiac arrest for the third time. CPR was continued with medications to try to start the heart beating again on its own. The situation went from bad to worse when Susan realized the young man was Richie Pierce, her daughter's best friend. The highway patrol officer didn't know for sure but speculated Richie had swerved and hydroplaned on the wet road. The car appeared to flip twice, hitting a tree on the driver's side. For reasons unknown, Richie had not been wearing a seat belt. The car was almost unrecognizable. The convertible top had torn off, leaving him vulnerable to the elements of the crash. Susan consulted with the other physician who'd stayed to assist after they'd gotten the call, and they both agreed there was nothing they could do at this point. Richie's heart would not beat on its own, and his head injury was of such severity there was no visible activity. Both lungs appeared to be damaged from multiple broken ribs, and it was suspected his heart was severely damaged as well. They determined the time of death for the death certificate. Susan left the examination room and walked into the office. She closed the door, sat down, and cried gut-wrenching sobs.

The highway patrol officer was able to contact Rick and Donna quickly from Richie's driver's license, and they ran into the hospital, hardly stopping to check in at the desk. They both screamed that their son was there, and they could not stop. Susan and Dr. Perry met them in the hallway. Susan could see they knew something was terribly wrong, but she didn't think they expected the news she would deliver to them.

"I'm very sorry, but Richie has passed."

Before Susan could go any further, Donna screamed and fell to her knees on the floor. She kept screaming, screaming at the top of her lungs. Blaming God, blaming Rick for buying Richie a car, blaming the weather; then turning to Susan and Dr. Perry, blaming them. She jumped to her feet, rushing at both of them, grabbing their scrubs with her fists. She didn't try to hit them, just grabbed their clothes and shook them, asking why.

Donna was taken to the hospital chaplain's office shortly after her outburst. She became a threat to the staff of the hospital and herself; she'd threatened to hurt herself and anyone who came near her. Before Rick could take her home, he and Susan talked.

"I am so sorry, Rick. We did everything we could. The severity of his injuries was beyond help. His heart stopped twice with the paramedics, and we did everything we could to start it when they brought him in." Susan explained the technicalities with all the courage she could gather without breaking down herself.

How was she going to break the news to her daughter? How was she going to explain she'd let her daughter's best friend die, even though fate was responsible? Susan and Dr. Perry had done everything in their power to no avail.

"I'm sure you and the hospital staff did everything you could. I just don't know what to do next." Rick hesitated, looking around the room; then he looked back at Susan and Dr. Perry, adding, "Can I see him?"

"Rick, I really don't know if you want to do that just yet. Um, he doesn't look good right now." Susan made an effort to explain that his son's physical condition was dire. There were multiple injuries, broken bones protruding from his body, and blood. His son's blood. But he was persistent, so she okayed his viewing. She was somewhat relieved to see that the attending nurses had cleaned Richie's body to some degree, which was of some comfort. Susan had seen things at their worst.

CHAPTER 59

Unanswered Questions

Six weeks before graduation—a time that should have been full of hope for an exciting future, college, and adult life with family and friends. Now it was marred. Richie's family and friends were left in a state of confusion, unable to fathom how or why this tragedy had taken place. The sensation of loss and grief was overwhelming. Susan's daughter was distraught to the point of locking herself in her bedroom and crying for hours.

Why, more often than not, was an unanswerable question; there was no explanation. Susan could not tell Julie why. No one could. It was a trick question. No answer. No solution.

The evening before the funeral brought the task of dressing and preparing Julie for the visitation at the funeral home. The Carsons wanted to pay their respects to Richie's family but knew it would be difficult. They'd sent a wreath to the funeral home with white chrysanthemums, greenery, and Carolina Blue bows and ribbons inscribed with *UNC* and *Tar Heels*. Richie and Julie were both going to Carolina in the fall and were both Carolina fans. Susan speculated his friendship with Julie had veered him toward the pale blue of Carolina and away from the darker shade of Duke blue.

As the receiving line inched toward the family, they saw the Carolina blue ribbons of the wreath, and Julie suddenly halted in her tracks, staring at the floral arrangement. Susan and Bob didn't know if Julie would be able to view the casket containing her best friend's body. She and Bob stood on each side of Julie and held her tightly, supporting their daughter both physically and emotionally. As they reached the casket, Susan's emotions threatened to overtake her as she viewed Richie's body. He appeared as if ready for church or a formal event, dressed in his black suit, starched white button-down–collar shirt, and light-blue striped tie. His acceptance letter from Carolina was strategically placed in his right hand, displaying the university's bold letterhead. He was such a handsome young man, and it was nearly impossible to stand there and believe he wouldn't open his eyes and smile.

Susan spied Rick, and her heart sank. She realized in that instant that he was a childless parent. She'd not thought of the baby she'd put up for adoption in some time, so when the memory came flooding back, she felt as though she'd been hit with the shocking sensation of a good dousing of frigid water. Susan drew in her breath. She mentally willed herself to relax and keep her composure; her daughter needed her. But thinking these thoughts was easier than acting on them. Her heart wept for Rick, knowing this had been his only chance to be a parent, and it was gone in the blink of an eye. Time would not be a forgiving factor. Time would be a constant reminder of what had been lost, whether Rick realized it or not. He would never know he'd lost two children.

"I am so sorry"—the watch words spoken as the mourners inched their way through the line. Rick and Donna clung to Julie for a long sixty seconds before releasing her. They asked if she would sit with the family at the funeral the following day. She numbly nodded her head, and the Carson family moved on to Donna's parents. Devastation was evident on each family member's face. Next in the receiving line were Rick's parents. Richard Pierce thanked them for coming and hugged Julie tightly and told her not to be a stranger. She would always be welcome in their home. Janet Pierce hugged Julie, kissed her cheek, and thanked her for being Richie's best friend. She shook Bob's hand and thanked him for coming. Susan was nervous about seeing Janet, and her fears were well founded. Janet hugged her, which Susan found interesting. Susan knew Janet had never cared for her, let alone touched her in any way beyond a handshake.

And then Janet whispered in Susan's ear. "I know you are the doctor who worked on Richie. Why did you let him die?"

Susan stepped away, taken aback by Janet's statement. Susan pulled herself together and leaned over and whispered in Janet's ear. "Mrs. Pierce, I don't think this is the time or the place to discuss this, but I will say his injuries were severe, life-threatening, and Dr. Perry and I did everything we could. I am sorry for your loss. It is a great loss not only to your family, but to his friends and the community as well."

Susan pulled back and walked away, not daring to glance back. She wasn't sure what she would see, but knew it would not be a look of compassion or caring.

The next day was Sunday. Susan was on a three-day break so she, Bob, and Julie went to church together but left early. They intentionally sat on the back pew in case they needed to leave early and were thankful they'd made that decision. Julie broke down, softly crying as the second hymn began playing, so they quietly slipped out of the sanctuary and drove home in silence, except for Julie's soft weeping. Susan knew her daughter was crying without looking at her. She understood Julie was doing the best she could under the circumstances.

The funeral was scheduled for two o'clock in the afternoon, so she and Bob decided to go through the drive-through lane of the nearest fast-food restaurant for lunch. This was not the time for sitting in a restaurant. Julie chose her meal, and they ordered, paid, and drove home. They each picked at their food, throwing most of it away. They each sat listening to the clock tick away the seconds, slowly and precisely.

The afternoon was beautiful, the sky a clear blue with no cloud to mar its perfection. The wicked weather front, a major contributor to the accident, was churning far off the coast of North Carolina, leaving a picture-perfect day. An ugly, tragic, picture-perfect day.

The church was filled to the brim, standing room only in the back, with chairs brought in from the fellowship hall and placed in any space that could accommodate a person. As Susan peered into the sanctuary, she couldn't help but notice the open coffin with Richie's body. She sidestepped to stand against the wall with her husband and daughter. They waited in the entryway for the family, with blank, lost looks on their faces, conveying the staggering grief weighing on their hearts. Richie's family arrived at the last minute and were escorted down the carpeted aisle—the aisle where Richie should have marched, honored as one of the church's high school graduates in just a few Sundays; the aisle where he should have walked someday, clinging to his bride with love and devotion in their eyes. None of this would happen. This was it. This was all there would ever be. The end.

As the Carsons trailed Richie's family into the sanctuary, Bob and Susan took opposite sides of Julie, leading her down the aisle, not sure if she would be able to support her own weight. As they walked, Susan noted the lid of the casket had been closed, with the spray of white roses, the color of innocence, centered meticulously on the polished bronze lid. She lowered her head, allowing warm, salty tears to slide down her cheeks. This beautiful child was gone. Everyone loved him so. What would they do without him?

The service was filled with only the good that could be gleaned from such a tragic loss. The good of a child, the good of his life, the good of his love of family and friends, the good of his baptism, the good of his eternal life in Christ. It was impossible for any of those sitting in the congregation to see any semblance of good in any of this. A life wasted, a future wasted, grieving childless parents, grieving grandparents and friends, an empty space in a world searching for hope and kindness. It was a loss, plain and simple.

Susan and Bob did not allow Julie to go to the cemetery for the graveside service. She did not protest. Seeing her friend lowered into the ground would be far more than she could endure emotionally, and Susan didn't know if she or Bob could witness it either. It was akin to their own child being lowered into the depths of death—too heartbreaking to consider, much less witness. They slowly walked toward the car and promised their daughter they would come back later to visit Richie's grave. She nodded numbly in agreement.

They drove home, changed their clothes, and lay down, hoping for sleep, desperately in need of an escape from the grief that lay heavily on their family and community. This was a day they would long to forget but a day that would be played out again and again in a world of imperfection.

CHAPTER 60

Class of 2006

In the weeks leading up to graduation, Julie's personality shifted from bubbly life-of-the-party to a more reserved, quiet wallflower. She returned to school on Monday following the funeral, saying she needed to be with her friends. Susan gave her a hug and an encouraging smile, agreeing this would be for the best. Julie assured her parents that if she became upset at school, she would go to the guidance counselor's office and take a few minutes to compose herself.

When she arrived home from school that afternoon, she said she'd made it. She'd received lots of hugs and condolences from friends and staff members. She thought she would make it okay the next day.

Graduation day arrived with much fanfare. Bob and Susan were filled with parental pride, watching Julie walk down the aisle closest to their seats. They were her only family. She'd given her extra tickets to a friend who had more family members than was allowed. Susan noticed Rick and Donna Pierce sitting a few rows below them, about thirty feet to their right. She'd suspected a diploma would be presented to Richie's family. There would not be a dry eye in the gym, and she dreaded the moments to come. Julie had just begun to return to her old self, and Susan was afraid this would be the setback she did not need. A summer of grieving would be more than any of them could take. It was obvious that Rick and Donna were sitting apart, not touching or talking with one another. He appeared to be looking over the audience as Donna looked down at her hands, occasionally wiping her eyes with a tissue. As the graduates were called to the stage, each one happily walked across—one with crutches from a failed slide into home plate during the final baseball game; girls in high heels, each step made precisely, trying their best not to trip and leave their last memory a comical, embarrassing fall in front of their classmates. It was a joyous occasion, until the name Richard van Allen Pierce III was called. A hush fell over the audience and graduates. One could see the clenched jaws of the boys and the simultaneous rise of white tissues by the girls, dabbing stray tears. A chair had been left empty in the alphabetical lineup, with Richie's baseball jersey draped over the backrest and his baseball cap on the seat, the illusion hinting he would walk out and place the cap on his head, with the voice of the announcer in the background bellowing, "Play ball!"

Rick stepped down from the bleachers and walked to the podium, head held level. He climbed the metallic steps and walked across the temporary stage. He shook the principal's hand and took Richie's diploma. A red rose was handed to Donna, which she accepted graciously. All it took was the clap of one set of hands to set off a round of thunderous applause, with a standing ovation for their fallen classmate. The class of 2006 would remember this moment. The loss of the first classmate was always the most difficult, and for this to have occurred just weeks prior to graduation made it all the more heart-rending. Richie was the senior class president and undeniably the most popular student at Cabot High School, making his death all the more tragic. He was loved and respected by classmates and teachers alike. As Rick returned to his seat, parents and guests shook his hand along the way, sharing their condolences. This would be the last time Rick and Donna Pierce would be recognized as parents.

CHAPTER 61

From Bad to Worse

Rick and Donna's marriage had been precarious in the months and years prior to Richie's death and deteriorated at an accelerated rate in the weeks that followed. The initial shock and long-lasting repercussions of that horrific event was more than either of them could have imagined.

For the first few weeks, Rick opened his eyes each morning, and his heart immediately plunged into the pit of his stomach. He dropped his head into his hands in disbelief, reliving the fateful morning again and again, praying for a different outcome. The sensation of grief was overwhelming to the point of his questioning life itself. *They say karma is a bitch*, he thought. *Well, fate is a bitch too.* She'd robbed him of the will to exist. His mornings began silently; the melody of the usual family chatter had died with his son. Each morning dawned with unbelievable grief, the finality of death having no equal. His days ranged from partial sanity to pure, unadulterated insanity. Every breath was a chore; every step a nightmare. The whole debacle was made worse by the absence of closure—there'd been no goodbyes, no chance to say I love you,

I'm sorry if I ever disappointed you, please don't leave me. He was convinced any one of his surviving family members would have gladly exchanged places with his son, giving their lives in his place. But that's not how the world worked.

The graduation ceremony put his and Donna's already rocky marriage over the edge in a terrible way. Donna had not spoken to him for three days. During the past few weeks, their dinners had been eaten in silence. She slept—or at least he thought she was asleep—in the mornings as he dressed for work. The last four evenings, he'd come home to an empty house. One place setting was neatly arranged on the breakfast bar with a plate of cold food sitting in the microwave. There was no sign of whether she had eaten, but he suspected she had not. He dumped the food down the garbage disposal, choosing to make a sandwich for himself. He couldn't be sure how long the food had been sitting in the microwave. The last thing he needed was to be sick from spoiled food.

Rick noticed his pants had loosened, and he knew he'd lost more than a few pounds in the weeks that followed his son's death. Food held very little interest. He didn't know how he would get past this. He thought each day would get easier, but he was wrong. Time was not the healing balm he'd expected. His grief clock was on hold, unable to get past the moment he'd run into the hospital with his worst fears realized, and it would not move, would not budge, no matter what he did or thought. He was firmly convinced he would never experience a shred of happiness again. Richie had been his happiness, the heart of his soul. Rick's willingness to live died that rainy April morning. His life would never be the same.

His friends were supportive and as helpful as one would expect, perfunctory smiles and gestures in place, but nothing would bring his son back from the dead. Grief had a way of bringing a couple together or being the knife that severed the precarious knot of marriage. Rick not only lost his son that day; he lost his marriage, or at least what was left of it. He was drawn into a swirl of grief that took him under and, just when he thought his life was over, offered him a shallow, gasping breath before plunging him into its icy depths again—a constant struggle. The problem was, he didn't know which direction he truly wanted to go, which direction would give him peace. He contemplated his own death more than once.

Rick heard the door open from the garage and knew Donna had returned. It was nine thirty at night. He had no idea where she'd been, and at this point, he didn't care.

Donna spoke first. "I need to talk to you."

He thought, *Okay, let's talk.* They hadn't spoken in three days. What he didn't expect was the direction the conversation would take.

"I want a divorce."

"You want a what?" The shocked response jumped from his lips.

"A divorce. Rick, I'm not happy; you're not happy. Richie's gone, and I think it's time we both stopped fooling ourselves. I've decided to move back to Raleigh with my parents. There are a few things I'll take with me, things that were mine before we were married … and other things. You can have the house; I don't want it. While Richie was here, it held wonderful memories, but there are no happy memories now. Right now, our feelings toward each other are indifferent, but I'm afraid we will come to hate each other, and this house will be an emotional prison for both of us. That's why I'm giving you an out. I would appreciate if you would sleep in one of the guest rooms until I move out. It won't take long. I promise."

Rick replied with a forced voice, "How long?"

Donna answered matter-of-factly. "A couple of weeks, just long enough to make moving arrangements. I promise I will leave you alone. I will not make this any more difficult than it already is for either of us. I don't want alimony, only the property I take with me and my car. I won't claim any of your inheritance from your parents as long as you do the same. When everything is settled, don't call me, ever. I've already talked to your mother. I've asked her not to be angry with you and to be understanding of my decision. And yes, she's upset; she cried and begged me not to leave. I told her it was better this way and to leave it alone."

Rick found it interesting that he was the last to know of his wife's decision—his mother, if not both of his parents, and Donna's parents undoubtedly knew of her decision. He realized, though, it was the best way out for both of them.

"Okay, I'll agree to it. Honestly, I'm sorry everything worked out this way. I don't think either one of us will ever be the same. I know I won't. I agree we have no future, and maybe this will give both of us a chance to find some sort of peace, somehow, someway." Rick watched as Donna walked away, climbed the stairs, and went into what would temporarily be her bedroom, shutting the door behind her.

Rick had known for some time things were not good. He'd suspected problems as soon as he and Donna returned from their honeymoon. He'd heard his friends talk about their marriages and how they'd found they loved their wives more as the years passed. This was how Rick pictured a successful marriage, based on love and companionship. He found that his and Donna's marriage evolved into financial power and the influence gained from the union of two upper-crust families.

He should have run from Donna after their initial meeting. He knew he'd required too much from someone who had no capacity to give, only take. His case of cold feet in the weeks prior to his and Donna's wedding had screamed at him to back out. He should have listened.

He had to admit Donna seemed to perk up when Richie was born, giving their marriage hope. Donna appeared to enjoy being a mother, although a full-time nanny was hired and spent far more time with Richie than Donna did. She loved bragging about him and showing him off to her friends and both sets of grandparents.

Janet Pierce adored her grandson, doting on him at every opportunity. She offered to babysit him anytime, except for her bridge or golf days. Nothing interrupted her bridge or golf days. Rick recalled that many years ago, his grandmother's funeral had to be postponed for a day because of his mother's weekly bridge game. His mother garnered all of her lady friends' sympathy, and, as his mother put it, she'd suffered through it. She didn't want to ruin the day for her friends. They needed her, and she needed them.

After Richie's death, Rick knew he and Donna were finished. It was just a matter of time and patience. Would they pretend to be happy on the exterior while living in misery for the remainder of their lives? That seemed like a waste. The hole left in their marriage was far too deep to be filled by anything he could imagine. No words or actions could ever take the place of their child.

Donna never mentioned a serious relationship with anyone in her past. No mention of old dates or boyfriends. Rick had seen a few prom pictures, but she acted as if they were nothing. He'd surmised from conversations with Donna's parents they were somewhat worried with her choices of dates until he came along. Rick never brought up the topic of Susan Anderson with Donna; never saw the need. If she knew about Susan, she never let on. He doubted his mother ever mentioned Susan to Donna; he was convinced she was happy to be rid of the past.

His only conclusion was that Donna appeared to be in love with herself, what he came to term a narcissistic love affair. She was unaware that a whole world existed outside of her wants and needs. She had no comprehension of a world of give and take. The quintessential saying that it was better to give than receive never entered her mind. He would have seen it, had their courtship followed a longer path. Rick guessed he should take the responsibility for that mistake. All the signs were there, but he was blinded by the loss of Susan, and Donna filled that temporary void—it should have and probably would have been temporary.

A true loving relationship between two people was dependent on mutual love, companionship, sacrifice, and trust. He and Donna had none of these. He'd heard it said that in a successful marriage, ego is left at the door when a couple returns from their honeymoon. In his and Donna's house, ego sat at the head of the dining room table, smiling a devilish grin.

Everything had been about Donna and then Richie. Rick was always the odd man out. He and Donna loved Richie much more than they ever loved each other, yet their love for him was very different. Donna saw Richie has an extension of herself, a possession to be shown to the world. She wanted full control of his life, and Rick knew Richie eventually would rebel against her. Their arguments were spurred by their differences in opinion, which grew more frequent as Richie grew older, the intensity measured by increasing decibel levels.

As long as Donna was in control of her environment, she was happy. When she lost control, life was miserable for everyone. In hindsight, Rick realized his mother shared that same narcissistic, controlling mentality. Her control issues with him were a problem from day one. He guessed that his father realized he was playing a losing game long ago and had given up on his mother. He'd given up on his own marriage as well.

Rick made a concerted effort to give Richie some freedom when the two spent time together as father and son. Rick taught him how to drive on a family friend's farm. Donna would have disapproved, had she known; she'd have said they were breaking the law. Rick talked to Richie about sex and using condoms—that would have resulted in another tantrum, had she known. He and Richie kept their father/son conversations in the strictest confidence. Richie knew he could trust his dad, and Rick knew he could trust his son. He was a great kid, the best son anyone could ask for. He was never in any sort of trouble, spent his life with a smile on his face, and was genuinely loved by everyone. He was smart but also possessed common sense and a great sense of humor and wit beyond his years. He exuded kindness and generosity. He would have gone far in life, but Rick didn't think Richie's adult life would have been happy with Donna in control. She would have hung on as long as there was a thread to grasp. Her guilt trips would've made his life miserable. The only way Rick could see his son becoming the person he was meant to be would be moving away from Cabot. All hell would break loose, and he was sure part, if not all of the blame, would be placed on him. It would have been the only option for his son's hope for independence. Rick would have wished him well.

But today was today. Donna was moving out. The moving truck had arrived to take all of her belongings—the antique mahogany dining table with matching chairs, buffet, and china cabinet; wedding gifts from her parents; the china, silver, and crystal; all of the artwork and paintings; and—oddly enough—all of Richie's furniture and belongings. Rick had gotten wind that Donna planned to take Richie's belongings when he overheard her making arrangements with the moving company. Rick had taken a look around Richie's room while she was out and chose a few items he hoped she wouldn't miss—Richie's senior baseball jersey and cap, which had been draped over his chair at graduation; a picture of him and Julie; and the Little League baseball he'd hit for a grand-slam home run in the third grade, signed by his coach and dated, commemorating the game. There were many choices among his son's belongings, but these seemed to speak to him as a parting message from his son.

Donna would not allow anyone to enter Richie's room after his death, and it looked just as it did when he left for school that fateful morning. His T-shirt and pajama pants were across the chair next to the window, and his bed remained unmade. He'd dropped a small bit of toothpaste on the bathroom cabinet that had transformed into a tiny globule of green-and-white sparkled glue. Donna had gone so far as to lock the room and hide the key. Little did she know, Rick had a key that fit all the interior locks in the house. With his treasures safely tucked away in his study desk drawer, he didn't care what she took. *Take it all; there's nothing left for me here anyway.*

Rick was surprised she didn't want the house. She said she wanted no part of it, said the only happiness she had here was their son. By her actions, he would agree with that statement. She'd wanted this house and would not settle for any other. She'd cried, begged, pouted, and went so far as seduction to get him to buy it, so her response to the lack of happiness seemed self-imposed. This was the prison in which she'd placed herself, always wanting more, never realizing material possessions were not the keys to true happiness. In his experience, letting go of the trappings of society seemed to bring the most happiness. A simple life with the right person was the key to true love and lifelong satisfaction.

Rick heard the moving truck backing up to the front door, the incessant beeping making a poor attempt to synchronize with the ticking of the hall clock. A separate van with half a dozen men unloaded stacks of boxes, tape, and other supplies. It seemed only a few minutes had passed before all of the china, crystal, and silver was packed. Richie's belongings were stuffed into boxes, and Donna's dresser and closets were emptied and packed into boxes ready to be strategically placed into the moving truck. Furniture was disassembled and carried to the truck, resembling pieces of jigsaw puzzles. In all, three hours passed in the blink of an eye, and it was gone. The moving truck and van exited the drive in a cloud of diesel exhaust and disappeared toward the main road. Donna walked down the stairs carrying a matching suitcase and toiletry bag. She set them down by the door and walked toward Rick. She took her house keys off her key ring and handed them to him, along with her security system key fob.

"I won't be back. Here are the keys to the house. You can change the security code if you so desire. There is nothing else I want. If you need to speak with me, call my cell phone or my parents' phone. I'll be staying with them indefinitely. If you have any other questions, call my attorney; here is his card." She handed the card to Rick without touching his hand. She paused a few seconds, tears welling in her eyes. "You may not think so, but I am sorry. I think we both made a mistake getting married. We tried to right that mistake with Richie, and it worked for a while. He was the glue that held this family together. But now that he's gone …" She paused, composing herself. "There …" Donna sighed. "There's nothing left. Rather than our pretending to be happy in a loveless marriage, I want to make this as easy as possible for both of us. Like I said, I'm sorry."

Donna didn't make eye contact with him. She reached up, kissed his cheek, and walked out the door. She loaded her few belongings in the back seat of her car and drove the length of the driveway before turning toward the same direction as the moving van. As far as Rick could see, she never looked back.

He stood at the door for a few moments and then stepped back, thinking, *Even a bad loss is a loss*. He'd give in to the pain of losing his family, grieve as long as he needed, pick himself up eventually, and hopefully move on, finding some degree of peace in the process. He had a choice—he could lie down and give up or head in the direction of the future, whatever that might be. He was in no hurry, and the future was nowhere in sight, a darkness that held no hope or light. He had more grieving ahead of him.

Rick had experienced loss before; he'd lost Susan years ago. He was glad Susan found love. He'd seen her with her family frequently during the last thirteen years. He'd survived without Susan; he'd thrived without her, or at least he'd thought so. He wasn't sure of anything now. He knew he could not endure this sort of experience again and maintain any degree of sanity.

He wandered through the house, no longer referring to it as *home*. A home was a family, ties that bound one to life within the walls. All ties he'd possessed were now severed, splintered for eternity. He would sell—yes, he would sell this house. He could no longer add any happy memories to the soul of this monstrosity. The life that bound this house together was gone. The family that made this house a home had disappeared in the guise of death and abandonment. He gazed through the rooms at the emptiness. Empty walls, empty rooms, without soul, sterile, no life. Every nail embedded in the empty walls appeared as a painful, stabbing hole left in his home and in his heart. The indentions in the carpet of

Richie's room reminded him of scars. No matter how many times they were vacuumed, they would never fully disappear. *That's how scars work*, he told himself. *You never forget the pain, and though you heal, there is always a mark left in that very spot, reminding you of your suffering.*

Later that evening, Rick made a sandwich from week-old bread and smoked ham he found in the refrigerator. It tasted good, maybe because the meal was consumed in peace, a peace he hadn't experience until now. Peace was an interesting commodity. It was something most people in his family needed right now. There was no rhyme or reason to its discovery; he wasn't sure if he could hang on to it, or if it would become illusive again, hiding behind a tenebrous cloud shrouded by the night sky. He guessed time would tell. He finished the sandwich, put his plate in the dishwasher, and walked to the bar. He chose scotch, a numbing escape. He poured the amber liquid into a glass—heavy on the scotch, light on the ice—and sat down. He took the first sip, frowned, took another sip, frowned again. In that moment it dawned on him—he really didn't care for scotch. He'd never truly liked it, only tolerated it for the sake of his wife's happiness. He'd used it as an alcoholic escape from the problems he faced at home. The mind-numbing effect on his empty stomach helped ease the tensions he faced daily between him and his wife.

Donna wouldn't allow him to drink beer in the house. She was okay with beer outside by the pool or grill, but she said drinking beer inside the house was what rednecks did, and she would not be married to a redneck. He thought a few minutes and realized he'd never seen his father drink beer in the house either. His father's inside drink of choice was bourbon and lots of it. He'd observed his dad enjoying more than one beer outside, grilling or eating on the patio. So it appeared the two Mrs. Pierces had joined forces, conspiring against him and his father without their knowledge.

Rick promptly walked to the small sink located at the end of the bar, dumped the glass of scotch, and then proceeded to dump the rest of the bottle down the drain, watching it swirl in a clockwise direction. It felt good. Control—maybe he was regaining some semblance of control over his life. He walked outside to the patio kitchen that Donna had insisted they build, though she'd failed to use it once, and took a beer out of the refrigerator. He popped the top, took a long swallow, and toasted every man who'd suffered life under the rule of a wife who was impossible to please. He walked into the den, sat down in his leather recliner, turned on a baseball game, and proceeded to sit back and enjoy his first taste of freedom.

Morning dawned with sunny blue skies, illuminating wispy clouds resembling angel wings. Rick awoke at 6:56. His alarm clock was set for seven, so he lay in bed for the next four minutes. Silence. Pure silence. He had a light day at the law office—actually, he'd had an abundance of light days recently. His dad and the other partners had taken on the more in-depth cases, leaving him with a few real estate closings and other relatively easy cases. Now that Donna had moved out, he hoped life would settle down, and he could get back in the law office and bury himself in work. He had nothing else in his life.

His alarm went off, startling him with a classic rock song that was a little—well, a lot too loud. He stood, stretched, and walked downstairs to the kitchen. He turned on the mini-television—same news, different locations—and made a pot of coffee, all twelve cups. The grinder whirred, and the rich brown liquid softly dripped, the elixir that made most adult mornings bearable, allowing him to face the day. The newspaper was on the front step. Rick brought it in with every intention of reading it, but it lay forgotten on the breakfast bar beside the gray linen placemat.

Later that morning, he took a break and phoned his friend, James Baker of Baker and Associates Realty. He and James had been friends in high school. James had been a groomsman in his and Donna's wedding, and the two had remained good friends throughout the years. James had gone to Carolina, and they enjoyed joking about the other's alma mater. They made silly bets, usually involving lunch or a drink paid for by the alumnus of the winning team. They'd decided, years ago, the loser of the bet would be the actual game winner. James's voice mail picked up, and Rick left his name and number with a brief message to give him a call at his earliest convenience. It took ten minutes for James to return his call. Rick explained that he and Donna had separated and planned to divorce, and he was looking to sell the house. He thought he might look for an apartment or a condo, something small, with no outside responsibility, until he decided what he wanted to do. James agreed to drop by that evening and look over the house, take some pictures, and work on an appraisal. Rick was ready to end the call when James stopped him.

"Man, I'm really sorry about all of this. I appreciate the opportunity, but if I had my choice, there wouldn't be any reason to sell in the first place," James said with a tone of sadness.

"Thanks, James, I appreciate that. I'll see you at six o'clock." Rick hung up the phone.

James arrived promptly at six o'clock, examining the outside of the house first, making notes on his legal pad. The two of them went through the house, noting upgrades and items to point out when prospective buyers toured the house. When they finished, James spoke with sadness in his voice.

"Rick, I really cannot imagine what you're going through right now. You do not deserve any of this, but I guess it doesn't work that way, does it?"

"No, it doesn't, and I appreciate your saying that. You know, James, you're the first person to say it like that. Everyone else says they can just imagine what I'm going through. No, they can't. No one can imagine this kind of grief until they experience it personally. And I wouldn't wish it on my worst enemy," Rick said with conviction.

After James's visit, they agreed on a listing price, and Rick's house was officially on the market. It was amazing how quickly one's life could change. It'd been a short two months since Richie's death, and everything was different. If someone had told Rick his future a few months ago, he would have stared at them in shocked disbelief. There were still moments he found it difficult to believe the turn of events that began with Richie's death. What would his future hold now? He didn't know, but he was sure of one fact: if given the opportunity to see into the future, he would pass. The sadness would far outweigh any joy.

CHAPTER 62

An Equal and Opposite Reaction

Richard and Janet Pierce's reaction to the news of Rick and Donna's separation offered some unexpected results. His father, Richard, expressed his sincere condolences and hugged Rick. Rick gained a new respect for his father that day. He couldn't remember his father holding or hugging him as a child, and they seemed to only speak in passing. Their relationship always seemed more businesslike. His dad had spent most of his evenings in his den, working on legal cases or watching television. Weekends were spent on the golf course, weather permitting. He'd occasionally inquired about Rick's grades or participation in sports teams, but Rick never felt as though he cared; it was just his responsibility as a parent. The change in his father's behavior following Richie's death and today was comforting in a fatherly sort of way. Rick gained a new appreciation for his father and thought this might be a turning point, bringing the two of them closer. They'd worked together for years in the law office, yet they'd never had a typical father-son relationship. As his father released Rick from his embrace, they looked at each other, their eyes filled with tears. Rick felt he had an ally now, someone on his side for a change.

On the other hand, his mother reacted exactly as Rick thought she would. It was all about her. What would she do? What would people think? How could she show her face in public? Rick stared at the floor during her tirade. Never once did she look at him with concern, never once did she hug him, though he had the feeling she would have slapped him if given the opportunity. Never once did she look at him as her son. She expressed no love or concern for her only child. Rick didn't know whose face had a more stunned look, his or his father's. His mother ended her outburst by dropping to the sofa and wailing into her handkerchief.

Rick had taken all the abuse he could stomach and chose to quietly walk out the door. He got in his car and backed around the driveway. As he put his car in drive, he looked forward and saw his mother standing in front of the car, hands on hips, waiting for him to stop. She walked around to the driver's window and motioned for him to lower it. Her tirade would continue.

"What are you doing? No one walks out on me, especially my own son. I've done everything for you. I've made sure you were happy all these years, and look what you've done. This is the thanks I get. This is all your fault!"

Rick made an attempt to explain why things were as they were. "Donna and I haven't been happy for a long time. The only thing that held us together was Richie. Without him, there's no reason to go on acting. We're miserable together. We should have never gotten married."

After making that statement, Rick drove out the driveway. He could see his mother in the rearview mirror, screaming at him to come back. He felt sorry for his dad, who would feel the brunt of her tantrum.

CHAPTER 63

The Awakening

Tuesday morning dawned just like every morning. Susan had the seven a.m. to seven p.m. shift at the hospital, and her alarm clock went off right on schedule. The power had blinked off the previous night as a result of a severe thunderstorm, and she'd been sure to check her alarm; she didn't want to be late for work. The strikes seemed right on top of the house, with lightning and thunder occurring simultaneously. She reached over, hit the button, and stretched, a yawn escaping her relaxed body. The morning was quiet—a little too quiet. She felt a sense of peace that would be shattered by a loud gasp. Her hand recoiled when she touched her husband. She'd reached over to wake him, but found his skin cool to the touch. She grabbed his arm and shook him with no response. She jumped out of bed and ran to the light switch, flipping it on with a click so loud it should have awakened him. It didn't. She could tell by the light that he was pale. Susan knew he was dead.

She called 911, explaining that her husband was not breathing, and she assumed he was dead. There was no need for CPR. No amount of chest compressions would bring her husband back. He'd just had a stress test a week ago, and everything looked okay, but the doctor wanted him back in a month for another test. He'd been scheduled for a sleep apnea study next week. It was now apparent no tests would be needed. He was gone; he'd probably been dead for a few hours. He'd died in his sleep. She'd heard it said that everyone should be lucky enough to die in their sleep. It might be lucky for the person, but it was a nightmare for loved ones left wondering and regretting any last-minute actions or words said or unsaid. No chance to say goodbye.

Susan ran down the hall to her daughter's room. Julie slept with her door closed and often wore earplugs so it took a moment for her to realize her mother's panicked state. Susan woke her daughter and, not knowing any easier way to say it, told her something had happened to her dad, and he was dead.

"Oh my God, Daddy!"

She jumped out of her bed and ran past Susan down the hall to the master bedroom. She sat on the bed beside her father. She shook him repeatedly, calling, "Daddy, Daddy, wake up, please wake up." He didn't wake up. As she sat beside him, she appeared to progress through the stages of grief in a matter of minutes. Her anger kicked in. "You cannot leave me. I will not let you." She held him by the shoulders. Then she bargained. "Daddy, if you'll only just wake up, I'll never leave you. I promise."

She finally dropped her head in defeat, tears streaming down her face. She stood, asked when the ambulance would be there, and went to her room to get her slippers and robe. Susan watched as Julie returned with a handful of tissues, using them in rapid succession. They heard the siren of the ambulance approaching their driveway. Susan and Julie walked downstairs, forgetting to turn off the security system. As Susan opened the front door, the alarm sounded, a loud screeching sound emitting from the assortment of speakers strategically placed inside and outside the house.

"Well crap!" It was all she could say.

Susan ran to the kitchen, typed in the code, and returned to the front door. The EMT personnel came in and followed Julie upstairs. At the same time, the phone rang, and Susan remembered the security company would call to make sure everything was okay. She answered the phone, gave the thumbs up and code word, hung up quickly, and ran up the stairs. The paramedics were bending over Bob and checking for any signs of breathing or heartbeat, but none was detected. Susan told them what she'd found when she'd awakened and that she was an ER doctor. Susan explained she hadn't tried CPR because she saw no need. They loaded Bob's body on a gurney and carried him down the stairs and out the front door to place him in the waiting ambulance. Susan knew from experience the decision would be made at the hospital for the death certificate. She'd made that decision many times. She called the hospital, explained the situation, threw on some clothes, pulled her hair back into a ponytail, and grabbed her keys. Without realizing, Susan found Julie had performed the same ritual and was waiting by the door to the garage. Susan hugged her daughter quickly, and they both ran to the car, jumped in, and rode in silence to the hospital. By the time they arrived, the ambulance had unloaded, and Bob's body was placed in an examining room. The consensus between Susan and Dr. Johnston, the doctor she was supposed to replace this morning, was that Bob had suffered a heart attack.

Susan called Jones Funeral Service, and they picked up Bob's body within an hour. At that moment, she realized death had changed her life drastically again.

Susan and Julie rode home in silence. There was nothing they could say to each other to make their situation any better. No amount of conversation would bring Bob back. They walked through the kitchen and then upstairs to their respective bedrooms. Susan heard Julie's shower running, but the rushing water failed to drown out her sobs. Susan knew how her daughter felt; she'd lost her mother in 1969 and though the tears poured, no amount of grieving would bring loved ones back.

Susan began a search for the dreaded envelope she knew existed. Bob had informed her years ago that he had an envelope with a letter and instructions in case of his death. Susan knew it was in his dresser, but she didn't know which drawer. It didn't take long to find it. She located it in his sock drawer. She pulled it out from under a mound of work socks and turned it over in her hands. Tears ran down her cheeks, dripping onto the smooth, white business envelope, staining it with the brine. She sat on the bed and sobbed, dropping the unopened envelope on the cool sheet. She sat until she could work up enough courage to pick up the envelope again and slipped her finger under the sealed edge.

Susan pulled out a sheaf of papers, maybe half a dozen or so. The first three sheets were account numbers and insurance documents. Next to the last piece was a certificate with the grave site where he wished to be buried. The last sheet was a letter. It stated that, first of all, he was sorry. It would be obvious that he had died. He talked about his love for her and Julie and the home they'd made together. He asked to be buried in a mahogany casket to reflect his love of the outdoors and nature. He reiterated his desire to be buried in a single plot; he'd included the certificate from the cemetery that was paid in full, including all fees and his headstone. Even in death, Bob took care of everything—everything but her grief.

The next seventy-two hours were a blur, and Susan's days and nights flipped. During the day, she was bone tired, no energy. At night, she lay wide awake for hours. She didn't think she'd slept more than a couple of hours during the first two days. Staring at Bob's pillow was painful, she could see the indention where his head had lain that last night. It was a tragic reminder of what she'd lost, and she finally had to fluff the pillow—well, she beat it; she just couldn't take looking at it anymore.

Susan and Julie walked into the funeral home thirty minutes before the visitation. There were flowers placed around the room from friends, customers of Bob's company, and colleagues at the hospital. They were beautiful, but their scent was so overpowering; it was all Susan could do not to be sick. Julie appeared to be holding up much better than Susan. Their roles appeared to have reversed from the time of Richie Pierce's death. Now, Susan was distraught, and Julie was in control of her emotions. Susan was concerned that her daughter's reaction seemed too calm and businesslike. Was she numb? Was she in denial that anything had happened? Her behavior concerned Susan far more than the outpouring of grief she'd experienced in April. Would this leave a scar on her daughter emotionally that would take years to overcome, just like for her? Would Julie learn she couldn't numb her life away, refusing to feel? Susan didn't know how long this would last, but her greatest fear was that it would haunt Julie, bringing with it a lifetime of depression.

Standing beside her husband's casket was more than Susan could bear; she just couldn't do it. Susan was relieved when Julie asked if she could stand by her father. They'd viewed his body earlier in the day, and Susan had not handled it well. Just a few days ago, they'd talked of going to the beach house for a long weekend since her three days off landed on a Friday, Saturday, and Sunday. Yet here she and Julie stood, preparing to say goodbye to her emotional rock, her love, her best friend, her dearest husband. She was too young to be a widow; Julie was too young to be fatherless.

Susan and Bob accepted the probability that he would most likely die first since he was sixteen years her senior. Susan was not ready for that end to their marriage. Yet here it was, and she didn't know what she would do tomorrow.

Susan and Julie were Bob's only family members, which meant they stood alone in the receiving line. Bob had no siblings or cousins, and his parents were deceased. That left the mother and daughter to face the myriad visitors alone. It seemed the whole town of Cabot shuffled through the receiving line. Everyone had nothing but wonderful things to say about Bob, his family, and his work. Their condolences made Susan feel a little better, knowing how much respect Bob had in their small town. The one person she was unprepared for was Rick Pierce. Two months ago, he'd stood here in this same spot, mourning the loss of his son. Susan, Bob, and Julie had trod the mournful path, grieving the loss.

Rick's presence unnerved Susan, and she knew why. They shared a history, more of a history than he knew. Her life would have been much simpler, had their lives never intersected. He hugged Julie and told her all she had to do was ask, and he would do anything he could to help her. Then it was Susan's turn. She was emotionally prepared to take Rick's hand, shake it, and move on to the next person. When he reached over to hug Susan, her heart plummeted. A mix of grief and guilt from the last thirty years combined with the loss of her husband. It was too much. Susan found herself reaching for the chair behind her, and she sat, abruptly. Her legs would no longer support her physical weight, much less her emotional weight.

"If you need anything—and I mean anything—you call me," Rick said as he leaned over, taking Susan's hands in his, whispering in a most sincere manner. All she could do was nod. She dropped her head, tears falling.

At the end of the evening, the funeral home staff counted over two thousand signatures in the guest register. Susan and Julie were astounded that so many people thought of them in their time of grief. It was obvious Bob had touched many lives.

Before Susan left the funeral home, she walked to the casket holding her husband, her rock in this crazy world. Julie had said her goodbyes in private, and now, it was her turn. She slipped off her wedding ring and placed it on his little finger, next to his wedding ring.

"I want you to have this, sweetheart. You gave it to me, and I want you to have it, to keep it safe for me until we meet again. I know you'll be waiting for me. I love you," Susan whispered. She kissed the fingertips of her right hand and placed them on Bob's lips. She turned away but stopped and looked back one last time, her tears creating a foggy, distorted scene. She pulled a tissue from one of the scattered boxes, wiped her eyes, and walked away, knowing she would never see her husband again.

Julie was waiting for her in the funeral home lobby, and the two of them walked to the car. They spoke few words as they rode home. The night was warm and muggy with a dew point in the low seventies. The air conditioning felt cool and soothing. They were exhausted. They both slept soundly that night after the past two sleepless nights.

Susan awoke around eight the next morning, knowing she didn't need to hurry. Julie walked down the steps not long afterward, yawning. The funeral was set for three o'clock that afternoon. Their church would be bringing lunch at noon. They both sat with a cup of coffee and a cinnamon roll from the platter a neighbor had dropped off the day before. They didn't talk about Bob, death, or life, for that matter. Susan had turned on the television above the breakfast table, and they watched a sitcom rerun they'd seen a dozen times, both smiling at the punch lines. The one thing they didn't do was look at each other. That would have been disastrous. They were two entities who could only look outward at the world around them, not at their own. They were the only two left, and Susan couldn't bear seeing her sorrow mirrored in the eyes of her daughter.

"Mom, where is your wedding ring?" Julie asked, picking up Susan's left hand with a concerned look on her face.

Without making eye contact with her daughter, Susan answered, "I put it on your dad's finger last night. I think he should have it. He gave it to me twenty years ago, and I think it's fitting for him to have it now, to keep it safe for me."

"Okay," was all Julie said, taking a sip of her vanilla-cream and sugar-laced coffee. She stood without a word, lifted her cup in her slightly shaky hand, and walked up the stairs to her bedroom. Susan dropped her head and wept.

Bob Carson's funeral was solemn and respectful. The church was filled with many of the same faces who'd greeted Julie and Susan the night before. The mother and daughter held tightly to one another during the hour-long service. Susan remembered a time when she and her mother were the only members of their tiny family; then her mother died, leaving Susan alone. She vividly recalled sitting on the pew of the funeral home chapel at her mother's funeral, surrounded by her mother's friends but no family. When Julie left for college this August, she would be alone again. She already missed Bob. They would never enjoy growing old together, laughing together, loving each other. He would never be a grandfather or enjoy a day of retirement. Susan found that she felt as sorry for him as she did for herself and her daughter.

CHAPTER 64

For Sale

The weeks following Bob's death were filled with moments of sorrow and wading through legal issues. Bob's company would have to be sold. Susan had no idea how to run a concrete and landscaping business. Fortunately, a buyer came forward quickly; the company was appraised and sold with the agreement that the new owner would change the name. Both Susan and Julie agreed that the Carson name should not continue to be associated with the company. They would have no control over it, and it seemed more advantageous for the new owner to rename his company and make it his own. The day the new signage was installed, Susan and Julie drove by on their way to the grocery store. They drove home in tears.

Bob had recently talked of retiring in the next few years and had expressed interest in selling the company. He said when he retired, he wanted to be free of responsibility. He wanted to spend his free time with his wife and daughter. It would be some time before Susan retired since she was forty-nine, but they'd take time to travel during her vacations from the hospital. It didn't matter now. There would be no retirement or travel. Julie would be leaving for college in the fall and Susan would be alone. She felt her chest tighten at the thought of the solitary days ahead, and tears filled her eyes. Susan knew she could count on Bob to be her companion when Julie moved away, but that was now a moot point. What would she do? How would she handle living alone again, surrounded by so many memories of her family?

CHAPTER 65

A Future?

Just when Rick thought life was settling down after his son's death and the breakup of his marriage, the news of Susan's husband's death brought painful emotions back to the surface. He'd meant to shake Susan's hand at the funeral home, had every intention of quickly voicing his condolences and moving on, but things seldom went as planned. As his eyes met hers, feelings he'd pushed to his subconscious came flooding back. He needed to touch her. She'd been there with her husband and daughter in his time of need, and he would be there for her as well. The more he thought about her, the more he knew his life would have been very different, had he married her instead of Donna. To hell with his mother; he should have stood up for himself years ago and spent his life with the one woman whose memory he'd never been able to fully escape. He would spend much of the near future grieving his son and the failure of his marriage. Susan would need time to grieve the loss of her husband. He was in no hurry and had plenty of time, but he would eventually approach her in a friendly and comforting way, letting her know he wanted the best for her future, whether it included him or not. He loved her, plain and simple. He would love her until the day he died.

CHAPTER 66

Grief is Fickle

Two months had passed since the sudden death of Susan's husband. She couldn't help but ask why? She was content, happily living each day with her husband, daughter, and a fulfilling career. Her world had finally righted itself after a tumultuous adolescence and early adulthood. Now everything had fallen apart again. Though she worried about herself, the person that concerned her most was Julie. Julie had lost her best friend in April and her dad in June. Julie was putting on a brave face, but it was an act, and Susan knew it. Julie's facade was covering up a sad, depressed teenager.

Julie was not a slob, but she wasn't the neatest person either. Susan went in to straighten her daughter's room a few days earlier and had found a sizable amount of wadded tissues in the bottom of her trash can. Behind the scenes, Julie was letting her emotions escape.

Grief is a fickle thing, Susan thought. Everyone's experience with grief was different, each person reacting uniquely to the same set of circumstances. To all outward appearances, Julie was hiding it well. But grief was like a soda can—once shaken, it will explode; it just depends on who or what pops the top. Julie's emotional can was punched with a tiny hole with a tiny plug, only to be released when she allowed it. It was almost a relief to find the soggy, damp tissues. Julie was grieving in the privacy of her own room, her home territory. She didn't talk about her dad or Richie and quickly changed the subject when someone did. Susan didn't know if that was good or bad.

Julie would be leaving for Carolina in two weeks. Susan noticed her daughter stayed busy, shopping for all the supplies she thought she'd need and seemed generally excited. She'd picked out a new laptop, and Susan upgraded her daughter's cell phone to the latest model. Julie had been in touch with her roommate, Lindsay, who lived in Blowing Rock, North Carolina. They'd met in Greensboro, shopping for matching bedspreads, with each paying half for a dorm-sized refrigerator. They seemed to hit it off when they met with, a few smiles and laughter thrown in.

Susan talked privately with Lindsay's mother, just general conversation, but she felt the need to tell her about their family and their recent losses. Lindsay's mother promised she would discuss the situation with Lindsay, and if the subject of Bob or Richie came up in conversation, Lindsay would be a kind and understanding listener. Susan felt some degree of relief after their meeting, knowing Julie had a friend and confidant who would support her if—more than likely *when*—she needed it.

CHAPTER 67

Julie Carson

Julie had known since she was a little girl she wanted to go to Carolina. A Tar Heel Blue girl she would always be, despite her father's best efforts to turn her into an NC State Wolfpack fan. She would have been excited if the tragic events of the last few months had not occurred. With the deaths of her best friend and dad, she wasn't so sure she should leave home. Maybe she should take a semester off, delay her entrance until the spring, take care of her mom, decompress. It was obvious her mom needed her, and she needed her mom. Julie and her mother didn't talk specifically, but based on her mother's actions, Julie sensed her mother wanted her to go. Her mom said she'd been alone before and would be okay. Julie started to protest, but her mother seemed sure of herself. Julie knew time would help both of them. Their days would not be easy, but they would survive. She and her mother were made from strong stuff.

Julie didn't like to think about her losses, liked to talk about them much less, and a change of scenery would be good. She didn't want to hurt her mother's feelings, but she needed time away from home. The everyday routine of walking by her parents' bedroom reminded her way too much of her dad. Julie would never admit it to anyone, but she found herself driving by Richie's house frequently—too frequently. She wanted him to be there, needed him to be there. She was too young to be living in the past. She had a future and would drive herself crazy if she didn't get away and remove herself from this morbid existence. She couldn't begin to move on with constant reminders everywhere she looked, in her own home and the neighborhood where she'd grown up. Yes, a change of scenery would do her good.

Julie planned to stay in Chapel Hill when there were home football games and worried whether her mom would agree with her plans. She and Richie had planned to stay at school most weekends, but now he was gone. She approached her mother and explained her intention of staying in Chapel Hill most weekends. She was relieved when her mother wholeheartedly agreed and supported her decision, saying her dad would have wanted it that way.

Moving day came, and amid all the craziness, Julie and Susan set up her room with Lindsay and her parents. Julie could sense her mom didn't want to leave, but they both understood the time had come. The mother and daughter held on to each other for an extraordinarily long time, tears falling with no attempt to stop them. They couldn't care less who saw them; they'd been through immense emotional upheaval in the last few months, and they simply didn't care.

"You be careful, and call me anytime—I mean anytime, okay?" Susan whispered in her daughter's ear.

"I will. I love you, Mama," Julie choked out.

"I love you too, sweet pea. I'll love you forever."

And with that, her mother stepped back and turned to walk to what had been her dad's SUV. She drove away, waving to Julie as she disappeared down the street. Julie hadn't expected the day to be as mentally draining as it was turning out to be, so she decided, rather than make a spectacle of herself any further, she'd walk into the dorm, shut her door, and cry it out. And that she did.

Julie lay awake in her dorm bed later that night. The muted moonlight filtered through the window, claiming her attention. Lindsay had fallen asleep, and Julie could hear her softly snoring. Julie was exhausted, but sleep was illusive. She was worried and sad. She worried about her mom. She missed her dad. She missed Richie. Richie should have been here with her, maybe living in her dorm or one just a short walk away. They would have been inseparable, just like home. Their lives would have been filled with unimaginable adventures. Tears welled in her eyes, and she sighed, sadly contemplating her lone presence here and Richie, buried in the dirt of a church cemetery back home.

Julie eventually found that sweet spot, the moment between consciousness and slumber. It was then she saw him. Was it a dream, was it her imagination, or was it his spirit? She could not discern. Whatever it was, Julie recognized her best friend. He didn't smile, didn't speak. He looked older, wiser. He peered into the distance without making eye contact. He was at peace. He was filled with wisdom, a knowledge of the world and the universe. She, on the other hand, had the sensation of lacking the most basic knowledge. He knew everything, and she knew nothing. She felt insignificant, minuscule. She would contemplate the vision for a lifetime. She would never glimpse his visage again.

CHAPTER 68

Starting Over, Again

They say you can't go back in time, but Susan felt as though she'd achieved the feat. She seemed to be heading backward to a time when loneliness was her watchword. The first few days after Julie left for college, she was lost. She hadn't lived alone in twenty years. She shouldn't have been alone now. She and Bob should have been relaxing in the evenings or taking walks in their neighborhood. She should have been learning to cook for two, instead of one. It would take a while to go through all the food in the refrigerator by herself; most of it would probably be thrown out.

Susan buried herself in work but concentrated on sleeping in and relaxing on her days off. The job she dreaded most was disposing of Bob's clothing. She decided to keep a few pieces of her favorite outfits that he'd worn and donate the rest. He had some expensive pieces, and maybe there was someone less fortunate who would appreciate them. It took two trips to the drop-off site, driving his oversized SUV, loaded to the brim. Susan threw away his undergarments and socks, since they were not considered viable donations. Most of his shoes were in good condition and were donated. The emptiness in their walk-in closet was unnerving. The size of this house was unnerving. With her husband and daughter, it seemed just right; now it felt wrong—wrong for her, wrong for her life. The silence was deafening, and the house seemed to bear down on Susan, as if scowling at her. She'd lived here for close to twenty years, but right now, she felt like an outsider in her own home. She would have to consider what she wanted to do and consult Julie. She wouldn't make any decisions about selling their home without her daughter's consent.

A trip to the grocery store would do her good. Well, at least it gave her something to do. Susan didn't need much, just some salad ingredients, cereal, soy milk, and maybe a rotisserie chicken. The aroma of the fresh apples smelled appetizing, so she picked up a bagful to eat for dessert or as a snack. Her appetite had not fully returned, but she knew she needed to eat something, no matter how small. She walked around the corner to the refrigerated section to pick out a carton of soy milk and was met with a warm male voice.

"Hey, Susan."

She stood in silence as she recognized the voice from her past.

"I hope you're doing okay," Rick Pierce said.

"Yes, yes, I'm fine, sorry. I didn't see you at first. How are you?" Susan quickly recovered, not expecting to see anyone she knew, much less Rick Pierce.

"I'm okay. I guess you're out shopping for groceries like me."

"Yes, it's just me now that Julie has left for college. I must admit I really miss her." Susan thought for a moment, twisting the past-present-and-future ring Bob had given her on their tenth wedding anniversary. She wore it in place of her wedding band.

"Where's Donna? I hope she's okay. I haven't seen her in a while. With the children … um … well … you know." Susan looked down at the ring, nervously twisting it, afraid of the tears that threatened.

Rick replied with some hesitation. "Donna and I have separated. She moved out in June; moved back with her parents in Raleigh."

Then he added, "We'll be filing for divorce when our year of separation is over."

"Oh, I am so sorry. I didn't know. I'm really sorry to hear that."

"It's okay. Things were not good and hadn't been good for a long time. Richie's death was the last straw, you might say. I think we're both better off."

The conversation had led into deep waters.

"Um, do you cook?" Susan asked, trying to change the subject. The conversation had gotten way too personal, and she wasn't sure she could keep up a happy face with the direction they seemed to be heading.

"I eat out for lunch and usually eat a sandwich for dinner during the week. I cook a little on the weekends, mostly grilling. I have an outdoor kitchen, and I've put it to good use lately," Rick replied. "Do you cook much?"

"Some. With just me, I eat some salad and chicken." She dropped her gaze to the ingredients in her cart. "I seem to have lost my creativity in the kitchen since … you know what I mean." She shrugged her shoulders.

"Yes, I do," Rick said with a sad undertone.

"Well, I guess I need to finish and check out my groceries. It's really good to see you." Susan looked into Rick's eyes and smiled. She didn't smile much these days, but this one felt right.

"Maybe we'll run into each other again. Take care of yourself."

Susan reached over and hugged Rick. That felt right too. He hugged her back, said goodbye, and they went their separate ways to finish their shopping.

Susan glanced back at Rick and found him staring at her. She smiled and turned, nearly running her cart into a display of precariously stacked Styrofoam coolers. Rick Pierce had a way of unnerving her every time their paths crossed.

CHAPTER 69

A New Friend

Julie's first semester of college was going well. She had four A's and a B, which she was hoping to bring up to an A. She liked her classes, especially psychology. The professor was an effective communicator, his lectures interesting and thought-provoking. A doctoral student, David Ellison, was assisting in the class this semester. He was in charge of undergraduate sign-ups for graduate school students' projects. Psychology 101 students were required to volunteer for participation in three projects. Julie scanned the descriptions and signed up for three that looked interesting. One of them involved a small portion of Mr. Ellison's dissertation. After she'd participated in the group activity and the other participants had left the room, Mr. Ellison called her over.

"What did you think of that?" he asked in a businesslike manner.

"Well, do you want the truth?" She eyed him quizzically.

"Yes."

"I thought it was sort of weird. Who would do that in real life? I mean, not me."

He smiled, nodding his head. "That is the response I was looking for, just what you said. All the other participants said it was great and were interested in my findings. I know they were saying that to earn brownie points" He laughed and Julie laughed with him. "Thanks for being honest."

"Oh, you're welcome. My mom always tells me I'm way too honest, but I've found people would rather hear the truth. I'm not good at sugar-coating anything."

They both laughed again.

"I'll see you in class next week."

"Yes, you will." And Julie walked away with a grin.

Julie's first visit home from college was Labor Day weekend. Her mother was thrilled to see her and hit Julie with a barrage of questions about school before she hardly had time to put her bag in her room. How were things going with her roommate? How did she like dorm life? Was she studying enough? Julie was happy to report everything was going well, she'd made new friends, and was eating mostly healthy food. She and Lindsay had bonded quickly and shared one of their classes.

Julie was curious as to whether her mother was eating healthy as well, checking the fridge and pantry. It didn't take long for Julie to see her mother was not eating much.

"Mom, where is the food? There's not much in either the fridge or the pantry. What are you eating?"

Susan replied rather sheepishly, "I eat out some days. I buy a little at a time, and once I've eaten it, I buy more."

"Are you sure?" Julie eyed Susan as if their roles had switched, with Julie taking on the role of mother, and Susan, the troublesome teenaged daughter.

"I'm sure," her mother replied, not making eye contact.

Julie let it drop, but she would monitor her mother's food intake while she was home. If she wasn't happy, she would have a talk with her mother and mildly threaten to come home if she didn't eat.

During her Labor Day visit, Julie and her mom visited her father's grave. The new headstone had been erected and was inscribed with his name, dates of birth and death, and a simple cross surrounded by trees and flowers. Julie was puzzled when she spotted the single grave plot, not a double as she'd expected. She should have noticed when they had her father's graveside service, but she was far too upset to see the single plot with all the funeral home equipment laid out for the burial. She'd assumed her parents would be buried together. She questioned her mother about the single plot, and Susan explained that her father wanted to be buried by himself. He'd buried his first wife in a single plot, not wishing to see his own name for years, forced to contemplate his own death. He'd decided against a double burial plot with her mother's name on the opposing side. Her mother explained he didn't want her to have to look at her name for years, inscribed on a headstone in the cemetery. She'd agreed reluctantly with him. They'd discussed this some years ago, realizing her father would most likely die first. Her dad had bought a single grave plot for himself soon after his first wife died. It wasn't until after a fall in which he'd suffered a concussion and a broken arm on a landscaping job that he came clean about his intentions to be buried by himself. Since her parents had not discussed his wishes with Julie, the discovery of a single headstone had come as a surprise. His request to be buried there was reluctantly honored by her mother after his sudden death.

Julie placed a bundle of mixed summer flowers on the soft grass in front of her father's headstone. She kissed her fingertips, touched the warm granite, and silently mouthed *I love you, Daddy*. She wiped away fresh tears as she and her mother walked to the car.

Julie returned to Carolina after the long weekend and jumped back into the swing of college quickly. Her classes were going well, with her favorite being psychology. She would have to consider a psychology minor.

Julie found herself occasionally staying after class, talking with Dr. Lakeland and Mr. Ellison. Her interest sparked many questions, and they were willing to speak with her, eagerly answering her questions. Mr. Ellison inquired, more than once, if she would be interested in majoring in psychology, but she didn't think that was her future career. She planned a career in corporate accounting. Math and business were her strong suits. She'd been actively involved in her dad's company and loved the business and accounting end of his concrete business. Sadly, she had no trace of the green thumb her dad possessed. He'd attempted on multiple occasions to teach her about plants, flowers, and trees, each to no avail. He could take dirt, seeds, and small plants and perform horticultural miracles. Julie seemed to kill every plant he placed in her room in a matter of days. Too much water, not enough water—it didn't matter, they all perished under Julie's seemingly poisoned touch. He laughed and disposed of each pitiful plant, saying they'd try again another day. He was such a good sport.

The university had one dining hall that served healthy selections of salads, grilled meats, steamed or roasted vegetables, and fresh fruit. A number of faculty and staff members ate there, choosing the healthier alternatives. For most college students, this dining hall was not the most popular place to eat, since most college students ingested the most unhealthy food imaginable, surviving on greasy pizza and burgers. Julie hadn't seen research, but she was willing to bet college years were the most unhealthy four years, food wise, of a person's life. Most of the dining choices consisted of greasy burgers, breaded chicken sandwiches, pizza, and french fries. All of these choices tasted fabulous but wreaked havoc on one's circulatory and digestive systems. Julie chose to indulge sparingly and ordered a healthy salad with vegetables, sprouts, and grilled chicken. The house dressing was a mix of tangy and sweet, with a tiny crunch of poppy seeds. Most days this was the place to be, but for some reason, it was packed today with no empty table in sight. She peered around the large room and noticed Mr. Ellison sitting alone at a table with three empty chairs. She didn't see anyone else she recognized, so she thought she'd ask him if it was okay if she sat with him. He smiled, nodded, and motioned for her to sit down.

"Thanks for the seat, it's really crowded today." Julie said.

"Yes it is."

"I try to eat here most days, my mom doesn't like me eating junk food all the time."

"Well, she's right, you know?" Mr. Ellison replied and Julie nodded her head in agreement.

"So, how do you like Carolina? Did you go here for undergraduate?" Julie inquired.

"I like it here. I'm from Atlanta and I went to Florida State for my undergraduate and master's program, but wanted a change of scenery for my PhD. I hope to finish after three more semesters, depending on my dissertation. How do you like Carolina?"

"I love it, I've wanted to come here since I was a little girl. I wasn't sure I would be here this fall, I had to leave my mom home alone. My dad died in June and my best friend died last April, so things have been tough without them. I must admit I worry about my mom."

"I'm sure she misses you, but she wants you to be here in school."

"Yes, she does." Julie took a long breath and knew it was time to change the subject. "So what do you do for fun, where do you vacation? We have a beach house at Oak Island. I hope my mom and I can go there for a weekend this semester. I miss it during the school year."

"I've been busy since moving to Chapel Hill, not much time for fun with all of my graduate school responsibilities. I do enjoy traveling. I've vacationed at Tybee Island and Hilton Head. Most of my vacations growing up were in Europe, though, cities like Paris and London. My parents enjoyed traveling and usually took me on their trips abroad, even as a small child." Mr. Ellison replied.

"Wow, that sounds exciting!" Julie was impressed. "The most exotic place I've vacationed was a cruise my mom, dad, and I took two years ago. We went to Mexico, Grand Cayman Island, and Jamaica. I loved the blue water and the white-sand beaches."

"Those are beautiful places, nice and warm. Makes you want to go there when the weather here is cold and damp. Hey, why don't you call me David instead of Mr. Ellison? It sounds like you're talking to my father, and that would be difficult since my dad is deceased."

"Oh, I am so sorry," she said and added a little too quickly, "May I ask what happened, if it's not too personal?" And before he could answer, Julie caught herself and apologized. "I should not have asked you that. My parents have chastised me a hundred times for being way too blunt and asking far too many personal questions. I'm really sorry."

"Oh, it's all right. My father owned Ellison Broadcasting out of Atlanta. He and my mother were flying to a business meeting. The weather turned bad, fog set in at the airport, and the plane missed the runway. They were both hurt pretty bad. Dad passed after two days, and mom lived a week. Neither ever gained consciousness. That was my senior year in college. I had a bad few months. I had to get my head back straight, you know? I've been a workaholic ever since. I'm still involved with my dad's company and a full-time grad student. The CEO and other board officers are very trustworthy. I sit on the board, but I don't want to run the company like my father did. He was a great businessman. I am more of a behaviorist. I like studying human behavior."

Julie looked down at her plate and found it empty—she'd been so involved in her conversation with David she didn't recall eating most of her lunch. He was an interesting person, not in a romantic way, although he was quite handsome, but in an interesting-person way. She wasn't sure what that meant, but she guessed she'd figure it out.

"Well, Mr.—oops, David, I need to go to my next class, but I enjoyed our conversation. Thanks for the seat. I guess I'll see you in class tomorrow?"

"Yes, I'll be there, reminding students to sign up for projects. Some haven't signed up yet, and time will run out if they're not careful. College time passes very quickly."

"Yes, it does. I'll see you tomorrow." Julie walked away to return her tray, thinking, *David Ellison is one nice guy.*

The semester continued to fly. It seemed like only yesterday Julie had moved into her dorm, and now it was Halloween. She'd written more research papers in her short college stint than in all of high school. She was getting pretty good at it, she admitted. Her first paper had left a little to be desired, but she perfected her skills with practice. She was managing all A's in her classes. High school AP and honors classes had been excellent preparation for the intense college curriculum. Julie had taken a number of the advanced classes and qualified as a second-semester freshman. She was okay with one less semester of college. It wasn't that she didn't like school; she just didn't want to be there forever. She was not a professional student. She would need a master's degree, so graduation would be anticlimactic. She would make an effort to take as many graduate classes as she could as electives, making her graduate school experience shorter and, hopefully, less stressful.

Julie and David became Wednesday lunch companions. Julie's psychology class met on Tuesdays and Thursdays, so they met for question-and-answer sessions on Wednesdays in the healthy-food dining hall. They found that they shared many common interests, including sports, especially football and basketball. Julie's favorite pro football team was the Carolina Panthers, and his was the Falcons, having grown up in Atlanta. Though he'd graduated from Florida State, he admitted he was slowly converting to the Tar Heels.

"Carolina has grown on me since I came here. I may be a little more Tar Heel than Seminole in the end." They both laughed, knowing his fraternity brothers at Florida State would disown him if he admitted this to them.

David described a girl named Angela he'd dated back in Atlanta during the hiatus between his study at Florida State and his move to Chapel Hill. They'd gotten to be what he considered serious, but then he'd decided to go to Carolina, which was a long distance from Atlanta. She'd just started a new job and wouldn't consider moving with him. They mutually agreed to let the distance between them either push them apart or pull them together. Right now, it seemed to be pushing them apart.

Julie admitted she'd never had a serious boyfriend. She'd dated a couple of Richie's friends a few times, but they didn't amount to anything. She and Richie had so much fun hanging out as friends that she didn't miss being in a dating relationship. They practiced dancing together and could out-dance anyone in their senior class. Together, they'd attended cotillion classes from middle school through high school. She did find it interesting that she and Richie were never able to slow dance; it just didn't feel right, and they usually found other partners. Julie didn't know why, but there was a difference between the closeness of being friends and being romantic. Their feelings were not romantic. Though she and Richie dated a few other people, they always seemed to gravitate back toward each other. None of their romantic relationships survived past a few weeks. Would their friendship have evolved into a romantic one? Julie didn't have an answer to that question. She'd heard of friends of the opposite sex sort of waking up one day and seeing each other in a whole different light. It really didn't matter now anyway; he was gone.

Most days Julie held her emotions in check, but every so often, she found herself teary-eyed, reliving her losses and missing her mother. She discussed her feelings with David, finding that she could trust him to understand her mix of good and bad days. She explained how, out of the blue, emotions overtook her without warning or explanation.

"I don't know how to explain it. I'm walking around feeling fine, you know, pretty good, and then it hits. I feel sad, but I also feel guilty," she explained to David over lunch.

"You feel guilty? Why do you think you feel guilty?" he asked in his serious professor voice.

"I don't know. I feel guilty that I'm alive, and my friend and my dad are dead. Why are they gone, and I'm still here? I try to make sense of it all and then grief overtakes me. Does that sound crazy?"

"Well, in my experience, every person reacts differently to grief. Sometimes people get stuck in the stages. Some people charge through the stages; others crawl with no end in sight. Some get caught in a stage, experiencing it for weeks, months, or maybe years. It doesn't matter; everyone is different. It's okay to have these feelings. Though they may never go away completely, it will get better. You're not crazy; you're normal. Plus, you have a supportive mother and friends, like me. You can talk to me anytime. I've had my share of grief, losing both my parents, so I understand," David reassured Julie.

Julie reached over and hugged her friend. For a brief moment, she could feel Richie and her dad, rolled into one. She closed her eyes, allowing a tear to fall with the knowledge that she would be all right.

The holiday season was fast approaching, with Thanksgiving and Christmas, and Julie looked forward to spending time at home with her mother. She'd have classwork, but it didn't seem so bad with time thrown in for a little shopping the day after Thanksgiving. She and her mother made it a habit to begin their Christmas shopping on the craziest shopping day of the year. Her mom usually took a vacation day if she was scheduled to work, and off they'd go.

Julie looked at David over lunch the week before Thanksgiving and asked what he had planned.

"I guess stay here in my apartment and have a takeout pizza," he replied solemnly.

Before she could think it through or ask her mother, she blurted out, "Why don't you go home with me? My mom is going to make a huge turkey dinner, and I'm sure she wouldn't mind a guest. What do you say?"

"I don't want to be a bother. Your mother may not want to share you with another person," David replied hesitantly.

"Oh, she'd be cool with it. We have a big house, plenty of room."

"I tell you what: you ask your mother, and if she says yes, I'll go home with you—as friends, right?"

"Of course, friends!" Julie said excitedly, shaking her head in approval, her smile wide and bright.

CHAPTER 70

Man, Not Boy

Susan's first reaction to Julie's request was, "You what?"

"I have a friend at college. He's the assistant in my psychology class and is working on his PhD. He doesn't have anywhere to go for Thanksgiving, and I invited him to come home with me. Please, Mom, he's really nice, and I promise it is only friendship, nothing romantic. And besides, we've got plenty of room. He can stay in the guest room downstairs; it never gets used."

"I don't know, Julie. I'd planned for you and me to spend some time together, just the two of us. I don't know this boy—"

"Man, Mama, he's a man!" Julie shouted over her cell.

"Okay, *man*, but I don't know this man. Why are you so interested in him?"

"We're just friends, and I didn't want him to spend Thanksgiving alone. I sort of feel sorry for him. We have plenty of room, and we could use a male point of view at our dinner table, you know, since Daddy won't be there."

Susan closed her eyes and pursed her lips, none of which Julie could see, thankfully. Susan could envision Julie rolling her eyes and saying something about old people. At that thought, Susan couldn't help but smile. Oh, how she missed that girl.

"Okay, since he is your friend. I'll get a room ready for him. Just let him know we are not gourmet cooks, and the turkey will probably be dry and the dressing mushy. Oh, and the pumpkin pie will come from Evelyn's, so tell him not to mistake me for a trained pastry chef."

"I love you, Mom. Thanks; you'll like him. I promise!"

"I love you too, sweet pea."

Her daughter just said she'd like the man she was bringing home for Thanksgiving. A man in the house. Susan hadn't expected to host a man in her home so soon after her husband's death. Richie had been a permanent fixture, no matter the occasion, whether a holiday, birthday, cookout, pool party, or just the kids hanging out. Susan thought all that had come to an end. But here they were, and she had no real idea who this boy—correction, man—was, or where he came from, which bothered her a little. She thought about it, realizing Julie would start bringing men home at some point, and she might as well get used to it. Julie was technically a grown woman and wouldn't stay an innocent little girl forever. She would have relationships with men, whether Susan was ready or not, and they would be sexual. She'd never thought about it while Julie was living at home.

Susan surmised she'd better get accustomed to having visitors and stock the pantry with edible food and buy a turkey and all the fixings for a traditional Thanksgiving dinner. She'd be off work Thursday, Friday, and Saturday and would need to shop early for all the ingredients for their dinner. She sat down, ready to start her list.

CHAPTER 71

News

Rick's emotional state had made some progress in the waning days of summer and early fall but spiraled downward the week before Thanksgiving. There was something about holidays that renewed feelings of depression after the loss of a loved one. He found himself mentally reliving his son's death and the breakup of his marriage during moments spent alone. His house continued to bear down on him with an air of disapproval. He considered moving to a smaller place in an effort to escape the loneliness of the prison-like abode.

Rick's friend James had shown the house about a dozen times during the last five months but hadn't received any offers. Rick understood it would not sell quickly. The economy wasn't looking good, and with the price being in the mid-six digits, it could take months, if not years, to sell. The average homebuyer did not have that kind of cash lying around, even for a down payment.

He found that he spent most of his time in the den, bedroom, or kitchen. The dining room remained empty; he wouldn't replace the furniture. As a matter of fact, he would have to downsize and sell most of the remaining furnishings, since the majority of it would not fit into a smaller space.

Rick was working in the office when the phone rang. It was his mother. She was agitated and demanded that he and his father come home right away. It was an emergency. She wouldn't elaborate, so neither he nor his father had any idea what was wrong. They both rushed to the parking lot, taking separate cars. Rick wanted to be able to leave when the emergency was over.

Rick had spent very little time at his parents' home since the day of his mother's outburst. It wasn't worth the arguments and questions about his soon-to-be ex-wife. She wanted to know when he'd last talked to Donna, were they getting back together, and when was she moving back home. His mother could not comprehend that he and his wife had no intention of living together again. He had not spoken with Donna since she'd moved out, only communicated with her attorney. He'd signed paperwork transferring the deed for the house, removed his name from her car title, and separated their bank accounts.

His last conversation with his mother had rehashed the subject of Donna again.

"We are not getting back together. I haven't talked with her. I've only talked with her attorney," he'd repeated to his mother.

"But how are you going to get back together if you don't talk? You could try again for another baby."

"Oh my God! What is wrong with you? That is the most absurd idea you've ever had! Donna and I are not getting back together—ever!" And he'd stormed out of the house.

Rick had not answered his mother's calls for two weeks after that conversation. She left message after message on his home phone, office phone, and cell phone. Without listening, he deleted all of them.

Rick didn't bother to speed on the drive to his parents' house. Whatever emergency his mother had concocted could wait. She'd probably had a bump-up with her car or locked herself out of the house again. She was like a cat; she always landed on her feet. Nothing seemed to knock her down.

Rick and his father walked into the house together—at least she wasn't locked out again—and found her in the living room, sitting on the edge of the sofa, nervously wringing her hands together.

"Okay, what's the emergency?" Richard asked flatly.

"I just got home from the doctor's office. I have cancer," she blurted out quickly.

"You have cancer?" Richard asked, with more concern this time.

"Cancer, I have lung cancer. I don't smoke! How can I have lung cancer?"

"Mother, people have lung cancer who don't smoke. There are different kinds of lung cancer. But may I remind you that you were a smoker years ago. Remember, when I was little? I know you quit, and really that's neither here nor there." Rick hesitated; then a thought hit him. "By the way, why is this the first time I've heard anything about this?" He turned to his father. "Did you know about this?"

"No, your mother hasn't said anything."

They both turned to Janet, and his father said, "Janet, I don't understand."

"I haven't been feeling well; my whole body hurts. I've been a little short of breath, and I can't shake this nagging cough. I didn't tell you, Richard, but I've been coughing up a little blood. The doctor ran some tests. He didn't say anything about cancer until today. Some spots showed up on the x-rays. They are planning a biopsy the week after Thanksgiving. That will give us more information. I'm really worried." Janet coughed with a wheezing sound, alerting her husband and son.

"We are too, Mother," Rick replied, feeling a tinge of sympathy for his mother. He leaned over, hugged her, and sat down beside her. This was the first time he'd seen his mother vulnerable. He didn't like it any more than he liked seeing her selfish tantrums.

Cancer. That was a word that could knock the breath out of you in a hurry. It made no sense. He admitted his mother was a pill—*pill* was putting it mildly—but the woman he saw sitting on that sofa today was humble; he'd never seen her like that. She was scared, and he was, too. The two of them did not see eye to eye most days, but that didn't mean he didn't love her and want her to be safe and healthy.

Rick thought of Thanksgiving the next week and the medical procedures that would take place the week afterward. It did not bode well, in his opinion.

Rick drove home that evening and opened the refrigerator, hoping to make a sandwich or something quick, but found it near empty. His head was still spinning from his mother's news. He decided on a quick trip to the grocery store and sat down to write a list—he would forget half of what he needed if he didn't make one. Coffee, milk, bread, eggs, sandwich stuff, beer, and cereal. Maybe a couple of steaks for the freezer. He ate simple meals at home. Rick's main meal was lunch in one of the dozens of restaurants in Cabot, and he generally ate light at home, finding any excuse not to cook. He'd gained back a few pounds, but his clothes continued to hang loosely on his tall frame.

He walked out the door to his car, opening the garage door. He hoped his trip to the grocery store wouldn't take long; he was tired, mentally and physically. The evening's weather was cloudy with the threat of rain or drizzle. The weather had cooled considerably in the past few weeks. Fall had arrived.

To his relief, the grocery store parking lot was nearly empty, and he pulled into a parking spot next to space set aside for handicapped customers. He pulled out a cart and set out to get his groceries. As he walked through the meat department, he noticed stacks of turkeys, frozen solid. He thought about his mother. What would they do for Thanksgiving dinner next week? He couldn't say celebrate. There would be very little celebration this year. He looked down at his hands clenching the handle of the cart, relaxed his grip, and looked up again to see the familiar profile of Susan Carson. He hesitated slightly, but his voice came out strong.

"Susan."

She turned at his voice. "Rick, hey, how are you?"

"I'm doing okay, surviving. It's good to see you." He smiled.

"It's good to see you too. I thought I had the grocery store to myself." She laughed. "I guess you have big plans for Thanksgiving."

"Actually, no. I'm not sure what I'll be doing," Rick replied with some hesitancy. He contemplated telling her about his mother but thought better of it. His mother had never treated Susan well—actually treated her badly when given the chance. He wasn't sure she would feel much sympathy for his mother, so he didn't say anything.

"I guess Julie is coming home for the holidays. I know you'll be glad to see her," Rick added, trying to keep the conversation light.

"Well, yes, and she's bringing a guest. A boy she's met at college. Let me correct myself; she says he's a man. He's a doctoral student, and he and Julie have befriended one another."

Susan seemed a bit hesitant, so Rick asked, "Well, what do you think of her bringing home a man she's just recently met?"

"I don't know. I really don't. She says it's friendship, nothing romantic, but I'm not sure how to interpret that."

"I don't blame you. Do you know anything about him, other than he's a graduate student? Where is he from? Why isn't he going home?"

"I don't know. Julie seems very excited about bringing him home and says, 'Mom, you'll really like him.' How am I supposed to interpret that?"

"Well, I can't help you there, but I trust Julie's judgement. She picked my son as her best friend, and that was a good choice."

Susan smiled. "Yes, she did, didn't she? I guess I should trust her choice of friends. I wouldn't question her if she were bringing home a girlfriend."

"Everything will be fine, I'm sure. And if things don't work out, call me. I'll have him arrested."

Susan burst out laughing. "You could always make me laugh!"

"That's my number-one job, making you happy." Rick said, peering into Susan's eyes. They stood in silence for a brief moment, transfixed, unable to look away. They both startled when the loudspeaker made the announcement that a blue Camry had left its lights on in the parking lot.

Susan looked away first, blushing. "I think I'd better finish my shopping. I have to work Monday, Tuesday, and Wednesday and really don't want to shop for groceries after working three straight twelve-hour days."

"That's understandable. Happy Thanksgiving, Susan." Rick walked to her cart and hugged her, wanting the hug to last longer.

"Happy Thanksgiving to you too." She smiled and turned to continue her shopping.

Rick smiled as he watched her walk away. The simplicity of her touch had sent his senses soaring.

CHAPTER 72

David Ellison

David wasn't sure he should be going home with Julie Carson. She was nice and he'd grown quite fond of her, but he wasn't sure what she expected. He was under the impression they were just friends. So far, their friendship had been platonic. He hoped it stayed that way.

He had no brothers or sisters—an only child, just like Julie—and had grown up in a quiet house with only his parents. Maybe that was the common thread in this relationship. At least he had aunts, uncles, and cousins, whereas she had none.

He was concerned that she'd lost her best friend and father in such a short time. She seemed to be handling it as well as could be expected, but what one observed on the outside could be the opposite of what was happening on the inside. Plenty of people walked around the world whose exterior appeared happy and content while they inwardly suffered emotional turmoil and depression. He had to admit he secretly analyzed her behavior, based on their conversations, and was amazed at how well she seemed to be coping with her recent losses. *Occupational hazard, I guess*, he thought.

David and Julie planned to drive to Cabot on Wednesday afternoon once their classes concluded. He had a meeting with his adviser that could not be rescheduled, so by late afternoon, Julie was fidgety and ready to leave. She was excited to see her mother and introduce the two of them.

David was a little nervous. He didn't know how Dr. Carson would interpret his and Julie's relationship, and he decided in advance that he should keep a little distance between the two of them. He didn't want her mom to get the wrong idea. They'd grown to be friends but nothing more.

His parents had been quite protective of him, growing up, and his friends were carefully selected for him. He'd never been close to any of them. Julie was his first female friend since his undergraduate days at Florida State. He'd formed close friendships with many of his college fraternity brothers, drawn together by circumstance and similar interests. He hadn't allowed himself much time for socializing since he'd moved to Chapel Hill, but he liked the area and thought he might put down roots when he finished his degree. Atlanta had outgrown its boundaries, and he wasn't interested in returning there on a permanent basis. He'd thought seriously about selling his interest in the company his father founded.

Julie was fun, smart, and cute. Why he didn't feel romantic toward her didn't make sense, but he speculated it probably had something to do with her being much younger. He honestly had to admit his affection for Angela had not wavered. She hadn't communicated with him over the past few months, but he continued to hold out hope. He still had strong feelings for her and sensed she was the girl he wanted to marry someday.

David was convinced that Julie was a good influence on him, making him smile and laugh with her bubbly personality. The two of them could talk for hours. Her eyes grew wide with his descriptions of faraway places and foreign cultures. She grounded him with stories of her exploits with Richie, her friends, and her parents. The two of them seemed to round out each other's world.

It felt good to have someone he could talk to without feeling the pressure of romance.

The drive to Cabot was accelerated by Julie's constant chatter. Julie described the sights during the trip, and the closer they grew to her hometown, the more excited she became.

"That's my high school! That's Evelyn's, the nicest restaurant in town. Oh, there's the bookstore—we'll have to go there Friday!"

Another five minutes, and they turned into the driveway of a beautiful two-story home with breathtaking landscaping, and though the sun had set, David could see the grounds in the bright car lights.

"You didn't tell me your home was so beautiful," he said to Julie.

Laughing, she said, "You didn't ask." And she giggled again.

The two of them walked up the intricate brick-paver sidewalk, and before they reached the front door, it flew open, and there stood Julie's mom, Dr. Carson.

"Mama!" Julie yelled and grabbed her mother in a bear hug. "Mom, this is David. David, this is my mom," Julie gushed.

"Hello, Dr. Carson. Thank you for having me." David extended his hand to shake hers.

"Oh David, please call me Susan. Come in."

Julie and her mom chattered on, and he stood there, looking at the two of them, observing their openly expressed affection for one another.

"Julie, we need to move so David can get out of this drafty foyer," chided Susan. "David, you can take your bag and put it in here." Susan led the way to the guest bedroom on the first floor down the hall from the living room. "This is one of our guest rooms. The bathroom is over there, and if there is anything you need, just let me know."

"Thank you, Dr. ... um, Susan. Thank you for inviting me into your home. I would have spent Thanksgiving alone, and I think Julie felt sorry for me. She and I have become good friends. You have a very special daughter."

Susan smiled, "Yes, you're right; she is special. Go ahead and put your bag away and come in the kitchen. I'm cooking dinner. I apologize it's so late. I worked until seven. I did some prep work last night, so dinner shouldn't take long."

"Thank you. I'll be there in a minute."

David put his bag on the floor beside the dresser. He looked around the room at the pale blue curtains and matching comforter. The furniture was antique white—quite beautiful, in fact. The sitting area appeared comfortable, with a plaid arm chair and matching ottoman in shades of blue and cream. He used the restroom and washed his hands with the citrus-scented hand soap. He turned off the bathroom light and walked through the well-appointed bedroom.

David couldn't stop the vision of Dr. Carson's face; it had run through his head from the moment he met her. He hoped she didn't question the puzzled look on his face as they were introduced. She looked familiar. He knew her from somewhere. Perhaps they'd inadvertently crossed paths when Julie moved into her dorm, though he didn't remember being on campus during freshman move-in day. He would have to think about it; it was definitely a poser.

Dinner was chicken-and-steak stir-fry with peppers, onions, broccoli, and carrots. A one-pot meal, Susan called it. She steamed a bowl of basmati rice, and the meal was complete. She'd cut a ripe pineapple into large chunks, which served as a healthy dessert. Tomorrow, everyone would splurge on a home-cooked turkey dinner with all the trimmings and Evelyn's decadent pumpkin pie.

After dinner, they each said good night, and Susan and Julie climbed the stairs to their rooms. David walked to his bedroom, thinking he might watch TV before going to bed. He couldn't shake the feeling he'd met Susan before. He found himself staring at her during dinner. Why did she look so familiar? He couldn't imagine where their paths could have crossed, other than the university.

He took his wallet out of his pants pocket and laid it on the nightstand. He'd bought it a few weeks earlier and was not happy with it. His old wallet had fallen apart from years of wear and tear, and he finally had to throw it away when there was more duct tape than leather. On more than one occasion since he'd purchased this one, his credit cards and driver's license had fallen out onto the dresser or the floor. He was afraid this was going to happen in a store or restaurant, and he would eventually lose something of importance. It appeared the slots holding the cards were cut too long, and his cards would continue to fall out; there was no adjusting it. He reached over to lay the ill-fated wallet on the antique white nightstand and a few of the cards fell out again. He bent down to pick up all the cards and rearrange them, and swore on the spot he would chuck this one as soon as he had a chance to purchase a new one. Anything would be better than this. He began placing the cards back in order when he noticed a picture had fallen out as well. The picture was taken in the hospital at some point after his birth. The teenaged girl didn't seem very happy; she looked as though she'd been crying, and the infant appeared to be ready to fall asleep. This was a photo of him and his birth mother. His parents were honest with him from the time he was old enough to understand, telling him he was adopted. He was grateful for their honesty. It was much easier to live his life when his past was an open book. His parents were not able to have a baby of their own, so they adopted him when he was two days old. They said other parents did not have the privilege of picking their children, but they had, and they were always proud of him and loved him no differently. He had everything money could buy and all the love to go along with it. He was spoiled in all the good ways, leading to a happy and confident adulthood. He never questioned his heritage or birth parents. He didn't feel the need to; he had everything a child could want. He lacked for nothing.

His parents, Charles and Catherine Ellison, traveled extensively and usually carried him with them on trips within the United States and many abroad. They traveled the world. He should have been with them the night of the plane crash. He was in college, though, and they didn't want him to miss any classes. They valued education and drew the line at allowing him to go on business trips when school was in session.

Following their deaths, David was given full access to their possessions, including bank accounts and safe deposit boxes. There were three safe deposit boxes, two with mostly legal papers and one with his mother's expensive jewelry pieces.

It took a week to go through all the papers with the attorneys. Among the stacks of contract documents, deeds, and titles, David found a business envelope labeled David's Adoption. In it, he found legal papers, three copies of his adoptive birth certificate, and this picture. The only name on the picture was his and the initials SA. He assumed the girl in the picture was his birth mother, and her initials must be SA. He had no plans to pursue an identification. The past was the past, and he had no desire to find her.

His parents were Charles and Catherine Ellison, not some teenaged girl in a picture. He didn't know what her situation was or why she didn't want him. His guess was that she was an unwed mother and, for whatever reason, she couldn't take care of him and had found a family that would take him and love him. David studied the picture for a minute and sharply drew in his breath, realizing why Julie's mother seemed familiar. The girl bore a strong resemblance to Dr. Carson. Was it just a coincidence? The initials were SA—could that be Susan? David didn't know her maiden name. Maybe it was a relative of hers or just a coincidence. People matured, their features changing over the years, but this girl certainly looked like Julie's mother. What should he do? Should he say something or stay quiet? Would he risk making a fool of himself by showing her this picture or spend the rest of his life wondering? He would sleep on it and wait until tomorrow to decide. He didn't want to scare her or make her feel threatened. She'd been nice enough to invite him into her home. He could blow it in a hurry, and destroy his and Julie's friendship in the process. But what if Susan was his birth mother? Why didn't she try to find him? She was now an accomplished physician. She had the means to search for him. What if she didn't want him? What if she didn't love him? Had she forgotten him? His breathing began to race, and his heart was pounding. He needed to think about this rationally. There had to be a perfectly good explanation. Could it simply be a coincidence? What would she say? How would she react if placed on the spot? And if she was his mother, would she admit it when presented with the evidence? So many questions with no answers.

David closed his eyes, and his breathing started to slow, reverting back to a normal rate. Forgetting the TV, he lay down on the smooth cotton sheets in an attempt to get some sleep. He knew it would be a restless night, and he would be proven correct. He tossed and turned for an hour before finally falling asleep. He had no memory of dreams that night, but he awoke drenched in sweat, heart pounding. He'd dreamed something, and he knew it wasn't good. He was thankful his memory failed to recall whatever had sent him into this panicked state.

CHAPTER 73

The Dawn

Thanksgiving morning dawned sunny and unseasonably warm. It was going to be a beautiful day. Susan tried to look at the bright side. Julie was home, they were healthy, and they didn't want for any material wealth. She pushed sorrow and self-pity from her mind for the day. David would add a male voice to their day with the absence of Bob.

They were celebrating their day of thanks with an early dinner. Susan would rest this morning, with the majority of cooking to be done in the afternoon. She enjoyed watching the Thanksgiving Day parades on television each year with the beautifully decorated floats, bands, and comical balloons.

Susan shuffled into the kitchen and started the coffeemaker. She was a coffee snob, laughing at herself. She'd purchased one of the coffeemakers that ground the beans and brewed the coffee in one sitting. It was better; no one could convince her otherwise. A little French vanilla creamer, and she was set to sip and enjoy.

The kitchen was quiet, so she turned on the local morning news program to add a little background noise to the expansive kitchen.

The solitude of the early morning sun shining through the blinds was comforting. Julie would sleep late; she always did on days when she didn't have to rise early and go to school. Susan didn't expect her up before ten or so. She'd just poured her coffee and sat down when David walked in the kitchen in his T-shirt, pajama pants, and robe, looking a bit disheveled. He seemed hesitant, which Susan thought was perfectly understandable. He was in someone else's home for the first time, a foreign place, surrounded by women. She chuckled silently to herself, feeling a bit sorry for him, and offered him a cup of coffee. He accepted, said he took it black, and slowly sat down at the breakfast table. He remained quiet for a bit, then opened his mouth as if to say something. He seemed to think better of it and closed his mouth again, letting out a breath ruffled with emotion.

"Are you okay?" Susan asked him softly. He didn't look so good—actually, he looked a little washed out. She hoped he'd slept comfortably, considering he was in a foreign environment.

"Oh, I'm sorry, yeah, I'm okay," he replied without making eye contact.

"If I can say something … you don't look okay. You look like you've seen a ghost. Did you sleep all right last night?" Susan didn't know what was going through his mind, but he shifted around in his chair and looked like he would rather be anywhere but here.

He took a deep breath. He'd placed his hand in his robe pocket but pulled it back and placed it on the table. He reached back in his pocket and pulled out a piece of paper, placing it on his lap. "I really appreciate your inviting me to spend Thanksgiving with you and Julie. My parents passed some years back, and I generally spend holidays alone or with my aunts, uncles, and cousins in Atlanta." He swallowed with much effort and then continued. "Something I haven't told Julie is that I'm adopted. It never came up in conversation, and it's not something I think or talk about very often. When my parents died, I found a picture of my birth mother and me as an infant. I carry the picture in my wallet for some reason—I don't know …" He drew in his breath and let it out slowly, deliberately.

Susan didn't know where this conversation was headed. Maybe he needed to talk to someone. Maybe he was feeling a little blue to be spending the holiday away from home in a strange house. She could identify with him; she'd woke up realizing this was the first Thanksgiving she'd spend without her husband. She'd teared up this morning when she awoke but made up her mind this would be a happy day, not a sad one. She had to concentrate on roasting a turkey and preparing dinner. Bob had been in charge of frying their turkey each year, having perfected his method of preparation over the years. She knew her baked version would not be nearly as juicy and mouthwatering as his, but she would put forth good effort, if nothing else.

"David, do you need to talk about something? I'm a pretty good listener. I understand about your parents. My mother died when I was twelve." David did not look good; the color had drained from his face, and Susan thought he might pass out. "Can I get you something? Maybe a glass of water?"

David shook his head and then reached out a shaky hand to pick up his coffee, almost tipping it over. He drank a swallow and immediately choked, spewing the dark liquid down his shirt.

"Oh, my goodness! Seriously, are you okay?"

"Yes," he sputtered, wiping his face and shirt with a napkin. He took another sip of coffee. This time, the warm brew stayed down, and he seemed to relax. "I'm okay, I promise. Dr. Carson …" He hesitated slightly. "I need to ask you a question."

"Sure, you can ask me anything. What is it?"

"Actually, I need to show you something. Please don't get upset with me. I'm just curious about something, and maybe you can help me. It's really very simple, and I would appreciate your help."

"Sure, what is it?" Susan couldn't imagine what could have made him this nervous and discombobulated. They'd just met yesterday. What could be so upsetting for him this morning?

David slowly reached to his lap and pulled out the piece of paper. He handed it to Susan. He didn't have to wait for any verbal response. Susan gasped when she saw the picture, her eyes wide with recognition.

"Where did you get this?" She looked at him with fear in her eyes. "Where did you get this?" she repeated with desperation in her voice. "I need to know—now!" She jumped up and stood behind her chair, gripping the back as if holding on to a sinking ship, alternating her gaze between David and the picture.

"I found it in my parents' safe deposit box after their deaths. Like I said, I was adopted, and this is me as an infant, with who I assume is my birth mother. I thought the girl bore some resemblance to you and maybe is someone who is related to you—or someone you might know?"

"That's me." Susan continued to stare at the picture, at the nineteen-year-old she'd been once upon a time. Alone and pregnant with Rick's son. Why hadn't she noticed it? How did she not recognize it? David had dark-blond hair and blue eyes, just like Rick. He had the same build as Rick. Susan didn't know what to do next.

"Dr. Carson … Dr. Carson …"

She looked at David in disbelief. This was her son! "I don't know what to say, David. I really don't. You're sure this is you. Are you really sure?"

"Yes, ma'am, it is. I have lots of baby pictures, and this is me. I'm sure."

"You look just like him. How did I miss it?" Susan said quietly to herself, not making eye contact.

"What?"

"You look just like him," Susan mumbled, unable to tear her eyes away from the photo.

"Look like who?"

"Your father."

Susan finally looked away from the photo. She sat down and glanced at David, speechless. No words formed. Her brain was a blank slate, fear and confusion wiping away all logical thought. She turned the picture over, reading the caption, "David and SA."

"I didn't think I would ever see you again." She pulled herself together, directing her remark more toward the picture than to David.

"Is that you in the picture?" David asked, barely above a whisper.

"Yes, that's me and my baby." Susan's voice was strained, producing words she'd convinced herself she'd never say.

"What does SA stand for?" David asked.

"My name was Susan Anderson," she replied with sadness in her voice. "Those were my initials."

"You're my birth mother."

They both sat with eyes downcast, coffee forgotten, each waiting for the other to say something. But there was only silence. The world had ended as they knew it. Life would never be the same.

CHAPTER 74

Caught

The silence was broken by a happy, bouncy voice calling from the staircase. "I'm up, Mom! And it's before ten! Aren't you proud of me?"

Julie danced into the kitchen, humming a song she'd heard on her playlist a hundred times. Susan and David first looked at Julie and then looked away, silent.

"You two are awfully quiet. What's up?"

Susan cleared her throat nervously, "We were just sitting here watching TV. Did you sleep well, dear?"

"Yes, my bed here is so much more comfy than my bed in the dorm. Dorm beds suck. Sorry, Mom, I know you don't like the word suck. I slept like a baby."

At the mention of the word baby, Susan and David sharply turned to face Julie, their eyes wide with guilt.

"Are you two all right? You have strange looks on your faces. Am I missing something?"

"We … saw a weird video on the morning news," David said, "and we're both grossed out."

"Yuck, don't tell me what it was. I don't want to know. Mom, I don't know how you work in the emergency department. You should be used to seeing gross stuff by now, shouldn't you?"

Without waiting for an answer, Julie flitted from cabinet to cabinet to the pantry, balancing a cereal bowl, spoon, box of cereal, and cup of coffee.

"Mom, do we have any French vanilla creamer?"

"Yes, it's in the refrigerator door," Susan replied sheepishly, directing her gaze to her cup of coffee.

"Hey, Mom, when are you going to start cooking? David and I will be glad to help with anything. Just tell us what you want us to do."

Julie continued her chattering, mostly to herself. Susan and David had not fully recovered from their conversation and tried to act as though interested in what Julie had to say. They both smiled and laughed when it seemed appropriate, though neither comprehended whatever joke Julie was sharing.

As the day progressed, Susan's and David's moods lightened, albeit with some degree of caution. It was difficult to be around Julie for very long without being drawn into her perky, happy world.

Julie didn't notice it at first, but as the morning turned to afternoon, she sensed a tension between her mother and David. There was something going on; she didn't know what it was, but it was … weird. They looked at each other suspiciously—that was the only way it could be described. Maybe her mom didn't like David; maybe David didn't like her mom. Her mother looked almost scared. Why would her mother be scared? Julie sensed David had something to do with her mother's emotional state and was puzzled by it. David was harmless. Maybe something happened early this morning she didn't know about. She would keep an eye on them during dinner.

CHAPTER 75

Can't Hide Forever

Thanksgiving afternoon passed quickly; dinner would be served within the hour. The turkey was removed from the oven when it was golden brown and the meat thermometer registered the appropriate temperature. Susan set it on the counter to rest while the rolls baked. Susan was in charge of carving the perfectly cooked bird, and once she completes her task, the group of three would sit down for dinner.

Susan observed the table laden with food; it could be best described as a feast. They'd prepared mashed potatoes, gravy, green beans, candied sweet potatoes, cranberry salad, deviled eggs, turkey, and yeast rolls. The spiced pumpkin pie from Evelyn's promised to be a delicious ending to their meal.

Susan topped the hot rolls with melted butter, and they sat down to their meal, with Julie offering a short prayer of blessing. Susan had to admit it was good, and they devoured their dinner. After the conversation with David this morning, she was fearful her appetite would wane, but the decadent aroma of the feast drew her attention. She hadn't eaten all day. There would be a mountain of leftovers, but what was Thanksgiving without them?

Susan, Julie, and David pitched in to wash the dishes after they'd finished dinner. Their conversation was short and to the point, with Julie providing most of the chatter. After the dishes were clean and placed in the china cabinet, the three sat in the living room watching whatever football game was playing on the television. Thankfully, they were all football fans. There was little need for conversation with the constant dialogue of the sportscaster's play-by-play.

Neither Susan nor David were expecting the accusatory statement that burst from dear, sweet, innocent Julie as half-time rolled around. She grabbed the remote, muting the TV, and stood, facing the two of them.

"There is something going on between you two. I don't know what it is, but I know something isn't right. Spill it."

Susan guessed the shocked look on her and David's faces gave them away. Their expressions were a mix of guilt and fear—guilt for what they knew to be true; fear that their secret would be exposed. Susan hoped to continue the discussion with David this morning, but Julie's early rising nixed that opportunity. They couldn't lie to Julie; she would see right through it. Susan made a point of not lying to her daughter. She'd never been good at it. Even as a child, Julie had an uncanny ability to see through Susan's untruths. Julie was one smart cookie.

Susan looked at David, and he slowly nodded. She took a deep breath, patted the spot beside her on the sofa for Julie to sit, and began her story, keeping it as simple as possible. Susan didn't name the boy she was dating at the time; she just said it was a boy at school, and she was in love with him. It wasn't just Julie hearing this story for the first time, Susan realized, but David as well. This was his past, the story that defined his birth and his life.

"I was pregnant and unable to contact the father. In the meantime, I heard he had become engaged to someone else, so I was alone. I was a freshman in college at UVA. My doctor suggested that I might consider giving the baby up for adoption. I had no means to support myself or to support a child. The arrangements were made and when I went into labor. I drove myself to the hospital."

Julie had sat in stunned silence, but at the last statement, she jumped to her feet and shouted, "You drove yourself! Mama, how did you do that? Oh my God!" She slowly sat back down, staring at Susan in astonishment with her hand over her mouth.

"Yes, I drove myself. I was alone. I had no family, no one to help me. I gave birth to a baby boy. He was beautiful, with sapphire blue eyes and fuzzy blond hair. The hospital offered to let me hold him, but I declined. I kept my distance because I thought it would be easier. He would have a mother and a father and would be well cared for and loved." Susan sighed heavily. "You can imagine my surprise when the nurse brought him into my room, laid him in my arms, and pulled out a camera. She told me the adoptive parents wanted a picture of me with the baby. David and I are pretty sure I am his birth mother. He has that picture in his possession. I'd hoped I wouldn't see him again; it would be too painful. I knew I had a job to do. I had to finish college and become the person I was meant to be—a doctor. There was no way I could do both—be a parent and a college student. I did what I thought was best for both of us." Susan looked away, closing her eyes momentarily, reliving a past she thought she'd buried forever. "Julie, you know I was the child of a single mother, but my situation differed greatly from my mother's. She was a nurse with the means to care for me. I had none of that, so the option of keeping my baby was out of the question."

Susan paused, and after a moment, Julie spoke, "So in other words, there is a good possibility that David and I are brother and sister? Or at least half brother and sister? Tell me the truth, Mama."

"Yes, that's true."

"And David has a picture of you and a baby that David thinks is him?"

"Yes."

"Can I see it?"

David went to his bedroom and retrieved the picture. When he came back to the living room, he handed it to Julie.

She needed only a few seconds to recognize her mother as a teenager. "That's you, Mama; that's you when you were young." She then looked at David. "And the baby—that's you?"

David replied matter-of-factly, "Yes, that's me."

Julie studied the picture as if it was something to be digested. "Oh, Mama, I'm so sorry this happened to you. Did Daddy know?"

This was the question Susan dreaded. "No, honey, I never told him."

"Why not?"

"I was ashamed and embarrassed. Not because I was ashamed of you, David, but because I let myself get into such a terrible situation. And Julie, I loved your father so much. He came along at a time when I needed him. He saved me, and he told me I saved him. Together, we gave each other the opportunity to be happy as a married couple. He told me he was meant for me and I was meant for him. And together, we were meant to be your parents. I think he suspected I had a past, but he never pushed it, never questioned me. He accepted me just as I was; he never tried to change a thing about me. He loved me unconditionally, and I loved him unconditionally. I'd hinted that I wasn't a virgin, and as I was thirty when we married, I think he would have been surprised if I had been. Maybe someday I would have told him about David, and if he were here today, he would discover the truth now, I guess."

Susan inhaled deeply and looked at her children. Her children— she'd never thought of being the mother of children. She was Julie's mother; that's all she thought about. She seldom thought of the infant in the picture. It brought back far too many sad and unsettling memories, and she'd pushed the image to the far recesses of her mind, buried as deep as her emotional shovel could dig.

"Dr. Carson, can I ask a question?" David said. "What day was the baby born? What is his birthday?"

"August 11, 1976," Susan responded, her voice strong and unflinching.

She didn't need a response from David; the look on his face gave her all the confirmation she needed.

But then he said softly, "That's my birthday," and dropped his face into his hands, rubbing his face, then peering into every corner of the room, every nook and cranny, everywhere except at Julie and Susan.

The seconds ticked off the clock; the room was silent. Susan's heart was broken. What would the next minutes, hours, and days hold for her and her children?

"Both of you, please forgive me," Susan said with a note of pleading in her voice. She was afraid of their responses but needed an answer.

No one spoke. No one made eye contact. No one moved. The silence was excruciating.

David finally said, "You have explained a lot here, but I still have one question."

Susan knew what his question would be, and he deserved an answer; he deserved the truth.

"Who is my father? Do you still know him. Do you know where he is? What happened to him?"

"Yes, I know him, and I know where he is."

Julie jerked her head to stare at her mother, her eyes wide in anticipation of her mother's answer.

"Then, who is he?" David asked in a businesslike voice.

Susan knew she might as well say it; she couldn't hide it any longer. It'd been thirty years, thirty long years of hiding the truth, thirty years of secrets, lies, and deceit.

"His name is Rick Pierce."

Before David could react, Julie jerked her head, staring at her mother. "Rick Pierce! Mama, that's Richie's dad!"

Susan sighed and nodded her head in acknowledgement. "He and I dated in high school. He doesn't know about any of this. I'll tell him; I promise." Susan turned to David. "He'll want to meet you."

CHAPTER 76

Tick, Tick, Tick

Thanksgiving Day would be a somber one for the Pierce family. Rick's once-talkative, outgoing mother was subdued and quiet. He'd suggested he and his parents go out for lunch at Evelyn's, saving his mother the responsibility of cooking. The absence of Donna and Richie would be too much for the three of them in the quiet setting of his parents' dining room. An overwhelming grief would take the day, turning it into a day of mourning instead of a day intended for giving thanks.

Evelyn's was offering a traditional Thanksgiving meal, but reservations were required. His parents didn't appear excited about lunch but accepted his invitation.

The morning was quiet, and Rick drank his coffee in silence without bothering to turn on the television. He wasn't sure how he felt about taking his parents to lunch. The dark cloud hanging over his mother was troubling. He'd never felt much pity for his mother, considering her self-centered behavior. She'd never raised a hand to him, but verbal abuse and neglect left deep emotional scars, invisible to the outside world. Internal scar-pocked pain faded much slower than outward wounds. His mother often made life miserable for everyone around her, and it was difficult to have sympathy for her. But things were different now. She was scared, truly scared. She appeared to have aged ten years in the last week. She'd always taken great care with her appearance. She'd caused him and his dad to be late for dinners and events more times than not, but she always looked beautiful. The past week was a rude awakening; her hair was disheveled, her makeup sloppily applied, no lipstick. That worried him more than anything. It appeared she'd given up on herself. That was bad. If she gave up before she started, her chance for survival would be greatly diminished in a worst-case scenario.

Rick showered and put on a suit and the tie his mother had given him for his birthday. He hoped she'd notice.

He drove to his parents' home with the intention of driving them to the restaurant. He had a reservation for twelve thirty, but told his mother noon so she would be ready on time. He didn't want to miss the reservation. The menu would be an enticing blend of traditional choices infused with a modern twist—herbed-citrus turkey, garlic mashed potatoes, Parmesan roasted asparagus, sweet potato purée with pecan maple glaze, oyster dressing with gravy, and honey-butter yeast rolls. The appetizers were listed as a choice of escargot with garlic butter or crostini with pesto tomatoes. Dessert would be Evelyn's homemade pumpkin pie with cinnamon-spiced whipped cream. It was rumored there were more Evelyn's pumpkin pies served at Thanksgiving in Cabot than homemade. They were delicious, and no one had been able to replicate the recipe. The menu would inspire one's appetite on a good day, but Rick wasn't so sure their meal would be fully appreciated with the events that had transpired in recent days, weeks, and months.

He arrived at his parents' home and found his mother seated on the sofa, ready to go. She was dressed in one of her best dinner dresses, hair done, makeup applied, and ready to leave. He stammered a bit and admitted to fibbing about the reservation time. She smiled, saying she understood. His father walked into the living room dressed in his navy suit, the one Rick admired the first day he wore it to the office.

His mother looked Rick over and said, "I really like that tie. That's the one I gave you for your birthday, isn't it?"

"That's right, Mother, it is. I thought you would enjoy seeing me wear it."

"Yes, I do."

And that was the end of the conversation. They stood in silence, the clock ticking away the seconds, minutes, and hours. There comes a time when families would give anything to get those seconds back. Next week's results would determine how many seconds this small group would wish to retrieve.

CHAPTER 77

Changed Lives

David said good night and walked to his bedroom. He said nothing in reference to their conversation, and Susan didn't know how he felt about the day's events. Was he happy, sad, mad, disappointed? He showed no emotion and was a little too matter-of-fact and businesslike for her liking.

Julie appeared to be in a state of shock. She leaned over, kissed her mother's cheek, said *I love you* without emotion, and left the room. Neither of Susan's children made any move to say they understood or offer any form of forgiveness. Susan would be the loser in this game of confession.

Oh, my God, what have I done? Susan thought. She'd ruined two lives, Julie's and David's. *Well, three, adding mine.* And then she thought of Rick. *Four—four lives ruined.* She had no idea any of this would come back to haunt her. No clue. Never would she have imagined the day's turn of events.

Susan practiced great care over the years, never letting on or offering any hint of her lost child or her pregnancy to anyone, including her husband of twenty years. Her love for her child never faded, and she'd pushed her feelings of regret to the far recesses of her consciousness. Once she realized David's identity, she wanted to hug him, say I love you, and tell him how sorry she was for the past. His reaction was cold, sterile, dismissive. His reaction did not bode well for a future relationship. She'd probably ruined Julie and David's relationship as well. Would she see David again? She highly doubted it, considering his reaction.

She tried lying on her bed, but sleep was illusive. She finally fell asleep but slept fitfully in ten-minute stretches and then hour-long breaks where she replayed David's birth and adoption over and over. She lay in her bed and cried. She was heartbroken. She didn't mean for any of this to happen. She'd never meant to hurt anyone.

When her alarm clock sounded the next morning, Susan was more than happy to escape her bed. Her usually comfortable bed had served as a nocturnal prison.

She walked downstairs, shuffled into the kitchen, and halted suddenly. David was sitting at the breakfast table, fully dressed in khakis and a burgundy striped shirt—not a good sign. She could only imagine he was packed and ready to drive back to Chapel Hill, leaving the events of yesterday behind. What would she do, knowing she'd lost her child again?

Susan drew in her breath and said hesitantly, fearing the worst, "Good morning."

"Good morning," David replied softly.

Susan didn't know what else to say, so she went with the old adage, *If you can't say anything good, don't say anything at all.* She didn't think there was anything she could say that would fix the awful mess she'd created or improve her chances of redemption. So, awkward silence it would be.

She brewed a pot of coffee and placed a cup in front of David, hoping this would be the start of a lifetime of peace offerings.

"Thank you … Mom," he whispered without making eye contact. He stared at the cup and had spoken so softly, Susan didn't know if she'd heard him correctly.

"What did you say?" she said with tears rapidly forming, her voice softly quivering.

He repeated, louder this time, "Thank you, Mom."

Susan looked at David; he looked at her; and they spoke at the same moment.

"I'm really sorry, Dr. Carson. I'm sorry, Mom. You are my mother, Susan. I've thought a great deal about the events of yesterday, and I've contemplated all the ways I could react to this. But, you know, life's too short. I've been given a second chance to have a family—a family I think will accept me. You are my family; Julie is my family; and this gentleman, Rick Pierce, is my family." He sighed. "My parents taught me family is important. When all else is lost, your allegiance should lie with them. Most people don't get a second chance when they lose their parents. For some reason, I've been given this opportunity. I'd be a fool to deny it."

Susan sat down at the table, reaching over to place her hand gently on her son's. "Oh, David, I am so sorry. I've loved you since the day you were born and always felt a part of my heart went with you. I hope someday you will understand why I did the things I did. Please find it in your heart to forgive me."

"I want to ask you a question," David said, looking at her. "Can you forgive yourself? If you can forgive yourself, then I can forgive you."

Susan thought about David's response and how wise he seemed. It would take time to forgive herself, though she knew deep down in her innermost being that she'd done the best she could in the terrible situation she'd found herself in thirty years ago. She had to forgive herself, though it would not come easy. Guilt was the enemy of forgiveness.

"Let's cook some breakfast. What do you say?" she asked her son with a smile and a wink.

"Sounds like a winning idea. I'm actually a little hungry," David replied with a smile.

"Me too," Susan said happily, and she leaned over to give her son a long hug, which he reciprocated. She walked to the pantry and dug out the pancake mix and syrup. Her eyes filled with happy tears.

CHAPTER 78

Out of the Blue

Thanksgiving lunch progressed without incident for the three members of the Pierce family. Their table was mostly quiet throughout the meal, so much so that the waitress asked whether everything was okay. Rick assured her everything was delicious, but they were missing some family members, so their meal was a little somber.

"Oh, I'm sorry. Maybe you'll see them next year," the waitress replied with a convincing smile as she left to retrieve dessert.

The silence was deafening, and no one made eye contact. No one uttered a word regarding the waitress's comment. There was no need to say anything.

Rick dropped his parents off a little after two thirty, said his goodbyes, and drove home. *Well, it's not really what I'd call home*, he thought. *It's just a house.* He hoped next year at this time, the house would be sold, and he would be settled into a new apartment or condo he could call home.

There would be no dinner; he was stuffed from a lunch that lived up to its advertising. He wished he'd enjoyed it more, but considering the circumstances, he'd eaten as much as he could.

He settled in his recliner to watch football and fell asleep. He spent most of his evenings in his den these days; this was the only comfortable room in his monstrosity of a house.

He awoke the next morning and made a last-minute decision to go to the office. He needed to work on some research he probably should have given to one of the paralegals. His life as an attorney kept him busy, leaving him little time to mull over the past months. As he worked, the phone rang in his office, and he answered it, "Law office of Pierce, Grant, and Morehead. You have reached the office of Rick Pierce. How may I help you?" He immediately regretted his decision to answer the phone. None of the staff was in today; all were out getting an early start to their Christmas shopping. The Friday after Thanksgiving was traditionally a paid holiday for the law staff. Maybe he should have let the answering service pick up. Answering the phone on a holiday or weekend was akin to stepping on a verbal land mine—as soon as you answered the phone, you were all in, whether you wanted to be or not.

"Rick, this is Susan Carson. I didn't know if you'd be in the office today, but I called your house and didn't get an answer, so I thought I'd try you here. I hope you're doing good today."

Rick's voice stuck in his throat for a moment. He cleared his throat and answered, "I'm fine. I hope you had a good Thanksgiving."

"Yes, we had a nice day yesterday. I hope you had a good Thanksgiving too."

"It was interesting, but I survived."

"I understand." Susan paused momentarily and then said, "I was wondering if you'd like to come over today. Julie is home, and I know she would love to see you."

"Well, I'm here at the office for a while, but I could drive over later. Would that be okay?"

"That sounds great. Can you give me a call before you leave your office so we'll know when to expect you?" Susan gave him her number, said goodbye, and hung up.

Susan Carson was the last person Rick imagined he would hear from today—or any day, for that matter. His heartbeat sped up, his hands were suddenly shaky, and he dropped his pen on the floor. As he bent to retrieve it up, he hit his head on the corner of his desk. He slowly sat up, rubbing his head, realizing Susan still had the ability to topple his emotions, leaving him as giddy as an adolescent boy.

CHAPTER 79

Nerves

Susan's nerves frayed into a tangle of loose ends as the day unfolded. She dropped a pitcher of sweet tea at lunch, spilling the contents across the Italian tile kitchen floor. She'd be cleaning sticky grout for months, though she was thankful the container was plastic; it would have been much worse had she broken her expensive cut-glass pitcher.

The phone rang at one thirty. Susan startled at the sound, her emotions on edge. It was Rick Pierce; he was on his way. She, David, and Julie discussed over lunch how to proceed with the conversation that could not be delayed. Susan suggested talking to Rick alone, but she was quickly vetoed by David and Julie. David was thirty years old, and Julie was nineteen. They knew where babies came from and how they got there.

Susan worried that Rick would get the impression he was being put on the spot with the presence of David and Julie. How did one begin a conversation of this magnitude? She came to the realization it really didn't matter; there was no right or wrong way. Rick's reaction could be positive; he had a son. He would no longer be a childless father. He had a son—a grown son but a son. *Congratulations, it's a boy! Thirty years late*, she thought.

If Rick's reaction was bad, this would be a bad day—a very bad day indeed—for everyone. What if he didn't believe her story? She had to consider that possibility. What if he didn't believe David was his son? What if he questioned whether someone else could be David's father? That would be heartbreaking. David's likeness to Rick was uncanny. His dark-blond curly hair, blue eyes, athletic build—all were identical to Rick. Would Rick be suspicious when he spotted David? So many questions, with only speculation and theory serving as answers.

The doorbell rang, and they all jumped. It was unanimously decided beforehand that Julie should answer the door. She'd not seen Rick since summer, and he would be happy to see her. Rick and Donna had treated Julie like family, as if she were their own daughter.

Julie invited Rick in, showing him to the living room. Susan and David were seated on the matching floral sofa and chair. Susan stood to receive a hug from Rick and gestured to an empty twill armchair.

"Rick, I would like to introduce you to David Ellison. He's a friend of Julie's from Carolina. He's studying toward his PhD and is visiting us over the Thanksgiving holiday."

"It's nice to meet you." Rick shook David's hand as David rose from his chair. Rick took a seat in the empty chair, and Julie sat on the edge of the sofa beside her mother.

"So Julie, how is school going?"

"It's going well. Grades are good, not too much partying." Julie laughed nervously. She looked toward her mother and David. They smiled at her, and she continued more confidently. "The football games have been fun. I guess we'll have to see who wins the Carolina–Duke game tomorrow. Go, Heels!" She grinned again, pumping her fist, and they all laughed.

"So you're in the enemy camp, huh?" Rick replied with a smile, raising his eyebrow at her in jest. They all laughed at the quip. "So

David? Susan said you are a PhD candidate at Carolina? What are you studying?"

"Psychology."

"What do you intend to do with the degree?"

"I'm hoping to teach at the college level. I assist in one of the classes now—that's how I met Julie. I'm in charge of undergraduate participation in graduate projects."

"That sounds interesting. Where did you go for your undergraduate degree?"

"I got my undergraduate and master's degree from Florida State. I took a couple of years off to work in my dad's company but decided to pursue my doctorate."

"Where do your parents live?" Rick inquired.

"Well, my parents died when I was a senior at Florida State, and I don't have any siblings. My home is in Atlanta. Julie and I have become good friends, and she invited me to join her for the long holiday weekend since my Thanksgiving dinner would've probably consisted of takeout pizza." David chuckled softly, looking at Julie. She gently laughed and nodded in agreement. "I think she felt sorry for me."

Julie burst out laughing as she replied, "Yes, I did!"

The conversation waned temporarily, and Susan spoke up, taking a deep breath. It was now, later, or never. She chose now.

"Rick, we need to talk to you." She looked at her son and daughter, each giving her an encouraging nod.

Susan went on to explain how much she'd cared for him in high school and how much she'd enjoyed Richie and Julie's friendship. This was an important beginning to her story. He needed to know that her love for him had been genuine. She needed to reinforce how important Richie had been to her family. She explained to Rick there were mitigating factors that had deterred her teenage relationship with him. She didn't mention his mother's interference; it wasn't worth the hurt it would impose on him, and it would place him in the middle of a nonexistent battle.

Susan continued her explanation and then said, "Please hear me out before asking any questions. I'll be glad to answer any questions when I've finished because I know you'll have plenty." She then explained that their Thanksgiving getaway in 1975 had resulted in a pregnancy, and she'd done everything she could to get in touch with him. Without modern communication, such as cell phones, computers or the internet, she was unable to talk to him about her pregnancy despite her best efforts. "I left messages with your mother and your college roommate. I assumed you didn't receive the messages or chose not to reply. I wrote letters but got no response. When my friend Debbie sent me the newspaper clipping in the spring, announcing your engagement to Donna, I knew it was over. I was being seen by a doctor in Virginia, close to college. I explained my predicament and my inability to care for a baby. My doctor suggested adoption. He told me there were wealthy couples who wanted babies but were unable to conceive. They would pay for all the birth mother's expenses and compensate the mother.

"I took two days to think it over. My baby would be taken care of, and I would be able to continue my college education. I hated the idea of never seeing my child again, but I had to be honest with myself. I could not take care of a baby and myself. I tried to keep my weight gain to a minimum, which was easy in the beginning, since I suffered a severe case of morning sickness, but eventually my friends noticed I'd put on a few pounds. I laughed it off and said I needed to cut down on the pizza. When school ended in May, I rented a small one-bedroom apartment, paid for by the adoptive parents, and waited out the summer. I went into labor the morning of August 11 and gave birth that evening. I drove myself to the hospital while having contractions."

"By the way, I do not recommend doing that. I parked my car and was helped into the emergency room. The staff could not believe I'd driven myself. My labor progressed quickly, and you"— she looked at David—"were born that evening. I didn't see David after he was born and had no intention of seeing him at all. If I

313

didn't see him, I wouldn't know what I'd missed. Out of sight, out of mind. You can imagine my surprise when the nurse walked in, handed him to me, took out a camera, and snapped a picture of the two of us. It was then I realized what I would miss. It was painfully clear what I'd done. I'd lost the one thing that was truly mine. The day before I went home, I asked the nurse if the baby was still at the hospital, but she said the adoptive parents had taken him. The next day, I was released from the hospital and drove home."

At this point, Susan hesitated, looking at her audience with a questioning look. No one spoke; no one moved. Rick sat in silence. Susan looked to David, and he responded with a knowing nod of his head.

David pulled the picture from his pocket and handed it to Rick. "I found this in a safe deposit box after my parents died. It was in an envelope with my adoption papers. I knew I was adopted from an early age. My parents were honest with me, assuring me I'd been chosen by them, and they loved me. For reasons I cannot explain, I carry the picture with me, and, upon meeting Dr. Carson, I sensed that I'd seen her before. By accident, the picture fell out of my wallet on Wednesday night, and I recognized what I thought was a young version of her. I showed her the picture yesterday, and she admitted the teenager in the picture was her and the infant was her child. I know from pictures of me as a small infant that the baby in the photo is me. And my birthday is August 11, 1976, the day of her baby's birth. So we can only assume I am her child. And since you and she engaged in a physical relationship, we can assume you are my father."

Rick sat back, silent. Susan found it nearly impossible to hide her fear in anticipation of how Rick would respond.

"I don't know what to say. I really don't. I'm not sure what all of this means. Susan, I didn't get any messages from anyone. I didn't get any letters after … oh, I don't know, a week after Thanksgiving, except for your goodbye letter. You'd typed it, remember? You explained that you were involved in school and didn't have time for me."

"A letter? I didn't send a typed letter. All my letters were handwritten. I don't understand. I didn't send it." Susan shook her head no slowly.

"It was typed and sent from the post office in Charlottesville where you were in school. I saw the postmark. You wished me well and said you knew I would be a successful attorney someday. I was crushed. I loved you … I still love you." With this revelation, everyone stared at Rick, wide-eyed.

"What?" Susan said.

"I love you. Susan, I've always loved you. My and Donna's marriage was in trouble from the start. I don't think we were ever truly in love. You were the one I wanted." He hesitated and then said, "I think I know what—or who—intervened in our relationship. I think it might have been my mother. I don't know how, but I think she found out about our night at the hotel on the way back to college. I need to talk to someone right now, but David, I want to see you again before you and Julie go back to school. Would that be okay?"

"Yes, would you like to have dinner with us tomorrow evening?" David looked at Susan for her approval and she nodded.

"Dinner tomorrow sounds great"—Rick smiled at Susan and Julie—"especially with two of my favorite ladies." Rick walked to the door, shook his son's hand, hugged Julie, and then turned to Susan. He hugged her and kissed her on the cheek.

"I'll see you tomorrow. And Susan, I want to say I'm truly sorry. I'm sorry I wasn't there for you. I should have cut class and driven to Virginia when that damned letter came." Rick then turned to his son. "David, I'm sorry I didn't know about you. I will make it up to all of you. I promise."

Rick walked out the door. He knew his next destination. It would be the conversation that would define his future relationship with his mother.

CHAPTER 80

The Confession

Rick struggled to keep his temper under control. Driving while angry was akin to driving while impaired. The sympathy he'd felt for his mother this past week had vanished in one fell swoop. It was three thirty in the afternoon, and he knew his father would be out of the house on the golf course until late afternoon on this warm, sunny day. His mother would be alone. It would take a great deal of effort on his part to keep his emotions under control. Maybe he was wrong; he hoped his conclusions were misguided because someone would be held responsible—the person who'd ruined his life. And his guess was his mother.

Rick didn't bother ringing the doorbell of his childhood home. He'd rarely appreciated the beauty of the historic house. The columns, garden, the elaborate brickwork—it was considered one of the most beautiful homes in Cabot. It had been in his family since it was built. He'd been told by many that he was lucky to live in such a beautiful home, but he didn't see the beauty everyone else saw. The mental anguish of living with his mother made this house more of an emotional prison, a nightmare of sorts. He'd never been allowed to live a normal life without interference from the person who should have protected his future, not poisoned it.

"Mother! Mother! Where are you?" Rick yelled as he opened the door. He halted mid-stride, noticing his mother sleeping on the sofa in the living room. Her frailty stood out, and he hesitated. Then, remembering why he was here, he dove headfirst into a conversation he would vividly recall for years to come.

"Mother, I want to know what you did thirty years ago. I want to know what you did to Susan Carson. I know you kept us apart. It had to be you. What did you do?" He ground out each individual word of the last sentence between clenched teeth.

"What do you mean?" His mother blinked, groggy from sleep, slightly confused by his accusations, but the truth slowly dawned on her. He could see the look of concern on her face, likened to someone caught in a lie of enormous proportions—trapped.

"What did you do?" he repeated with the same intensity.

Janet hesitated at first but then began speaking. "I did it to save you from marrying the wrong person, that girl," she said with her head held down, still feeling the effects of the afternoon nap. She refused to make eye contact with her son.

Rick's anger was at a fever pitch, and his mother was both the source and his target.

"Well, Mother, knowing what you know now, don't you think I married the wrong person? Tell me!"

"I only did it because she was a threat."

"A threat? A threat to what? I don't understand. I loved her. I still love her. I will always love her! We could have been happy, had children together. You would have been happy, surrounded by grandchildren. Instead, you're alone. Richie is dead. Donna and I had a miserable marriage with nothing to show for thirty wasted years. No love, no companionship, no child, no life! What do you have to say for that?" Rick was shouting at his mother, frightening her. He'd never given her a reason to be frightened of him until now.

"I'm sorry," she said softly, staring at her aging hands on her lap.

"What?" Rick shouted again.

Janet replied, louder this time, "I'm sorry. I only did it because I love you!"

"Love me?"

"Yes, I love you. You didn't need that girl in your life. She was not good enough for you, for our family."

"Not good enough? In other words, not good enough for you!"

"I had to protect you; no one else would. Your father told me to leave it alone. He said he liked her, but I knew he was lying."

"My father is a smart man, except for his choice in marrying you. I don't know what he sees in you. I truly don't. You are conniving, you lie, your cruelty knows no bounds, and you torment people with a smile on your face."

"No, I do not."

"Yes, you do. I want the whole story. I want to know what you did to Susan, and don't you dare lie to me."

His mother took a deep breath and began her story about the letters, calls, and events; it turned Rick's blood to ice. He'd never realized what his mother was capable of, what she did with no thought to the futures of Susan, Donna, or him. She'd sacrificed them all in her game of control, lies, and deceit.

"I ask that you forgive me someday. I did everything because I love you; you must understand that." Janet coughed, uncomfortably clearing her throat. "I never understood what you saw in her. She was nobody. She had nothing. You were somebody, and you were going to be somebody. You deserved a girl who was the daughter of a doctor or a lawyer, someone like us, someone of high standing in our community. I could see the two of you getting closer every day. I couldn't let it go any further; I just couldn't. I decided to do whatever it took to separate the two of you. You must understand; I had to get rid of her." Janet hesitated before continuing. "I'm the reason she didn't get into Carolina. You know my college roommate, Paige Donovan? You remember she was married to the dean of admissions at Chapel Hill at the time, and I called in a favor. I asked her to convince her husband to deny admission to Susan. I told her that Susan was known for cheating in high school, and her grades were not what they seemed. I told her Susan was under investigation at the school, but she'd applied before it went on her record. I thought that would keep the two of you apart while you were in college, seeing as she would have to go somewhere else, hopefully far away."

Rick stood in silence, eyes wide with the discovery of the depth of his mother's lies and deception.

"When you came home for Thanksgiving, I saw you and Susan together. I was frantic. It was as if time had stood still during the months between August and November. The two of you were together the entire time, inseparable. I know the two of you left early to meet at a hotel, and I know you spent the night together. I saw the charge on the credit card bill. You broke something—oh, I don't know, a lamp or something. I was incensed. How could this happen? After that weekend, Susan called here three or four times, and I didn't tell you. She seemed anxious to speak with you."

Rick was astonished by her confession. He had no idea his mother had sunk to this level to keep him and Susan apart.

"I contacted your roommate, Dan, and paid him one hundred dollars to take any mail that came to you. He stole your mailbox key so he was the only one who could get into the shared mailbox. He took all the letters from Susan and destroyed them. He asked me if I wanted them, but I told him no. I didn't want any trace of them left."

At this point, Janet stood and paced the carpeted floor, making very little eye contact with Rick, seemingly speaking more to herself than to him.

"I decided I had to end this thing between the two of you, so I typed a breakup letter and mailed it from Virginia. I drove to Charlottesville to mail the letter so you wouldn't question the authenticity of it. A Cabot postmark would have been suspicious. I told no one. Your father nearly caught me, I put quite a few miles on my car, and he questioned me about it. I told him I'd gone out

319

of town, shopping, and I guess he believed me; he never questioned me about it again."

Rick stared at his mother, slack-jawed. He was making every effort to comprehend the story she was telling him. Why had she hated Susan so much? Just because Susan wasn't wealthy? It didn't make sense. He didn't understand how someone could be this cruel and vindictive. Susan was an innocent girl who had never done anything wrong. She'd taken a bad situation and made the best of it for herself and, later, for her baby.

Janet continued her story. "I planned the Christmas in Florida. You had a wonderful time, didn't you? I had to get you out of town, you see. I couldn't risk you and Susan seeing each other over the long winter break. I was thrilled when you brought Donna home to meet your father and me. I thought this was a young lady worthy of our family. She was attractive, wealthy, and a part of our society. Your marriage was my dream come true for you. I know it took years for the two of you to have Richie, but I loved him so much. My life was complete—a daughter-in-law who made me proud, a handsome grandson, a successful son in his father's law firm. What more could I hope for, right? And everything was perfect—until Richie died. Everything was ruined. I know you may never forgive me, but I am sorry. I truly am. Maybe you would have been happier with Susan. I don't know, though you don't know that either." She shook her index finger at Rick.

"Well, don't you think you could have at least given us a chance? Anything with Susan would have beaten the debacle of a marriage between Donna and me. Have you considered that? The fault lies solely on you." Rick's voice raised with each word.

"Yes, it's my fault you and Susan didn't have a chance. I take full responsibility." Janet abruptly sat down on the beige chintz ottoman. Rick could see she was beginning to cry, but this didn't make him feel pity for her, only disgust.

"I did it to save you because I love you, if you can only understand that, dear. I love you."

"If this is what you did to prove you love me, then I think I would have fared better had you hated me." Rick walked to the door and left without another word, slamming the door behind him. His walk to his car was purposeful, channeling a bitter combination of anger and regret.

He realized, after starting the engine of his car, he'd failed to tell his mother about David. Should he go back? Should he tell her? Should he ever tell her?

She'd made his life miserable. He would carry the emotional scars for a lifetime.

Thinking back on her emotional torment, he thought she could wait to hear she had a grandson, a bright, handsome grandson. He then considered his father. His father deserved to know. He blamed his father, in part, for his mother's behavior. His father had allowed her to behave this way. If he'd stood up to her, maybe she wouldn't have been so difficult and headstrong. Was it possible that his father had given up on her years ago? He guessed his mother would have taken his father for everything he had if a divorce had been considered. Maybe his father stayed with her to keep her satisfied financially, as long as she gave him his space—a fair trade.

Just as Rick backed his car into the wide circle of pavement at the top of his parents' driveway, he saw his father turn into the wide, brick-paver entrance from the main road. Rick debated whether he should go back and tell his parents about David. He weighed his options, deciding they should know.

"Hey, Rick, did you go to the office today?" Richard asked Rick.

"Yes, I did until a little after one this afternoon. I've probably had the most enlightening afternoon of my life. Why don't we walk in and talk to Mother? You will not believe what she's done."

"What has she done now?" Richard Pierce said with a growing anger in his voice.

"Come on, Dad. I think you deserve an explanation."

As they walked in the door, Richard called out, "Janet, get in here—now!"

A tear-stained Janet Pierce stepped from the small powder room under the stairwell and hung her head in what appeared to be a combination of dejection and embarrassment, sniffing into a handkerchief. Rick would force her to repeat her story, and he knew it all. He would not let any fact go untold.

She took a deep breath and recounted the story to her husband, omitting no detail, just as she'd told Rick. Richard stopped her a couple of times, but otherwise listened in shocked silence.

"Oh my God, Janet, what is wrong with you? Do you have no morals at all?" He glared at her. "Rick, I wouldn't blame you if you walked out and never darkened our door again." He turned to Janet. "Honestly, Janet, what could have possessed you to do these heinous things? Have you lost your mind?"

"I only did them because I love him."

"Well, that's one hell of way to show it!" Richard said in an accusing voice.

"I know. I'm sorry. I am so sorry." She dropped her face into her hands.

Rick decided now was the time to tell his parents about David. "Well, I have some news for both of you, and I think you may want to sit down. Susan Carson called me today; she wanted me to drop by since Julie is home for Thanksgiving. Julie brought a friend home from school. His name is David Ellison. He's a graduate student at Carolina. He's thirty years old. He lives in Atlanta but was adopted by his parents in Virginia. His mother was a young college student in Virginia. She was not married and had lost touch with his birth father. Does any of this story sound familiar mother?" He glared at Janet.

Janet sat unmoving on the sofa, her eyes wide and unblinking.

"Anyway, his adoptive parents gave a maternity nurse a camera, and she took a picture of David with his birth mother. His birth mother is Susan Carson. He's my son. I'm his father."

At this, Janet and Richard simultaneously shouted, *"What?"*

"I'm David's father. His resemblance to me is uncanny, and Susan confessed that she became pregnant when she and I spent the night together at Thanksgiving. She made multiple attempts to get in touch with me, but, Mother, you know why she was unable to talk with me, don't you?" He continued, eyeing his mother. "Susan eventually gave up and decided to put the baby up for adoption, knowing she could not take care of an infant and continue going to college. She completed her medical degree, and as you know, she's a doctor in the emergency department at the hospital. You have a grandson. He's an intelligent young man who will make you proud to know him. I just wanted you to know what you've missed, thanks to your interference in our lives." He glared at his mother who appeared too shocked to speak.

"Can we meet him sometime, your mother and I?" Richard asked cautiously.

"Yes, at some point. Mother, you owe Susan an explanation and an apology, a big apology. I wouldn't blame her if she refuses to forgive you or speak to you again. I'm going now." Closing his eyes and shaking his head, still in disbelief of the day's events, Rick said, "I'll see you before you go to the hospital Tuesday." He looked at his mother as he said this. He made no move to touch her as he left, shutting the door behind him.

CHAPTER 81

A New Family

Saturday evening's dinner brought with it a sense of excitement and anxiousness for the new family. The conversation was sparse during their meal of grilled balsamic glazed salmon, roasted potatoes, and green salad. They toasted their newfound family while remembering lost loved ones. As the evening progressed, everyone relaxed, and laughter echoed throughout the house.

For the first time, loved ones were mentioned without tears. David recounted stories of his parents and their world travels. Rick, Susan, and Julie sat glued to his every word while he described his adventures. Rick was impressed with David's business sense regarding his father's company and was happy to hear David speak of his involvement.

Rick, Susan, and Julie talked of Richie and his and Julie's antics, particularly their science experiments that had gone terribly wrong. All it took was for someone to say the word *volcano*, and everyone burst out laughing. The patio table at Richie's house had been destroyed. They were lucky they still had hair after it blew out the side instead of the top.

By the time the new family realized it, they'd been sitting at the dining room table for three hours. Everyone pitched in, and the dishes were washed, dried, and put in their respective places. They began taking turns yawning and knew it was time to say their goodbyes and get some rest. The last few nights had been restless ones. Everyone agreed tonight would be their best chance for a good night's sleep.

David reached out his hand to shake his father's. As soon as they shook, each looked gratefully toward the other, ending with a hug and hearty pats on the back.

Julie hugged Rick with tears ready to spill, but he looked at her, tapped her nose, and said, "No more tears, just smiles." Julie burst out laughing, wiping her eyes with the back of her hand. Everyone joining in with her infectious laughter.

David and Julie excused themselves, giving Susan and Rick some degree of privacy to say their goodbyes. Susan walked Rick through the foyer to the massive, mahogany-paneled front door.

Rick turned to Susan at the door. "Thank you, Susan."

"You're welcome. Julie and David helped cook, so I can't take all the credit." She smiled at Rick.

"Susan, there is so much more. Thank you for David, thank you for Julie, thank you for loving Richie like your own, thank you for being such a kind, generous person. I know you're still healing from the loss of Bob, and I respect that, but I want you to know I've never stopped loving you, and I'll love you till my dying day. I hope at some point you will give me the chance to show you how much. I also hope that, in time, you'll love me too."

Rick took Susan's hands in his, and her voice was a little shaky as she replied, "I do want to say this—a little part of me always cared for you. Every time I saw you, my heart fluttered, and my stomach dropped to my feet. Being in your presence always unnerved me a little." She sighed. "I know we should take whatever relationship we have slowly. Neither of us should be in any hurry. Don't you agree?"

"I totally agree," Rick said calmly.

Susan smiled at Rick as he leaned down slightly, kissed her lips softly, and bid her good night with a smile and a wink.

Her heart fluttered, just as it had the day he walked into their freshman biology class.

CHAPTER 82

Pieces of the Puzzle

Rick drove home from Susan's and decided to relax in his study for a while. He had no words to describe the revelations of the past two days. He was still in a state of shock. His thoughts wandered to Richie. He missed his son. A part of his heart died with Richie that rainy April morning. *No one escapes the agony of a loved one's death,* he thought. *The hurt may fade, but a tiny hole in one's heart continues to exist into eternity.*

It is often said that when a person recovers from a serious accident or illness, that person has cheated death. Rick held the opinion that no one cheats death; it's not their time. When death comes calling, you do not cheat it. It reaches out its cold, deadly talons and grabs you in its clutches. No turning back, no sympathy, no pity, and no second chances.

Death came calling that day for Richie, and his death was followed by the death of the remnants of Rick and Donna's marriage. Death did its best to destroy not one life that day but all the lives associated with that being. In order for their family to survive, all parts were required to remain viable, living, breathing. For when one piece of the puzzle went missing, the family could no longer maintain itself. Richie was that piece, the glue that bound the family together. It became unhinged quickly, falling into disarray, pieces that no longer fit and would never fit together again, imploding upon itself.

Rick thought how the loss of Susan's husband didn't have the same effect on her family. Of course, their resulting family consisted of two parts, Susan and Julie. But they appeared to be bound together more tightly, rather than a disjointed, hodgepodge of a family the Pierces had become. *That's how a family is supposed to react in a crisis*, Rick thought. *A tragedy should bring a family together, not tear it apart.* He'd witnessed scenes in the law office with families becoming unhinged when a member passed away.

Had his family ever truly been a unit of people with a common goal? His answer came quickly. No, they were not. Every member had their own agenda, whether it was control, emotional absence, narcissistic tendencies, greed, jealousy—the list went on. It was not surprising his family had disintegrated. It was never a stable entity.

Some degree of peace settles over a person when they discover answers to emotional questions, and Rick knew he had discovered answers today. He'd somehow been given the chance to be a father again. He and Susan were bound together by their son. He hoped this would be a turning point, a new beginning. His life had changed dramatically today. He had to move on, give himself a chance to find happiness again, a place where his heart and mind could live in peace and contentment. Susan Carson had offered him life again, and for that, he was grateful.

CHAPTER 83

Who's the Boss

Time all but stood still for Janet Pierce. Would Tuesday ever get here? Then again, was she all that eager for the dreaded day to arrive? She could answer that with one word—no. Not only was she worried about her future but the future of her family. She had to be all right; there was no other option.

Richard had given her a good dressing down after Rick left Friday afternoon. He'd yelled at her and accused her of terrible things. He'd never yelled at her or questioned her before. She'd written one silly letter and dodged a few phone calls. She'd apologized; what else was she to do? She was still firmly convinced she'd saved her son from a disastrous marriage to Susan that would have resulted in a divorce long ago. Susan would have taken their family for everything she could, using her child as a pawn in a game of money. The poor child would have been dangled in front of the Pierce family but kept just out of reach. Janet would not have enjoyed a moment with her grandchild without interference from his mother. Why was everyone jumping to the defense of that girl? Why was no one on her side? Janet saw herself as a victim too. She'd been cheated out of her grandson.

Richard had been so bold as to say her days of doing as she pleased had come to an end. She would be listening to him from now on, no exceptions. If he found that she'd caused Susan Carson any more grief, he would deal with her severely. What did that mean? No one had ever spoken a cross word to her, not her father, her mother, or Richard, for that matter.

Janet truly believed she was different. She was entitled; her parents had told her so from the time she could comprehend their meaning. She was better, she was smarter, and she had the money to back it up. No one could convince her otherwise, and with this in mind, she gained a new determination. If she had cancer, she would beat it and show them all. She would take over her family again and show them she was still the boss.

CHAPTER 84

Back to You

Rick arrived at the hospital Tuesday morning to sit with his mother before her scheduled biopsy. He didn't have a good feeling about the procedure. He didn't know why, just a nagging feeling that refused to go away. His inclination was that something was terribly wrong. He'd noticed his mother appeared to have lost a few pounds, which could be attributed to worry and stress. She looked older, with lines appearing overnight on her face. Her cough had not improved. She had developed a habit of trying to clear her throat as if it would help. It did not.

He was cordial with his mother and hugged her when she reached for him before the procedure. He decided to stay and sit with his father during the one- to two-hour wait. The sample would be sent to a lab, and they should hear within a couple of days. His mother was given a mild sedative and would rest for the remainder of the day.

He planned to head back to the office when the procedure was completed and his mother was ready to go home. Her friend Margaret volunteered to sit with Janet for the remainder of the day so his father could go in to the law office. He was preparing a critical case representing the firm, and it was too late for one of the other partners to take over. There would be no vacation days until the case was concluded.

Rick called Susan on Wednesday, the day after his mother's procedure. He needed a friend, and he couldn't think of anyone he'd rather see than Susan. He reiterated his intention for them to be friends, but he silently hoped for more. He wanted her, needed her. He didn't think he could live without her again. Since the discovery of his son the previous week, the door had been opened for him and Susan to reestablish their relationship. They were permanently bound together by their son. He was pleased to find her open to a relationship between the two of them. Friendship would be a good start, but he had a much higher and more intimate goal. Susan ended their conversation by inviting him for dinner the following Friday, her last day off before a long weekend of work.

Rick found his heart beating a little faster than usual on the drive to Susan's house. Nothing could wipe the smile off his face; his anticipation of his dinner with Susan was all he could think about. He was acting like a lovesick teenager, but he didn't care. He'd returned to the life he was convinced he was meant to live. He was meant for Susan Carson.

Susan greeted him at the door, and Rick took her hands in his and placed a kiss on her cheek. She smiled the smile he remembered from high school, her dimples forming perfect creases in her flawless features. She'd changed very little over the years. Maturity seemed to only enhance her beauty.

Susan opted to set two place settings at the breakfast table in her warmly accented kitchen. Rick complimented her on the meal of sautéed pork chops, stewed potatoes, and steamed broccoli with a lemon-butter sauce. She blushed at his compliment, happy to cook for an appreciative guest. Their conversation was happy and full of laughter. They caught up on each other's lives like two old friends. Though they'd crossed paths frequently while their children were growing up, their lives had been on parallel paths. They'd kept an awkward distance between them, neither willing to expose their teenage love affair.

Rick spoke of his mother's lung biopsy and his uneasy feeling. Susan didn't attempt to assure him everything would be all right, simply because it didn't sound good to her. She wasn't an oncologist but had made recommendations for patients to see their primary care physicians when she'd detected shadows on x-rays in the emergency department that appeared unrelated to the illness or injury at hand. She had a good track record in her discoveries of cancer from ER x-rays.

She asked him how he felt about his mother's condition without appearing to judge him or his mother. He appreciated her concern, not only for his mother but for him as well. No one usually cared how he felt; the only aspect that mattered to his mother or to Donna was how his emotions affected them. It was nice to talk to someone who put his feelings first and truly cared about him.

Susan talked about Bob—how they met, their marriage, their early days prior to and after Julie's birth. Rick knew him on a social level but not personally. Susan's descriptions of him were such that Rick had the feeling he and Bob could have been friends. Bob made Susan happy, and likewise, she made him happy. They had a fulfilling marriage, cut short by Bob's untimely death.

"That's the kind of marriage I wanted, you know?" Rick looked into Susan's eyes and then looked down at his hands.

"That's the kind of marriage you deserve." She smiled.

"You think so? I thought my job was to please others, never being happy myself. I sacrificed myself so my family would be content. I put their feelings first, always hopeful they would be satisfied. The problem was—it didn't work. Nothing I did worked." Rick appeared sad and downtrodden.

Rick explained his marriage to Donna, that he thought he loved her, that he thought she was the one for him. His mother loved Donna from the moment they met, just as he thought she would. He confessed his reservations from the start of his and Donna's marriage. He'd almost called the wedding off in the last couple of weeks before the ceremony.

He suddenly drew in his breath, recalling the dream with Susan and the baby. He'd almost forgotten. He described the dream to Susan, leaving her speechless. She'd given birth to David just a few days before Rick and Donna's wedding. It became a night of personal confessions and revelations.

"I think it's time for you to be happy and to have some peace," Susan said with a gentle smile.

"I agree, and I know who can help me find it." Smiling, Rick took her hand and gazed into Susan's eyes, the mirrors of her soul. She returned the smile, the warmth of her brown eyes settling his mind and heart.

"Susan, I'm not going to mince words. I love you. I've always loved you. I've tried to deny it, but I always come back to you. I'm a middle-aged man, and I'm tired of lying to myself. Can I tell you why I married Donna? No. Maybe it was on the rebound, maybe it was hurt and loneliness, maybe it was just plain foolishness, but it was a mistake. The only good that came from that debacle of a marriage was Richie." Rick's voice softened, never letting his eyes leave Susan's. "But now I come to you—or might I say, I'm back to you. If I had my choice and could turn back time, I would've never let you go. You see, you are my life and my love. I cannot and will not deny my love for you ever again."

CHAPTER 85

Determination

The call came first thing Friday morning. Dr. Long wanted Janet and Richard to come to his office to discuss the results of the biopsy. He had an opening in his appointment schedule in the late afternoon. Janet called Richard at the law office, and he came home early. They rode to the doctor's office in silence.

The news was not good. The biopsy results were worse than expected. More testing was needed, and Janet would need to be hospitalized for a couple of days. She and Richard sat in silence, gripping each other's hand. *Worst-case scenario*—it was all she could think.

Janet refused to let the news deter her. She made up her mind she would undergo the tests. The hospital and Dr. Long would form a plan, and she would get better. That's all it would take. She would get better, and go on with her life. She was not going to die.

Janet had a grandson to meet. She was upset with Rick for not bringing David to see her. She could not understand why Rick wanted to keep him away. Now was the time she needed her family rallying around her. She planned to meet David during Christmas, and she made up her mind she would see him then, one way or another. He would love her just like Richie. How could he feel any other way?

CHAPTER 86

The Request

Susan's day at work had been slow. Slow days were good for humanity, in general. That meant people were not in pain or injured or worse. A nurse from the oncology wing came into the office of the emergency department and caught up with Susan.

"Dr. Carson, there is a patient in room 219 that has asked to speak with you."

"Who is it?" Susan asked, puzzled by the request; she continued examining a chart.

"They told me not to tell you," the nurse said matter-of-factly.

Susan looked up, and the nurse shook her head and shrugged her shoulders.

"Well, that's interesting. They didn't tell you anything?"

"Nope, not a hint."

"I have a break at three. I'll go then."

When the clock hit three, Susan walked to the opposite side of the hospital, her curiosity piqued. Who would want to talk to her? She sensed it would be an interesting conversation, based on the nurse's reaction. She would find out soon enough.

Susan stepped into the room and stopped abruptly when she recognized the woman in the hospital bed. It was Janet Pierce.

Susan braced herself for whatever Janet had to say. What was she up to now? Janet Pierce had a way of making Susan's life miserable when given the chance. She steeled herself for whatever Janet dished out. She would promptly exit as soon as she had the chance.

"Hello, Mrs. Pierce," Susan said cautiously.

"Come here, Susan. Richard and I talked with Rick, and he said you had some very interesting information." Janet didn't mince words.

"Yes, that is correct."

"I want to know the truth, from the beginning," Janet said coldly.

"The truth?"

"Yes, the truth—the truth about you and Rick, the truth about David."

Susan knew the inevitability of this conversation. The cat had been let out of the bag, so to speak. She took a deep breath and began to recount the chain of events that had transpired thirty years earlier. A secret no more. Susan told Janet the entire story, from the time she'd gotten pregnant until David showed her the photo of his birth mother.

Susan explained that she called Rick after sharing her story with Julie and David. Rick deserved to know he had a son. He met David the day after Thanksgiving. "I didn't think I would ever see my child again. No one would have ever known."

Susan stared at the floor, afraid to make eye contact with the one person who had the ability to turn her world upside down with a simple glance.

"Let me begin by saying you were not my favorite person for my Rick to date. I was not happy when he chose you. But you have proven yourself to be a smart, independent woman who has taken an unfortunate situation in life and turned it into an opportunity to better yourself, and I applaud you for that. I am sorry for not giving

Rick your messages. He didn't get your letters because I intervened with his roommate. I paid him to take the letters and destroy them. I typed a letter and sent it to Rick at college. I signed your name. It was the letter breaking up with him. I knew it would hurt him, but it would pass. Time would heal his wounded heart. He met Donna shortly after your breakup. I thought I had succeeded in my plan until problems began for Rick and Donna. It took them years to have Richie. Our family's world was righted after his birth." Janet coughed, reaching for a tissue to cover her mouth. She then wiped her eyes and continued. "But then Richie died, and Donna left. My punishment will be all of the lost years when I could have spent time with David."

Janet paused again but then continued her explanation. "When we lost Richie, I thought my life had ended. I loved him so, and I blamed you for his death at first. I thought, if you were such a good doctor, you could have saved him. But I know he was dead before he arrived at the hospital, and I know you did all you could. You lost your daughter's best friend that day. He spoke very highly of you and your husband. He loved you both like a second set of parents. Now I find that I've been given a second chance to be a grandmother. I think it is a good thing, and I'm thankful for the opportunity."

"David is a wonderful young man. He and Julie are already like brother and sister. I think we have a good chance to be a family," Susan said awkwardly. She paused momentarily and then said, "Well, I need to get back to the ER. Thank you."

Susan was ready to leave. The conversation had taken a much different turn than she'd anticipated. Maybe the threat of illness had softened Janet Pierce. She turned and walked toward the door, reaching for the handle.

"I have one more thing to say." Janet swallowed hard, coughing a deep, strained cough, then slowly cleared her throat with a wheezing sound that concerned Susan. "I know who your father is."

The color drained from Susan's face, and her world stopped spinning as she turned slowly, deliberately, facing Janet. "What did you say?"

"I know who your father is—or was, anyway." Janet cleared her throat again. "He was my best friend Margaret's husband, Jack Penninger. He was a doctor here in this hospital." Janet gestured to the room. "Before he died, he confessed to Margaret that he'd fathered a child with a nurse back in the 1950s. Her name was Barbara Anderson; that is your mother's name, isn't it? He placed a secret trust fund for that child in an attorney's care when the child was born. The child's mother died some years later. He kept it secret for years; that is, until he was dying."

"And you've known this for how long?"

"Jack died in 1996, so ten years, though I'd suspected long before that. I knew something was going on between the two of them. I caught them in his office when they thought no one was looking. She was obviously pregnant, and they were kissing. They didn't see me, but I saw them. He and Margaret separated for a while, and that's when you were conceived. I saw Jack give your mother an emerald ring that same day. I've seen you wear it, right? You wore it the first evening Rick brought you to our home for dinner. I saw it and recognized it. Your mother held it up, admiring it as I stood outside the door. He'd never given Margaret any piece of jewelry like that. I could tell it was expensive. He should have never done that." Janet finished her statement, almost to herself, her brow knotted with disapproval.

So many answers dawned on Susan in the blink of an eye, giving rise to her response to Janet's confession. "That's why you've disliked me from the moment you laid eyes on me, isn't it? I never understood why you treated me so coldly when Rick and I started dating. You suspected I was Dr. Penninger's daughter, didn't you? You've hated me all these years for something that wasn't my fault. To you, I was an ugly reminder of past indiscretions. And it's your fault that I was forced to give up my child." Susan was visibly upset with the shocking revelation, but she found the courage to continue, clenching her fists at her sides. "You must be a miserable person to want to hurt everyone around you to such a degree because you certainly stole the love of my parents, Rick, and my child from me!"

Susan turned to leave, not giving Janet a chance to respond. As she reached the door, she turned to face Janet, "Goodbye, Mrs. Pierce."

Susan headed straight for a private restroom. She made sure the door was locked as she walked to the sink. She faced the mirror as scalding tears raced down her cheeks. She'd worked with Dr. Penninger—her father—in this hospital! He knew who she was and never let on, never said a word. She remembered him as being kind and smiling at her occasionally when they met in the hallway, but she never suspected a thing, never noticed anything out of the ordinary. How could this be? Why hadn't he said something? How could he let her, his own daughter, be placed in an orphanage?

Susan recalled his early retirement due to some heart issues, and she remembered attending his funeral. She also remembered his wife, Margaret. She'd treated Susan with kindness at the children's home. Hadn't their church provided cookouts and Christmas parties for the children?

Susan drew in her breath sharply as she remembered Sandra Penninger's wedding. Dr. Penninger asked her for a dance at the reception, complimenting that same emerald ring she wore, asking where she'd gotten it. She'd told him it'd belonged to her mother, who'd died in 1969. He expressed his condolences, saying he was sure Susan missed her. Susan assured him she did, and that was where the conversation ended. She hadn't been suspicious when he neglected to ask about her father. Susan now concluded he didn't need to ask because he knew he was her father. That was his chance to talk with her under the guise of a simple dance. She remembered finding it rather odd when he approached her at the reception. He'd smiled and said she looked like she could use a dance. She remembered smiling at him, appreciative of his kindness. Their encounter was comfortable, not awkward as one might expect.

Susan couldn't help these newfound revelations from racing through her mind over and over. She checked her watch and saw that she'd been gone for thirty minutes, well past her fifteen-minute allowance. She didn't know how she could concentrate, but she would do what she had to do. She hoped there were no additional surprises in a day full of them.

As Susan walked back to the emergency department, a puzzling thought entered her mind. Why was Janet Pierce in the hospital?

CHAPTER 87

Right and Wrong

Rick was skeptical of his mother's return to good humor. Something was up, and he knew it wouldn't take long to figure out. She was happy but not in the typical way most people exude happiness. This was different, like a cat when it has eaten the proverbial canary. What had she done? He knew her well enough to know whatever it was, she was not behaving herself. His father had given her an ultimatum to be on her best behavior. Rick guessed she would go down swinging if history had taught him anything about his mother's behavior. It would take less than twenty-four hours for him to have his answer.

Rick invited Susan over for dinner the next evening. He wanted to talk but mostly to simply see her. Being in the same room with her gave him a sense of peace. She made him happy. As the evening progressed, she seemed preoccupied, so he asked what was wrong.

"I wasn't going to say anything, but your mother requested a meeting with me yesterday in her room at the hospital. By the way, may I ask why she's in the hospital?" Susan asked.

"Mother had a lung biopsy. Her doctor says lung cancer. She's undergoing testing for a couple of days. I don't think the results are going to be good. I have a bad feeling about all of this," Rick answered, eyes downcast, shaking his head.

"I'm sorry to hear that. A diagnosis of lung cancer isn't as bad as it once was, but it is still serious and almost always requires treatment, usually aggressive." Susan was matter-of-fact in her response, keeping the rest of her thoughts silent. Depending on the type of lung cancer and whether it had metastasized would play a part in treatment and survival. At some point, if the cancer had spread into her body too aggressively, there would be little, if any, treatment. The diagnosis would be terminal.

Rick hesitated but continued his questioning, sensing Susan had withheld prognosis information.

"So what did she say to you?"

"Are you sure you want to know?"

"Yes, obviously she's upset you. My father will want to know, and I will not stand for her causing any more emotional damage to you or anyone else, for that matter. What did she say?"

"Well, she started the conversation by wanting to know the story behind David. I knew you'd explained what happened, but I told her everything. I held nothing back. I didn't know what her reaction would be or what she would say. She admitted to breaking us up, writing the letter, and destroying the letters I sent you. She complimented me on working to be a doctor, and she appreciated the relationship Bob and I had with Richie. I must admit I was pleasantly surprised at her comments and thought the conversation was over. As I was walking toward the door, she dropped the bombshell of a lifetime. She said she knew who my father was."

"She knows who your father is?" Rick gasped.

"Yes, she said my father was Jack Penninger. He and his wife were separated for a while, and she caught him and my mother, pregnant with me, in his office when they thought no one was looking. Before he died in 1996, he admitted to Margaret that he was the father of Barbara Anderson's daughter. Your mother has known for ten years and suspected since the 1950s. She admitted she witnessed Dr. Penninger give my mother an emerald ring. You've seen the ring—you know the one I wore in high school? I wore it the first time I visited your home when we were seniors. She said she saw the ring and became suspicious."

Rick stared wide-eyed at Susan. "She'll pay for this."

Susan clasped her hands, her eyes filled with tears. "You know, I worked with Dr. Penninger at the hospital. He was always nice to me, but I never suspected anything, nothing at all. To know he's my father, well, I really don't know what to think. Why didn't he say something, anything? How could he let me be sent to an orphanage?"

"Susan, I don't know why he didn't claim you. I honestly don't. I don't understand how a father can abandon his child. I know the situation was out of the ordinary, but he should have stepped up."

"I don't know what to think," Susan said, her voice barely above a whisper.

"My mother had no right to tell you something as important as this the way she did. My father is going to disown her. He gave her an ultimatum to be on her best behavior. I don't know what he'll do."

"I didn't tell you this to get her in trouble. But you're the only person I could talk to about it. Julie will have to be told, but I don't know how to tell her something like this. The conversation you and I are having is not a mother/daughter conversation. She knows her grandmother was an unwed mother, but an affair with a married man …" Susan sighed. "I'm at a loss. This is something I need to tell a friend who will listen, and I guess you're it." Susan felt a little better, having unburdened herself of this shocking turn of events.

"I'll talk with my father. He'll want to know what she's done. He and I'll have a chat with her. Well, the good thing about her being in the hospital—she can't escape. She will have to sit and listen to us for a change."

Rick and his father visited Janet in the hospital the next morning. There was one test left to perform; she would be out of her room the majority of the afternoon.

When faced with the conversation she'd had with Susan, Janet didn't understand why it was so bad. She'd complimented the girl and told her valuable information to help Susan understand who her father was; it was not meant to hurt her.

In their conversation over lunch later that afternoon, Rick and his father came to the realization that Janet did not understand the difference between right and wrong—never had. She lived in her own world, a world of her making, a world designed by her self-centered personality. Her life was built around how the world conformed to her standards, not how she conformed to it. Janet Pierce thrived on the attention and love bestowed on her by the those around her, unable to return that love to the people closest to her. They knew Janet would not change. Richard Pierce made the decision then—if she survived the illness, she would see a therapist. Janet truly felt what she did was right, and everyone else was wrong.

When the tests were completed and the diagnosis was made, Richard didn't have to worry about therapy. Janet was given a few months—maybe as many as six months to live. The cancer had metastasized quickly. Extensive-stage small-cell lung cancer, and the additional scans determined it had spread to the point that treatment would offer little to no benefit. He and Rick decided it was best to let her behave as she pleased. All of her friends were warned not to take anything she said seriously. Janet's behavior would not change; it would be between Janet and God in the end.

As the fall semester came to an end, David drove to Cabot for a visit during the Christmas holiday. He met Janet, and she gushed over him as if he were a child. He took it in stride and let her hug and kiss him, holding his hand for the duration of his visit. She told him repeatedly that she loved him, her mood swinging from smiling to tear-filled. This was good for Janet. She needed something to live for, and David seemed to be the key. He described, in vivid details, his worldly exploits and adventures. Janet was amazed and thrilled to hear him speak of visiting various parts of the globe.

Janet talked endlessly of David and all the ways he made her happy and proud when her friends visited. As expected, her explanation of his presence made her out to be the person who'd been wronged; she had a gift for describing an event and placing a spin on it that worked to her favor. Rick and Richard could see, in her friends' eyes, that they knew the truth, yet no one said anything different in front of Janet. No need to upset someone facing death.

Margaret Penninger later explained to Susan and Rick that after Jack's death, she'd confided in Janet about Jack's illegitimate child. Janet encouraged her to keep Jack's confession a secret, convincing Margaret it would only hurt her children and Susan. Margaret apologized through tears, her eyes drawn to her vein-lined hands clutching her handkerchief, begging Susan to forgive her. Susan did not hesitate, remembering the fondness Margaret had shown her from the time she was twelve years old, living in the children's home.

Margaret confessed she had no idea, until Jack's death, that anything had happened in the 1950s. She and Jack had separated for a short time; he'd moved to a small apartment in town. She became pregnant with one of the boys as soon as Jack moved back into the house. Jack kept the secret of Susan's birth hidden, confiding in no one. With this revelation, Susan realized she had a family, and they welcomed her with open arms. Her best friend, Sandra, was her sister.

The spring of 2007 brought with it new life for some and end-of-life preparations for others. No words were spoken, but the Pierce and Carson families were caught between the joy of Rick and Susan's newfound love and the imminent death of Janet.

Janet continued to decline, with the effects of the cancer making a mark on her daily life. Her daily activities slowed to a crawl, then to a standstill. Time was the enemy.

Janet Pierce succumbed to her illness on a Saturday in May, the day before Mother's Day. She died peacefully, surrounded by her husband, son, and grandson in hospice care. One moment, irregular, shallow puffs escaped her lips, and in the next moment, they ceased. A calmness overtook the room, each man lowering his head, tears sliding down each masculine cheek. The length of time each man had spent with her made no difference; their grief was the same. Janet Pierce had left her mark on each of them.

Janet was buried on a sunny Tuesday morning in the church cemetery, surrounded by her family and friends. Her grave lay next to her grandson, Richie. A sea of wreaths and floral arrangements highlighted with red roses covered her grave. Red roses were her favorite.

Rick and his father sorted through his mother's belongings in the weeks following her death. In the process, Rick came across a yellowed cello bag with what appeared to be the torn remnants of an old photo in the bottom drawer of his mother's dresser. After careful inspection, Rick recognized the fragments of Susan's picture he'd ripped apart on the day he married Donna. How did his mother find the pieces of Susan's photo? Why did she keep them? Why didn't she say anything? She must have been concerned, or was she scared? Scared that he was still in love with Susan Anderson? He would never know. The answer to his questions lay buried in the church cemetery.

CHAPTER 88

Thanksgiving 2007

The doorbell rang five times in fevered succession. The heavy front door flew open, and Julie burst in, calling to her mother. "Mom, where are you? We're here!"

Susan walked around the corner and wrapped her daughter in a fierce embrace. "I have missed you so much, sweet pea." Susan refused to let her daughter go, hugging her tightly.

"Mama, let me go. You've got all weekend to hug me. I want you to meet someone." Julie turned away, motioning to the shadows. "Come here, Michael," Julie impatiently called to the young man standing in the foyer, and he hesitantly stepped forward.

"Mama, this is Michael Harrison. Michael, this is my mom."

The young man reached for Susan's hand, shaking it confidently. "It's my pleasure to meet you, Dr. Carson," he said formally.

"It's a pleasure to meet you, Michael. Julie hasn't stopped talking about you since the two of you met." Susan laughed, eyeing her daughter, knowing she'd embarrassed her by Julie's wide-eyed expression. During their recent phone conversations, Julie excitedly described her new boyfriend, and Susan knew her daughter was smitten. "Please come in and make yourself at home," Susan added.

"We're sorry we're late; my last class ran over, and I swear my professor did it on purpose. He drives me nuts. What's for supper?" Julie jumped from one topic to another in the same breath.

"It's taco night. I thought a taco bar would be good for everyone and easy for me. Your brother should be here any minute. He's bringing Angela." Susan winked. "I have a feeling there is an announcement coming sometime soon, if you know what I mean," Susan whispered, grinning.

"You think he's going to ask Angela to marry him?"

"I think so, he's picking her up from the airport, and they should be here before long. We'll just have to see, won't we?"

"Yes, we will. Is Rick coming?" Julie asked her mother.

"Not tonight, but he's coming over tomorrow to spend the day with us. All of you will be helping cook Thanksgiving dinner—thank you in advance." And with that, Susan laughed a slightly evil laugh. Julie and Michael joined in, knowing their Thanksgiving meal would be a joint effort between all the family members.

Thanksgiving morning dawned cloudy and cool, but the interior of the Carson home was warm and cozy. The dining room table was set with Susan's best china and seven place settings, including one for Richard, Rick's father. It didn't seem right for Richard not to be included. Susan found that she'd grown quite fond of Richard. They'd spoken soon after Janet's death, and he'd apologized for his indifference in years past. He explained that he was impressed with her life and career and hoped that the two of them could get to know each other better. Susan was happy with his acceptance of her, and the two of them were growing to be good friends. He was becoming the father figure she'd never had.

The men of the family continuously sidled into the den to watch football, and the ladies were forced to keep a constant vigil, rounding them up and bringing them back into the kitchen to complete some menial task. As the dinner hour neared, Susan, Julie, and Angela gave up, leaving their male counterparts to the comfort of the leather sofa and recliners in the den.

The family gathered promptly at six o'clock. Susan stood, looking out over her family and guests. "Well, here we are. This Thanksgiving is quite different from last year, don't you think?" Everyone agreed, laughing softly. Even Michael understood, since Julie had spent one of their dates describing the events of last year, the loss of her friend and father, and her newly discovered brother.

"It gives me great pleasure for all of us to be together. Our lives have not always been easy. We've all experienced the loss of our loved ones. But we are here, and we are together. I am thankful for each of you. I'm happy to have my children"—Susan looked at Julie and David—"and Angela and Michael, God bless the two of you for bearing with our comical group." Everyone laughed. "Richard, I consider you like my dad, if you don't mind."

Richard nodded his head, his blue eyes twinkling as he raised his glass in a silent toast.

"Rick, I can't say enough for your kindness and the love you've shown me this past year. I love you, sweetheart."

"And I love you, too," Rick replied with a gentle smile.

"Okay, I've gotten a little sappy." Susan wiped a tear that threatened to slide out of the corner of her eye with her napkin while everyone laughed. "Rick, will you say grace?"

"I'd be happy to." Rick proceeded to give thanks and bless the first of many Thanksgiving dinners their family would share.

David did not disappoint, and following dinner, he pulled a small, silk-covered box from his pocket that contained a diamond engagement ring and proposed to Angela, his longtime girlfriend. Susan pulled a bottle of champagne from the refrigerator—she'd placed it there in anticipation of the evening's announcement. Each family member offered congratulations to the newly engaged couple with toasts and well wishes. Susan and Rick shared a wink and a smile; their hearts filled with joy for their son and future daughter-in-law. Wedding plans began in earnest before the first dinner plate was washed.

It was a happy day indeed.

EPILOGUE

Rick and Susan considered their renewed attraction as an opportunity for a fresh start. More often than not, teenage love affairs fail to translate into mature love and companionship. They were fortunate to discover the foundation of love they'd began as teenagers transformed into a powerful, loving relationship filled with hopes and dreams for the future.

In retrospect, Susan truly believed Rick loved Donna in the beginning. She'd loved Bob from their first date and grieved his death deep in her soul. A part of her died with him, just as a part of her died with her mother. She grieved the memories she would never make with Bob or her mother. Death not only robs families of their loved ones, but it steals their future.

Susan and Bob often spoke of second chances, each considering the other as a second chance for love. In a time of loneliness, Bob saved her, and she saved him. With Julie's birth, they were complete. They were a family. It brought Susan great sadness knowing he would not see Julie graduate from college or walk her down the aisle on her wedding day. She truly hoped God allowed the souls of loved ones occasional glimpses into the lives of the ones they'd left behind, not in sorrow but in joy and love.

Rick and David gave Susan a second chance by forgiving her, and, in turn, she was able to forgive herself. Forgiveness would be the only path that allowed her to move forward with any degree of peace.

Fate had dealt emotional blows to each member of the Pierce and Carson families, but it seemed to be smiling on them now. The past could not be changed, but the future of their family held much joy and promise.

Susan was puzzled by the ambivalence of her father and his motives, which led him to skirt his claim of her parentage. So many questions, with only theory and speculation as answers. She ultimately concluded she must learn to leave it behind. Rehashing it time and time again would lead to no good. Susan happily found solace in the form of Margaret Penninger. Margaret welcomed her into the Penninger family with open arms.

Most members of humanity consider themselves lucky to find love once. Susan felt especially blessed to have found it twice. She and Bob were like an old married couple from the start, mature, always thoughtful in love and decisions. Their relationship was comfortable and predictable, very seldom spontaneous, always planning ahead. It worked for them. Her relationship with Rick, on the other hand, was quite different. Their days were often spontaneous and filled with laughter. They each sensed the other's thoughts and often finished each other's sentences, leading to smiles and giggles. He surprised her with beautiful bouquets of flowers for no reason—pinks and purples, her favorite. They made it a point to say I love you each time they left for work or some other destination. Each day was filled with joy and hope. It worked for them.

Rick and Susan were married June 4, 2010, on a beach in North Carolina, surrounded by their loving family. David stood as his father's best man, and a newly engaged Julie stood with her mother as maid of honor. The small group of guests included Rick's father; Julie's fiancé, Michael; David's wife, Angela; and David and Angela's infant son, James Richard Ellison. They stood with the happy couple as they pledged their love for one another on a sunny, windswept afternoon. The dazzling Atlantic Ocean provided the perfect backdrop for the intimate wedding.

Susan and Rick were thrilled to be grandparents and found it amazing how much joy a baby could bring to a family. They looked forward to growing old together, sharing the life and family they were meant to be.

Susan smiled as she considered her life and the promise of a future filled with love and adventure with her husband and family. She was firmly convinced she and Rick were meant to be together. The fates had interfered in the form of Janet Pierce, but Susan knew she must forgive and move on from memories that had the power to destroy the future. She understood all too clearly that life seldom goes as planned in an imperfect world. Perhaps the ill-fated events of their past would strengthen their future, bringing with it an appreciation gained from lessons learned. Susan's past was ancient history, clouded with bits and pieces of good and bad, but her destiny was as clear and bright as a Carolina blue sky. Nothing but happiness awaited her and Rick. Together, they could face anything.

Each morning, Susan's heart nearly burst with affection as she gazed upon her sleeping husband. It was in those quiet, early moments that she sighed and couldn't help but think …

I was meant for you.

CPSIA information can be obtained
at www.ICGtesting.com
Printed in the USA
BVHW030403290519
549522BV00001B/5/P